THE LAST DAYS OF MADAME REY
A Stephan Raszer Investigation

Carroll & Graf Publishers
An Imprint of Avalon Publishing Group, Inc.
245 West 17th Street
11th Floor
New York, NY 10011

AVALON
publishing group incorporated

First Carroll & Graf edition 2007

Library of Congress Cataloging-in-Publication Data is available.

ISBN-10: 0-7867-1881-1
ISBN-13: 978-0-78671-881-8

9 8 7 6 5 4 3 2 1

Interior book design by Bettina Wilhelm

Printed in the United States of America
Distributed by Publishers Group West

Dedication

For three muses:

Kimberly Cameron (my agent)—*Fidelity*
Michele Slung (my editor)—*Fortune*
Valerie Hill (my mate)—*Fortitude*

(Each of them has been an April Blessing)

And to the memory of Dorris Halsey

Acknowledgments

The author wishes to acknowledge the contribution made to this book by the writings, research, counsel, and support of the following individuals: Professor John R. Hall of the University of California at Davis; Dr. Ralph H. Abraham of the Visual Math Institute, Santa Cruz, California; Frank D. (Tony) Smith, Maverick Physicist; John Dobson, peripatetic physicist and founder of The Sidewalk Astronomers; Professor Oscar Bruno, California Institute of Technology; Bishop Stephan J. Hoeller of the Ecclesia Gnostica; Randy Sorbet; Patricia Kenny.

Prologue
0

THE FOOL.

"LET me tell you something, son—about the men who truly run this world."
The old man brought a handkerchief monogrammed "R.V" to his chin to dab away the spittle, then rolled his wheelchair to within an inch of the boy's foot. "They hold to three maxims: The old order must prevail. Thule must be restored." A phlegmy chuckle. "Heh-heh. The rats must be kept in the sewers."

Young Fortis Cohn blinked behind his thick glasses and looked to his doting mother for encouragement. At ten, old age seemed to him a kind of disease. He liked when his mother called him her "little man," but he had no desire to grow up, much less to grow old. Old men smelled like pee. But Fortis had been admonished to show respect. Betty Cohn nodded with pursed lips, then shared a proud and—to Fortis's way of thinking—improper smile with the elegantly attired man who stood behind the wheelchair, a man with the eyes of a monitor lizard.

The invalid cocked his ear to the door, through which could be heard the reverberant voice of an orator. "That man," he said, "will be President of the United States. Know why?" Fortis shook his head, though his impulse had been to nod: he liked people to think he was smart. "Because the Fraternity has sanctioned it, that's why."

The year was 1979, the place a political rally in Orange County, California. They were in a V.I.P. room behind the stage, just the four of them, and a Secret Service agent. The old man's bones cracked like twigs as he leaned in and fingered Fortis's lapel, which, like his, bore an American flag pin. "And you, boy," he said, sen-sen masking his stale breath. "You've also been chosen to serve. All you must do is to retain the knowledge of your true paternity."

After the speech, the candidate stopped to pay his respects to the old man before being whisked off to the next appearance. What fun, *Fortis thought!* How exciting, to stand so close to power. *It was, he decided, where he always wanted to be.*

Once the room was clear, the remaining agent disarmed the emergency exit and motioned the four of them into the alley, where a limousine stood, engine idling. In spite of his frailty, the old man insisted on getting into the car under his own power, aided by a fine wooden cane with a steel tip. At that moment, an agitated woman of indeterminate age turned into the alley, wearing an onion-skin ensemble of rags and waving a placard that read: Matthew 7:20—By their fruits, ye shall know them, turned into the alley. She got to the old man before he could be shielded from her assault, which consisted of a pungent odor and a blast of invective. Betty Cohn clamped her hands over Fortis's ears. Wielding his cane like a foil, the old man feebly poked at the woman's belly, but she would not retreat. With heroic dispatch (so thought Fortis), the reptilian man now interceded, scooping up the patriarch and depositing him gently in the limo. Taking the old man's cane in hand, he turned to the woman, and with one deft and businesslike swing, cracked her skull like a nut. She staggered for a few seconds, and then dropped.

It had sounded like a cap gun, but bigger and deeper, the splintering of bone. Fortis had not heard such a sound before. His eyes widened as the woman's limbs twitched and blood oozed from her head onto the pavement, but he concealed his disgust when he saw that neither her assailant nor his mother gave the slightest indication of alarm. He knew that his father, Abel—had he been there—would have reacted quite differently, and he wondered: What was the right way to behave in the face of such things? He went to his mother's side and took her hand without a word.

Twenty-four years later, to the day, Abel Cohn stood at the picture window of his Hancock Park home (were Betty still alive, she'd have reminded him that it was, after all, her home) and watched as the private investigator descended the front steps and got into his restored Avanti, carrying with him a ten-thousand-dollar retainer and Abel's fondest hopes for the return of his wayward son, Fortis, now thirty-seven. The P.I. had an excellent track record—this much Abel had on good authority—but his methods were highly unorthodox. Cohn hoped to God that Stephan Raszer wasn't going to carve a magic flute and attempt to charm his son back from Hell.

PART ONE—GAIA

1

THE MAGICIAN.

Omni solum forti patria
("All nations are Home to the Strong")
—the "motto" of Victorian British explorer, linguist,
and Sufi Sir Richard Francis Burton

OCTOBER, THE PRESENT DAY

STEPHAN Raszer lay belly down on the massage table, just inside the open French doors of his bungalow at the Korakia Pensione in Palm Springs. "Empty your mind," said the dark-eyed woman, as her strong hands worked his Achilles tendons, "and picture the name of your true father." She had earlier driven down Mt. San Jacinto from Idyllwild at Raszer's special request; it was his habit to get an energy-balancing massage before commencing a new assignment, and this Chippewa girl who called herself Serena Mankiller was the best—and the smartest—masseuse he'd found: the only one who could provide any extended relief from the otherwise constant discomfort in his left ankle. Her brains and the quality of her hashish only enhanced her ministrations. She plowed up his calves to the inner thigh and groin muscles without lifting her palms, leaving the bottom half of his body feeling weightless. He unclamped his eyelids enough to allow the unfiltered desert moonlight to expose the neural tissue behind his retina, and a name etched its way across: A-B-R-A-H-A-M. "Wow" he thought, reaching for his gin and tonic, "How the hell did I come up with that?"

Raszer was culturally predisposed to dislike Palm Springs. It was Bob Hope, golf tournaments, and old Republicans with facelifts and tummy tucks. It was a long way from Whitley Heights, the funky-but-chic sector of Hollywood he called home, and a longer way still from the gas-lit back streets his mind wandered in waking dreams, seeking the one red door of promise in a monochrome night. Yet Palm Springs had become a guilty pleasure for him in recent years. When he wanted to combine the austerity of bruised pink rock formations and bitingly dry desert air with the hedonism of poolside and shrimp remoulade, there was nothing quite like it.

On an evening like this, with the Santa Anas sweeping all the air pollution westward into the moneyed canyons of Pacific Palisades, the skies pulsed with starlight and the air was fragrant with sage and coconut suntan oil. The Korakia, a Moroccan-style villa built in the 1920s by a Scottish expatriate, was a world apart. In its perfumed garden, set right up against the jagged base of the San Jacinto ridge, one could feel like D. H. Lawrence in the land of Liberace.

"So you're off to track another stray, hmm?" said Serena, handing Raszer the hash pipe. "Think this job will turn into another vision quest?"

Raszer took a hit and exhaled the words in smoke. "A vision of Hell, maybe. It's a young Jewish lawyer—half-Jewish, I guess I should say—who's gotten himself messed up with a cult of neo-Nazis up north. Pretty hard to figure, huh?"

"Not so hard," she said, pressing the heels of her hands into his buttocks. "I know plenty of Indians who call themselves Smith and play Anglo to deny who they are."

"You have a point," he said with a contented groan, opting, for the moment, not to discuss his own altered surname. "On top of it all, the stray is gay."

"The stray is gay," she sang. "I like that. My father once told me a Seminole story about a turtle who wanted to be a crocodile so that the others would fear him."

"What became of him?"

"The crocodiles tricked the turtle into leading them to his own village. Then they made him watch while they devoured his family. In shame, the turtle climbed into a Seminole stewpot, and this is how they got turtle soup."

"Some days," said Raszer. "I wish I'd chosen another line of work."

Raszer's métier was the infiltration and analysis of religious sects, doomsday cults, and other extremist groups that operated in the shadow sector between free exercise of religion and organized mayhem. His specific mission was usually the retrieval of a family member who had somehow come to be caught in the sticky embrace of such a group. These were the poor souls who had clipped out the ad that read "Is Your Life Out of Control?," attended the first meeting, and never come home. Because the work was difficult, the preparation exhaustive, and the risks relatively high, Raszer's services did not come cheap, though he was considerably on the shy side of what either good lawyers or *feng shui* practitioners charged these days. The money was usually not a problem for his clients, whose missing loved ones were the living proof of an axiom to which America-the-bountiful had yet to orient itself: that spiritual hunger seemed to grow in direct proportion to material success. If it was not tended to before the organs of the spirit began to atrophy, the hunger would manifest as depression, depravity, or delusion. Raszer's lost sheep fell into all three camps. They were the neglected Bel-Air wives whose despair lithium could not leaven, the children who came of age without benefit of real parenting, and occasionally, the breadwinners themselves, who one day woke in panic to find themselves wholly unsuited for their role.

These were the borderline lives, the lives without a convincing story, the stories without a worthy protagonist. Their numbers were growing exponentially. The consumer society was breeding them like rabbits, and Raszer's business had grown.

The masseuse kneaded her palm into his tailbone, igniting a faint orange glow on his eyelids. She worked up his spine, fitting the pads of her long fingers into the spaces between his vertebrae. The color in his mind's eye shifted to pink.

"This neo-Nazi," Raszer said, his words slurred. "This crocodile that my turtle has gotten himself mixed up with—believes that his enemies live inside the Earth."

Serena braced herself, kicked up her left leg, and dug her bare brown heel into his lower back. "The Anasazi people," she said, with an incantory grunt, "the ancestors of the Hopi—they had stories about cities beneath the ground."

"Do you ever wonder," Raszer asked, "if there might be worlds . . . curled up in this one . . . that most of us just don't have the eyes to see?"

"I asked my father once," she replied, "if the shaman could really become a raven and fly to other worlds. He said that when spirit and will are joined as husband and wife, new worlds are made."

"Yeah," said Raszer, with what little breath she'd left in his lungs.

Raszer saw nothing ignoble about the appetites that drove his "strays" into the spiritual netherlands: he was a hungry man, too. He considered himself a tracker rather than a "deprogrammer," and though he'd once taken a course in "exit counseling," he rejected most anti-cult hysteria as agnostic envy. What fueled his rescue missions was his recognition that the growing market for the sacred was spawning a whole new kind of con man. The spiritual huckster had been around for centuries, but now he spoke in a pseudo-scientific jargon that spun heads and bedazzled souls. Raszer, who shared the desire of every boy who'd ever thrilled to an issue of *Amazing Stories* or an H. Rider Haggard tale to peek behind the veil, had set himself up to expose the religious racketeers, in hopes that by shoveling away shit he might find a truffle. It takes a thief, a wise man had told him, to show you where the jewels are stashed. He wanted gnosis like a junkie wants skag, and gnosis—as the ancients knew—rarely came without a trip across the River Styx.

Seven years earlier, on the edge of an oblivion fueled by methamphetamines and a failed acting career, he had nearly lost his adored and adoring three-year-old daughter, Brigit, to a rare disease of the liver. Her death was all but foregone; there was no cure, so Raszer's wife, a Connecticut Brahmin turned Beverly Hills Buddhist who had just completed *A Course In Miracles*, called in a Malibu healer who claimed to have cured Whitney Houston's polyps with crystals. Hands were laid-on and facile exorcisms performed, but in the end, Brigit was still going to die, and Raszer, after rising to one last howl of impotent outrage, had decided to die, too.

While Brigit lay wired up to life support at Cedars Sinai, his wife and her new lover in attendance, he curled fetally in the back seat of his car, waiting for his heart to burst, wishing himself away. He did not think to pray, though there was religion in his past, even a youthful flirtation with a monastic order. He knew that only what the physicists call a counterfactual—something that didn't happen in fact but might have in an altered reality—could cheat fate. And so, with all the doped-up, delusional power he could muster, he fashioned that other reality in the matrix of his mind, and offered his own soul as its guarantor. Brigit recovered, and though the skeptic in him refused credit for the miracle, he limped out onto La Cienega Boulevard with an itch at the base of his skull, a burst vessel in the iris of his right eye, and new faith in the phantasmic.

Two years later, after a scholarly immersion the field of "emerging religions" and a required stint with the LAPD's Missing Persons Unit, he received his P.I. license and opened the offices of Raszer's Edge, a lost and found service for misplaced souls. On this very day, in Palm Springs, he was celebrating his fifth year in service, and the enterprise could be deemed a modest success. Raszer had pulled off what few men can: he'd turned his quest for personal salvation into a career.

Serena Mankiller turned Raszer on his back and worked toward the last movement of her tactile sonata. Thoughts began to break apart and fly out to the edge of his centrifugal mind. He was relaxed and meta-stoned. She cradled his ash-blond head in her arms and began to hum one of those plaintive, tuneless chants the Plains Indians were known for, rippling the surface of his mind like wind bending Kansas winter wheat. He was now able to perceive his own face from an angle above the massage table, the first sign that he was slipping into dreaming the way the shamans dream. His nose was hawklike and reddened by the desert sun, the angular masculinity of his features subverted only by the sensual curl of his upper lip, leaving him somewhere on the ragged edge of handsome. She worked his solar plexus and some part of him leapt through her hands.

He plunged into a dark, narrow place, feeling and smelling the closeness of earth against his shoulders as he burrowed headfirst. As a boy, Raszer had loved caves and tunnels, and was forever crawling into storm drains and heating ducts. *Had he once gotten stuck?* Now, he was a boy again, and the tunnels were sprouting branches faster than he could negotiate them, as if he were an antibody rocketing through a network of blood vessels. He liked the antibody simile so well that he stayed with it, increasing in size each time he swallowed up one of the ugly viruses which he now imagined were his real-life adversaries. He became so fat with the disease he'd ingested that the walls of the vein, though pliant and yielding up to a point, began to offer resistance to his passage. With the resulting friction came heat, and Raszer began to perspire.

The masseuse, standing at his head, gathered the cotton sheet about his torso and rocked him to and fro in a makeshift cradle: a technique for nurturing the soul. Now a serpent, he could not escape his tunnel dream, and was so engorged with earth and organic matter that he began to feel nauseous. With nausea came a metamorphosis of his dream self into the sulfurous head of a column of molten lava moving up through the fumaroles of a volcano. The urge to vomit all he'd swallowed grew so great that consciousness intervened and he found himself sitting bolt upright on the massage table, the sheet draped around his shoulders, dripping sweat.

"Wow!" said Serena Mankiller. "Strong one, huh?"

"Jesus!" he gasped. "What was that?"

"You have to sweat it out sometimes, Raszer." He wrapped the sheet around his midsection and slid off the table. His climbing khakis were hanging on a chair and he fished his cigarettes out of the right pocket.

"Especially with that poison in your system," she said, eyeing the pack disdainfully. "C'mon. Let's get you in the hot tub."

"I don't know if I'm up for the tub, Serena. I'm pretty overheated as is."

"You need the sulfur, baby," she said. "Like heals like." She came to where he stood near the open window, plucked the cigarette from his mouth and, holding it aside, dabbed the sweat from his brow with a cool washcloth.

"Coming in with me?" he asked, with a schoolboy smile. The tip of her nose was within a millimeter of his. She smelled good, like burnt sage and sandalwood. For the duration of a heartbeat, their lips brushed, and he felt a twinge of desire. Then she gave him an Eskimo kiss and withdrew.

"That," she replied, taking him by the hand, "might not be a good idea. But I'll stay with you a while." She led him out into the tiny hotel's private plaza and a single redwood hot tub which bubbled as odiferously as a primeval marsh. She took the towel from him, and as he stepped in naked, seemed to reconsider her abstinence.

Just four days earlier, Raszer had met with Abel Cohn, senior partner of L.A.'s oldest labor law firm, at his home in the equally venerable Hancock Park. Abel's son, Fortis, a junior partner—though clearly of an age beyond the paternal leash— had been AWOL from the firm of Cohn, Gottlieb & Schuyler for more than two months. Moreover, he was freelancing on a case that his father had emphatically refused to take.

Raszer had gotten the meeting by referral, which was how he worked. His number was unpublished, his services discreet. The senior Cohn was a Democrat of the old school who'd made his name over forty years of trying personal injury suits on behalf of the workingman. He had been a counsel to former Governor Pat Brown, and—by evidence of his trial record—a staunch opponent of the old Southern California plutocracy that had quietly and copiously endowed Nixon and Reagan's political fortunes. Nonetheless, the atmosphere within his vintage house hummed with an oddly reactionary dissonance that puzzled Raszer at first.

A Latina maid answered the door. She had a stern face and a dark mole the size of a Fresno raisin on her chin. She led Raszer to an old-fashioned smoking room, where he was invited to sit but not to smoke. Raszer sat, then stood and explored. He was no good at waiting. The decor could only be described as Hollywood Con-quistador, like the set for an old blood and sand movie with Lupe Velez and Ramon Navarro. Images of the sun blazed from oversized urns and ornately framed oil paintings; a brass spittoon adorned the bookshelf and there was a full Spanish suit of armor at attention in the corner. None of this was of a piece with the bearlike but decidedly humble man of sixty who then entered, his brow furrowed and hand extended.

"The, uh, art direction," he said, having caught Raszer examining the suit of armor, "is Betty's. My late wife. I'm not much on decor, so I leave it alone. I'd have probably furnished it from a Levitz showroom, but she, well . . . she had decided tastes."

"So I see," said Raszer. "I remember stories that were run at the time of her death. Wasn't she some sort of California royalty?"

"She was descended on her father's side from one of the 'founding families' of L.A. She was a Hancock Park Catholic who married a Mar Vista Jew. A marriage of wealthy tribes." Cohn paused. "Hmm. I don't think Fortis has ever much liked belonging to mine." His voice trailed off, then regained its strength. "I loved her like crazy, though, even after the booze took the best of her. And for a while, she loved me, probably because I was everything her father wasn't. But they all go home to papa eventually." Raszer lowered his eyes. "Love isn't rational, is it, Mr. Raszer? It's Ray-zer, right?"

"Right," Raszer replied. "And Stephan rhymes with even. And, no. It's not."

"If it was," said Cohn, "her politics alone would've been grounds for divorce. Now I'm dealing with her legacy. This poison she . . . "

"You're speaking of your son . . . "

"Fortis was his mother's creation," Cohn affirmed. "He was lost to me from the moment he first clamped his gums down on her nipple. There were days when I'd look at the two of them and have to wonder where I . . . " He left the thought incomplete. "Anyhow, I tried to be a father to him. Fishing trips, Boy Scouts, Little League . . . none of it took. He rejected everything I offered. There was—if I can speak 'biblically'—an enmity between us. He was only mine when his mother had no use for him . . . or when he was in trouble." He chuckled wryly. "Some things don't change." Cohn mopped his brow with a handkerchief. "But you're not here to be a shrink, are you?"

"No, but these things are important," replied Raszer. "Especially in light of what you told me on the phone." Raszer looked about for an ashtray, and seeing none, continued. "So, after Mrs. Cohn died, you tried again with Fortis? You got him through the California Bar and brought him into the firm . . . "

"Yeah. What can I say? I'm an idealist. I truly thought if I put him on a few industrial injury cases or into the eye of some labor-management disputes he'd begin to develop empathy with the underdog. I gave myself five years to make a human being out of him. Instead, he identified with the adversary every time and wrote briefs that sabotaged his own clients. Lately, he's been moonlighting with shady Hollywood types, trying to be a player. I blew up. Put him on notice. Three months ago. Right after he got the call from this fellow Vreeland and brought me this *meshugge* land use case."

"Bronk Vreeland," Raszer repeated. "Yeah. I've heard stories."

"Some name, huh?" said Cohn dryly. "Probably born Leroy Lutz or some such thing. Anyhow, Fortis pitches me this case as a 'David vs. Goliath' type thing that he wants to do pro bono. Only his David is this neo-Nazi thug Vreeland and Goliath is a consortium of regional Indian tribes who've filed a class action suit to reclaim the sacred land that Vreeland is using as a proving ground for his militia."

"Where's the real estate?" asked Raszer.

"A hundred acres on the southern slope of Mt. Shasta."

"Shasta … Jesus." Raszer whistled. "There's privately owned land up there?"

"This is the last parcel," Cohn replied. "Incredibly valuable. Vreeland claims it was deeded fair and square to his 'organization' by the assigns of the original landowner: the Klamath Mining Company. So, for my son, that makes it one more case of Native Americans overplaying the guilt card and trampling property rights so they can build a casino. Open and shut. Only, as usual, he didn't tell me the whole story."

"Uh-huh," said Raszer. "Go on."

"First of all," Cohn said, taking a folder from the credenza. "The tribes don't want title. Just guaranteed access via the Forest Service for their ceremonies." He handed the file to Raszer. "Here's the brief. Read it at your leisure. My son has a thing for big stars. Always has. What breaks my heart is seeing him hitch his wagon to the same kind of monsters who murdered my father at Bergen-Belsen. To a guy who calls himself 'Supreme Commander' of a private army of goons known as the Military Order of Thule. Why, Mr. Raszer? How could he hate me that much?"

"Maybe because you're a bigger star than he'll ever be." Raszer let a moment pass. "You say it's a private army?"

"They're sitting on a fucking arsenal up there. And that's not the worst of it."

"Tell me," said Raszer.

"I had an old friend in the A.G.'s office run a background check on the Order of Thule. This is no loose-knit bunch of survivalists in flap-bottom long johns. Vreeland was Special Ops in Desert Storm and an advisor in Somalia before he hung out his gun-for-hire sign. He has a local radio show. His 'High Command' are all crackerjack mercenaries with notches on their belts from places you and I only go in nightmares. Fifteen years ago, ATF and the FBI would've been hassling them to death, but ever since Waco and Ruby Ridge, the feds have handled these home-grown Huns with kid gloves."

"I hear you, Mr. Cohn," said Raszer. "They've pretty much abdicated on the home front. Too busy chasing guys named Mohammed. The thumbnail I've seen on Vreeland is that he's extremely charismatic, has the undying loyalty of his boys—mostly reconditioned Pentecostals—and that he's not just playing war games." Raszer cleared his throat. "So the question is . . . what is he really up to? And of all the ambitious young neo-con lawyers in the country, why was your son chosen to defend his citadel?"

"I don't know, Mr. Raszer," said Abel. "That's what I'm hiring you to find out. But I fear for the answer. I truly do."

A little shudder ran through the house—an everyday California earthquake, hardly enough to budge the needles at Caltech. The suit of armor in the corner began to rattle, then clank a few times before settling. Some lesser god playing stage manager, thought Raszer. Abel Cohn's brow knitted up tight; he appeared to be genuinely afraid that he'd fathered a monster, but like all fathers, unable to stop loving his creation.

"You're certain that Fortis is up there? With Vreeland in Shasta?"

"I'm sure," Cohn replied. "He's personally filed documents with the court. But I'm not convinced his presence there is entirely a matter of free will. I'm leaving room for doubt . . . or hope . . . that this maniac has him mesmerized. Your baili-wick, right?"

Raszer only smiled.

"I haven't had contact in over a month," Cohn continued, "and that's one thing I can count on with Fortis. He likes for me to know that he's shitting on everything I care about. If he cares enough to hurt me, I can even persuade myself he still needs me."

"Has the Indian case come before the Court yet?" Raszer asked.

"No. There's a lot of pre-trial discovery involved. Old documents. The tribes claim there was fraud in the original 1875 transaction. The first recorded challenge to the Klamath Company's deed is by the Modoc tribe in 1882."

Raszer let it sink in. "You said Fortis was doing this pro bono?"

"Not any more. He made sure I knew he was getting my hourly rate."

"Any idea who's bankrolling it? These guys don't make enough off their Web sites to fight class actions."

"I've done some poking around," Cohn replied. "The land that the Order of Thule now holds changed hands for exactly one dollar, which indicates to me that the Klamath Mining Company—whoever they are—is still running the show."

"So the Order of Thule could be the paramilitary wing of some bigger bird," Raszer speculated. "And the Klamath Company—a front—since, as far as I know, they don't mine up there anymore. Not on a dormant volcano. It's puzzling, but . . . " He looked at Cohn straight-on. "Given your son's contrarian history, what makes you think this is cult-style manipulation? Why hire me and not just a good surveillance man?"

"Because they say you can keep a poker face in a card game with the Devil, Mr. Raszer. And because there's something else I learned from Sacramento."

"What's that?"

"There's a pedophile doing time on a prison farm near Stockton. Karl Lodz is his name. He claims he and Vreeland merc'd together in Somalia and fell out over someone named Ori. Lodz swears that while they were playing war games in Utah four years ago, Vreeland had a 'vision' that the earth was honeycombed with tunnels inhabited by an antediluvian race. And that these ancient trolls—whoever they are—plan to resurface through Mt. Shasta, at which point they'll impose a New World Order in cahoots with the United Nations and the European Union. That's Vreeland's bogeyman, and now it's my son's crusade."

Raszer shook his head. "When God made fascists, he shouldn't have given them imaginations. He must be talking about the Lemurians."

"Le-what?" Cohn asked.

"Stop anybody on Main Street in Shasta village and they'll tell you about the lost continent of Lemuria. It's their local mythology, like Bigfoot in the Pacific Northwest. According to nineteenth-century theosophy, Lemuria was the Atlantis of the Pacific. Depending on whose account you hear, the inhabitants were either furry giants with telepathic third eyes or tall, blond, clairvoyant vegans."

Cohn rolled his eyes. "But they don't . . . take this literally?"

Raszer offered an enigmatic smile. "Shasta's an unusual place. I spent some time up there a few years back. Time stopped in 1967. It's almost as if the mountain creates a paranormal low pressure zone."

"Hmm," said Cohn. "All the more reason to make you the weatherman."

"I hope you're right. Anything else you have to tell me, Mr. Cohn?"

Cohn opened a drawer and took out a folded sheet from a yellow legal pad. He let it sit on the desktop for a moment, as if having second thoughts, then pushed it across to Raszer.

The note was written in a textbook longhand, almost compulsively neat, but it was clearly a draft, as certain words had been crossed out in favor of others and there were odd scribblings in the margins. It read:

My Commander: You have become more than a brother, more than a ~~teacher~~ *father to me. You have entered my soul and opened my eyes to the destiny of the* ~~planet~~ *race. Please do not doubt me. I salute your command. 010101 will be my own restoration,* ~~too~~ *as well. Yours* ~~For,~~ *Fortis.*

Raszer glanced at the margin for just long enough to see the notation "23.5" and a few other disconnected fragments, then looked up at his host.

"So, tell me, Mr. Raszer," said the older man. "Is that a love letter?"

"It suggests a bond that's considerably deeper than attorney-client privilege. Devotion, yes. Love? I don't know."

"Right. And the zeroes and ones. What? Some kind of code?"

"Too basic," Raszer replied. "And since he speaks of it in future tense, it can't be a date." He shook his head. "In any case, it sounds like they've got plans."

"I want you to go up there and find my son. And if you can get me something criminal on this scum Vreeland, I'm prepared to pay a substantial bonus."

Raszer had accepted the job and a generous retainer. Before walking out the door, he'd turned to Cohn. "Does Fortis have . . . any history of homosexual activity?"

"Until a year ago," Cohn replied, "I would've said no. True, he never was big on girlfriends, but he coughs up more homophobic bile than Rush Limbaugh. I would've said he was just socially ill adapted, but recently—" He paused. "There's a young executive at Paramount he was seeing a lot of before he took off. Something to do with a movie deal. His name is Christopher Rose. Let me give you his number."

Raszer pocketed the slip of paper before shaking Cohn's hand. He turned to leave, but there was something that needed saying. "Mr. Cohn . . . the only thing we understand as little as religion is sex. That's why—for my money—they're connected. Connected in the search for identity. And it doesn't take a shrink to tell you that in that search, what we exclude is usually what we fear we are." He looked his new client in the eye. "We'll meet again before I leave for Shasta. Thanks for your trust. I will find your son. If I can, I'll bring him home."

The jagged San Jacinto Ridge was bejeweled with stars. Raszer tipped his head back and found Polaris, pulsing faintly. Serena was singing again, beside the hot tub. He'd just begun to drift when he felt a tremor and watched a small wave form and splash onto the Moorish tiles.

"Earthquake," she said, squeezing his hand. "A little one."

"C'mon in," said Raszer, smiling. "Bound to be an aftershock."

Without much hesitation, she slipped off her dress and joined him.

2

THE HIGH PRIESTESS.

The Road to the Western Lands is by definition
the most dangerous road in the world
for it is a journey beyond Death, beyond the basic
God-standard of fear and danger.
It is the most heavily guarded road in the world,
for it gives access to the gift that supersedes all others:
Immortality.

—William S. Burroughs

EARLIER that evening, Raja Zlatari, known on the street as Madame Rey, had stepped outside her Hollywood tarot parlor to sniff the air for customers. She'd shuddered as it entered her nostrils. It smelled of desert scrub and bleached bone, borne into Los Angeles on the back of the ill winds now coming down hard through the canyons. It smelled of *bibaxt*—"bad luck" in her native and ageless Romany tongue. Luck and fate were a Roma woman's tireless accompanists, rolling out the chords and urging her to sing the next note in the prefigured melody. It was as if she had spent her entire life waiting for the shadow that followed, even in the brightest sunlight, to finally overtake her. The shadow was her own *mulo*—the ghost of an evening yet to come.

It was early autumn and prematurely dark, for Los Angeles had just switched back to Standard Time. The day's warmth had quickly risen into the cloudless sky, a sky from which not a drop could have been squeezed, leaving behind the typical California chill which puzzled so many tourists from the east who arrived expecting balmy nights. Without warning, the Santa Anas had swept in with their oddly perfumed heat, creating a weird ambiguity of season. As an undulating swarm of leaves and debris sailed past the front of her rundown establishment, she found herself thinking, *the earth will shake sometime in the next twenty-four hours.* She had not felt such certainty in many years of practicing her profession-by-default as a *drabardi*—a fortune teller. The sign in her window, its garish colors now faded from the unsparing Southern light, read "Madame Rey's Palmistry & Tarot," and in smaller print: "Destinies Revealed."

Raja turned wearily and put a hand against the doorframe. Over the years, a habit of staying open well past standard business hours had formed, mostly in consideration of the fact that her little Franklin Avenue strip included a theater, a few restaurants, and an offbeat bookstore that remained open to midnight, all of which meant potential passerby business for her. These days, though, it was simply habit. Business was bad—so bad, in fact, that she was in danger of losing the lease to yet another trendy but inevitably short-lived restaurant.

The Roma people themselves—whether those who formed her own large *kumpania* of expatriate French-Romanians or those who rolled into L.A. day after day from other parts of the world—never consulted fortune tellers. Since gypsies accepted predestination as a given, it was of little value to ask another gypsy to affirm it. But now, even the *gadjes* were staying away. New Age bookstores and crystal emporiums served their spiritual interests. After thirty years of near respectability conferred by the children of the sixties, the last decade of the old century had once again reduced the "gypsy woman" to a black-eyed charlatan in a faded sari who'd tell you anything to get her rent paid. All too often, Raja thought to herself, the description was apt. She'd given some lousy readings lately. As she pulled the door open, Raja felt something brush her shoulder and then heard a throat being cleared.

"Ma'am?" said a voice from her left. She rolled her head in its direction without shifting her stance and beheld a nicely dressed young man of about twenty-nine with the dewy eyes and smooth but faintly lined skin of a child actor past his prime. He was wearing a wedding ring and looked spooked. She nodded a mute greeting.

"You're, uh . . . closing. I-I'm sorry," he stammered. "Do you think . . . could you give me a reading? I've never done this before, but I . . . I don't know where else to go." He cast an apprehensive glance over his shoulder.

He was clearly distraught and anxious to be ushered in before being spotted. He wore that look that nine-to-fivers have when they are casing a sex shop in broad daylight. Perhaps, she thought, he's embarrassed about seeing a fortuneteller. But there was something about his trembling jaw that moved her. She led him to an overstuffed loveseat with a musty gold slipcover and asked him to sit. The parlor had a large picture window which normally offered a view of the street scene, but was now masked by a drawn velvet shade. The simple decor had not been significantly altered in years, although she had collected about her an impressive number of talismanic knick-knacks: rattles, bells, and even a few Navaho dreamcatchers. Raja pulled the chain on an antique floor lamp with a shade discolored by the patina of tobacco smoke, tinting the off-white walls in amber and throwing a stooped shadow that cast her as an old woman well beyond her sixty-two years.

From a lacquered Chinese box on the bookshelf she took her tarot deck, carefully unwrapping the silk scarf that shielded the cards from unwanted vibrations. She crossed the room, expertly and effortlessly shuffling the cards from hand to hand as if she were playing the musette. It was a hand-painted Marseilles deck that she had picked up seven years earlier during the annual May pilgrimage to the festival of Saintes Maries de la Mer in coastal Provence. The festival's first day was an homage to dark Sara, handmaid to the sister of the Blessed Virgin and to Marie-Salome, mother of the Apostles James and John. Sara was patron saint of the gypsies, and her dusky statue, gazing eternally on the blue sea, was just one of the Black Virgins of the Mediterranean, those cryptic Madonnas whose images were found in grottos and cliff sides throughout the old heretical enclaves of Southern France and Spain. The Gypsies of Europe had swallowed Catholicism as an antidote to persecution, but Raja had been taught that the artisans who'd fashioned such likenesses as Sara's had found a clever way to cloak the old faith in the guise of the new one. For the Roma, all is concealment. Raja still thought of her tarot deck as the gift of "Sainte Sara," for it was in the shadow of her statue that she'd traded her gold ring for the cards she now held.

She drew her armchair closer and sat, facing north, at a small, glass-topped coffee table opposite the young man. She noticed that he alternated between kneading his hands and fidgeting with his right earlobe, which had been pierced but was currently without an ornament.

"My name is Madame Rey," she said. "A pleasure to meet you, uh . . . ?"

"C-Christopher," he stammered. "Christopher Rose."

"Try to relax," she said. "And please uncross your legs. You will find yourself more receptive to the vibrations."

"Okay, sure," he replied, with a nervous giggle. "Should I . . . how do we begin?"

"You're troubled . . . probably by more than one thing. But see if you can form all of the things which are troubling you into a sort of spinning wheel, and then ask me the question which is at its center."

"All right," he said. "I'll do my best."

As her client considered his query, Raja spread the seventy-eight cards face up with a single pass of her hand. Her deftness was the product of a lifetime of practice. She considered the timeless images, allowing them to tap her own psychic energy so that their potency could be aroused while she remained suitably passive.

A ferocious gust roared down Franklin Avenue like a hell-bound train, followed by a wake that shook the storefront window and loosened a few more chips of brittle putty from its decaying frame. Raja raised her eyes as she shuffled the cards and discreetly observed her subject. He was a pretty man, genteel, but with a certain glassiness in his eyes. The pilot light had gone out; the oven was already cold. She shivered. A shock of golden brown hair fell over his forehead and came to rest on his twitching right eyebrow. He was the sort of man who wouldn't make it safely through a day in prison, she thought, and hoped for his sake that he wasn't going to confess a crime. When she dropped her gaze once again to the cards, they had begun to hum for her. *That's good,* she thought. *Haven't felt that in a while.*

"This is the Significator," she said, placing the Page of Wands in the center of the table. "It represents you, the querent, in the present moment." Her impression was of youth, damaged—perhaps by ambition—and now, by doubt. She raked the remaining seventy-seven back into a pile.

"Have you a question, my friend?" she asked.

"It's actually—" he began. "More of a . . . problem. I'm, uh, involved with someone . . . something that maybe I shouldn't be. And I don't know what to do. There's really no one I can talk to, so I thought—"

"Are you concerned about—" Raja observed his ring finger with the poker-faced attentiveness which had long been her forte. "—your marriage?" He lowered his eyes and affirmed. He wore an expensive Armani tie, out of place against an Arrow shirt. "And perhaps, your career?"

"Both, I guess. I have a choice to make. The hardest one I've ever made."

"So, then . . . " She leaned her shoulder to the left while inclining her head right. "Make it a question. I don't need the details."

He sighed. "Am I giving up . . . more than I'll gain?"

Raja was more affected than she'd expected to be. Although her practice tended mostly to women, it was not uncommon for a man with a guilty conscience to come begging karmic indulgence for his faithless prick. But there was something else here, something that unsettled her. This man was anxious for his soul.

She handed him the deck and instructed him to shuffle three times while considering his question.

"Now," Raja said. "Separate them into three equal stacks."

When he had done so, she picked up the stack on the left and began to lay the cards in the Celtic Cross spread. The cards were alive now, and so was Raja. She dealt from the full tarot deck rather than only the twenty-two cards of the Major Arcana. The fifty-six cards of the Minor Arcana—a standard poker deck plus four in the Suit of Knights—were the fine-tuning. She covered the Significator with the Judgement card.

"This covers you," she said. "It is the 'climate' surrounding your query." The card came off the deck upside-down. She crossed the Judgement card with the Two of Swords, saying, "This crosses you. These are the forces which oppose you." *Deadlock,* she thought to herself. *Indecision. He can't see what's ahead, and it scares him.*

"This crowns you. This is what you hope for." Her psychic radar ricocheted off his reaction as she placed the Ace of Pentacles just above the center of the cross. It's power he wants, she realized, not pussy. "This is beneath you," she proceeded. "This is the foundation of the matter in question." She laid the sixth card of the Major Arcana—The Lovers—as the lower support of the cross, but once again the card was "reversed." *Sexual confusion?* Raja was beginning to sniff something. To the left and right of center she laid the cards signifying, respectively, what lay behind and ahead of this pensive junior mogul (for she was now certain that was what he was or wished to be). Bringing up the rear was the Knight of Rods, a born opportunist. Up ahead, however, lay a more portentous sign. The sixteenth key of the Major Arcana: *The Tower.*

Okay, she thought, *big changes ahead. For good or ill? Divorce? Maybe. No, definitely.* How could she be certain? Because she was now riffing off her client's own response to the images on the cards.

Raja sat back for a moment and inhaled deeply. The Santa Anas had raised the outside temperature by a good four or five degrees and her headscarf was damp with perspiration. Now came the final four cards, laid out vertically alongside the cross, which represented the forces that would be brought to bear on the events described by the spread. The seventh card was the subject himself. She laid the Death card calmly on the glass, as if it were any other card, and waited for his reaction. The scant color drained from his cheeks and the air left his lungs. "Sshhit . . . "

19

"Don't be alarmed," she counseled. "In this position it usually means that an old way of being is ending and a new one beginning." He seemed unconvinced. It was a little like a doctor telling his patient that there was a reasonable chance the ten-ounce tumor in his colon was benign.

The eighth card was the effect of others—family, colleagues—on the resolution of the question. Raja placed the Four of Cups above Death. It was ambiguous, but she made a call. Acceptance. "Those whose approval you seek are more like you than you know." It was not a particularly exciting card, but she thought she owed him some relief. The ninth and penultimate card had always been difficult to read. It reflected the subject's own feelings regarding the outcome. In her young man's case, the possibility for error was compounded by the fact that she dealt The Wheel of Fortune, the card most closely linked with the Gypsy's abiding awareness of fate. When the Wheel card was dealt upright, it meant to her that the querent believed that his own actions would govern. When it appeared upside-down, as it now did, it suggested that outside forces were in control. The pivot was the final card, the one which—nuanced by all before it—pointed to the denouement of the drama. Raja noticed that his eye was twitching.

She laid the card and sat back against the worn, rose-embroidered damask, exhaling through puckered lips with a dry, unconscious whistle.

"Am I screwed?" asked the young man, with what seemed resignation. It was difficult to draw another conclusion from the Ten of Swords in this position. The hand-illuminated image on the card's face was of a callow young dandy being shown through a door by a princely rake; on the dark side of the door lay a deep pit containing ten sabers with upright points. One could interpret this as a warning—the young man had not yet crossed the threshold—but following the Four of Cups and the Wheel, it should almost surely be read as treachery already afoot, trust foolishly given. These were the moments of truth for a *drabardi*, the crux between craft and artifice. Should she send him out to the ill winds of evening with a twenty-dollar fix, betting that he would return for another, or share her apprehension and risk his not coming back?

She lost herself for a few moments in the card's beautifully sinister design. It was said by the man who had traded her the deck to have been painted by an old Kabbalist in Fez, who must by now have gone to meet his mulo. She considered the correspondences, for each of the cards in the Major Arcana could be linked with a letter in the Hebrew alphabet, and with a number that had its own special resonance. Tarot was a system, a way of divining the bigger picture, and at her best, Raja was an able seer. She recalled her father holding her aloft after she'd given her first reading at ten, crowing proudly, "This girl will make us the richest kumpania in France!"

Raja had a talent for the cards because she accepted them for what they were said to be: an encoding of every possible permutation of life's journey from blindness to wisdom etched on the face of seventy-eight paper rectangles. She had an affinity. If only she could utilize it now, for this sweetly desperate young man with the terrible secret.

"Is it over?" he asked, his voice oddly serene, his fears validated.

"This is what I can tell you," she replied, meeting his eyes and holding them. "You asked about the effect of your choice on two important parts of your life: your marriage and your career. Your marriage . . . may suffer. I do see an ending, perhaps the ending of a chapter, not the book. In the next chapter, you will not be the same, and this frightens you. As for your career, I sense that those who hold the key to your success would not reject this new person." He lowered his eyes. "But—" she ventured, tapping the Ten of Swords with a long, slender index finger. "There is a danger. Someone you have trusted is not worthy of your faith." He sighed, slipped his hand inside his suit coat, and glanced at the door again.

"Are you expecting someone?" she asked.

He finessed the question. "In what way do you mean . . . not worthy?" he asked instead.

"It's not clear." She observed that his fingers had now gotten hold of something, and recalled that he'd said he was involved in something he shouldn't be. "Has someone recently given you something of value?"

"Can I ask you something?"

"Of course," she said. He drew out a folded piece of yellow legal paper. It had a red wine stain on it and was faded from perspiration, having lain against his heart.

"Can I ask you to keep something for me? I can pay you. I mean, on top of your fee."

"Yes," she replied, "but you should probably tell me why you fear having it. Or at least, how you came to have it."

"It's going to sound crazy."

"Try me," she said.

"There's a kind of war going on," said the young man, his hands trembling. "One that nobody sees. But once you know about it, you have to choose sides. If I've made the wrong choice, then I shouldn't have this. And I think I have. Made the wrong choice."

Raja held out her palm.

"Give it to me," she said. She accepted the folded note, rose with a sigh, and crossed the room to the shelf she had taken her cards from. There was a lacquered Russian box bearing the saintly image of an old babushka; she opened it and placed the note inside. "There," she said. "It is off your chest! It will be safe until you return for it."

"It doesn't look like much," he said, anxiously folding Raja's twenty dollars in a hundred-dollar bill. "But he—They . . . say it's important. And I—" He paused, and she was suddenly aware of the mortal intensity of his fear. His tongue clicked against the dry roof of his mouth. "Thank you," he said. "I do feel a little better."

She lowered her penciled eyelids and accepted the money with a nod of gratitude, though she had the distinct feeling that she'd just been passed a curse. The young man stood up to leave, and she had just begun to collect the cards when the door blew open and a wild lick of wind, carrying a day's worth of exhaust fumes all the way from San Bernardino, scattered them to the four corners of the room. Raja sprang to her feet and stooped to grab the Devil card which had landed nearest her chair. A train of crisp leaves tumbled across the faded carpet and the squared-off toe of a black riding boot clamped the card to the floor before she could retrieve it. Raja looked up.

The intruder was easily six feet tall, wearing a buzz cut and a set of Gold's Gym muscles. The tattoo on his left bicep read M.O.O.T. above a depiction of a sword pinning a writhing serpent to the ground. His feral eyes connected with the young man as if the latter was a shank of beef.

"Let's go, bitch," he commanded. "We're late."

"How did you—" the young man stammered, then turned to Raja with a mint julep gentility totally at odds with the moment and said, "Nice to meet you, ma'am." In an instant he was gone, dragged out the door with the blind suddenness of a shark attack. Stupefied, Raja stared after him for a long moment before she resumed picking up the cards.

Shortly after ten o' clock, Raja locked up the shop and began to walk the scant block home, to a small flat she had rented for years in the grandly named but visibly decayed apartment building known as Villa Carlotta. Like the lavish chateau across the street that had been claimed for the Church of Scientology, the Villa Carlotta owed its existence to William Randolph Hearst. It was rumored to have been built with hush money paid by Hearst to a man he'd shot and wounded aboard his yacht. The Carlotta's manager, Ric Proust, who acted the baronial caretaker, swore by the story. He told also of how in the thirties, when the building was in its prime, it had been known as Barrymore's bordello. Whatever it had been, the Carlotta was now a refuge for Raja and fifty-two other "practitioners of the unusual," as Ric referred to his tenants. There were penniless poets, painters of grotesques on glass, Balkan pianists, magicians, and what seemed an entire subset of the L.A. goth scene, all distinguished by their inability to pay the rent with any regularity. Ric had said that "any tenant who could be counted on to make the rent on time was not worth having," and he had generously allowed Raja to fall three months behind on hers. It was her pride, more than her landlord's insistence, which demanded that she pay her debt soon.

As she set foot on the first of two worn stone steps leading to the building's heavy wooden doors, Raja was unaccountably overcome. She staggered, and fell back against the gothic stonework that cloistered the entrance. Fearing a stroke, she put her fingers to her temples and slid down the curve of the archway to sit. Her sight was gone for what might have been two seconds or two minutes, and she found herself utterly unable to form a single coherent thought or impression. She reached out for one of the cool, stone ribs of the ogive, gripping it for balance, because the stoop was shaking and she felt as if she might fall off. For a moment, her auditory sense shut down as well, and it was as silent inside her head as in those moments when one's ears plug up on an airplane's descent. Then it came, like a diesel freight through a mountain tunnel: a synapse-shattering burst of electronic noise, roaring in one ear and out the other and tailing off with a Doppler effect.

She looked around as her pupils dilated and the street once again reflected light. The sputter of a passing moped reminded her that her hearing had returned as well, and that the world was back to normal. As she stumbled to her feet, she thought *the earth has moved, all right . . . but did it move only for me?*

3

THE EMPRESS.

NINE thousand, three hundred ninety-six feet up the SW slope of Mt. Shasta, Professor Niall Mathonwy sat at his desk in the spartan climbers' hut which had been commandeered by the U.S. Geological Survey for his use. As was his habit when he was prepping a lecture for his Tuesday night classes at the community college, he had been scribbling in his journal and (as there was no one to hear him at nine-thousand feet) thinking out loud. Head to toe in Scottish woolens (the temperature in the hut rarely made it above 62 degrees), Mathonwy had been musing about science's efforts to find mathematical stability within apparently chaotic systems. Science, a masculine passion, would not stop seeking order, but Mathonwy felt pretty sure that Mother Earth would confound any attempt to comprehend her behavior which did not take karma into account. He was a volcanologist, so chaos was something he'd had to accommodate himself to. But he was also a scholar of myth, and it was in myth that he saw the ceaseless interplay of human foible and planetary fate, distant action and intimate consequence which, finally, brought some "order" to the jumble of history. "Chaos is karma in the disguise of fortune!" he announced, to no one in particular.

Precisely as the last word left his lips, the mountain's internal organs seized up and his clatterbox began to shake. He waited for a moment, then rose from the desk, leaving his journal open, and went to the door. If his theories about the source of the seismic disturbance were correct, there might be something of a light show waiting for him outside.

The door had a heavy wooden core with sheets of corrugated tin nailed to both sides, making it groan mightily each time it was opened. He stepped out into the dry, windless night and shivered. It always seemed to be winter on the slopes of Shasta, though tonight's 50 degrees Fahrenheit was relatively mild for October. His vision tracked up the Casaval Ridge to a snow-caked depression, about twelve hundred feet below the summit, which was known as "The Heart."

Sure enough, there they were.

Blossoming to the left and right of The Heart's topographical dimple were hemispheres of luminescent deep red and green, sometimes mounting a ridge like rising harvest moons, sometimes quivering in midair like levitating Jell-O molds. Min-min lights, they were called by the locals, and Ezekiel's Chariot couldn't have been more wonderous. Less fancifully, they were electromagnetic emissions from the deep fissures near the volcano's twin cones, brought on by piezoelectric activity within the crystal-veined core.

The famous ghost lights of Mt. Shasta. For nearly a century, there had been folks down in the village below who attributed their appearance to the nocturnal ramblings of the Lemurian mountain dwellers or else of Theosophy's "White Brotherhood," who had long since found a place on the slopes thanks to resident seers like Elizabeth Clare Prophet. Mathonwy did not judge them entirely wrong: science did not negate magic, any more than sex obviated love. He returned to his journal and wrote: "Science laid a Cartesian grid over the mischief of daemons, but even Descartes knew that the daemons had merely been caged." He read the line over, satisfied. Maybe he would use it in tomorrow's lecture, maybe not. He decided to make himself a cup of tea.

Professor Mathonwy stretched his long frame while waiting a small eternity for the water's high altitude boil. His fingertips, protruding bonily from the knit climber's gloves he wore habitually in the hut, touched the ceiling. He had lived in this eight by seventeen foot shack for more than a decade, assigned there after the St. Helens eruption had put the Geological Survey on alert for the possibility of more volcanic activity along the Cascade chain. Remarkably, the station, with two narrow cots and two cramped desks, had been designed for a pair of geologists, but Mathonwy had never put in for a partner. For most people, that would suggest either sociopathy or penitence; for the crowd, such an existence would epitomize loneliness. But he was not a sociopath and was seldom truly lonely. There were his students, both those from his current classes and those from his days at Caltech with whom he'd kept in touch. The more intrepid of them occasionally paid visits. There were the mountain goats that nudged his door open when it rained and stood demurely on his threshold as if waiting to be invited in. And there was Shasta herself, a mountain so massive that, like some huge star, it seemed to bend all light in its direction, to warp its own small sector of space-time. The Modocs and the Wintu had sensed this, and had made it the seat of their gods.

The water reached a simmer; the best that could be hoped for at this altitude, and Mathonwy removed the dented saucepan from the hotplate, pouring his tea with Zen attentiveness. Yes, he was all alone up here, but only in solitude could one truly monitor a volcano. The closest "neighbors" he had he would sooner have done without. They were twelve hundred feet down the ridge in a military compound, the jackhammer report from their automatic weapons violating the mountain's sanctity with every round. Bronk Vreeland. Now *there* was a man courting chaos.

No, he was not lonely, but Mathonwy did sometimes long for rapport, for the sound of a voice like his but not his, and he found himself keenly anticipating the arrival of the private investigator from L.A. who, with the support of the State's Attorney and the wary assent of the USGS, was to share his shack for a time and make use of its vantage to survey Mr. Vreeland's garrison.

He took his tea and returned to his journal. Tomorrow evening's lecture, he had decided, would address the multifarious and often conflicting legends of Mt. Shasta by way of the mountain herself. Here was chaos gowned in fifteen thousand feet of snowy serenity, and here, too, was potential instant karma. The Greeks had made Earth a Woman and called her Gaia: Gaia-Ge-Geology. The Greeks had known whereof they spoke. "Where does She live?" he jotted down. "She lives inside," he whispered.

Only after the ink had dried did he rise, cross the hut, and examine the array of instruments that were positioned against the north wall. The readings were more or less the same as those from the last event, and the one before that. The seismograph had tracked at a magnitude of just below 3.2, hardly enough to rouse the slumbering inhabitants of the village below, but significant when recorded on the haunches of one of the Geo Survey's "Top Ten" volcanoes. Once again, the temblor's signature was uncannily constant: you could lay a ruler across the peaks. It was as if somebody had flipped a switch, delivered a precisely measured jolt of voltage, and then killed it. Earthquakes, Mathonwy well knew, didn't usually behave that way.

Within the hour, Caltech, Berkeley, and the USGS field office in Redding would have a fix on the epicenter. If this event were related to the recent swarm, it might lie anywhere along an arc from Yreka to Bakersfield. Seven small earthquakes in as many weeks, with epicenters hundreds of miles apart and on no known fault line. It was as if they had been plotted—too disciplined a performance to have been delivered by the chthonic goddess of chaos. And there was more. Mathonwy had not yet shared a salient fact with his field office: each of the seven had registered with identical strength on his mountain.

He stretched out on his cot, reading himself to sleep for the umpteenth time with Jules Verne's *Journey to the Center of the Earth*, the book which had inspired his vocation.

4

THE EMPEROR.

Los Angeles . . . a place where the genius loci
is favorable to the visions of old.
A new Alexandria . . . perhaps.
In any case, a good place for gnosis—
> —Bishop Stephan J. Hoeller,
> Ecclesia Gnostica, on Los Angeles

INTERSTATE 10, from Palm Springs back to L.A., was a hundred miles of exurban dreariness, relieved only when—as on this day—the air was clear enough to reveal the San Bernardino and San Gabriel Mountains leaping out of the basin to the north. During the pristine winter months, the desert floor shimmered, and Raszer always had a sense that he was moving across a vast seabed on which leviathans had once rested. Now, at the ragged end of summer, the "Inland Empire" was usually veiled by a milky haze that obscured everything but the freeway and the endless tracts of commercial property that bordered it. This day was unusual. The Santa Ana winds had blown the inland smog out to the coastal enclaves of the rich, sweeping the county and its working class pre-fabs clean in a natural redistribution of wealth. Off to his right, the sun glinted off the glass-faced office buildings of the City of San Bernardino, a foothill metropolis built foursquare on top of the San Andreas Fault. If and when the "Big One" came, San Bernardino would likely be the first domino to fall. The whole of Southern California's tenuous Eden seemed to Raszer one audacious act of tempting fate. And that was its thrill, as if Eve, hearing the heavy footfalls of a wrathful God in her garden, had said, "Fuck off!" Raszer felt keen, reasonably centered, and just hyped-up enough for the show. Restored by the previous evening's treatment, two days on the rocks, and two nights balancing the ingestion and purging of toxins, he was ready to go to work on the Fortis Cohn case.

He pushed in a cassette of some Berber folk tunes a friend had recorded for him in Tangiers and grinned as the music transformed his scrubby, familiar surroundings into the Maghreb. The weave of the nasal voice around the slap of the gut strings moved his mind into cruise mode. Leaving the 55 mph zone of San Bernardino, he lit a cigarette, goosed the speedometer up to 87, and held it. With the speed came an erotic surge; he recalled his masseuse, Serena, shedding her dress, the "little earthquake" having triggered abandonment of her professional discretion.

The memory of her body, still new, released a time-lapse retrospective of sexual history into his bloodstream. There were those encounters—urgent, sticky, and often as not, disappointing—which had occurred B.C. (Before the Crash). Since his experience of near-death metanoia, however, sex had been perfumed with grace. From each lover he'd received gifts, and each gift amplified his conviction that Western religion had gotten sex wrong. As a college boy, he'd been spellbound by the exploits of Sir Richard Francis Burton, the Victorian adventurer who had both discovered the source of the Nile and translated the *Kama Sutra*, but he hadn't been able to square Burton's spiritual yearning with his prodigious promiscuity: they'd seemed at odds. Now, he knew that one should never, ever take fucking for granted. Sex and mysticism were kissing cousins, but you couldn't tell that to a Baptist. What Raszer's adversaries seemed invariably to share was a quaking fear of the carnal expression of divine love. *Ah, Serena.*

His car phone bleeped and shot the replay to pixie dust. On the other end of the line was the one person other than his daughter Brigit he couldn't reproach for intruding on his reveries: his research assistant and one-woman Directorate of Operations, Monica Lord.

"Hey, Raszer," she said. "You all toned up? Ready for combat?"

"I'm a lover, not a fighter."

"Right. Did you get some climbing in at Joshua Tree?"

"Just a little bouldering," he said. "My ankle's still not right."

"I'm afraid you're gonna have to make an unpleasant side trip before you head up to Shasta."

"Uh-oh," he said, and cut the music. "What's up?"

"Detective Borges from Homicide just called. Wasn't he—"

"Yeah. He was in Missing Persons when I was earning my license. I guess they bumped him up. Jesus. Homicide? Those guys never call me. Who's dead?"

"I don't know," she replied. "He was pretty cryptic. Said it was 'up your alley' . . . He wants you to look at a body." Raszer shifted out of overdrive and moved into the right lane.

"At the morgue?" he asked, a little apprehensively.

"Nope. Still fresh. They're at the crime scene. Bronson Canyon. Up at the Bat-Caves. How far away are you?"

"Another forty-five, at least. Tell him I'll get there as quickly as I can. I guess I can't refuse the LAPD."

"Right," said Monica. "Sorry, boss. Anything you want me to prep?"

"Open a bottle of that '87 Rioja," he replied drily. "Any more calls?"

"Yep. On your private line. I'd have called you but . . . well, you know how you are about your retreats. That Paramount exec you've been trying to see? Christopher Rose. He finally called you back. About seven last night. Sounded like he needed to unload."

"Shit. I should've . . . Well, good. I need to see him before I leave. Any time, any place. Abel Cohn seems to think that Rose and his son were involved in some way, and I need any keyholes into Fortis's psyche I can get."

"Got it," she said. "I'll put it in your appointment book. Behave yourself with Homicide, boss. I'll see you in the morning."

"Hey," he said. "Before you sign off, partner. Was there another earthquake last night? Around ten-thirty?"

"Not that I felt in Silver Lake. But you know me. I sleep through anything under 5.0."

"'Blessed are the sleepers, for they shall soon drop off.' Thus spake Zarathustra."

"Some of us have to sleep, Raszer. Not everybody's engine runs on vapors like yours. *Ciao,* baby."

The Bronson Caves were located on a wildfire-denuded hillside in a lightly trafficked section of Griffith Park, about a quarter mile north of the Franklin Avenue strip. They were not true caves, but Hollywood artifice, a three-branched tunnel blasted through the granite hills years before, reportedly to provide a location for the Batmobile's secret garage on the vintage TV show. The surrounding canyon, however, was authentically rugged. Raszer hiked up the fire road that ascended from the dirt parking area and was struck by how L.A.'s schizoid topography provided a haven for malefactors in the chaparral which backed right up to the barbecue pits of the rich and famous. If they ever combed through these hills with a backhoe, he thought, they'd come across more than a few things you wouldn't want to mention at dinner.

A square hundred yards had been hastily cordoned off with police tape and a small cluster of sunset joggers and dog-walkers had gathered at the barricade along with a frustrated camera crew from Channel 9. A single uniformed patrolman stood guard, but fifty yards distant, through the tunnel opening, Raszer spotted the tan and charcoal suits of the Homicide boys. He approached the cop casually, displaying his P.I. license in his palm, and beckoned him a few feet away. Raszer did not like to announce himself in public if he could help it, and not with a news crew standing by.

"I'm here at Detective Borges's request," he said softly. The cop gave both his license and his casual attire the once-over.

"Oh, yeah," he practically bellowed. "You're the 'cult guy.' Borges is over there." He waved him through and Raszer ducked quickly under the tape and made a beeline for the mouth of the cave, hoping that the cameraman was slow on the trigger. A tall, Latino man with a thinker's creased face, whom Raszer recognized as Detective Borges, turned as soon as he heard boot soles crunch on the rock-strewn floor of the cavern. He approached Raszer with a huge, bony hand extended.

"Thanks for coming."

"My pleasure, Lieutenant," said Raszer, admitting his insincerity with a wry grin. "Sorry I couldn't get here sooner."

"That's all right," said Borges, cocking a thumb over his shoulder. "It wouldn't have done him any good. Come have a look."

"Belated congratulations . . . on your promotion."

"If you can call it that," said Borges, without inflection. "Thanks."

As soon as they had passed through the dark tunnel into the muted light of the box canyon, he saw what had been hidden from the view of the onlookers. In the dust and parched grass of the canyon floor, a forensics team and a medical examiner squatted beside the corpse of a sandy-haired, slim-built man who lay face down in the dirt. To his death, he'd worn a designer suit the color of poached salmon.

Raszer had a bad feeling almost instantly, but kept it to himself.

"Time of death: around ten-forty P.M. last night," said Borges. "Cause: strangulation, most likely a garrote. It appears—although the lab will have to confirm this—that he was sodomized either just prior to or *during* his murder. There's so much damage down there it's hard to tell if it . . . the sex, I mean . . . was consensual or not."

Raszer felt the pulse in his throat. He had encountered brutality, depravity, and even death in his pursuit of latter-day Svengali's, but at the heart of his mission was a play of abstractions. Articles of faith were abstractions; murder was not, and he knew that he would never be as composed in the face of its stark ugliness as this veteran cop.

"He was killed in there," Borges continued, pointing into the cave, "and then dragged out here. My guess is that the killer figured that the coyotes would get to him during the night and make both the ID and the m.o. more difficult to nail down. Coyotes will eat just about anything they don't have to work for . . . and yet, there's not a coyote track within ten feet of the body. They didn't touch him."

"Ten-forty, you said?"

"Right," Borges affirmed.

"There was an earthquake about that time."

"News to me," said Borges. "But things are always shaking in Boyle Heights."

"Well," said Raszer, "I don't know how strongly it registered here, but it may have spooked the coyotes—thrown off their feeding instinct. I have a Chumash friend who tells me that even a 3.0 will keep them crouching in the brush for hours."

"That would explain it, I guess," said Borges, a little skeptically. "Glad to know we can still rely on you for the odd bit of information. Anyway, we have a clean corpse." He studied Raszer for a beat. "But there *is* something here outside normal parameters, and that's why I called you."

"What's that?" Raszer inquired.

The detective motioned Raszer closer and tapped the medical examiner on the shoulder. "Burt, do you mind if we have a look at that wound?" The older man stood with a sigh and wiped his hands. Borges turned to Raszer. "I hope you're not having oxtail soup for dinner."

"Never touch it."

"Ah," said Borges. "You would if you tried my mother's."

Raszer took the examiner's place beside the body and felt a rush of vertigo as he squatted down. The pink Pacific light at first caused him to question his vision. The tails of the victim's single-vented sport coat had been folded out of the way and the shirttail rolled up; his trousers and bikini briefs had been pulled down to the thighs, exposing the buttocks and lower back. The corpse was not exactly "clean." The sacrum had been opened up like a zipper and the muscle tissue carved away to reveal the spine. The gaping wound had the shape of an arrowhead, its point where the tailbone would be, except that the tailbone was missing. It appeared to have been snapped cleanly off, leaving a stub of bone and cartilage.

"Jesus H. Christ," Raszer said quietly.

"It has to be ritualistic," said Borges, squatting beside him. "It's post-mortal, and if the killer just wanted to draw scavengers with the scent of blood, he could have gone to a whole lot less trouble. What do you think, Mr. Raszer? Know of any cults with a tailbone fetish?"

Raszer shook his head numbly. "Not that I'm aware of, and I thought I had most of them in my rolodex . . . "

"It's sure not Santeria," said Borges, "although some Anglo reporter will probably go for that. I thought about vodoun . . . we've got a sizable Haitian community in the Valley. And these hills are full of weekend Wiccans, but I'm guessing they order their eye of newt from Gelson's. What are we dealing with here?"

"I dunno," said Raszer, fishing in his pocket. "Okay if I smoke?"

"Sure," said Borges. "It's a free country. For now."

"The groups you mentioned . . . if they *do* use animal sacrifice, it's to effect some kind of sympathetic magic. This just looks like retribution." Raszer flipped open his Zippo and spun the wheel. "What do we know about his last hours on earth?"

"He bought a drink at Prizzi's down on Franklin at around nine P.M. A rum sour. The receipt was in his pocket. Guys in suits like that don't drink rum sours alone. Not in L.A., at least."

Raszer surveyed the body, the delicate hands.

"He's wearing a wedding ring," he observed.

Borges smiled. "He's also got a ticket stub from the Rialto in Boys' Town."

Raszer ran his eyes down the body from fingers to feet. The shoes were

Merrells, new, with a deep tread. Something twiglike and dung brown had wedged in the sole. He leaned in and gave it a sniff.

"That's dedication," Borges observed dryly. "What do we have?"

"Incense. Maybe somebody held last rites for him." He pivoted on his heels in the red dust. "Any I.D? A picture of his wife . . . or his boyfriend?"

"Nope. I'll bet the wife doesn't have a clue. Tells her he's working late, drives over from the studio lot to get sloppy with some leather boy he met in a chat room."

Raszer's jaw tightened. "You said he wasn't carrying I.D. How do you know he worked at a studio?"

"The killer took his billfold, but he missed the inside pocket of his suit coat. One of those little business card holders the studio players never leave home without. Paramount. A vice-president of development. I still haven't figured out what they do."

"Do you mind," asked Raszer, "if I see one of them?"

Borges shrugged. "Sure," he said. "But there's nothing written on them. No phone numbers." He snorted. "No secret passwords." He retrieved the evidence bag from a second detective and displayed the small white cards with the familiar blue logo. For Raszer, who expected the pre-ordained the way most people expect the merely predictable, it did not come entirely as a surprise that the name on the card was Christopher Rose. Nonetheless, it knocked him back. He squinted reflexively and handed the business cards back to Borges without a word.

"Do that again," said Borges.

"Do what?" asked Raszer, concerned he might have betrayed his interest.

"The squint thing."

Raszer chuckled. "Even when I was acting, I couldn't mug on cue."

"That's o.k. Now I remember. Steve McQueen. That's who you used to remind me of. The only Anglo actor I ever really liked." Raszer stood and brushed the dust from his knees. "Any ideas, Mr. Raszer?" Borges asked.

"Nothing I'd put in a police report," said Raszer. "But here's how my mind works, for what it's worth: in Tantric yoga, the root of the spine is the seat of the serpent power, Kundalini . . . creative force, libido . . . the urge to, uh, merge. The trick is to get the serpent to rise through the chakras—the energy centers of the body—and into your brain, until it blows through the top of your head. Now there's a sexual variant of this yoga, which is done with a partner . . . where the object is to contain orgasm until Kundalini floods both of your heads with the blinding light of illumination."

The detective blinked. "You've tried this, have you?"

"If you, uh, lose control, you've blown it. You've let the snake out of the bag, so to speak. So maybe Mr. Rose, metaphorically speaking—"

Borges nodded. "Spilled something he should've kept bottled up?"

"Right. Some kind of inside knowledge. And this . . . is his comeuppance."

Borges raised an eyebrow. "You're an original, Raszer."

"Like I said," Raszer repeated. "I wouldn't put it in a report." He stamped out his cigarette and pointed at the wound. "It's an inverted pyramid. That . . . and the missing tailbone . . . sure makes it a signature of some kind. Let me look into it. I'm leaving for a job up North, but your guys know how to find me." Raszer offered Borges a hand up.

"Thank you for coming by, Mr. Raszer," said the Lieutenant. "I would appreciate anything you come up with." He smiled. "No matter how weird."

As he crossed paths with the medical examiner, Raszer put a hand on the old man's shoulder. "What about you, sir?" he asked. "Ever seen this kind of wound?" The examiner was an Asian man who looked ancient enough to have autopsied the Black Dahlia, and Raszer figured that a life's work in L.A—a city where death imitates art—must have shown him some grisly handiwork.

"I've seen bloodier and messier and meaner," came the reply. "But I've never seen anything as cold as this. This was a beast."

Leaving Bronson Canyon, Raszer made a right on Franklin Avenue and surveyed the store fronts on the block-long bohemian strip, looking for anything that might suggest that Christopher Rose had come there for more than a rum sour and rough trade. There were three or four small restaurants, including Prizzi's, where Raszer sometimes went for the antipasto; a few little shops, one of which traded in Asian exotica and might well sell incense, a coffee house, a bookstore. And there was Madame Rey's Tarot Parlor, which brought back memories as bittersweet as her honeyed lemon tea, for at the nil point of his life he had briefly been a client.

He made mental notes of it all, and decided to come back that evening when the night crews would be on duty and someone might remember the pretty young man in the pale salmon suit. Raszer did not entirely buy the notion that the victim had visited the edgy and highly visible Franklin strip for romantic purposes, but he might have come to meet someone, and that meeting might have gotten him killed, yogic serpents aside. He hoped for Abel Cohn's sake that the meeting had not involved his son, Fortis. He shot through the Highland intersection and made a steep right turn onto Whitley Drive, heading up the chronically fractured pavement at a forty-five-degree slope.

Whitley Heights was an enclave of Tuscan-style homes built into the hills in the 1930s and recently designated a "historical overlay." The artifacts of Golden Age glamour were what passed for ancient history in Los Angeles. Raszer himself had come to embrace the town's mythos through a sort of willful self-delusion. His Hollywood was not the tawdry border town that had disappointed so many over the years who came expecting a cross between Palm Beach and Carnaby Street. It was a free zone of magic, equal parts Nathaniel West, Raymond Chandler, and Madame Blavatsky, where people clutched talismans and wished themselves into being. It was not a place for realists. Even the bums here could recite Bogart's best lines from memory. In the serpentine braid of the canyon streets, in the live oak and laurel greened hollows—oddly backwoodsy considering their nearness to the most modern of cities—Raszer had found a new skin.

Raszer's house on Whitley Terrace was partially masked from the street by a stand of cedars. The longest section of its wraparound balcony faced the canyon, and from there he could smell the sage and wild fennel and hear the maniacally gleeful yip of the coyotes when they were feasting on a rabbit, or a housecat that had strayed onto their turf. Now, as he pulled into the garage, he could not help thinking of how those scavengers might have torn at the soft tissue exposed by Christopher Rose's attacker, and wondering if it had indeed been the earthquake—and not some more inscrutable magic—which had kept them at bay.

There were three bedrooms, one of which served as his library and one of which belonged to his daughter when she came to stay for summers and Christmas. Three bedrooms and a balcony with a view was about all a half a million had bought at the time of his purchase. Now it bought far less. In the third and smallest bedroom, Raszer slept on a futon he'd had since his divorce. Although he was not particularly sentimental, Raszer had a historical attachment to the first piece of furniture he'd owned after the machinations of his ex-wife's lawyer had siphoned off everything else. He had never bothered in the years since to restore his material estate to its former bounty, and the house still had the airy, teahouse quality of a place just moved into. The exceptions to this were the office—a former sunroom that opened onto the balcony—and his library of esoterica.

He unlocked the twin deadbolts, disarmed the security system, and stepped into the office. The darkened space was eerily pin-pricked by the dozens of glowing green and red indicator lights of the computer and telecommunications equipment that formed the nexus of his increasingly global enterprise. Monica had only recently left, as evidenced by the still-warm cup of tea at her station. He picked up the cup and sniffed it. Ginseng. Raszer wished he could pick her brain at this moment.

He credited himself with having managed only two strokes of real genius in his erratic professional life. One was to have ramped onto the "information superhighway" long before any speed limits had been posted. Under thirty-two different e-mail aliases and through the strategically baited traps of eight different Web sites, he received information from all over the wired world. Much of the data was worthless Internet dreck. Occasionally, however, some useful chatter came his way via the more clandestine newsgroups. He had once warned Interpol, four days in advance of the event, that the notorious French-Canadian "suicide cult," the Temple of the Sun, was planning a Yuletide mass exit in an Alpine pass near Grenoble, France. Interpol hadn't listened, and sixteen people had died. After that, international police agencies began to take Raszer more seriously, and now he was networked into a dozen of them.

His smartest move, however, had been to lure Monica Lord out of a promising career as a Hollywood publicist, at a time when she was young and hungry enough to take two-hundred dollars a week for the dubious privilege of managing his on again/off again career as B-movie actor in the early 1990s. Why she had come to work for him was never stated; one day she just said, "Okay. Let's do it." She knew he was no actor, or rather, that he was an actor because he did not yet know what else to be. He guessed they had clicked because they were the rare two people who could begin a conversation in the parking lot at five P.M. and still be talking at two A.M. She was the yin to his yang, a stealth blond surfer from Huntington Beach, fluent in four languages and possessed of a maternal fierceness that had seen him through many skirmishes. She had once convinced National Guard helicopters to pluck him out of a crop circle in Paradise, Kansas within scant seconds of his being pitchforked by a mob of angry farmers, convinced that he'd not only trampled their corn but abducted their daughters.

Try as he might, Raszer could simply not imagine having this kind of connection with a man. His relationship with Monica was not, had never been, overtly sexual (despite his ex-wife's smug certainty), but there was no denying its erotic energy. Raszer was something of a traditionalist regarding gender issues, though he took grave offence at any suggestion of sexism. He simply believed that the planet spun in response to the friction generated by men and women in conflict and in congress, and that without this store of bipolar energy, the world might grind to a halt. There was no more conclusive proof of Monica's devotion than the fact that she had remained at his side throughout his breakdown, throughout his bruising divorce, even when he did his deranged utmost to drive her away.

He returned to her desk and switched on the antique reading lamp with the cobalt-blue hood. She had left him the usual well-ordered stack of notes and resource materials, place-marked and highlighted. He would dive into them in the morning with his first haze-burning cup of coffee, but now was the evening. He had dinner and a few more contemplative tasks to attend to before heading back to the strip where Christopher Rose had ordered his last rum sour. He scooped up from Monica's desk the dog-eared volume she'd obviously been reading, and smiled approvingly. It was Frederick Spencer Oliver's oddball chronicle *A Dweller On Two Planets*, written in 1894 in the "channeled voice" of "Phylos the Tibetan." The book described how Mr. Oliver had discovered his true karmic identity as Phylos only after meeting an Ascended Master by the name of Quong on the snowy slopes of Mt. Shasta. The story had absolutely nothing to do with Raszer's present assignment, except in the way it demonstrated that Shasta had been inducing visions—or delusions—for more than a century. Raszer wondered if Supreme Commander Bronk Vreeland knew of the book, as Timothy McVeigh had known of *The Turner Diaries*. Even lunatics feel obliged to quote some gospel in defense of their madness.

Raszer moved on through the converted bedroom that had become his library. Here, in a scant hundred and fifty square feet of room, opening through weathered French doors onto a fern-shaded terrace and therapeutic herb garden, were over three thousand books. Only a few, such as a first edition of Sir Richard Francis Burton's translation of *A Thousand And One Nights*, were rarities. Many were well-thumbed paperbacks. Each title, however, had been selected with great care, and in aggregate, they catalogued a good portion of what was known about man's trips to the hidden regions. There were alchemical allegories, Gnostic histories, shamanic field guides, volumes of Sufi and troubadour poetry and Renaissance grimoires. If Raszer was not yet himself quite a magus, he possessed the library of one. Like his darkly chivalrous hero Burton, he made no journey without that was not also a journey within.

And what had the books taught him? There was this: something had gone wrong. Eons ago—not just in "real time" but in the clockwork of the human soul. Something violent and sacred. It could rightly be thought of as a crime, and though it was recounted in all the myths of our species, it was yet the best-kept secret in the Universe. It was the *magnum mysterium*, and each time an acolyte of Orpheus had descended to the underworld, a knight had forsworn comfort for quest, or an intrepid Nancy Drew had entered an abandoned ware-house with no more than a hunch and a cheap flashlight to go by, it was this mys-tery they pursued.

And every worthy book of the occult on every shelf in every library of the world was an attempt to rectify the crime and doctor to its blunt trauma.

Some of us hurt more than others. Some felt it like a phantom limb or a stillborn twin; some drank, some gambled recklessly, some debased themselves out of shame. Others felt a morphic resonance: an unsettling ripple in the veil of comforting illusion.

One way or another, humankind was suffering post-traumatic shock disorder, and this was why people sought healing, even at the hands of quacks.

He navigated the house, turning on table and floor lamps as he went. Raszer was drawn to little pools of light that created their own distinctive shadows. Shadows kept him company in this canyon house where he lived alone for most of the year. Like many solitary people, his routines held an element of ritual. He switched on the lamp beside his sofa, where he'd once read Brigit *Through The Looking Glass*, and thought: "In this house, I have learned to love." He lit a hurricane lamp on his mantle and thought, "In this house, I have learned to pray." He nudged up the recessed lighting in his floor, recalling the lessons he'd taken here in the use of a combat knife for self-defense, and thought: "In this house, I have learned how to kill." Finally, he pulled the chain on the swag lamp over the curly maple and inlaid slate bar where he took his meals, executed a tango move his Argentine housekeeper had taught him in trade for English lessons, and thought: "In this house, I have learned to dance."

On his way to the kitchen, the telephone sounded a muffled ring. He scooped it up from the overstuffed armchair he'd pushed to within four feet of the fireplace the last time a woman had spent the night. The chair would not return to its ori-ginal spot; it was now invested with memory, and had thereby obtained a ceremo-nial right of place.

"Hello, Pops," squeaked the voice on the telephone. It was Brigit, calling from her mother's home in Mystic Seaport, Connecticut. Her radar was even stronger than usual.

"Do you know what time it is, muffin?" he reproached her gently. It was after ten in the east. They chatted in father-daughter shorthand for five minutes. Then she revealed but the true purpose of her call.

"Have you been watching CNN today, Daddy?"

"No, baby . . . why?" He could feel that she was ready to burst.

"People have been seeing UFO lights all up and down California."

Raszer ended up, as he often did, in the kitchen, which sat on stilts sunk into the steep side of the canyon at the rear of the house. It was not particularly spacious, but he rarely hosted more than a guest or two. Its centerpiece was a magnificent Wolf stove, cast iron and heavy as a tank, which took up far more space than suited the square footage. For a man who valued precision and old-world craftsmanship as Raszer did, it was well worth the expense in elbowroom. He located the uncorked bottle of Rioja and poured himself a generous glass. Then he turned on the small black and white pro monitor he had mounted under the cupboard, the only television in the house. Although he received all sixty-seven channels of noise that the local cable distributor provided, the set was tuned more or less permanently to CNN. While the day's numbing financial news droned on in the background, he set to work, still meditating on the weird conjunction between Lt. Borges's investigation and his own, surely as good an example as any of chaos being other than wholly chaotic.

He removed a ten-inch copper sauté pan from the rack, set it on the front burner, and poured in just enough cold-pressed virgin olive oil to cover the bottom. *There had been an earthquake, one of a recent swarm.* He turned the flame to medium-low, and just as the oil began to ripple, he crumbled in about a teaspoon of oregano which he'd dried himself out on his back deck. The herb was followed by a half teaspoon of cracked pink pepper. *As an indirect result of the earthquake, Serena Mankiller had offered him her body and its secrets.* While the oil was absorbing the spices, he set a heavy pot of water to boil for his capellini. *Christopher Rose had offered his body, too, but as a sacrifice to some lesser demon.* He completed the culinary ritual on autopilot, adding a handful of chopped plum tomatoes and a liberal shake of kosher salt to the sauce, and was about to leave the kitchen for his habitual perch on a high stool at the bar when his ears pricked up at CNN's mention of "triangular patterns of light witnessed by beet farmers in the San Joaquin Valley." *And now people were seeing flying saucers.* The report went on to say that sightings had been reported as far north as the Cascades. He was due to leave in days for Mt. Shasta, a trip that would take him straight up the San Joaquin Valley into the lower Cascades. Raszer began to plot each occurrence as a point in space, and then watched them interconnect in a lattice of possibility.

He lit another candle and set it on the slate bar top not far from his plate. Raszer ate habitually by candlelight, not only because he enjoyed the ambience but because the candle's gauzy glow created the sense of another presence sitting opposite him. It made him feel less self-conscious about talking to himself. He dropped an Arabic language tutorial cassette into his bar top boom box and swung onto the stool. The tape had been prepared for him by the same friend who had recorded the Berber music, and it employed a distinctive teaching method. Over the continuous droning thrum of North African musical instruments, a soothing female voice alternated Arabic words and phrases with their English equivalents, in sets of six. "River. *Nahr.* River. *Nahr.* River. *Nahr . . .*" Learning Arabic was Raszer's current project. After Arabic would come Russian. He'd now tackled the rudiments of six languages, but he had a long way to go before he matched the three dozen or so in which Sir Richard Burton had been fluent.

The light meal, good red wine, and the repetitive intonation of words in a still alien tongue set his brain waves in phase, and he found himself in the mood to work on a mind-into-matter exercise he'd been practicing for almost a year with erratic results. There was a small, portable vise that he had attached to the end of the bar, and into its jaws he set the handle of an antique silver spoon he'd inherited from his grandmother. He tightened the vise until the spoon was secure, with five of its six inches visible, and moved the candle so that its flame was reflected in the deepest part of the spoon's concavity. Keeping his posture erect and his breathing regular, he allowed his eyes to cross lazily, their vectors converging on the flickering mirror image. He tried not to concentrate in the usual sense, but simply to observe the spoon and—this was the trick —urge the atoms of silver into directed motion. It was, of course, irrational to think that they'd respond, and yet the technique had been subjected to experiments in which the brilliant physicist David Bohm had tested the celebrity spoonbender Uri Geller, yielding results which suggested that Geller and his spoon were linked in a subatomic syzygy.

After what seemed like a minute but was, in fact, seventeen of them, Raszer felt a sudden shift and realized that the light now sharply refracting off the spoon was not coming solely from the candle. He moved his head subtly from side to side and the light moved with it. Here it was again: the physical legacy of his psychic crash. His "re-birthmark." From the dull brown spot that had appeared in the iris of his right eye on the morning after Brigit's recovery, there sometimes came light, finely focused as through a lens. As if a second, dwarf iris had spun open, revealing some ancient ember glowing in the recesses of his brain. No doctor could make sense of it, and not even Monica fully believed it. He removed the spoon gingerly from the vise, expecting to see nothing, but aware that some had accused Geller of unconsciously exerting tactile force. He examined it skeptically: what he'd seen could have been a trick of the candlelight, and even if not, he doubted that the shower of photons from his eye could bend metal.

But doubt yields to quantum truth every time.

The little teaspoon was decidedly—if only slightly—bent. Was he learning to see—and shape—the subtext of reality? The possibility provoked a shudder. Much as he desired it, this kind of magic scared hell out of him.

It was about nine-twenty by the time Raszer sat down at Prizzi's and hailed the waitress, who from her rouged cheeks and thickly applied mascara he guessed had spent the better part of her day in an audition queue for extras. He'd chosen one of the small outside tables so that he could smoke, and because it allowed him to survey the strip in both directions. Right across the street was the Church of Scientology's palatial "Celebrity Center," a building more suited to the 16th *arrondissement* of Paris than it was to Hollywood. Some sort of gala was going on in its manicured gardens, featuring a regiment of frighteningly earnest-looking young men in the ersatz naval uniforms of L. Ron Hubbard's elite Sea Organization.

"Hi," the waitress chirped, smiling as if she were still working the casting director. "What can I getcha?"

"Hi." He returned the smile. "How about a double espresso, with something sweet on the side. Maybe a—"

"Biscotti. Sure thing. That'll be it?"

"That'll be it," he replied. "But I'm curious about something. . . . "

He took a twenty-dollar bill from his money clip and tucked it under the ash-tray, available when she needed it. Aspiring actresses always needed money. "Were you on duty this time last night?"

"Yep," she said. "Five nights a week. Are you with the police, too?"

"Nope," he replied. "Journalist." She relaxed her shoulders.

"L.A. Times?" she asked.

"Hollywood Reporter." Her eyes lit up. He beckoned her closer. "But if the police have been here, then you probably know I'm curious about the young fellow in the Italian suit who ordered a rum sour from you about this time last night."

"That was Karla. She works the inside tables, and she's the one the police talked to." She set her order pad on his table and leaned in. "But I can tell you more about the guy, 'cause I checked him out."

"Oh, yeah? Why's that?" She shrugged and shot him an impish grin.

"I'm single. Karla's married. I'm an actress. We get a lot of writers and producers here and——."

"I gotcha. How would you describe him?"

"Thirty-something. Married. Agitated. Gay."

"Two of those words don't go together."

"In this town they do."

"Why don't you go grab the coffee and settle me out," Raszer said, tapping the twenty gently. "Keep the change. Come back and talk to me after you take care of your other tables." She slipped the bill out and tripped off, ponytail swishing buoyantly. Raszer could see that he'd gotten her hopes up with his *Hollywood Reporter* charade, and felt a little bit guilty about it.

He lit a cigarette, faintly annoyed by the hubbub across the street. He glanced over and saw that the admirality had assembled on a riser and was performing an Andrew Lloyd Webber ballad in perfect four-part harmony and with cloying reverence. When he turned back to look down the strip, he caught the avian profile of Madame Rey, who'd poked outside her storefront two doors down to scan the street for customers. He smiled. It was, perversely, to her—rather than one of L.A.'s twenty-six thousand marriage counselors—that he'd come after first discovering his wife's infidelity. He'd felt silly about it at the time, but she had acquitted herself impressively and been, in a sense, his introduction to the world of suspending disbelief. He'd seen her a few more times, and had once even consulted her on an MP case in which his quarry had left behind a tarot card in lieu of a letter.

Sparks fired across his cortex . . . one . . . two . . . three . . . triggered by the chemistry of memory. The incense he'd found in the sole of Rose's shoe: a standard part of Madame Rey's *mise en scene*. Monica had said that Rose had sounded "like he needed to unload." Suddenly, Raszer understood. Rose had wanted to know about *consequences*. Raszer was pondering this when his coffee arrived with a mound of biscotti.

"Was he someone I should know?" the waitress inquired, on more familiar terms after his money. "The guy who got killed?"

"I'm sure he was trying to be," he replied. "Now we'll never know."

"It's creepy," she offered, with a dramatic shudder. "Right here, in Bronson Canyon. I walk my dog up there."

"You don't want to know," he said, stubbing out his cigarette, "half the stuff that turns up in these canyons. They can sanitize Times Square, but they'll never get the stain out of Hollywood's sheets. *Hell,*" he said, gesturing toward the singing Scientologists. "Right across the street, they could be plotting the overthrow of the United States government to the strains of 'Music of the Night.'" He drained his espresso in one gulp. "You didn't happen to see which way he turned after he left the restaurant?"

"Sure," she replied, pointing west. "That way. I saw him looking in the window of the tarot place, like he had nowhere to go. When I came back out, he was gone." Raszer draped his napkin over the cup and stood.

"Thanks," he said, foregoing the biscotti. "You've been a big help." Reconsidering, he snatched a cookie and locked eyes with her. "Don't beat yourself up if the parts don't come. Just pretend life's a Fellini movie and you've got the lead."

The night was again unseasonably warm, but with an undercurrent of approaching autumn and air so robbed of moisture and crackling with electricity that it felt like fever chills. The devil winds had retreated to the canyons, leaving the streets with a static charge that put nearly everyone on edge. Absent were the usual scents of jasmine and oleander. Raszer stepped into Madame Rey's Tarot Parlor and heard three sets of chimes announce his arrival. He'd just taken a bite out of the anise-flavored cookie when the gypsy appeared from behind a bead curtain, rubbing her temples.

"Madame Rey," he said, swallowing hastily. "It's Stephan Raszer." He offered his hand. "Do you remember me?" She approached him in an arc and with head cocked, as if inspecting a suitor. The crown of her gray head came to just below his chin; she could not have stood more than five feet tall. Her eyes, deep and dark as wells, searched his face and found a signpost.

"Yes," she replied. "Now I do . . . though you've changed. You're the man with the light in his eye."

"You read my cards a few years back, when I was trying to figure out what to do with my life."

"And did you figure it out?"

"I guess I did. I guess that's what brings me back to you. You told me that my life would move in a spiral . . . that when I thought I was repeating myself I'd actually be covering the same ground at a higher level."

"I said that?" She gave a rueful laugh. "I used to be good at this."

"More than good. And you still draw some pretty interesting clients. A young fellow who was in here last night about nine? Nicely dressed. Clean cut. Maybe a little edgy."

"Are you with the police?" she asked, a bit on guard. "Or are you his priest?"

"I'm a private investigator now," he replied, giving her his card. "Have the police been in to see you? A Lieutenant Borges?"

"No," she said, stiffening. "Why would they?"

"The man I described was murdered last night in Bronson Canyon. If I'm on the mark, he went straight from your session to his death."

"Mother of God . . . " Raja visualized the lay of the cards in her head, wondering how she could have missed a man with a dagger over his head. Maybe she had chosen to miss it. "How?" she asked. "Why?"

"I'd better leave the specifics aside, ma'am. The police might not appreciate my tampering. But a revenge killing is my guess. Did he say anything to suggest he was frightened, that someone might be after him?"

Her gaze turned inward. "I don't reveal what passes between me and a client, even when he has . . . moved on. This is my trust. But I will say that he was concerned he had made a mistake, and that there might be a price." Raja thought about the note tucked away in her Russian box. She had a strong urge to rid herself of its contamination immediately. The leavings of the dead were *marime* . . . contaminated.

"Did you see him arrive . . . or leave with anyone?" Raszer asked.

"A man came for him," she replied. "Not a nice man. Big. Shaved head. Leather. Tattoo. He may have been waiting outside. He was not happy."

"They left together?"

She nodded, seeing it all come horribly together in her mind's eye, knowing now that she would have to examine the note, for good or ill.

"You say the man was big. How big?"

"Oh ..." She shook her head. "At least six feet and over two hundred pounds. Big."

Raszer relaxed a little; this did not describe Fortis Cohn.

"May I ask your professional opinion?"

"You may ask."

"Did this young man—Christopher Rose was his name—fear that he'd been betrayed by someone he had cause to trust?"

"His cards indicated so, Mr. Raszer . . . but I think—" Her face tightened, but there was just the faintest hint of a smile. "I had also better leave the specifics aside. At least until I know that you're not what he was worried about."

"Fair enough," said Raszer. "But, in any case, the man is dead. His worries are over. And please call me Stephan. You once gave me reason to keep breathing . . . I think I owe you my first name."

"He is dead to your world, Stephan. Not yet to mine. His *mulo* will wander the place of his murder for many days. Perhaps as a coyote, or as a rattlesnake. It would not go well for me to betray his secret so soon."

"I respect that," said Raszer. "I've been employed by the father of another man with whom Mr. Rose may have been involved. My job is to find my client's son before he comes to the same end. If and when you feel able to help me, please call. Anytime." She examined his card, its newsprint block letters advertising RASZER'S EDGE—Specializing in Missing Persons.

"By the way, Madame Rey," he added. "Did you happen to feel an earthquake at about ten-thirty last night? I can't seem to find anyone—" She nodded slowly, her eyes on axis with his. "Good," he said. "Then I'm not crazy." He tipped his head and turned toward the door, then paused. Something demanded an explanation.

"How'd you know," he asked, indicating his right eye, "about this? My crazy eye?"

She began to close up the shop. "You don't remember . . . ah. You came to me one evening, mad with anger and grief. A child?" Raszer nodded. "Your daughter—" He nodded again. It was strange to hear his own history as if it were another man's. "—had been taken away from you. I wrapped you in a blanket and made you tea. I stayed with you. In the deepest part of the night, I woke up. There was a point of light on my ceiling. I followed its path, and it led to your eye."

Raszer nodded. "*Sastimos*, Madame Rey," he said as he left. Raja kept her dark eyes on the curtained door and wondered. The detective, now taken up by the gathering night, had used the Roma salutation, something rarely heard outside gypsy circles. Now, as three years earlier, she was certain that their fates were to be entwined.

Raszer arrived home a few minutes past midnight, returned to the bar to finish off the Rioja, and saw that he had an e-mail message on his laptop. The sender was april@blessingindisguise.com. The message was brief: *wart - all systems GO. come on up. xx morgan le fay.* He smiled and sipped the wine. His field operative had decided to assign each of them "code names" on this, her first serious outing with him. He laughed, but hoped that she was taking it all seriously enough.

While Raszer dashed a reply to his accomplice in Mt. Shasta, Abel Cohn paced his spacious bedroom. He had gone to bed at ten with a book, as was his habit, drifted off briefly, and then found himself wide awake and deeply anxious. It was the Santa Anas keeping him awake, he thought. They managed to insinuate their needling aridity even into a climate-controlled environment. They leeched all tenderness from the city. He wanted to sleep, but he did not want to take a pill yet, because it was about more than the winds. There was something he needed to remember.

Abel did not put a great deal of stock in the notion of "repressed memories." As a practical man and a practiced lawyer, he believed that people forgot what they elected not to recall, and that it didn't take a shrink so much as a good cross-examination to get it out of them. And yet, here he was, pacing the bedroom in his pajamas, agonizing like a man who after years of using a wall safe is suddenly unable to remember the combination. The memory had something to do with Fortis's birth, on another night when the winds had come; with the nursery at Glendale Adventist, and a reptilian face glimpsed fleetingly through swinging hospital doors. Abel had arrived late from a labor negotiation in Modesto. The sequence of events as replayed before his mind's eye was so compressed and charged with semiotic import that it couldn't possibly be anything other than a dream. That's it, he thought—I'm driving myself crazy trying to remember a dream. How neurotic is that?

Then the sweat broke out on his forehead, and he felt acutely nauseous. There was another man in the dream, and the man had a voice—"crying in the wilderness." A mental patient who had managed to escape his ward to come to the nursery, where he'd told Abel he was "looking for a baby boy." He'd appeared ordinary enough, except for the white smock that Abel had taken for what they issued fathers who chose to attend their child's birth, and the little gold medallion he wore around his neck. But then he had turned breathlessly to Abel, eyes black-rimmed, shiny and wide with fear, and said: "The boy . . . he belongs to them." And Abel had seen that the man's arm was extended, that he was pointing through the nursery window, and that he was indicating not his own son but the bassinet marked *Cohn.* "He's not—"

Then the orderlies and two burly men resembling plain-clothed cops had burst through the stairwell door and taken him down, offering muttered apologies.

Abel went into the bathroom and swabbed his face with a warm washcloth. He decided to take a pill after all. If the dream was still there in the morning, he would call the detective. If not, so much the better. Some combinations were better forgotten.

5

THE HIEROPHANT.

A ND in those days," Professor Mathonwy began, "there were giants in the earth." Mathonwy, no small man himself, stood before his adult education class at Siskyou Community College in the Northern California hamlet of Weed. "So said Moses," Mathonwy continued, "and so begins the handwritten draft of Richard Shaver's wild-eyed and utterly spurious pulp chronicle, *I Remember Lemuria*, published 1945 in Ray Palmer's *Amazing Stories* magazine. Most people wrote off the story as the ravings of a sexually troubled lunatic, but we would be poor investigators of the subterannean regions if we dismissed so persistent a myth as Lemuria simply because crazy people had given voice to it. Myths travel in good minds and bad minds alike."

The college was located about ten miles up Interstate 5 from Shasta village, the New Age Mecca masked as a rural tank town which lay nestled amid the ancient lava flows of the eponymous volcano. There were thirteen students enrolled in Mathonwy's Chthonic Mythologies of the Pacific Northwest class, but he directed his lecture with special ardor to the long-limbed young woman with the wheat-colored hair and ripped blue jeans who seemed to be listening more intently than the others. "Whether it's the wise Lemurians or the malevolent Shupchers of latter-day Wintun legend—who crush the life out of anyone foolish enough to venture underground—whether the Great White Brotherhood of I AM lore or the gentle titans of Telos . . . there has always been something about this area that inspires the wildest imaginings. *Why?*"

Mathonwy left the blackboard and walked toward the class for emphasis, his internal gyroscope bringing him to stand just in front of the pretty student's desk. His heels had already left their mark on this spot, where decorum required that she look up rather than stare at his navel, bringing her violet eyes into contact with his own in a right triangle of intimacy. Her name was April Blessing and she was twenty-seven, a Siskiyou County wood nymph whose adoption of another generation's tribal colors and feathery neo-paganism could not disguise the keenness of her intellect.

"Where have all the titans gone, Ms. Blessing? Allowing, for the sake of discussion, that the geological catastrophes of the early Holocene era—roughly 3200 B.C.E.—those cataclysms spoken of in Native legend, really did occur. Should we conclude that entire super-races were wiped out like the dinosaurs? They had, according to myth, highly developed cultures. It stands to reason that their efforts to preserve them would be no less strenuous than our own. Do traces remain, or is it all pixie dust? If we dig deep enough, do we find artifacts, or do all these alternative histories represent no more than periodic eruptions from a Jungian collective unconscious?"

"Couldn't both be true?" she replied, without blinking.

"Ah hah!" said Dr. Mathonwy, placing his palms on her desk, leaning in just close enough to whiff the sandalwood oil on her skin. "And how could that be?"

"Don't know," April said, and shrugged. "Memories of a parallel universe, beamed by gravitons through that interdimensional membrane the string theorists talk about?"

He lingered for a moment at her desk. His monastic lifestyle had all but drilled eros out of his system, but April Blessing was a post-modern Diana. Oh, to come upon her bathing in a woodland spring! "Or perhaps," he said, "memories of what might have been. Counterfactuals. The Klamath and Wintu Indian legends speak of Elam-MU, which was Anglicized in the nineteenth century as Lemuria, the lost continent of the Pacific. Now, a rationalist will tell you that it's just another Golden Age pipe dream: Atlantis, Arcadia, Shambhala—the Germanic racial fantasy of Ultima Thule. But there are hard scientists like Rupert Sheldrake who contend that the rocks and trees retain memories—a kind of molecular "tape recording"—and native peoples have always found a greater truth in Nature. Who's to say that 'giants' may not be sleeping beneath us tonight?"

An overweight fellow in the rear raised his hand, and Mathonwy somewhat reluctantly shifted his attention.

"Does all this have anything to do with the weird lights people see up on Mt. Shasta?" the man asked. "And the UFOs?"

"I'm glad you asked," the professor replied. "Because it is, after all, the mountain that causes all this fuss . . . the mountain that brings us all here. Yes, those eerie displays of red and green on the white slopes . . . those odd lenticular clouds that swirl above the mouth of the volcano like a mothership. I'll tell you this as a scientist: a volcano creates one hell of an electromagnetic field, and almost any sensory impression we can imagine can be conjured by the right kind of disturbance." He strode to the window and gave the shade a tug. For dramatic effect, he let it fly up, revealing the massive, faintly luminous hulk which, even fifteen miles away and at night, dominated the landscape by blocking out the stars. "As a plumber of local mythology, however, I'll say this: Shasta is our Mt. Olympus. Why, just this past week, a young boy—"

There was a groan from deep in the building's foundation, and the windows began to rattle. A couple of disaster-ready students in the back of the room slipped out of their chairs and ducked under their desks. Mathonwy watched the chalk vibrate out of its trough at the blackboard, then glanced back at April. She was alert, but not alarmed. He continued his lecture. "Jack Falconer was his name, I believe. He was sweating up the Old Everett Highway on his bike when he claims that a 'high-pitched sound' blew the circuits on his iPod and knocked him to the ground!"

Mathonwy noticed that April made a note on her legal pad. "This 'high-pitched sound'—according to another bit of local lore—is the pealing of the great Yaktayvian bells which hang inside the hollow mountain. Hogwash? There may be other causes, equally bizarre, if less quaint. Crystal oscillation induced by tectonic strain, for example. We are living next door to a natural atom bomb: a 'dormant' stratovolcano which last blew its top in 1786. Not long ago in geological time." He stooped to address the students who had ducked and covered. "I think the danger has passed, gentlemen."

"But the point of our Tuesday night meetings here," he told them, rising to his full height, "is not to determine what is science and what is fantasy . . . but to examine our local mythologies to see if they encode a truth far stranger than their concealing fictions. The point . . . " He leveled his gray eyes at April Blessing. " . . . is to learn another way of seeing what we look at each day."

Professor Mathonwy began to pack his briefcase. He glanced up to see that though most of his class was headed for the door, April remained in her seat, poised to take down the next assignment. "And along those lines," he said, his voice amplified for her alone, "I'd like you all to read the excerpt in my anthology from *The Journal of Augustus Leek*—one of the few nineteenth-century white men to whom our local Native Americans entrusted their stories. His account of the legend of the Modoc maiden Loha will give us food for thought as we contemplate the fireworks on Mt. Shasta." April shut her notebook and stood. Then she danced off like a doe, the fringe on her buckskin jacket swinging in time with the turquoise beads woven in her hair.

6

THE LOVERS.

*The world will change less in accordance with man's
determinations than with woman's divinations.*
—Claude Bragdon

APRIL Blessing fished an apple from her daypack and held it in her teeth while she opened Professor Mathonwy's anthology to page sixty-three and commenced her reading assignment. The mountain air was cool, the sky cloudless. Through the scrim of pine boughs two-hundred feet below, she could make out the blue roof of her cabin.

"Of all the maidens," began the story, as told on August 23, 1871 by the Modoc chief known as Lalek to the young Corporal Augustus Leek, "Loha was most beautiful."

Loha's feet fell upon the earth like a gentle rain, and like the rain, her dew penetrated the lower regions of Llao, God of the Underworld. It was this beautiful torment that finally brought Llao to the summit of Mt. Mazama to look upon her form, and it was that sight which drove him to possess her. Llao begged Loha to return with him to the Underworld, promising her eternal life, but the maiden refused, preferring a finite life beneath the sun to an eternal one in darkness. Llao pleaded with the elders of the Modoc tribe, but they would not turn her over, even when the god unleashed a storm of fire over their village. Hearing the commotion and the wailing of the people, Skell, god of the Heavens, descended from the sky to the snowy top of Mt. Shasta and warned his dark brother to cease his mischief. But Llao would not relent, so blinding was his desire, and so began a battle of our peoples' gods in which the earth shook mightily and fire flowed from both mountains for seven days and nights. Loha, in despair over the suffering that her beauty had brought upon her people, threw herself into the mouth of Mt. Mazama, and Skell was so angered by this needless sacrifice that he summoned all his strength and delivered a blow with the force of Heaven. When it was over, there was nothing left of Mt. Mazama but an enormous bowl, fit for Llao to grind his grain in. It is now what you call Crater Lake, and Loha's form can still be seen in its center. The forests were leveled for miles, and so Skell counseled the Modoc to move their people south. In the shadow of Mt. Shasta, he told them, you will find sanctuary, for it is sacred to the Great Spirit. It is called, in our tongue, IEKA."

April closed the book and shifted her position atop the boulder, seeking a spot warmed by the morning sun. As a concession to modesty, she wore a cotton thong beneath her hemp skirt, but on a brilliant day like this, with glacial breezes softened by solar heat, she might've hiked the scant quarter mile up the ridge naked if not for the chance of crossing paths with a backpacker returning from his night on the summit.

She had found herself a perch at seven-thousand feet on Mt. Eddy, a seat that placed her at the Western apex of an isosceles triangle, with Mt. Shasta and its dark little sister, Black Butte, at the other points. She had come here to do her assigned reading in the proper light. Moreover, she wanted to meditate on the job she'd eagerly agreed to do for her old lover, current friend, and occasional employer, Stephan Raszer.

About three miles across the valley as the crow flies, she could just barely make out a feather of gray smoke coming from the wood burning stove in the climber's hut occupied by Professor Mathonwy. It comforted her to think of him up there with his journal and his seismographs, listening to the mountain's heartbeat, tending its secrets like some medieval hermit. April liked her professor, in spite of his sometimes awkward attentions. Mathonwy's passion, she thought, was that of a Platonic scholar whose mind had dwelt for a little too long on an idealization of woman. For all her own Apollonian tendencies, April preferred her men to be a bit more on the Dionysian side.

The professor and the U.S. Geological Survey were to provide Raszer's "cover" as he sought to penetrate the gang of neo-fascist Neanderthals that called itself the Military Order of Thule for the purpose of "rescuing" Fortis Cohn. April was to assist him. Mathonwy was to remain unaware of her role, the better to insure him deniability should the mission be compromised. Raszer took great pains to protect those he referred to as his "allies." It pleased her to feel protected by him.

With the midmorning light, Shasta was just now emerging from silhouette, and from here April could survey better than one hundred-eighty degrees of its enormous base. She had climbed it three times, twice up Misery Hill with a guide and once up the perilous Whitney Glacier with a former boyfriend. It was the sheer mass of it, as much as anything else, which made the storied existence of a hidden city within seem physically imaginable, if not entirely credible. By some accounts, the mountain was home to the sister cities of Yaktayvia and Ilethelme, the "Secret Commonwealth" of Light. In others, the underground metropolis was Telos, a two mile deep by one-and-a-half mile wide cylindrical supermall with five distinct levels and a dome that rose to within a few thousand feet of the summit. She had read all of the literature: the Village Bookstore, where April alternated between working the register and reading fortunes, had an entire shelf devoted to the urban architecture of Mount Shasta's interior. It was all to be taken, of course, with a pinch of salt, but then again . . . something had to account for the accretion of such exotic worlds around the hub of a single natural monument.

It wasn't as if Shasta's mythos was only the psychedelic by-product of New Age cosmogenies. She'd learned from her professor that the Modoc, Shastika, and Wintun peoples had all considered it the root of the world, the axis between Earth and Heaven. Belief that the volcano had provided a refuge for Lemurians fleeing their sinking continent went back well over a hundred years, and was so widespread that even gas station attendants in nearby Dunsmuir could direct pilgrims to sacred landmarks. April neither fully believed nor disbelieved any of it; she simply refused to dismiss the possibility that her mountain was the matrix of something wondrous.

Her pale blue tie-dyed skirt, waist-length mane of straw-colored hair, and decoratively applied henna eyeliner (the only hint of makeup on her classically chiseled face) leant an impression of lightness, but April was at least as grounded as anyone in Siskyou County, and a natural scientist in her own right. She observed keenly, and sifted everything through the screen of her intuition. If empirical proof was lacking for the notion that Mt. Shasta represented some kind of nodal point on the vast underground network known in occult/theosophical circles as Agharta, it was clear that even as outwardly hard-nosed a character as Bronk Vreeland gave it credence. April felt sure that the Order of Thule hadn't commandeered its alpine fortress for the purpose of protecting Agharta's enlightened denizens. No, Vreeland was there to keep them down.

And too, she thought, every myth had its inverse, just as every god had his nemesis and every particle its antiparticle, and the two in each case are not necessarily opposites. The trick lay in seeing one through the other, but never mistaking the alias for the thing itself (that led to madness and worse). This was what made the prospect of working for Raszer so exhilarating: it was a trapeze act with her own shadow. If in some sense Vreeland, from the dark side of the mirror, believed as she did, it might be a way to get inside his skin.

She had first come to the town of Mt. Shasta on a vagabond's whim to commemorate the five-year anniversary of the Harmonic Convergence, a rare alignment of the planets which had purportedly augured the beginning of the New Age. Five thousand pilgrims had traveled north, drawn by the promise of spiritual and sexual fraternity and by the volcano's reputation as a telluric "vortex": a place, like Sedona and Stonehenge, where earth energies were uniquely focused. A few dozen, April among them, had never gone home. She had arrived as a precociously bright and prematurely jaded college student, one who'd been granted early admission to the UCLA psych program based on an essay entitled "Mental Illness And The Myth Of Family Values." She'd come as an observer and unexpectedly ended up a participant. Shasta had enchanted her. According to the old village woman who'd held her hand as the celebrants formed a human chain about the mountain's base, Shasta represented the "5th Earth Chakra," the terrestrial analog of the throat in the yogic energy chain: a geomantic voice box through which spiritual truths could be broadcast into mass consciousness. The mountain had spoken to her almost from the moment she'd laid eyes on it. "This is where you become YOU," it had told her, and she had believed.

Still, April had not entirely abandoned her jaundiced view of human nature; she'd simply decided one day that life on earth was a far more exciting affair if you believed in things like "energy vortexes" than if you didn't. Soon after, she formally dropped out of UCLA. Her closest friend, the older student with whom she'd hitchhiked north, begged her to reconsider, warning her not to abandon her scholarly efforts to grapple with a history of paternal abuse in favor of some airy-fairy notion of "healing." But April had been resolute in her neo-paganism. To her way of thinking, she'd simply found a less Freudian and more Jungian way to deal with her father's ghost, casting him as a demon from the underworld in her own myth. The danger for April lay in the fact that all demons are masters of disguise. Not even Jung could save her from a spate of bad affairs with men who looked like gods and turned out to be not so different from Daddy.

Raszer had attended the Shasta gathering as well, in search of some metaphorical hot spring in which to bathe his own wounds. The character he would become a few years hence existed then only in a germinal stage; April remembered perceiving him as a guy whose edges were blurry like an out-of-focus photograph. His face had been red and puffy from the ravages of gin, cocaine, and the soul blows he'd received from his unfaithful wife, but even then he was a stoic, and April could not recall his ever having faulted the woman who'd betrayed him. The strange and festal evening of the ceremony had been the first and only time that April and he had made love, but it was—she thought—what sex was meant to be. Their combustion had been so galactic and their thrashing around so beautifully savage that at one point a park ranger had approached her tent with his flashlight to make sure that a black bear was not mauling some helpless camper.

In the morning, when she awoke naked to birdsong and the smell of the mesquite fire he'd lit an hour before, she sat up and peered out the tent flap to find him standing six meters away at the edge of the clearing, rapt in contemplation of Shasta's snowy crown. When he turned to greet her, he was no longer the psychic wreck she'd met the previous night as Matthew Ross. He was already on his way to becoming Stephan Raszer.

"Good morning," he'd said. "How do you feel?"

"How do you think I feel?" she replied, blushing. "I feel great. Hungry."

"Good," he said. "Me, too. Let's go get blueberry pancakes."

April, then barely eighteen, was not yet aware of the alchemy that a woman's full-bore sexuality can work in a man's soul. Now she knew that she, along with Shasta, deserved some credit for Raszer's rise from the ashes.

Over the years, her gift had been reciprocated, as their friendship flowered and Raszer's own protean leaps of consciousness had catalyzed her determined but inchoate spirituality into a fully formed conviction that the world could be saved only through magic. He had first employed her to do background work on a bogus "Christian Youth Camp" for troubled adolescent girls, operating on the Tex-Mex border as a cover for a white slavery racket. She'd seen in that tutorial how easily the Devil slipped on the robe of high priest. She loved Raszer's notion of shepherding his "strays" into safer pastures, but there was something else, too. Something unsettling. Sometimes the proximity of evil fanned embers inside her that might have been better left to go cold.

Slowly, as if by some act of atmospheric conjuring, a vast, creamy cloud in the shape of a perfect ellipse began to form over the mouth of the volcano. April perceived it as underlit in pale rose, as if someone had turned on an arc lamp within the cone. Worth coming up for, she thought. She stood, strapped on her pack, and headed down the trail to her one-room cabin in the canyon below. At one o' clock, she was to report to her part-time day job at the bookstore on Main Street, where her services as a spiritual counselor were much in demand. For some customers—mainly the guys—it was less a matter of her psychic acuity than the fact that she was a stunning blond hippie chick with a bare midriff. For many others, however, April had proven herself a remarkably sensitive detector of emotional dysfunction. It really didn't make much difference which divinatory tool she used: tarot, palmistry, I-Ching, runes. She let the customer choose. It was what she did with them—the transference they effected—which had established her reputation among some in the village as a more than accidental sibyl. It wasn't unheard of for wounded (and, yes, often lovestruck) souls to make the 2.5-mile trek from town to her cabin and set rough camp among the junipers until she agreed to see them. In a very real sense, April had become, by other means, the talented shrink she might have become by certification of a UCLA degree.

It had been at the Village Book Store, some nine months earlier, that she'd first encountered Bronk Vreeland—long before Raszer's call for assistance had come in. The town, and especially the ecologically minded neo-hippie community, had been abuzz for weeks with the news of the tribal lawsuit and the militia's increasingly noisy "war games" at seven thousand feet. For Vreeland and his two farm-faced Pentecostal recruits to come barreling into a metaphysical bookshop, wearing Army fatigues and smelling of Right Guard and gunpowder, was not just provocative. It was perverse. The men from the compound rarely trafficked with the townies, let alone with the "enemy." But, like much she had since learned about the Supreme Commander, the incident had confounded her expectations.

She had watched him from behind the bead curtain of her tiny "consultation room," a converted storage closet at the rear of the store. She'd arrived only shortly before and had just lit a stick of hyssop incense in preparation for her first reading of the day. His two young lackeys stood dumbly by as he scanned the shelves with his hands on his hips, bare arms sun-leathered in an olive drab tank top, gunmetal blue eyes narrowed with something between contempt and fascination. He looked to her to be thirty-five, though in California older men could look as good by way of strenuous regimens and macrobiotic diets. His nostrils flared and he turned halfway, sniffing the incense which she realized with alarm was curling toward him with the stealth of a python. She'd felt a shudder run the length of her spine as he stalked across the plank floor and drew her curtain roughly aside.

"That's hyssop," he said. "They used that in Old Testament times."

"I know," she replied flatly. "I make it myself."

"Hmm," he grunted. "Don't usually smell that in hippie stores." He seemed to her oddly impressed.

"Is that what you think this is?" she shot back, self-surprised at the insolence of her tone.

He didn't answer, but cocked his thumb back at the shelves. "You have any books by Madame Guyon?"

"I don't know who that is," April said.

"You ought to. You carry this junk by 'Sri Rama-Lama-Ding-Dong' and '2-Pac Chopra.' Now, Guyon's the *real* deal."

"Really. Why don't you tell me about her."

"She's a nun. A quietist. She teaches *quietude*. I'm trying to train myself to hear what you can only hear when everything else stops."

April realized that her palms were sweating. She couldn't shake his stare. He dropped his eyes for an instant to the Viking rune stones she had laid before her on the table, and she regained her pluck, if temporarily.

"You any good with those?" he asked.

"I guess that's why they keep me here," she said.

"Look at me, then," he said, the register of his voice dropping to a hypnotic rumble. "Tell me where I died in 480 B.C."

The reply she gave impressed her no less than him. Perhaps the date had jogged some textbook memory, or maybe she'd just read his vanity correctly. In any case, she answered: "In the pass at Thermopylae, with the rest of the Spartan army." It was only after he'd been gone for two minutes that she realized she'd been, however briefly, in a kind of a trance.

The shingled roof of her cabin came into view through the junipers. The day's plan was set: she was a woman with a mission. After putting in six hours at the store, she planned to buy herself a salad and prepare for the evening's assignment, a job that paid better than the minimum wage she earned in town. April was duly proud of her initiative. Raszer had originally asked her to come on the Fortis Cohn case to snoop around and put together a brief on what she could learn of Vreeland's belief system. He knew she was a climber and had also asked her to do some reconnaissance of the militia's property. But April had persuaded Raszer to let her "go operational" this time. Ten days ago, she had auditioned for and won a job as one of the exotic dancers at The Pink Temple, a raunchy roadhouse on the remote woodsy backside of Mt. Shasta, accessible only by dirt service roads and known to be frequented by Vreeland's men. From the altar of its tacky stage and the power it lent to weaken wills, she hoped to gain a view of the Order of Thule that Raszer could never hope to obtain on his own and as a man. She was to be his mole, and he would dig her out if she got too deep. She had dubbed her stage persona "The Gypsy." She wanted to surprise the Supreme Commander as much as he had surprised her, and to show Raszer that she was fit for active duty. On the evidence of her debut performance, on a night when Vreeland himself had made a rare personal appearance, she was on her way to achieving both objectives.

The crocus-yellow shutters and periwinkle-blue flower boxes of her cabin beckoned. The colors gladdened her, as they had been intended to.

Her screen door was unlocked as always. She stepped in and greeted the scarlet macaw she called Diogenes, his perch on a branch of Coulter pine she'd dragged in from the woods and mounted near window that faced Shasta. *"Bonjour, ma'am-selle!"* Diogenes squawked. He plucked a grape from his bowl and offered it to her in his powerful beak. April leaned in and parted her lips, and on her nod the bird dropped his gift into her mouth.

"Thanks, baby," she told him, gave his beak a wet kiss, and turned to collect the things she needed for the long day and longer night. She was on her way to fetch a less-revealing pair of panties when a long shadow crossed the tiny room and she heard Diogenes flap his wings and croak, "Uh-oh!" She pivoted to the front door with only mild alarm; visitors were rare but generally benign. Before she could suppress her gasp, all six feet of Bronk Vreeland's fatigue-clad frame had eclipsed the sun. He strode into the room, owning it instantly. He was followed by a vaguely ferretlike younger man she recognized from Raszer's case file photos as Fortis Cohn. A third man—a heavyset, pock-marked recruit she'd seen at the Pink Temple—waited outside on the stoop. Vreeland pushed his fingers through the pale blond quills of his buzz cut and surveyed the decor of the room disdainfully.

"You put on some show the other night," he said, with implicit challenge. "My men didn't sleep a wink. Was it for real?"

"As real as you are," she answered, trying to still the trembling of her lower lip. "How did you find my place?"

"You're not that hard to track," he said, the corners of his wide mouth curling in a reflexive smile. "So what's your angle, 'Gypsy'? What's a girl like you doing at the Pink Temple?"

"I like to dance," said April. "It's no crime." She locked stares with him, her best shot at restoring her composure. Nothing remotely like him had ever been this close to her bed. "Besides that," she ventured, "I know about you. I've heard you on the radio. You seem like the only man around here who doesn't doubt himself. That intrigues me. I'm sick of doubt. Sick of abstraction. Sick of men who hide behind metaphors."

Vreeland picked up a garland of wildflowers from her table, considered it for a moment, then put it down. "You've got some strange ideas for a flower child." He stepped to within a foot of her face, smelling of saddle soap. "You say my ideas intrigue you. You told my men you wanted to hear more. But it doesn't square up with your whole . . . routine. Why should I believe you're not with ZOG . . . or even a spy for these Indians who are making my life so miserable? We're under attack, lady. I need to see some bona fides before I can trust you." His eyelashes fluttered, and for an instant, she'd have sworn he was wearing a light basting of mascara. "*Can* I trust you?"

She placed a hand on her hip. "If you need to see more than I showed you at the Pink Temple, you have a lot to learn about women." She felt a muscle twitch in her abdomen. It was a provocative thing to say and she knew it. Nonetheless, she pushed it. "You see things too black and white. I live this way because I like to live free. I'm surprised you don't get that. Maybe I was wrong about you. I've been wrong before."

"I don't think so," said Vreeland. "Go on."

"I can't blame you for being paranoid," April said, stepping gingerly through the minefield. One mistake and it would be over. She allowed a critical few seconds to pass. She'd been trying out personas, and that wouldn't do. Time to choose. In her mind, she pulled the handle on a slot machine and watched the tarot images spin. She settled on the High Priestess as written by Ayn Rand, a role she knew she could pull off. "I'm not with the Indians or anyone else . . . including the Zionist Occupation Government. I'm with me, and there's no way I'll be able to keep living free if we become a nation of slaves 'Freedom can exist only where the strong are free to rule,' right?"

"You quoted me correctly, Gypsy," Vreeland said, his growl a little silkier. April noticed, as she had on their first meeting, that a certain measured gallantry accompanied his macho bluster, the whiff, perhaps, of a maternal steel magnolia in his boyhood history. "But that doesn't make you a believer," he added, with a nod to Fortis.

She stepped into the opening. "You told me about Madame Guyon, remember? Well, maybe there are some things *I* can show *you*. Ever heard of Julius Evola . . . or Miguel Serrano . . . or Savitri Devi?"

"Savitri Devi I've come across," he affirmed. "But it's you I'm asking about. You say you can read the stones. Tell me what you see. Show me you're worth the risk."

"I'll get you the books," she said, sidestepping. A breath. "You need me, Commander, because you're more than *Guns 'n Ammo*. There's a reason you wanna hold onto Shasta. A spiritual reason. You're tuned in to something . . . or trying to be."

"What would you know about that?"

"I know Shasta like I know my skin. It's got secrets, but . . . " April now marked a path that went beyond what Raszer had charted. "It takes someone like me to get at them. I'm worth the risk. You just don't know it yet."

"Okay. We'll take your offer under consideration. I may have to twist some arms. But, hell . . . " He chuckled, and the little nerve in her belly began to twitch again. " . . . the Order could use a few breeders." He paused to see if April would flinch. "Along those lines," Vreeland said, gently placing his big hands on her shoulders, "you'll have to submit to a security check. A painless examination. Make sure you're not a carrier."

His lips curled into a smile that was almost fey, knowing he'd called her bluff.

"Blottmeier!" he called out to the front stoop, keeping his eyes on hers. "Get in here this instant and assist me with the evaluation of our prospective recruit."

April's eyes widened with the timeless feminine acknowledgement that all her tough talk amounted to nothing in the face of a man determined to use muscle. She felt something of the helpless dystrophy of prey as Vreeland turned her around and bent her over the table. She was not weak, but with the strength of one arm and a well-placed steel toe, he had her immobilized. *What the hell have I done*, she thought. She heard, and smelled, the arrival of the anxious young sycophant he'd called Blottmeier. It was a mixture of odors, none of them pleasant.

Vreeland kept her neck pinned with his left hand, while with the right he pushed up her skirt.

"Tsk, tsk," he clucked, evidently in reaction to her barely functional thong. "Dressed for work even in the daytime . . . " Blottmeier snorted. April felt sick.

Turning her right cheek to the table, she spoke icily. "I expected so much more. I should've known. I offer you my soul and you settle for my ass. Fuck you." The words were resolute, but her jaw was quivering. April had no neighbors; it wouldn't help to scream. Not even Diogenes's urgent squawking would bring the mounties to this neck of the woods.

A new voice, formal and weirdly affectless, made itself heard. "You've no cause for concern, Miss. You won't be harmed." It was the man she'd identified as Fortis Cohn.

It was faint reassurance, and she waited for the sound of a zipper. Her breathing was as shallow as a bird's, her skin flushed and her mind already at the abortion clinic. She knew this panic from beneath the scar tissue of memory, and she knew also the twisted consummation that could follow, the perverse relief that the deed was done and no longer threatened. *This is what you deserve, girl.* Say it. *Yes, Daddy, this is what I deserve.* Here it comes, she thought, as Vreeland shifted position, and she softly closed all the doors in her mind, waiting to be violated. Waiting to be negated.

Instead, she became aware of the surprisingly gentle pressure of his palm on the small of her back, and then something light and narrow being laid along her lower spine and tailbone.

"You underestimate me, April," Vreeland said. "Gangbangs are for mud people and third world miscreants, and a woman's womb saps a man's vitality unless she's ovulating. You'll understand my reasons soon enough."

From the discussion that ensued, April deduced that a fabric tape measure had been extended from the crown of her lower vertebrae to the tip of her coccyx. All three men leaned in to observe the result. She could feel their combined breath on her skin.

"Borderline," said Vreeland.

"She's over the standard, Commander," said the toady named Blottmeier.

"What would you know?" Vreeland replied coldly.

"Let's get a read from St. Joachimsthal," said Fortis Cohn. April's ears pricked up. She had not heard mention before of such a place or person.

"Keep your own counsel, Cohn!" Vreeland warned. "She's not clear yet. I'll make this call. I say she's close enough." He relaxed his hold on April's neck, and the three men stepped back simultaneously. She turned around, suppressing fury in favor of caginess, and smoothed her dress down. Part of her wanted to shiver off the contamination of his touch; the other part found itself transfixed by the little flecks of gold in the irises of his slate-blue eyes. He hadn't harmed her, and she did not know what to make of it.

"What the hell was that about?" she demanded.

"You're not ready to know," Vreeland replied.. "And when you are . . . if you are what you say you are . . . I won't need to tell you." He smiled and tipped his head to her.

Once again, April found herself without any frame of reference for his behavior. Was this little gesture a sign of consideration or simply a con? There was plenty of iron in his delivery, but no hint of irony.

The other two men preceded their leader to the door, and just before he made his own exit he turned back to her. "By the way," he said, "if you're going out, put something decent on under that skirt. There are maniacs in these woods."

April leaned into the cheap makeup mirror and drew eyeliner thickly across her lid, ending with a Queen of the Nile filigree a half an inch out from the corner. As a final touch, she painted an oversized beauty mark beneath the shallow smile line that separated her left cheek from her upper lip, and then stepped back to pull on her cigarette and survey the overall picture. Florence, a fleshy townie girl and tonight's only other act, was about to go on. She came to a dead stop behind April, drained the last of her Jim Beam, and whistled through her teeth.

"Wish I had your body, girl," she said enviously.

"Shit, Flo," April replied, turning to profile. "You can have it. It's more trouble than it's worth."

She looked down the length of her five foot, ten inch frame and saw fleetingly what Florence had seen. Then she tied her hair back severely, stuffed it into a net, and put on the auburn wig. *Fucking Delilah*, she whispered under her breath. April could allow herself the pleasure of vanity because, after all, it wasn't *really* her. There was a thrum of fear in her belly but just one thing in her mind: *he will give me what I want*. April shared a weakness with Raszer. She couldn't stand for there to be a secret she wasn't in on, and right now, Bronk Vreeland had a secret. Beyond the tailbone enigma, beyond the question of why a barely closeted gay Jewish lawyer was mixing it up with neo-Nazis, there was something more: Vreeland was waiting for something to happen inside the mountain, and April wanted to be the one to tell Raszer what it was.

She turned her backside to the mirror to inspect the henna tattoo she'd received just three hours earlier from a friend at the Dharma Bums Thrift Shop in town. It was a representation of the caduceus, the staff of Mercury, messenger of the Gods. Using her spine as the central rod, the tattoo artist had expertly fashioned the double-helixed serpents so that they spiraled down her backbone and merged into a single head which boldly outlined April's tailbone, its forked tongue brazenly seeking the shadowy recess of her buttocks. She had no idea yet what special significance the coccyx had for Bronk Vreeland's Order, but she intended to make a point of it nonetheless. April was playing the line: the line where affectation becomes persona and persona reflects a genuine piece of one's hidden self. The line between mind games and madness. By the time she got her summons to the stage, April Blessing had all but vanished.

At 10:31 that evening, a single blue spotlight crackled on at the foot of The Pink Temple's beer-lacquered "stage," followed by the report of drums from the cheap speaker system: goatskin drums with the exotic metric signature of the Middle East. There was a murmur of voices and some banging of beer mugs. The former bordello, garishly pink amid the tall pines, was seven miles outside of town via a treacherous network of old mining roads. It had been erected in 1901 to service the employees of the Klamath Company, and had then shut down for decades following the abandonment of their mines in the twenties. Now resurrected by Vreeland's troopers, it was the subject of some prurient gossip in town, and no respectable local ventured near it. There was little chance, especially given her disguise, that April's bookstore co-workers or clients would learn of her double life. In here, she was safe to transgress.

"Gentlemen and, er … boys!" croaked Grandpa Labin, the Temple's ancient proprietor, through the archaic p.a. system. "The girl you've been waiting for! All the way from An-da-loo-sia! The high priestess of the Pink Temple! The GYPSY!"

In the shadows just beneath the stage's rim, Bronk Vreeland took a sip of his boiled spring water and tapped his fingers to the Moorish rhythm. April was dancing for him, but he did not grant her the acknowledgement of a direct gaze. It wasn't anything like love he was feeling: it was destiny. This one, he mused, may just be the real thing. He scanned the tawdry surroundings and the rapt faces of his men, some of whom had probably never laid hands on a real woman. He smiled faintly, for no one but himself. Of all the fucking places to find his sibyl.

7

THE CHARIOT.

We must admire the wisdom of the initiates,
who utilized vice and made it produce
more beneficial results than virtue.
—Papus, The Tarot of the Bohemians

MADAME Rey sat motionless at a painted table in the back room of her shop, contemplating again the spread she had laid for the unfortunate Mr. Rose, wondering if her decision to put the best light on his cards had denied the young man a warning which might have saved his life. Remorse was uncharacteristic for Raja, for Roma people generally. It was regarded as a form of vanity, for no individual act, selfish or altruistic, could alter the set of probabilities which fate had set in motion. Nonetheless, she felt guilty.

The Judgement card had "covered" Christopher Rose. *"Lost soul,"* she had thought at the time, but now she saw other portents, evoked by the cards that followed. Fear of Death. The Two of Swords had "crossed him," and she had thought, *"He feels trapped."* But in the context of the lay, she should have read it as *"No Way Out."* Whatever club Rose had gotten himself into, it wasn't one he could unjoin.

The Knight of Wands had been behind him and she had seen only his youthful opportunism; now she saw that he had succumbed to a great and dreadful temptation. The Tower lay just in front of him, and Raja had glimpsed a divorce brought on by the Hollywood brand of bourgeois infidelity: he had cheated on his wife with another man.

Now, The Tower, placed as it was at the apex of a triangle formed by Death and the Ten of Swords, conveyed almost certain catastrophe.

Raja thought of the Russian box on her shelf, the contents of which she had not yet examined and which now seemed dangerously taboo. *Marime*. A shudder ran from the base of her skull to the bottom of her spine. She was suddenly very frightened.

Her shop door rattled, its prayer bells set jangling along with her nerves. She resolved in the name of St. Sara to do two things, providing she was not about to be murdered: she would read what Christopher Rose had given her, and she would think about calling Stephan Raszer's number. The boy was dead; he deserved an avenger. She drew a breath, adjusted her scarf, and prepared to face her visitor.

"Hello-oo?" a voice called from the other side of the bead curtain. "Anybody hooome?" It was a woman, and she sounded harmless enough. Her voice had a warbly, birdlike quality. Little trills ornamented the end of each phrase.

"Hello?" she repeated, more impatiently, running her fingers over the beads like a harpist executing a gratuitous glissando. "Are you op—?"

Raja parted the curtain brusquely. Not six inches from her nose, and not the least bit jarred by Raja's obvious irritation, was a face she recognized instantly, not so much from the movies (she rarely saw the new ones) as from the covers of the glossy celebrity magazines in the supermarket. It was occluded by oversized dark glasses and baby doll bangs, but unmistakable for its dark mole and crooked little mouth. Raja glanced past her visitor to the black limo that now commanded the two spaces in front of her shop.

After all these years, she thought to herself, *Hollywood has come to call.*

"Are you Madame Rey?" the actress inquired. Raja softened immediately. Her manner was childlike, guileless, and absent of condescension.

"I am," Raja said.

"I'm Bree Donahue." She extended her hand smartly and wasted no time. "Do you have time to give me a reading?"

"You're in luck," Raja replied. "I've just had a cancellation."

"Oh, great!" said Bree, parking her handbag, removing her glasses, and plopping down on Raja's loveseat as if she'd just arrived home after a day on the set.

"It looks like you know the routine," observed Raja.

"Oh, yeah," said Bree, with a self-mocking flick of the wrist. "I'm a veteran. I usually see a woman in Topanga, but I just had a meeting at Paramount and I'm a mess. I've got a huge decision to make, and I can't think straight with all this noise in my head."

It tickled Raja, even moved her a bit, that there were still people for whom one fortuneteller was as good as another. People who trusted the craft itself. "What kind of 'noise?'" Raja asked. She reached for the familiar place where she kept her cards, then remembered that she'd left them in the back room. She considered for a moment, then retrieved another deck and sat down opposite the actress.

"It's bizarre," said Bree, peeling off the vintage red vinyl raincoat she wore despite the cloudless sky. "Like radio static. And then, hums . . . "

"Hums?" Raja asked, more than a little intrigued.

"Hums," Bree affirmed. "You know, like—" She pulled her chin down to her chest and made the lowest sound her girlish vocal cords could produce. "Hum-mmmh." Then she laughed. "I'm either delusional or touched by God."

"Tell me the difference," said Raja dryly, shuffling the deck. "So . . . you've come from Paramount?"

"Uh huh," said Bree. "Big pow-wow on this go picture they want me to do. Big drama, too. The C.E. on the movie was murdered two nights ago."

Raja turned up the Five Of Cups. "That's terrible," she remarked, licking her cracked lips. "Do they know who . . . or why?"

"Well," Bree replied, leaning across the table as if she were about to share a secret with her oldest friend. "The word is that it was some kind of gay mafia thing. Real inside. Chris was leading a double life. If you ask me, he was sleeping with one of the producers. The whole thing stinks, which is partly why I'm *shvitzing*." She looked about the room. "Do you mind if I smoke?"

"It's better that you don't," said Raja. "Breathe . . . and tell me about the decision you have to make."

"Okay," said Bree, assuming yogic position and drawing a cleansing breath that sounded more like a gasp. "I've been offered this part they claim was written for Cameron, but she backed out. It's good money—my best payday yet—and the directors are this hot pair of *twins*—yeah—who call themselves the Buzz Brothers. May I have a glass of water, please?"

Accepting the non sequitur, which seemed in keeping with Bree Donahue's flighty but purposeful manner, Raja went to the bathroom sink and returned with a cup of water. She found Bree in suspended animation, as if she'd held her breath to complete the unfinished thought. "There's just one huge problem," she said, and then exhaled.

"What's that?" asked Raja, laying the next card.

"The contract. It's got all the stuff top actresses fight for, and my agent told me it was actually Cameron's deal! But then there are these two little add-ons . . . " Bree waited for Raja to look up from the cards. "One . . . is that I have to submit 'for insurance purposes' to a complete physical by a doctor of their choice . . . I mean, the works! I have never seen that before! It's like the contract can be voided if they don't like the looks of my plumbing! What's that about?"

"And the second?" Raja asked.

"If the deal makes, I'll also be taking on these producers as my personal managers. For fifteen years. Believe me—in this town—that's my whole shelf life."

"Perhaps you should be talking to a lawyer," Raja said calmly, and laid the next card. She said it calmly, but she noticed that her hand was shaking and that there was a persistent throbbing at the base of her skull.

"Oh, I have," said Bree. "But I don't go by lawyers. If I did, I'd never take a risk."

"So you want to know," Raja said, "if you should take this one . . . "

"Right."

When it was over and Raja had laid a European straight spread topped by the Judgement card, she announced, without the slightest hesitation: "There is another role waiting for you. One that will bring greater fame." She wasn't going to hedge her intuition a second time.

"H-how will I know . . . wh-which one?" Bree stammered, undone.

"It will be self-evident," Raja replied. "I can't say who will offer it." Having made her rent already and feeling a certain concern for the young actress, she charged only her usual fee of twenty dollars, though she could have asked far more. Her headache had gotten worse, but her conscience was clear.

Bree Donahue stood up, put on her raincoat and sunglasses, and then stooped to kiss Raja's rouged cheek. "You know," she said, "I'll bet I could get you a credit on that picture when it comes. 'Spiritual advisor' or something like that. They do that, you know . . . for serious actresses."

"Is that so?" said Raja absently, rubbing her temples and feeling suddenly faint. Bree leaned in and lowered her glasses.

"Are you . . . all right?" she asked softly.

"H-how . . . did you find me?" Raja asked. "I mean . . . why did you come to me of all the readers in Hollywood?"

"Well," said Bree, "you're in the neighborhood . . . We had lunch at Prizzi's. And— well, if I told you the real reason you'd think I was ready for the Betty Ford Clinic."

"Try me." Raja took another look at the cards.

Bree perched on Raja's chipped windowsill. "You know that noise in my head? The static and the humming that started Monday night after the earthquake . . . "

Raja stared, one eyebrow hiked up like Gloria Swanson. For the moment, her curiosity got the better of her dizziness.

"It got louder during lunch," Bree continued. "I almost gagged on my risotto. And then when my limo passed your shop, it got really loud."

"Something is happening," Raja said, rising unsteadily from the sofa, feeling a million miles away. "Something important. You sense it, too, don't you? Something that will bring great change . . . and danger. I'm getting the same—" She brought her fingertips to the bridge of her nose.

"Signals?" asked Bree. "The hums and the static?"

"Yes. I suppose so. Then again, at my age, it could be a tumor."

"*Listen*," Bree said. "The reader in Topanga—the one who usually does my cards? She's a channeler, a real one as far as I can tell. It's happening to her, too. She thinks it's something the Navy's doing in Alaska. Or else it's something called the 'Taos Hum' that's driven fifteen people in England to suicide. Or else she thinks it's—" Bree rolled her eyes in the general direction of outer space.

Raja blinked, and realized that her jaw had dropped. "Yes, well," she said, and cleared her throat. She rose, steadying herself against a chairback.

Bree came to her side and gently held her elbow, then suddenly turned and reached for the shelf where Raja's Russian box sat. "This is beautiful," she said, touching it and then drawing sharply back, as if burned.

Raja observed the reflex and knew she was in trouble.

They agreed to a consultation the following week, for the sake of comparing "hums," if nothing else. Now alone, Raja took the box from the shelf and retreated again to her back room. There, she removed Christopher Rose's unwitting legacy and laid it before her. The text inscribed on the piece of yellow legal paper that he'd been so eager to get rid of appeared to be in verse form: three four-line stanzas, tidily copied in block characters. There were notes in the margins, in an equally neat but nearly microscopic script, and some arcane doodlings that included a geometrical figure, but the verse appeared to be the main thing. It seemed likely that poor Mr. Rose had genuinely not had a clue what it contained, for its lines interspersed phrases in Sanskrit with isolated words in Hebrew. He hadn't struck her as the type to know either.

Neither language was entirely foreign to Raja, but for different reasons. Sanskrit was, for some conservative Roma people, a linguistic bequest, mother tongue of Dombari, the proto-Romany language of their North Indian origins. It was of little use nowadays, but during the pogroms of Europe, it had come in handy for subterfuge. Raja had learned it as a child from her paternal grandfather, who had always told her, "When they call you a dog, remember that you come from the same stock as the Brahmins of Delhi!" Hebrew, she knew less well, but it was her business to know the basics, for it was the language of tarot. Each letter of the Hebrew alphabet corresponded to a card in the Major Arcana.

Raja's surmise was that the poem was a cipher, with both an overt and an esoteric—possibly numerological—import. She stood, went to the front parlor, and pulled the curtains. Then she set to work. Nearly three hours later, at 5:35, she received a visit from Lt. Borges of LAPD Homicide.

The cop left shortly after six, having gotten little from her beyond a confirmation that Rose had indeed come to her for a reading on the night of his death, and a good description of the skinhead who'd hustled him out. Raja did not much like policemen, even polite ones like Borges. A distrust of them was ingrained in her Roma soul as surely as was her gift for the cards. She did, however, leave an urgent message for Stephan Raszer before collapsing to the sofa with another—and the most disabling—of the seizures she had suffered in the aftermath of her blackout during the earthquake.

The seizures were like electro-shock therapy. She felt utterly stupefied while they lasted—about three minutes—yet strangely recharged afterwards. In particular, her intuitive faculties seemed markedly enhanced, although there was hell to pay while they lasted. Anyone witnessing her in their grip would have suspected epilepsy or worse. This one had worn her out, and when it had subsided, she's fallen into a deep, trancelike sleep until after seven.

When she awoke, she returned to the table, where she found Rose's note, a steno pad with pages full of her nearly illegible efforts at translation, and a tarot spread, newly laid. She did not, in the usual sense, *remember* having laid the cards, but there they were. She sat down at the table, her eyes wide, her senses acute. She heard a clock ticking from behind a closed door; even the muffled traffic noise was deafening. The lay of the cards puzzled her at first. She often did them to pass the time, the way some people played solitaire, but such was not the case here. It was clear from her notes that the spread was linked to the cipher, though *how* was not immediately evident.

She had translated the better part of the first stanza, and now she began to glimpse the method. The Hebrew insertions had to be translated to Sanskrit by way of a three-step *gematria*, a Kabbalistic alphabet magic that gave numerical values to words and allowed substitution of any word with the same value. In her youth, she'd been able to compute gematria as facilely as some people do acrostics, but how had she found the right keys, and when?

She stood up and circled the little table, hoping that a different angle of view would yield a clue. She reasoned that she'd done most of the straight translation between the departure of the actress and the arrival of the cop, but beyond that, it was all a blank. She remembered lying down after Lt. Borges had left, her brain on fire, and then had come a weird repose—a suspension—accompanied by an sonic baptism in white noise, like the sound of a TV after the station has signed off for the night.

But it hadn't been "dead air." It wasn't only static.

It had been instead just as Bree described: her head like a ham radio receiver, auditing a dozen frequencies at once. But amid the cacophony, one channel had been more insistent in its transmission, and it was this frequency that she'd locked onto.

She knew this: that in both crytography and ritual magick, repetition connoted meaning. This had been her father's most persistent lesson: "Look for the things which repeat, Raja. Look for the patterns." And there had been, in fact, a pattern tapping itself out on a remote wall of her mind. Its urgency had been unmistakable. She knew that she would either decipher its signal or be driven mad by it.

Raja shook herself back into the present tense and looked down at her last page of notes. In her trance, she had ordered the first and last characters of each Hebrew word in a single column, and this alignment was the invisible hand behind her tarot spread. But by whose instruction had she done this? Had she been guided by the radio signal, by a will larger than her own, or was this the work of reawakened daemons within herself? Was there a difference? And most curiously: whose cards were these?

Professor Mathonwy sat stiffly at the computer terminal, contemplating the Send Mail icon on the screen. His fingers hovered over the mouse as he considered whether or not to commit the latest in a long line of scientific heresies. He had reached certain discomfiting conclusions about the seismic transients that were occurring on his mountain, and was about to send his report through to the USGS Cascades HQ in Vancouver, standard procedure when there was notable activity. In spite of the arid cold, he found himself perspiring. *Deus ex machina*, a reprieve came with the burp of his old fax machine. After pouring himself a brandy, he went to retrieve the fax.

It was on the letterhead of the Berkeley Seismological Lab, and it was from a former student of his: a brilliant, if congenitally hyper young quake jockey with the unlikely patronymic of Odd Meyer III, whose tastes ran more to comic books than scientific journals, and with whom Mathonwy corresponded sporadically. There are, he mused, no true coincidences.

Greetings Prof. Merlin-wy,

It's me, your old protege OM3. Bizarre stuff going on. Three little temblors with identical signatures and identical duration in the last 48 hours. Steady as smart bombs. Instant attack, instant decay. Something not right. Nobody else here gives a flying f**k. They're all hung up on their "size matters" magnitude bias, and these little guys are signing in at only 3.4. Just one problem. Computer keeps coming back with Shasta-Trinity area as the epicenter. If it hit here at 3.4, then technically you should be dead. The IT guys think the software's corrupted and have taken down the whole system for maintenance. Idiots. There's more. I picked up an ELF carrier wave each time on my Ground Radio (yes, I still worship at the shrine of Nikola Tesla) and it had an audible sideband. Way too stable and coherent for a quake. And check this. I graphed the events against the clusters of UFO sightings that the CHP has been logging up and down the state. Bingo. The sightings peak within an hour of each hit. So tell me. Has the Navy moved its HAARP Ops to NoCal? Is AUM Shinrikyo dug in on Mt. Shasta? I'd bet my D.C. Comix collection that somebody is firing off EM slugs on a Tesla cannon. O.K., I'm f**king nuts. But I'm sending my audio to the lab for analysis anyway. Your humble page, OM3.

Professor Mathonwy drained his brandy, and then threw back his head and whooped loud enough to vibrate the corrugated tin walls of his shack. Yes, indeed, Odd Meyer III was probably certifiable, but that's what they'd said about Tesla, too, and Tesla had been—if not quite a god—then not wholly mortal either.

Odd Meyer III wasn't the only borderland scientist to "worship at the shrine" of Nikola Tesla, the Victorian era prodigy who'd pioneered—among other things—alternating current, radio *(no, children, it wasn't Marconi)* and robotics, and had left behind baffling (and, in many cases, still classified) proposals for all manner of arcane devices. Among these were transmitters capable firing "slugs" of high voltage current into the Earth's crust and then—in a kind of geo-electrical echo of enormous force—back up into the ionosphere, a natural (and entirely wireless) conductor of electricity. The planet, he had argued, was one gigantic storage battery—a capacitor—and needed only to be properly tapped for a virtually limitless supply of electrical power. Tesla's divine madness had been inspired by the grandest sort of altruism—a scheme to provide free energy to all of mankind—but the idea was a non-starter with *fin de siecle* robber barons like J. P. Morgan and their cronies in the U.S. Government, who years before ENRON had seen vast profits in the controlled distribution of energy. Tesla had died a pauper in 1943, utterly marginalized, his research papers seized by the feds, his astounding legacy earning him barely a footnote in high school science texts.

And thus was born the most hair-raising conspiracy theory in modern science, a theory to which Mathonwy at least partially subscribed. For it was widely believed on the fringes of the scientific community that the same Teslian technology that might have freed humankind of its dependence on fossil fuels could, if employed differently, produce weapons of great destructive power. In the wrong hands, such technology could wreak global havoc, altering weather systems, manipulating brain waves, and causing massive earthquakes. Although Mathonwy reserved a measure of doubt (lest he receive the same treatment Tesla had), he knew that in Odd Meyer's universe, this dark science had long since found its way to the U.S. Navy, and quite possibly to groups like the AUM Shinrikyo cult of Japan, which some claimed had used "Tesla cannons" developed in the Australian desert to trigger the 1995 Kobe earthquake.

He reserved doubt, but as to the mysterious ELF (Extremely Low Frequency) pulses his former student claimed to have tracked, he had a few crazy ideas of his own.

Steeled by the brandy and heartened by Odd Meyer's maverick energy, Mathonwy returned to his desk, pausing on the way to glance at his thermometer. The temperature in the hut had dropped eight degrees in the last hour. He flexed his hands in their fingerless knit gloves and resumed his position at the keyboard. Once again, he reread the report he was about to file. He had made an analysis of Monday night's event and its mimetic replicates. And, like his protégé, he'd conjectured that the UFO sightings were attributable to a widely dispersed manifestation of tectonic "stress lights" caused by strain along certain fault lines in California's dark, empty interior. Just the night before, a hemisphere nearly two hundred meters across and the color of a Florida blood orange had remained in place over Avalanche Gulch for two hours, bobbing like an oil globule in a lava lamp. The existence of such phenomena was not quite orthodox science, but men in his field were as familiar with them as sailors had once been with St. Elmo's Fire. They were the result of massive discharges of electromagnetic energy.

Mathonwy wasn't particularly worried that seeing "spook lights" would cause his superiors to conclude he'd been in the thin air too long. There was something else, much stranger. Beginning with the second event, he had run the seismic waveform picked up on his magnetic field sensor through a frequency analyzer to break it down. After stripping away the collateral vibrations, he was left each time with two distinct "signatures." The first was characterized by short bursts at radio frequency, each one followed after about six seconds by a sort of smeared echo. The signals were masked by the roar of moving mountains, but they were there, and their regularity was striking.

This was all within bounds of natural science; it jibed with theories about how radiowave oscillation could be induced by strain on quartz crystal deposits in the volcano's interior, but what was causing the strain did not seem natural at all. OM III was right about that. What had drawn night sweat to Mathonwy's scalp was the second "signature." It was humming away at 39 Hz, below normal human hearing but easily impressed on the brain's temporal lobe and within the range of the mysterious Schumann Resonances, the rumbling "voices" of the Earth's own electromagnetic field, generated as it spun on its axis by friction with the upper atmosphere. The SRs were always there (some people claimed to hear them), but never at this amplitude unless something big was going on. At this level, they were the equivalent of an S.O.S.

Until now, Mathonwy had kept in check his own suspicions that whatever Bronk Vreeland was doing in his compound amounted to a deliberate scheme to aggravate the area's delicate geology. This was, he acknowledged, partly a factor of his ideological vanity: he couldn't bring himself to think that people who believed in international Jewish conspiracies were smart enough to pull off geoterrorism. But there were, indeed, malign forces at work in the world, and it was no stretch to think that the Military Order of Thule might be in their employ. For the moment, he decided to hedge his more paranoid conjectures and practice good science. If the volcano was going into labor, it didn't much matter whether it was induced or natural, and suggesting the former to his superiors before there was solid evidence might consign him to professional oblivion. He wanted to blow the militia off his mountain, but he needed unimpeachable cause, and from this need flowed his eagerness for the arrival of the P.I. from Los Angeles.

Even as it read, his report to Vancouver sounded like geomancy, and he would probably pay for it. Nonetheless, it was going, and for good reason: the possibility that Mt. Shasta was signaling the end of her two-hundred-year slumber meant that the lives of tens of thousands in the green valley below were at mortal risk, and among these was a young woman of whom he was very fond.

On her way back to the Villa Carlotta that evening, Madame Rey spotted a coyote that had wandered down from Bronson Canyon and was tearing through the contents of an overturned trashcan. Her scalp bristled when the animal turned and bared its teeth before scurrying timidly off. In the twilight world of Roma belief, feral creatures often served as "halfway houses" for the mulo of the recently deceased as it wandered the purgatory of raiyo. She hurried into the Carlotta to await Stephan Raszer's imminent arrival. In her handbag, she carried the Rose message and her attempted decryption of it. In her head, she carried intimations of apocalypse.

The call from Madame Rey, informing Raszer of her arrival at the Carlotta, came as he was watching the grains of dusk dissolve into darkness from the perch of his wraparound balcony. In the southeastern sky, Jupiter rose, sanguine and supreme. He'd mixed closing time margaritas for himself and his assistant, Monica, though it was past margarita season, even in California. It was to be his last drink before leaving on Sunday morning for Shasta, and he would have few during the term of the assignment. Bronk Vreeland did not drink—April had told him that—and Raszer was already well into the pre-deployment regimen of slipping into the psychic skin of his adversary.

He held the drink in his right hand; in his left was a cigarette he'd rolled when he found that his pack was empty. There had been some leftover Drum tobacco in his key drawer, and on impulse, he'd gone out to his herb garden, snipped off a couple of the more sun-withered leaves from his *Calea* plant, and rolled them into the cigarette. The plant, a Mexican neo-tropical from the sunflower family, was known as dog-grass to the profane and "leaf of God" to the initiated. Its effects, which were far more pronounced if one was patient enough to dry the leaves, was oneirogenic: it clarified the senses and, under the right circumstances, could induce lucid dreaming.

As Jupiter continued its ascent, Raszer observed how sparsely decorated the sky was on the edge of night—only the brightest stars and planets could pierce the screen of dusk. His own reconstituted self was a little like that. He'd cast off most of what had formerly burdened him with desire; only the high ticket items remained. Raszer truly loved just three things: his daughter Brigit, sly and slightly twisted women with old souls, and God. He was forever trying to figure out if they weren't, in fact, aspects of the same thing. When his paternal ache for the daughter he had raised and lost to divorce grew too intense, he would seek the company of a woman with whom he could just be, without pretense and without making apologies for his lapses into melancholy. All they asked in return for sanctuary was what should have been their birthright anyway: kindness, a practiced touch, and maybe a hint of worship.

When women failed to restore his light, he sought out God in places like Joshua Tree or even in the scrubby highlands of Hollywood, in hopes of raising the pillar of fire and engaging it in one-on-one dialogue. There were no back-ups for the Great Spirit. When it wouldn't answer your call, you had only the faltering retreat to booze, drugs, sexual excess and solipsism, all of which had been on Raszer's dance card at one time or another. He wasn't fool enough to believe they wouldn't ask for another spin if he dropped his guard. He laughed out loud and took a drag on the smoke. There was a spotted owl with the face of a rabbi perched in a nearby spruce. He heard the phone ring inside, and Monica chant "Hel-lo" in the interval of a minor third, a sure sign that it was near quitting time. It took a small eternity for her to reach the screen door.

"Whatcha doin', Raszer?" she asked rhetorically, her nose pressed into the screen's mesh. "Catching moonbeams?"

"Just thinking," he said. "How's the research going? Any bombshells?"

"Just that these Thule creeps have really learned how to use the Net. I'll bet that's where Vreeland finds a lot of his recruits. Hate gets almost as many 'hits' as porno, you know."

He pointed to the big spruce, its bows overhanging the driveway. "See that owl? In the tree . . . two branches from the bottom." She came out on the porch, stooped to bring her eyes to his level, and pushed a long strand of bleached hair out of her face.

"Yep. I see him," said Monica.

"Tell me he doesn't look like a Talmudic scholar."

"Ho boy." She sniffed the smoke leaving his nostrils. "You're not smoking Salvia, are you? You've still got work to do."

"No, mother," he said. "Just a little catnip."

"Bullshit. What is it? I don't recognize the scent."

"It's *Calea Zacatechichi*. Doesn't grow all that well here. Needs more humidity. Who was on the phone?"

"The fortuneteller. She'll see you at 7. At the Carlotta. She said you'd know—"

"Good! She's dealing me in."

"You mean on Christopher Rose's big secret?"

"Or whatever it is that he laid on her. I have to believe it relates to Fortis Cohn
. . . or a rationale for murder. There aren't a lot of reasons to kill a studio executive." He paused. "Well, some might beg to differ." He patted the seat next to him.
"Take a load off, Moneypenny. Contemplate Jupiter with me."

"I hate it when you call me that," she said, easing herself down.

"I only do it because you're so obviously light years beyond it."

"Yeeaah. There's still a smidge of paternalism in you."

"And wouldn't you miss it if there wasn't . . . " He leaned over and sniffed her
hair. "Cinnabar. You smell good. Got a date tonight?"

"As a matter of fact . . . " She gave him a look. "I do." Then she changed the
subject. "So, here's the latest from our girl April. Just came in. Vreeland wants to
'introduce her to the troops.'" She paused to gauge his reaction. "Like some
warped friggin' USO, right? She says she's convinced him she can clarify his
'calling.' I guess she passed the tailbone test . . . whatever that was."

"We don't have a clue what it was, other than the link between the exam they
put her through and the damage that was done to Rose's body. Shit. I really didn't
want her to move this fast. She got ahead of me. It's a good thing our server is
secure."

"You knew she was a cowboy, boss. I doubt you could've held her back."

"Well, I'll be up there on Sunday. I suppose I can clip her wings if she's too
close to the flame."

"I don't know, Raszer," said Monica. "You may be the flame."

He thought for a moment, and then said quietly, "I don't think so."

"You two were really close once, weren't you?"

"A long time ago. For a cosmic blink. But, yeah. We were close."

"Don't underestimate your knack for getting women to act against their
better judgment. Take me. I could be running a studio media relations department
by now."

"Yeah, but you'd hate it," he said. "C'mon. How many girls get to be both
Nancy Drew and Dorothy?" He smiled mischievously, and when he did that, the
crinkles came around his eyes. Monica sighed, drained her drink, and shot him an
accusing look.

"See what I mean?" She set her drink down emphatically and stood up. "Well,
I'm off in pursuit of a meaningful relationship. I left the material on Thule and that
guy Sebottendorf on the bar. I think you've walked into another hall of mirrors,

Raszer. And there's a file with a history of all the cases where Fortis Cohn was attorney-of-record."

"You're indispensable."

"Let's keep it that way. Don't forget to call April tonight. And——" She nodded toward the remainder of his spiked cigarette. "And don't forget your appointment."

"That's the last thing I'll do. Have a great date . . . don't do anything I wouldn't."

She turned before descending the steps. The unruly strand of hair had fallen back across her face and she wore a sly expression. "Which means 'all is permitted', right?" In another moment, she was gone in the trail of exhaust from her Toyota.

Raszer set his glass down and checked his watch. In half an hour, he was due at the Villa Carlotta. He was about to rise when something stopped him. A rippling of the field around his sensory antennae. A distinct warning.

His neighbor's St. Bernard, a big puppy named Bo, began to growl furtively. From the carport underneath the balcony, Raszer heard a spring in the suspension of his Avanti give out a telltale groan. A gentle canyon updraft brought with it the trace odors of sweat and leather. Raszer's scalp bristled. Nobody had any business in his carport. Could he have drawn trouble this early in the game? Could Rose have alerted Fortis Cohn to Raszer's snooping before being killed? Still, nobody knew where he lived. The deed was in another name, the coordinates as secure as an FBI safe house. It was only possible if he'd been followed home . . . but from where?

The intruder must have sensed he'd been heard, because all movement below ceased.

The St. Bernard bayed and was answered by a distant coyote. Raszer rose warily and cocked his ear. The Calea made all sensation register with the clarity of a dream. In fact, he realized with some consternation, he could be dreaming. *No, fool*, he reminded himself. Everything *is always real. Act accordingly.* The best thing to do was to wait. He didn't keep a gun in the house. The only weapons other than wits with which Raszer was adept were a combat knife and a set of tiny darts tipped with a paralytic agent that could either immobilize or kill, depending on the penetration point. Neither weapon was immediately at hand. He counted silently to sixty, inhaling . . . holding . . . and exhaling with each count of five, until his pulse had slowed enough to allow him some degree of control over his fight-or-flight instinct. Then, *ex nihilo*, he howled as loudly and savagely as he could while leaping up and down on the floorboards. He tore open the screen door, reached around the doorframe, and pulled his knife from the harness which hung on a peg just inside, leaping back out quickly enough to see, in the streetlight's hazy spill, the pink of a shaved head and the sheen of black leather blur down the brambled hillside and disappear into the pitch of the descending night.

The dog was quiet now, but the echo of Raszer's howl hung in the canyon. It was no wonder that many in the quiet Whitley Heights enclave felt both threatened and somehow shamanically protected by their reclusive neighbor.

He locked the house up tight and armed the office security system, rendering his computer and all of the communications equipment it controlled inoperable by anyone without world-class hacking skills. Lacking the time or the patience to check his car's ignition system for tampering, he kick-started his old Triumph motorcycle and sped down the hill to Hollywood. He would face the ramifications of the intruder's trespass on his return. He was certain they were not minor.

The fragrance of jasmine had returned to the air with the departure of the Santa Anas. With the psychoactive herb percolating into his brain and the Triumph's big engine beating away beneath him, past and future collapsed into a living present.

Madame Rey lived in a first floor garden unit off the Carlotta's hidden courtyard. It was there, in her flat, that he'd had a couple of readings years before, and he recalled it as redolent of frankincense and spilled herb tea, soaked up over the years by faded Persian rugs. As he stepped into the courtyard, masked by its gothic columns and jungle vegetation, a lank, pale young man in black silk perched on a wrought iron loveseat, joined shortly by a young woman with iron-straightened purple hair. She sat reverently and wordlessly at his side, the pair of them harbored by the translucent ferns in this little piece of Paris in L.A., a place hidden from the all-seeking California sun. Raszer stopped and watched them for a few moments from the opposite side of the central fountain, then padded across the tile to Madame Rey's flat.

"Sastimos," said Raja, nodding a greeting as he stepped across her threshold. "Would you like some tea?"

"Sastimos, Madame Rey," replied Raszer. "Thank you."

She was a birdlike woman with keen, dark eyes that registered every sound and shadow. It was apparent to Raszer that she'd once been very beautiful, but that she now bore the weight of a fate half-glimpsed but not fully accepted. She was not, he guessed, more than sixty, but the curve of her spine suggested an older woman. He eased himself into a velveteen armchair next to the half-opened

French doors. From the lobby adjacent the courtyard came the tinkling of a grand piano. A twisted little fragment of Satie or Scriabin. She brought him his tea and dropped to the sofa like a leaf.

"So," he began. "How's business?"

She shrugged. "It has been lousy . . . until the last few days. Something is in the air. People come for readings when they are uneasy. Something is making them that way. Maybe it's these earthquakes . . . or the winds."

"Maybe so. And Mercury is in retrograde."

"That never hurts," she said. "But still, I don't think business will ever be what it was. When my generation dies, the craft will die with it."

"Divination will never go out of style."

"Maybe not, but the tarot is a life's work, and it never made anyone rich." She paused, drumming her fingers on the edge of the ornately carved coffee table. "I had a visit this afternoon from a Lieutenant Borges."

"Oh?"

"He asked about you," she said, an eyebrow cocked.

"He did, did he?"

"Yes," Raja replied. "About whether you'd been in to see me."

"And you told him I had."

"Yes."

"Good."

"But I said nothing about your case."

"Also good. Did you tell him what you're about to tell me?"

"No. I might have. He seems a thoughtful man, not unkind. But still, a cop, and my father taught me never to tell the police the whole truth. They read it like a newspaper—in black and white—and this . . . this message . . . is neither."

"That may partly explain why it came to you and not the police."

Raja nodded with weary fatalism. "Something else came to me, too. In a black limousine. That young actress from television . . . Bree Donahue."

"I haven't seen the show, but I know the face. She's all over the newsstands."

"Yes . . . her moment seems to have arrived. But with fortune comes fate. She knew of the young man who was killed. She is involved with a movie that he was . . . what do you call it that men like him do?"

"Developing," said Raszer, a dozen questions sprouting. "How weird a coincidence is it that an actress involved—even peripherally—with Christopher Rose found her way to you?"

Madame Rey shook her head. "There are no coincidences in my line of work, Stephan. If she came here, it was in the cards."

"I take your point," said Raszer. "Still, I'd be careful. She might've been sent."

"She gave every appearance of being ignorant of my connection to that poor man. No, she was worried about her contract."

"Her contract . . . " He puzzled it out. "Her contract . . . on the picture . . . that Christopher Rose was in charge of?"

Raja nodded.

"Is it about money?" he asked.

"No," said the gypsy. "I think it is about her soul."

Her eyes locked onto his. He kept his silence for a good ten seconds before saying, "I'd give anything to know the name of the lawyer who drew up that contract."

His hostess poured herself some tea. The fragrance was as tantalizing as the questions left unanswered. "I'm concerned about her," she said.

"I'm concerned about you, my friend," said Raszer. "I had a visitor, too. A prowler. I chased him into the canyon. Didn't get a real good look, but I'd stake my license on the fact that it was the guy who came for Rose."

"And murdered him."

"That seems like a reasonable assumption. I'm inclined to think he's been watching your shop . . . maybe even suspects that Rose gave or told you something . . . that he saw me there Tuesday night, and tailed me home."

"Well, the police have his description. Maybe they'll get lucky,"

"Maybe. Nonetheless, if he's still around, he has unfinished business. Would you like me to find you a bodyguard?"

"No . . . no. But I will spread the risk around a little."

"I'll take my share."

"Come over here and sit by me."

Raszer came to the sofa as Madame Rey carefully unfolded the scrap of paper and opened her pad beside it. His eyes widened on seeing the amount of work she'd done.

"It's a kind of riddle," she explained. "Partly encrypted. I have only the first half. Tell me what you see."

"The characters are Hebrew and . . . Sanskrit?" She nodded. "The geometric form at the bottom—that lattice-like thing—there are diagrams of the internal structure of crystals that look a little like that. The numbers on the right—*those* I've seen before."

She traced her finger to the lower right-hand corner, where the penciled numeral 23.5 was connected by an arc to a zero, followed by the sequence 010101. Raszer had no doubt that the obsessively precise hand responsible for the figures was the same which he'd seen on a similar piece of legal paper. Fortis Cohn's.

"But I don't know what they mean," he said. "Tell me about the text."

"It was written out by someone who understood neither Sanskrit nor Hebrew. You can tell by how stiffly the letters are drawn, and because some are completely out of place. Probably copied from another source, but what that would be, I have no idea. At least . . . not yet." Raszer gave her a look, and she went on. "The Sanskrit makes up eighty percent of the text. Some of the expressions are archaic, some words are closer to the tongue of my ancestors, the Domba, than to classical Sanskrit. How odd that it should come to me."

"No argument there," he said. "Unless your linguistic skills are more widely known than you thought."

"No," she replied, somewhat absently. "This has the feeling of *kris*. Fate."

She drew her finger down. "These Hebrew words serve multiple purposes."

"How so?" he asked.

"Some fill in blanks in the verse. Some are dummies, designed to throw a novice off. And some . . . " She paused to clear her throat. "Well, here I am going on intuition, but I believe they may link to tarot. My father taught me the links between the cards and Kabbalah. About the old Jews in Morocco and their secret pact with the Sufis . . . "

"So you think," he interjected, "that the Hebrew letters represent a spread?"

"Yes . . . and the order in which they appear—" She paused and counted over the letters again, her lips silently forming the sounds. "—is the order of the lay. Nine letters." She indicated the verse. "First and last of these four words, plus the Aleph. Nine cards in the old European spread. Three for the past, three for present, three future."

"Have you done it?" Raszer asked eagerly.

"I'm working on it. A tarot spread read properly can mean only one thing, but this one will take me time. When I return to the shop tonight, I will continue working."

A worry crossed his brow.

She gripped his knee, suddenly assaulted by a new storm in her head. From where Raszer sat, it looked like a seizure, the sort not entirely unfamiliar to him.

He instinctively applied pressure to two points at the base of her skull. After a moment, Raja regained her equilibrium and turned to him.

"Where did you learn to do that?" she asked.

"From having it done to me," he said. "Aspirin won't cure that kind of headache."

Madame Rey pointed to her right eye, to the part of the iris where Raszer's little "flaw" resided. "Does it hurt?" she asked. "When the light comes . . . "

"Like a bitch," he replied. "And sometimes for hours afterward."

"I once met a man from Fez," she said, wistfully, "with a condition like yours. Long ago, in Marseille. I don't know what became of him." She turned from the memory, and Raszer, and opened her pad to a new page. "This is as far as I've gotten. I have tried to make it rhyme in English, since rhyming words are used in the Sanskrit, though the puns are never quite the same. The second verse, I still can't make sense of."

The tree of man has branches five
the shortest is the root.
Take its measure to discern
the wise man from the brute

"I was free with the translation," she explained, "but I think I have the essence. 'Wise man' is pretty close to the meaning of the original Sanskrit word. 'Brute' is actually closer to 'tyrant,' but that didn't rhyme. 'Discern' could also be distinguish. It doesn't make sense, though, that the shortest 'branch' of anything should be the root, so something is wrong. Does it add up to anything for you, Stephan?"

"I don't get the 'root' thing, either," Raszer said, "except maybe as it relates to the tree of Man, as in 'family tree.' Madame Blavatsky and the Theosophists had a theory about the root races of mankind. Let's see . . . the Lemurians were the third root race, after the Hyperboreans, and before the Atlanteans, who were the fourth. We're the fifth —and probably the lowest! But we presage the return of the Masters and—"

"The end of this wicked cycle," said Raja. "The Kali Yuga. And the start of the New Age, when man's inner eye will once again open."

"And if so, Madame Rey," observed Raszer, "I wouldn't write the obituary on your trade just yet." He smiled and took the document in his hands, pouring over it millimeter by millimeter, as if by conjuration he might cause something to materialize from the paper, as in the old trick with lemon juice and flame. As the intensity of his concentration and excitation escalated, the dark spot on his iris—no bigger than a dust mote—flickered almost imperceptibly.

Madame Rey leaned forward. "Ah," she said.

Without lifting his eyes from the paper, he asked, "Have you made any headway with the second quatrain?"

"This line," she said, indicating the first, "says something about the 'spinning of the earth.' And the last line contains a phrase . . . something like 'the old regime' or 'the old tyranny' restored.'"

"When you crack it, will you give me a call?"

"Of course, my friend."

"I don't suppose you'd let me make a copy," Raszer asked.

"Well," Raja sighed. "I should not. He entrusted it to me alone." She sat for a moment, rubbing her palms together. "But I will, because I have his death on my head, and you may be the one to bring him justice. Come by the shop in the morning."

Raszer drained his tea, nodded, and set the cup down.

"Okay." he said. "I'm heading up north tomorrow, but I can swing by around ten." He stood, still staring at the cryptic piece of paper. "That," he said, pointing to the lattice design, "would mean something to a physicist, I'll bet." Fortis Cohn wasn't much of a draftsman, but the figure he'd sketched betrayed its elegance. It was a complex of interconnected vectors, enclosed in a five-sided polygon: a geometrical house of mirrors. Unlike the verse, he could only have drawn it if he'd had some idea of its meaning.

"Did you know, Stephan," Raja said, looking over his shoulder, "that the word *gematria*—the key I used to decode the Hebrew—is the origin of the word 'geometry?'"

"Madame Rey?"

"Why don't you call me Raja," she said. "Madame Rey is a name on a sign."

He nodded, but was suddenly grave. "Raja. I want you to be very careful. I'd feel much better if you didn't go back to the shop tonight-"

"I will be careful," she said, putting a hand up. "*Les Gitanes* are always cautious, because they anticipate the worst. But if I am meant to be found, hiding will not make me invisible."

Raszer nodded.

She touched the back of her hand lightly to his cheek. "Don't worry too much for me. Whatever is to be, I am happy that fate has once again brought us into the same world. And I am certain that you will find the answers you seek."

"How do you know that? Have you read my cards lately?"

Her expression remained impassive.

"Do you remember, Raja," he asked, "telling me once about how every gypsy receives a secret name at birth?"

"The Oraga, yes. It is whispered in the ear of the newborn infant."

"Do you suppose that everyone has one?"

"I am certain that you do, Stephan."

Parked at the curb outside the Carlotta in an unmarked squad were Lieutenant Borges and his stolid partner. Raszer was displeased, but not entirely surprised to see them there on his exit.

"Good evening, Lieutenant," he said, as Borges emerged from the car.

"Evening, Mr. Raszer." He nodded to the building. "Having your palm read?"

"I'm not sure she does palms, Lieutenant."

"Thanks for not being coy with me." Borges joined Raszer beneath the Carlotta's gothic arch, and shook his head as a midnight-clad girl in a dog-collar choker emerged from the building and disappeared down Cheremoya. Looking after her for a moment. he said, under his breath, "They just ask for trouble, don't they?" Then, turning back to Raszer: "The two of you . . . " Borges cocked his thumb. "You and the gypsy . . . you know each other?"

"We're acquainted. I'm closer to her line of work than I am to yours."

"Oh, I don't know about that."

"I'm on a missing persons case up north," said Raszer. "The murder victim may have had an involvement with my stray."

"Well, that's awfully tidy."

"Life deals me the splits, Lieutenant. I just play them."

"I hope you get lucky. Does your MP have an alibi?"

"I'll know when I find him."

"And you'll tell me all about it when you do . . . "

"To the degree I can without disserving my client, or endangering the MP, who happens to be his son."

Borges whistled through his teeth. "It's always a small world with you, isn't it, Raszer? Did you know when you saw the corpse that he linked with your case?"

"Not until I saw his business card. I'd never seen him alive. He was on my list, though." He paused and surveyed the street, making sure that his Triumph was still where he'd left it, in the diagonal spot in front of the Daily Planet bookstore. Something had caused his scalp to bristle. "It *is* a small world when you bring it down to ritual revenge killings with a tarot reading as foreplay, Lieutenenant. And then there's the fact that you and I worked together and had a knack for picking up the same scent. Every connection narrows the field, right? You made one by calling me to the crime scene."

"Right," said Borges, stepping back into the car. "Let's keep those connections fresh. I'm Homicide now, but I'd rather be preventing it than solving it. I'll give you some room, but I'll need more next time we talk." He pulled the door shut and lowered the window. "With a killer on the streets, that may be sooner than you think."

Raszer waited for Borges' car to thread the traffic at Beachwood Canyon Drive before turning toward the Daily Planet, a low-level current still crisscrossing his scalp. By the time he'd reached his motorcycle, its voltage had been stepped up.

Raja examined the cards again. It was past midnight and she was spent. The images were beginning to blur. If her hunch was correct and the Hebrew letters spelled out a tarot spread, then the pictures ought to tell a story. It was one she couldn't yet read. A sharp pain traveled across the back of her skull like a crack in aging plaster, and she closed her eyes while it ran its course. Five seconds passed, and her eyelids popped open. "Of course," she said aloud. She knew what was missing. The querent. The querent had to be present at the table for the stream of divination to flow. Raja sighed, sat back and ran her finger around the familiar chipped rim of the china cup she'd taken her tea from for nearly forty years. Then the lights went out.

In the blackness came the clarity of fear. There had been a sudden metallic *click*, the tripping of a circuit breaker. She knew the wiring in her shop was old, but she couldn't have taxed it with a single lamp. She'd hung the CLOSED sign and curtained off the front reception area, so could not see the street to know if there'd been a power outage. The breaker box was in the rear of the building, easy enough to get to, if the blood had not drained from her limbs. *Snap.* The deadbolt turned on the back alley door.

"Blessed Sainte Sara," she whispered. "Make my peace with all those I have wronged. Remove all curses I have uttered. Grant my spirit speedy release from raiyo. I accept—"

There were heavy footsteps in the narrow hallway that led from the alley into her parlor, and an odor. Sour sweat and leather, and worse. Something feral. It was then that Raja realized that her grip had broken the china cup, and that her hand was bleeding.

A voice issued from behind the beam of a high-powered flashlight, military grade. "Don't move a muscle, Gypsy. Just tell me where it is." The voice had corrosion on it, like a machine gun left in some jungle theater of tribal war. The instruction was unnecessary, because Raja was paralyzed with dread. "I will kill you sure as your old man was a chicken thief," the man said. "I want that fucking piece of paper."

"Kill me, then," said Raja softly. "I don't have it."

"The fuck you say."

"I burned it. It had bad luck written all over it. Check the ashtray over there." Her fatalism bolstered her nerve, but it was disconcerting not to be able to see her killer's face, despite her certainty of his identity. The hot spot came a step closer to her eyes, shutting down her pupils. She could see nothing outside its beam.

"You're lying, you mutant bitch. But you know what? It doesn't matter. You've seen it. You die. That oughta cover it."

Raja's options were limited. She had no gun; she had no pepper spray. What she did suddenly have was blood in her extremities, and without forethought, she overturned the card table into his path and made a run for the door to the front room, the street, and salvation. But he was easily twice her weight and half the distance to the door. He stopped her cold and put the gun with its oversized silencer to her temple.

"Why do they run?" the killer purred, his mouth to her ear. "Don't they know that's what makes the juices flow?" His steroid-pumped forearm was around her neck, and Raja sensed he could just as easily snap it as shoot her. "Haven't you had this nightmare, lady? Don't you remember me? You don't get away. You can't even scream." Raja closed her eyes and felt herself slip out of her body. It was the oddest feeling, like a snake shedding its skin.

"You can kill me now," she said calmly, and it must have spooked him a little to hear her voice coming from the other side of the room. He shifted his hold on the gun grip, and for an instant, she felt the pressure of the muzzle ease.

"No, you can't," said a new voice. The headlock tightened and Raja felt her windpipe constrict as her feet left the floor. "Point the gun away from her head, asshole," said Stephan Raszer, only inches removed, "or I'll slit your throat." Undeterred, the assassin jammed the barrel to her temple once again. "You didn't hear me," Raszer said, low and fervent, and Raja felt the killer's grip weaken as a phlegmy, gagging sound issued from his esophagus. "One more chance," said Raszer. Drop your arm to your side. And let the gun fall to the floor. Got that?"

"Fuck you . . . whoever you are."

"I'm *your* nightmare," said Raszer, and put his weight into it.

"Jesus!" the skinhead gurgled. "You're cutting my——"

"You bet I am. Let her go, and drop the gun. Now."

The weapon hit the carpet with a dull thud. Raja remained against the wall, hollowed out, her feet on the floor but her body temporarily missing its soul. "Raja," she heard Raszer say with uncanny calmness. "I want you to reach down, and pick up the gun." She did so. "Good," he said, "Now go into to your parlor and close the door behind you. Dial 911. Ask the operator to connect you to the Wilcox Station, and tell them to get our friend Lieutenant Borges over here right away. Tell them I've got his man. When that's done, come back in here, if you'd be kind enough, and hold the gun on this creep so I can smoke a cigarette."

After the door had shut behind her, Raszer took a few measured breaths, said a short prayer, and began to drag his oversized captive back toward the center of the room. A rivulet of blood from the man's throat ran down the mirror-polished blade of Raszer's knife and past the hilt to his thumb. But for the faint light leaking in from the alley, the room was dark and Raszer wanted it that way until he'd had time to fix a blindfold. He kicked the chair away from the table and forced his captive down, remaining behind him all the while. Beginning at the nape of the neck and tracing down the spine, he cut the killer's black tank top with his blade, slipped it from his torso, and tied it snugly around his head. Only them did he step back.

"What's my name?" he asked.

No answer.

"What's my name, soldier?"

"Cocksucker."

"Close, but no cigar. You need a shave." With a quick upward stroke, Raszer sliced another millimeter of flesh from the man's stubbled neck.

"Rumple-fucking-stiltskin!" the killer yelped. "Fuck! I don't know your name!"

"That's good," said Raszer. "Let's keep it like that."

Outside, the howl of a siren cut through the intersection of Franklin and Vine, and Raszer silently rehearsed his presentation to Lt. Borges. A few seconds later, Madame Rey returned with the killer's gun, and Raszer smoked a cigarette.

PART TWO—EROS

8

Bene visit qui bene latuit
(One lives best by the hidden life)
—Francis Bacon

THE Berkeley Audio Lab did manage to clean up Odd Meyer III's "ground radio" recording, but the ELF pulses he'd registered were far too weak to be rendered as anything more than a low, cyclical warbling. The staff was dismissive; after all, ground radio was raw technology—nothing much more than iron rods in the earth—and the pulses might as easily have been generated by a neighbor's sprinkler system. It was only after a chorus of OM III's usually reticent colleagues had risen to his defense that the lab's senior analyst had agreed to examine the evidence. He concluded immediately that there was only one facility in the West with the resources to enhance a signal this dirty. It was at the Very Large Array Radio Telescope installation in Socorro, NM. There were SETI people there, still listening for ETs, who might be intrigued.

Under the brilliant dome of New Mexico starlight, with the Rio Grande slipping silently past and the Magdalena Mountains draped in violet shadow, the technicians stood and held their collective breath as the final enhancement came over the government issue loudspeakers.

"I don't get it," said one. "It's like a musical waveform, but . . . "

"Increase the pitch," suggested another. "By 3X."

"It's a voice!" cried a third. "Female! Jesus! It sounds like singing—"

As the SETI team stood spellbound, an unaccompanied chant filled the room: rich and reedy, the nasal contralto curling like an asp around the notes of her lament, notes sung in a language foreign to all.

After thirteen seconds, the voice broke off abruptly and degenerated into random noise. That was all they had, but it held them rapt as they played it repeatedly. Was it some kind of transient? A Yemeni toothpaste commercial picked up by the plumbing? Although the term was mentioned, no one seriously thought it could be the chimerical EVP, i.e., "spirit voices" wrapped in radio static. Procedure dictated that they digitize it and, if security was a concern, ship the sound file off to Washington, where it would find its way down the food chain to a G-9 level civil servant in Section 7 of the National Security Agency, a dozen savants who did low-priority code breaking. After some talk about the possibility that the ditty, given its "Middle Eastern character," might contain covert wake-up instructions to terrorist sleeper cells, that is exactly what they did.

The NSA cryptographer recognized in the chant certain phonemes that led her first to think that the language was proto-Hindi. Then she was thrown by odd little "glottals" which sounded more like an Altaic cousin of Turkic. A Harvard-educated linguist, she was reminded of the Medieval obsession with finding the original Adamic language, and laughed to shoo away her fear. The melody itself was another enigma. She ran it past one ethnomusicologist, who labeled it fifteenth century Berber, most likely a strain from the area of Morocco's Atlas Mountains, but this was contradicted by another who dubbed it Tuvan. She moved phonemes and roots around the computer program like a linguistic Rubik's Cube. By Wednesday at 9:15 P.M., this is what she had:

Ear to (hear, harken, listen to) the earth
(for) in her/through her veins (arteries? roots?)
sounds (vibrates, resonates, drones?) the song (incantation?)
to/that will heal (rectify? reverse?) the break/separation

Exhausted, but feeling that she'd unscrambled little more than a fragmented riff on something from Kahlil Gibran, she switched off the lights and went home for the night. At exactly three o'clock in the morning, she sat up in bed with the voice from the tape in her head. It was the voice of a mature woman, not a young chanteuse, and there was something both maternal and profoundly martial in it. It was laced with the chill of an autumn gale that announces the end of golden summer and presages winter. It spooked her like nothing had since childhood.

Somewhere over the Maricopa lowlands, the twin-engine Cessna carrying Raszer north found its cruising altitude. The Sierra Nevada was way off to the right, obscured by airborne dust but for the morning sun glinting off a few snow-caps. To the west, he could make out the voluptuous landfolds of the Coast Ranges, presenting one last barrier to the Pacific. He was traveling over the floor of the San Joaquin Valley, and everything here was measured in great distances.

On his lap and mostly unread were copies of Wilhelm Landig's 1971 neo-Nazi rhapsody, *Gotzen gegen Thule* (roughly, *Little Gods v. Thule*) and Miguel Serrano's 1984 *Adolf Hitler, The Last Avatar*, two books April had special ordered for Commander Vreeland in hopes of "teasing out" his personal mythology. The former, written in the dubious fact-disguised-as-fantasy mode of so much European occult fiction, posited the existence of "Point 103," a subterranean polar base and staging ground for a new Reich; the latter, authored by a Chilean diplomat/scholar, was precisely what its title suggested: a paean to the Fuhrer as the "tenth avatar of Vishnu." Both books cinched what Raszer had for some time believed: that in the borderlands of thought, the New Right and the New Age sometimes met. Their common ground was purity, a rejection of all that was carnal and essentially human. Supporting evidence was to be found in the three-ring binder Monica had prepared as his pre-mission brief. It contained her most recent material on Thule, Hyperborea, Rudolf Sebottendorf, and other subjects that April's reconnaissance had revealed to be near and dear to Vreeland's heart. As usual, Monica had done a good gloss on the material and burned a companion CD-ROM with hyperlinks that could be used for more in-depth study on his laptop.

Madame Rey's assailant had been arraigned that morning on battery and weapons charges. The D.A. had not yet charged him with either the attempted murder of Raja Zlatari or the Rose homicide, but Borges had assured Raszer that sturdier counts would be filed once the fortuneteller had picked him out of a line-up and a few more threads of evidence had been knitted. Raszer was not com-forted. If William "Buck" McGinty made bail on the lesser charges, there was every chance he'd head straight back to the house on Whitley Terrace. Hence, Raszer had spent his first week's fee to engage the services of a buffed-up Latvian bodyguard for Monica.

Borges had been officially displeased by Raszer's vigilantism at the scene of the crime, but was quickly mollified when Raszer offered to share the basics of the

Cohn case. It had occurred to Raszer that Borges might be helpful should he need to use the threat of misprision of felony charges to pry Fortis Cohn out of Vreeland's grasp. Borges had also promised to argue strenuously for denial of bail to McGinty, who had told the police nothing beyond his name and former rank in the United States Marines. Still, Raszer couldn't shake the feeling that he'd already lost his cover, and that was no good.

But something else was even more worrisome. Shortly after the arrival of the police, Madame Rey had collapsed and been rushed to Hollywood Presbyterian with an elevated pulse and all the signs of impending stroke. It had been directly from her hospital bedside that Monica had driven Raszer to Santa Monica Airport to board the chartered plane.

"Raja?" he'd whispered, clasping her hand. Her lids fluttered open. "How are you feeling?"

"Alive," she said. "Thanks to you."

He smiled. "That should give the doctors something to work with."

She glanced at Monica, who was wearing three-inch pumps and a slit seal-colored skirt with her white blouse, then registered her approval to Raszer with a lowering of lashes, like a matchmaker satisfied with her work.

"Oh," said Raszer. "Beg your pardon. This is my assistant, Monica Lord. She'll be checking in on you while I'm up north. I would trust her with my own blood. But for added security, Lieutenant Borges has been kind enough to detail a man to your hallway for the next few days. We want you to be able—"

"To rest in peace," Raja said, the wryest of smiles on her lips.

Raszer regarded her fondly and instinctively put his hand to her forehead. "Anyway, Monica will be able to track me down wherever I am. She's got a bead on me. And if you have any more brainstorms about that riddle . . . "

"I had one last night," Raja said, so calmly that it spooked him.

"Yes?"

"The cards are yours."

"Mine?"

"The tarot spread spelled out by the Hebrew letters. It's for you."

Raszer kept his hand on her brow and searched her eyes for any sign of either whimsy or delirium. He saw nothing but gravity. "How is that possible, Raja? Aren't we looking at a cipher that been around for ages?"

"It may be old, and it may not be. It doesn't matter. The past is as much aware of the present as the present is of the past. There are no *real* secrets in the universe.

Nothing is hidden from view once you are outside of time. And that . . . is where She is."

Raszer waited.

"The one who sings in my head," said Raja, growing more distant with the effect of the medication.

"You translated the second verse, didn't you?" he said.

She smiled, eyes closed. "Not all . . . not yet. But there is a kind of refrain: 'A man of light will see the ancient tyranny subdued.'" On the last few words, her voice diminished. Raszer leaned in and kissed her forehead, then took Monica gently by the arm.

"We'd better head for the airport," he said. "Let her get some sleep."

They were at the door when Raszer heard Madame Rey call out weakly, "Take care, Stephan Raszer. Those who track the Devil often end up walking in his footsteps."

The Cessna lurched over an invisible speed bump of turbulence. Once it had settled, Raszer opened Monica's binder to the summary she'd labeled *Ultima Thule and the Myth of the Polar Homeland.* He started to read, then shook off the residual anxiety he felt about the possibility that McGinty had been lying when he'd claimed not to know his name. For reasons both operational and deeply personal, being recognized was Raszer's recurring nightmare. He'd had it as a boy, in waking dreams in which teachers and authority figures singled him out, shrieking, "There you are!" Later on, in drug-fueled panics, there were blank-faced mobs chasing him through towns drained of color, and again the cry: *"There he is!"* How perverse that he had, for a time, been an actor. Now, his m.o. was that of a chameleon; everything he had planned for this mission depended on being able to pass himself off as a geologist, a faceless assistant to Niall Mathonwy, plumbing Shasta's arteries for whatever disease had infected Fortis Cohn.

Monica's file was not bedside reading, any more than a medical diagnosis was, but it showed a practiced hand in the etiology of virulent mythologies:

10/03/06 ML - Mythical accounts of a paradisiacal green land beyond the Arctic Circle date at least as far back as the voyage of Pytheas of Mas-silia (bet. 340 - 285 BCE), but were revitalized in the late 19th c. with the fantasy of Jules Verne (Purchase Of The Pole) and Edgar Allen Poe (The Narrative of Arthur Gordon Pym), the pseudo-geology of John Cleves Symmes (1779-1829), and the occult writings of H.P. Blavatsky (1831-

1891). Blavatsky's theories about the root races of mankind and her assertion that the First Race had had its genesis in Hyperborea, an ethereal
realm encircling the North Pole, inspired racially-motivated tracts like
those of the Odinist Rudolf von Sebottendorf (1875-1945). Sebottendorf
claimed that the Aryan race was descended from these proto-Nordic
Hyperboreans and carried in its genetic memory a longing for that same
Polar Eden which he knew by the name Thule. In primeval times, it was
conjectured, some cataclysmic event (a comet?) had knocked the earth's
axis off true north and covered Thule with ice, forcing its inhabitants to
migrate south, eventually to Lower Mongolia and Tibet, where still today
the Hidden Masters reside in the subterranean kingdoms of Shambhala
and Agharta. Sebottendorf, along with fellow Ariosophists Guido von
List and Jorg Lanz von Liebenfels, all of whom believed that the Master
Race had been polluted by contact with inferior races like the darker
Lemurians (already busy mongrelizing the planet by having sex with
apes), decided to set things right. At a meeting held on Pentecost, 1914,
they initiated the crypto-Masonic lodge called the Germanenorden,
whose purpose was to restore the German nation and counter the
growing power of the International Jewish Conspiracy purportedly
exposed by the Protocols of the Elders of Zion, ultimately uniting people
of Aryan descent in a purified spiritual community known as HAL-
GADOM. On 17 August 1918, the Germanenorden became the Thule
Society, its stated aim to "fight until the swastika (orig, a Tibetan sun
symbol) rises victoriously from the icy darkness." The Thule Society
embraced vegetarianism, "natural living," and "family values." All appli-
cants were screened for "undesirable" racial and psychological character-
istics, but curiously, of the 16 original members, 7 were of Jewish
lineage. Despite an insistence on sexual continence, covert homosexual
activity was alleged. In February 1920, Sebottendorf subsumed the
German Workers Party into Thule, forming the National Socialist
German Worker's Party, of which Adolf Hitler soon became president.
Among the more curious offshots of the Thule movment was The Vril
Society, which included member Karl Haushofer (1869-1946), father of
geopolitics. The Vril Society took its name from a mysterious "vital force"
possessed by the underground supermen described in Edward Bulwer-
Lytton's (1803-73) novel, The Coming Race. Others who embraced the

ideal of Thule included <u>Julius Evola</u> (1898-1974) and <u>Miguel Serrano</u> (b. 1917) All of these men saw their mission in terms of eternal struggle between <u>solar</u> and <u>lunar</u> principles, e.g.: "pure" North and "corrupt" South, "strong" masculine and "weak" feminine. Above all, they looked to the <u>celestial pole</u> as the source of all real power.

There was more in the diligently footnoted pages that followed, and in the scores of documents she'd photocopied at the library or pulled off the Internet, but her gloss was sufficient to explain Bronk Vreeland's adoption of the name Thule for his militia.

The timing of Raszer's arrival in Shasta—now delayed a good six hours by police procedures and concern over Madame Rey's condition—had been a critical element in his acceptance of April's dicey plan to gain access to Thule by way of the Pink Temple. He knew he'd have—at most—a few days before the risk of exposure rose to an unacceptable level. Part of him wanted to trust her instincts; another part saw that she would always come at a target from an angle very different from his own. She wanted so badly to look down evil's throat that she risked being swallowed, and it all seemed to come down to facing her father's ghost. Monica hadn't hesitated to express doubts.

"She's hanging way out there, Raszer. Have you weighed the possibility that she could end up a hostage if Vreeland gets wise to either of you?"

"Yes," Raszer answered, weighing it yet again. "I have."

Monica had a way of making Raszer second-guess his own intuition, a faculty he was intent on developing but which he conceded women had the better of. On the eve of his departure, immediately following Madame Rey's admission to the hospital, he'd phoned April and directed her to call in sick to both The Pink Temple and the bookstore, check into the room he'd reserved at the Shasta Motor Inn, and lay low for a day. April had gotten Vreeland's attention faster than Raszer had thought possible. Once he had arrived and was in place on Mathonwy's mountain, he could more capably monitor her descent into Vreeland's Hades. He could also, if necessary, shut her down.

Below him, the valley opened wide, quilted with sprawling produce farms, some of whose owners had doubtless witnessed last week's plague of UFO's. In about an hour, he'd have an unpleasant but potentially illuminating stop to make at the prison farm in Stockton. With Abel Cohn's help, he'd been granted an interview with Karl Lodz, the pedophile and former Vreeland comrade-in-arms who'd witnessed the Supreme Commander's Utah epiphany and the birth of the Military

Order Of Thule. Raszer wanted to know what Vreeland's "calling" was, and he wanted to know about *Ori*.

Bronk Vreeland tossed his copy of *Gotzen gegen Thule* on the plank floor of the officer's quarters. Its comic book cover art depicted a squadron of luminous, spherical flying objects emerging from what appeared to be a black hole in the North Pole. A knock on his open door brought in his ripe-faced aide-de-camp, Blottmeier, to announce that the MOOT high command had convened and were awaiting their leader's gavel. Vreeland eyed him and pointed toward the book now resting at his feet.

"It's a good thing, Blottmeier," he said, ignoring his summons for the moment, "that writers are such peacocks. Otherwise they might just let the truth slip out."

"Sir?"

"They always go for the kitchen sink," said Vreeland. "Bio-active flying saucers!"

"Yes, sir."

Vreeland stood and smoothed his trousers. "But the girl gets points just for knowing about it. How many people——" He stopped in mid-utterance, seized by a sudden thought, and walked to his impressively full bookshelf, pulling a copy of John White's *Pole Shift* from between a munitions manual and a primer on anthrosophical medicine. He handed it to Blottmeier. "This—on the other hand—is worth reading . . . if you've got the attention span."

"I have, sir."

"You have what, soldier?"

"I have read it," said Blottmeier, the tiniest hint of pride showing at the corners of his mouth.

"Well, now," said Vreeland. "You may just earn your stripes—and my favor—yet, Blotto." He slapped the recruit on his softly rounded shoulder. "If you can stay away from the chicken and dumplings. Lose some weight. It disgusts me to look at you."

"Yes, sir."

"Okay, then," said Vreeland. "Let's go face the lions." He straightened his vest, drew to full-chested attention and turned to a wall-mounted mirror in an antiqued gold frame. In the clean morning light, his freshly oiled scalp shone through the cropped corn stalks of his Marine cut; he took a moment to register his steel-blue eyes, as if confirming that their commanding qualities were intact. His cheekbones were high and burnished bronze; his mouth was wide and habitually drawn down at the corners. Something made him scowl, then he turned away from the mirror, muttering, "Screw it."

The members of the high command had gathered stiffly around a horseshoe-shaped table on the third floor of what had once been residential quarters for the Klamath Mining Co.'s regional boss and his family. The wraparound windows afforded a 180-degree view of the corral, the sloping meadow of wildflower and sheep grass, and the heavily guarded western approach to the compound. Behind the ranch house and the old stables and extending almost to the snow line was a boulder-strewn, two hundred acre glacial moraine where the militia conducted its exercises. Although the area lay at roughly nine thousand feet above sea level, its concave topography prevented its being seen from lower altitudes. That, plus the high degree of stamina required to perform in the thin air, made it uniquely suitable for drills.

On the east wall, behind the table, hung an oversized banner bearing the insignia of the Military Order of Thule. A muscular centurion stood supremely in his chariot as his three mares reared up in flared-nostril terror. In his left hand, the charioteer held the reins, while with his right, he thrust the lance which pinned a writhing serpent to the earth. Although the snake had coiled itself halfway up the shaft, her position was hopeless: her head had been run through.

Vreeland pulled out a chair at the head end of the table and sat down without offering a greeting. He drew the stub of a fat Cohiba from his vest, lit it, and squinted through the acrid smoke at the other six men. All but one, Fortis Cohn, were in fatigues, and all but Fortis had shaved their heads to the fuzz.

"At ease," Vreeland said perfunctorily, and blew a plume of smoke in Fortis Cohn's direction "I know what this is about—and I'll deal with your questions—but let's hear first from counsel about the Indian lawsuit." He aimed the cigar. "What gives? How long is it going to take to derail this thing? Did we get to that judge yet?"

"After some investigation," Fortis answered with quiet temerity, "I don't think that's the way to go, sir." Fortis Cohn was of slight build and had a face whose features seemed raked forward like an antique roadster's hood; his hair was pomaded back to an opaque sheen and he wore a Brooks Brothers suit. Vreeland sat forward.

"And why is that?" Vreeland challenged. "Every man has his weak spot . . ."

Fortis Cohn allowed his client's last assertion to stand uncontested.

"The judge is of Modoc descent on his mother's side, but there's no way they'll remove him for prejudice. He's ruled four times against his own people in similar cases, and he's all but dared us to try and impeach his suitability. His wife died five years ago and he has no mistress. He's clean, he's dry, and he doesn't have his hand out."

"Maybe you haven't offered what he really wants," Vreeland retorted. "Or threatened to take it away. There isn't a soul that doesn't beg to be stained with the right juice. If he's gone against his tribe, maybe what he wants is to be what he's not: a white man. Try planting an article in the *Sacramento Bee* about his noble Modoc heritage."

"With all respect, Commander," said Fortis. "I think there's a better way."

"With all respect," said Vreeland, mimicking Fortis's mannered legal tone. "There'd better be. By the way, counselor, you are looking very slick today. I might have to let you take me to lunch." The other men snickered as Cohn flushed and fingered his tie. They were used to this: their leader's habit of dispensing affection and abuse in equal measure. Pull them up, slap them down. It had made addicts of them all.

"The Klamath deed was ambiguously worded as to the return of the land to the tribes," Cohn pressed ahead, recovering his composure. "However, I think there may be a way to make it less ambiguous." Vreeland arched his brow.

"You work on that, then. And fast. We're getting close to the day we've all been waiting for, and I do not want the media focused on this mountain until it serves our agenda." He cast a confirming glance at Latimer J. Bloch, his second-in-command and a former fertilizer salesman and deacon for the Free Church of Christ in Festus, MO. Then, with a contemptuous expression, he turned back to Fortis. "Oh, and Cohn . . . your protégé down in Hollyweird . . . the one you nominated to the Fraternity? He flunked initiation. Didn't last a week. Told a dozen people he had something big going on, including a fucking actress. Leased a Porsche. Worse yet, he went and spilled his guts to a fortuneteller. I'd reckon your judgment was, uh . . . clouded."

"Wh-what are you saying, sir?" Fortis ventured.

"I am saying, Fortis, that he was not fit, that he betrayed your trust and has paid the price for your sins. You know the Fraternity wants a major stake in the movie business. We've got directors, writers—and most important—studio executives, because they're the ones who decide what gets made. When our moment comes, the world will be ready partly because they'll already have seen the movie version. It'll be ready because we've laid the foundation, not because we banked on sissies who run off to gypsies every time they have a little attack of nerves. We went with you on this, but you screwed up. All unplanned leaks must be neutralized at the source. Do you understand what I'm saying, counselor? Are we clear? Or do I send you back to Little Israel?"

The blood that had drained from Fortis's face upon realizing that Christopher was dead now rose in anger. These were not emotions he was able to conceal, much as he tried. It was the part of himself he hated most: the feeling part. His father's part.

"With all deference to your position, sir," said Fortis, "you cannot do that. I am a legacy, and there is a binding contract."

A red-tailed hawk screeched from somewhere over the meadow. Otherwise, there was not a sound save for the uneasy creaking of chairs.

"You are quickly using up your mother's grace, Fortis," said Vreeland, with soft menace, and for a few moments, there were just the two of them, and Fortis was as immobilized as the hippie girl had been, bent over the table with her skirts raised. "I told Voorhees I'd take you under my wing. Your 'contract' . . . your *mother's* contract . . . was with him, and now it's been assigned to me, and the fact is that it's a *service* contract. *Your* services to *me,* Fortis. So, you'd better remember that this is my command and my mission and that every man here is expendable if he jeopardizes it."

"Can I assume that includes you?" Fortis just could not help himself.

"Yes, you can," answered Vreeland, bristling. "I'm a soldier, asshole."

"Then why—" Fortis ventured, suddenly very conscious of the difficulty of swallowing. "Why would *you* risk it on this 'dancer?' April Blessing . . . if that's her real name. We have absolutely no reason to trust her, and every reason to suspect that she's allied with our adversaries. I strongly advise against bringing her onto the base."

There was a nodding of heads around the table as the advantage shifted temporarily to Fortis, and a bare instant when Bronk Vreeland's face reflected something almost like hurt—an ache he assuaged by puffing the Cohiba's ash into a red-hot coal. From the corner of his eye, he'd noticed that Aldo Zwieg, his field officer, was nodding in Fortis's direction with particular enthusiasm. Keeping his eyes leveled on the attorney, he pushed up from the table, took one last series of puffs on the cigar, and then crushed its glowing ash out on Zwieg's forehead.

Vreeland took his seat again, and Fortis Cohn quietly broke a sweat.

"Not one of you," said the Commander, "appreciates the hidden side of history. You think wars are won by taking the right hill? Not now, not ever. There are subtler forces at work. Spiritual forces. If you don't invoke and enlist them—or find someone who can—sooner or later you face them as enemies." He paused and regarded Zwieg, who was doing his best to hang tough, palms on the table, chin trembling. Bronk grasped his wrist. "There's some good burn ointment in my medicine cabinet, Aldo." He summoned Blottmeier over. "Blotto. Take this man to first-aid and attend to him."

Once the two men had left the room, Vreeland resumed. He left his place and made the circuit of the table, stopping to place his hands on Fortis Cohn's shoulders. "Seven years ago," he said, "I received a calling. I have obeyed that calling, even at great personal cost, and it has earned me the faith of the Fraternity. *Faith,* gentlemen."

Latimer J. Bloch cleared his throat. He was a square-cut forty year old with a flattened nose as gristly and quilted as a cube steak. He spoke tonelessly in an Indiana drawl that went straight from his barrel chest to his nasal cavities. "Not one soldier here questions the authority of your vision, sir," he said. "Not one. But we are sworn to protect you. We are your guard, Commander. Mr Cohn is our legal counsel and he is also sworn to protect our mission. I just feel like that we need some background on this girl. I mean . . . where did she come from and why—"

Vreeland held up his palm for silence. "Where *did* she come from?" he repeated. "Well, now, that's a good question, Latimer, and I'll try to answer it. Jesus counseled us not to throw our pearls before swine, but what the hell? The worst that can happen is that Fortis here will sell me out for thirty pieces of silver. She came down through the ages from Eleusis. You might've heard of that, or maybe not. Doesn't matter. She has the gift of sight. She's climbed this mountain to the summit three times. When's the last time any of you did that?" He dropped his voice. "She is the vessel of our lineage."

"Commander, I—" Fortis had a point to make, but Vreeland gripped his shoulders tightly enough to make him wince.

"She knows this mountain, gentlemen. *Inside* and out. Our satellite dishes are getting pounded with jamming signals just at the time we need them clear, and the Fraternity has given me ten days to find out where they're coming from before they pull us from Stage One. I don't know about you, but I don't intend to forfeit our place in history, and if she can lead me to the source of that interference, well . . . "

Bloch interjected, "I thought we knew the signals were—"

"An S.O.S. from the rodents, right," Vreeland came back. "Like the nursery rhyme Mr. Cohn here passed across the pillows to his boyfriend." He tousled Fortis's perfectly groomed hair to put the icing on his humiliation, and the attorney's chin dropped to his chest. "I know, Fortis . . . It was only a little show 'n' tell, right? You wanted to show him something only a plugged in guy like yourself could have. Impress him with your *bona fides* so you could close that big movie deal and up your status in the Fraternity. Or maybe you thought you'd be really clever: the old *'I could tell you but then I'd have to kill you'* routine. Well, we did it for you, counselor. And it's a good thing, because otherwise—" He leaned in close, lifted Fortis's chin, and slowly brought the lawyer's ear back to his lips. "You could've blown the whole damned thing." Stepping back, Vreeland wiped his hands and directed his summation to the rest of the brass, leaving Fortis to stew. "Yes, we know the rats are screwing with our relays from down below, but we don't know how they're getting past our filters and we don't know where their signal originates. Until we know, they're making hash of our transmissions. I'm prepared to employ extraordinary means to find out, including those powers that most of us have forgotten how to use." He paused. "And I have the full support of the Fraternity."

The chief technical officer, silent until now, spoke up. "She's been vetted then . . . by the leadership?"

"I'm the only leadership that matters here," Vreeland reminded them, "and I've 'vetted' her. And in case it slipped your minds, you can't make a new world without pussy. Not yet at least. A man can find a certain solace in the company of other men, but tell me . . . which one of you has hips broad enough to bear me a son?"

Vreeland inspected the faces of his advisors one by one, not moving on until each one had met his gaze with tacit assent. Only Fortis Cohn's eyes remained downcast, and Vreeland stayed on him.

"I'm bringing her in Tuesday night. Now, Fortis, you can take this to Voorhees if you want . . . that's your blood prerogative. You can pull rank on me, and maybe you'll win. But if you don't, I'll expect you to handle it graciously. You're under my watch for as long as it takes to beat this Indian suit. If you try to leave, it's treason, and you can join your boyfriend in hell. Do you understand?" He waited. "Are we clear, Fortis?"

Fortis glanced up from under hooded eyes, bit his lip, and nodded sullenly.

"Good," said Bronk. "Then buck up. You're still our lawyer. Let's show these Indians a little Manifest Destiny and send them back to the reservation. All right?"

"All right," said Fortis, smoothing his hair back into place.

Raszer left his pilot waiting at the small landing strip outside Stockton and took a cab to the State Prison Farm, eight miles south. After a brief meeting with the warden, he was escorted to a cluster of brown sheds at the far end of the compound, where a selected group of inmates were assigned to an experiment in hydroponic farming. Raszer shot his escort a look of disbelief. This seemed pretty light duty for a man twice convicted of sexual battery with minors. The guard led him into the climate-controlled cloister of Shed Number 6 and pointed to a figure halfway down a long trough filled with floating heads of Boston leaf lettuce.

"That's Lodz," he said flatly. "Warden says twenty minutes, no more. "

"Thanks," Raszer replied. "I'll take it from here."

The grow-lights overhead hummed and flickered sporadically as Raszer advanced down the plywood decking laid alongside the trough. The canned light and the ceaseless bobbing of the lettuce made him feel as if he were in steerage on a ship bound for a leper colony. Karl Lodz was the sole prisoner currently working Shed 6. He was wearing a white jump suit and leg irons, and something about him made Raszer think of a child's first attempts to draw the human figure: spindly arms that seemed to sprout from the thorax and a head like a cantaloupe. There was nothing of even passing distinction in his features. It was a face that would leave no mark; one that even a victim might have difficulty recalling. Lodz turned with unsettling calm and revealed that someone had carved a string of three linked sixes into his forehead. The scars were ragged.

Raszer announced himself. "Karl Lodz? I'm Roger Bacon. I believe your attorney told you to expect me. I've heard you might have something up close and personal on a soldier of fortune named Bronk Vreeland." Lodz left his hands dangling in the cool water and spoke with the joyless drone of hardscrabble Nebraska.

"You're the D.A.'s man, yeah? Thought you might be here to ask me about that little girl in Petaluma. Vreeland, shit. That's another universe altogether, now, i'n't it."

"That's the only universe I care about right now," Raszer said. "I'm going to try really hard to pretend I don't know anything about your little girls. You were with Vreeland in Utah, right? When he was 'chosen.'"

Lodz wheeled on him, his hands dripping. "I dunno what you were expecting, mister, but what could you possibly offer that would make it worth my while to earn another brand like this?" He spread his thumb and index finger across his forehead, stretching the translucent skin taut. "This is what I got last time I opened my mouth about Vreeland. This plus a length of PCV pipe up my ass."

"I can't offer you anything but a chance to put the story straight. But the D.A. might be grateful, and he's got a little pull with the governor. Are you saying that Vreeland has people here at the farm?"

Lodz puckered his little mouth. "Open your eyes, doc. The prison system is like a rabbit pen for the Aryan brothers. These are Bronk's foot soldiers, man. Come the restoration, they'll make one badass army."

"The restoration?"

"0-1-0-1-0-1. The Zero Point. The first day of history, when things are put to rights . . . if you b'lieve like he does. Just like the old hymn: . . . *and the prisons shall be opened.* Only I think Bronk intends to give the Lord some help."

"Whose side are you gonna be on?" Raszer asked.

"Me?" Lodz snickered. "Neither side'll have me."

"Would you go back to Vreeland if you could?"

"What profiteth a man if he gain the world, and lose his own soul? I may be a pervert, mister, but I'm not a fuckin' reptile."

"What do you mean by that?"

"Just what I said."

"Tell me about Ori," Raszer said, rolling the dice on Abel Cohn's obscure reference to someone or something that had "come between" Lodz and Vreeland. "Isn't that what sent you packing?"

"That," Lodz insisted, "is a little chicken I didn't pluck. Tempting, though. Always wearin' those Bugs Bunny pajamas with the footies in 'em." A shiver skirted Raszer's collar. Here was a man nominally of his species, and he wondered if having even that much common lineage wasn't enough to damn him. "Bronk's daughter," Lodz continued. "His ex-wife . . . so-called . . . dumped 'er at the compound one day and drove off. Vreeland kinda took t' the kid, but he kept 'er caged up like a mink. One day, he caught us playin' doctor in the barn." Lodz smirked. "I got a way with kids, see."

Raszer pictured his own daughter, then pictured lopping off Karl Lodz's head and placing it amidst the buoying hydroponic lettuce.

"Anyway," Lodz went on, "he figured I'd messed with 'er. He broke my thumbs, took away my stripes, and had me cleaning toilets for a month, but it was really Ori he couldn't forgive . . . "

"What happened to her?"

"Three weeks went by . . . then I didn't see 'er around no more. I figured maybe he sent 'er back to mom, maybe to a home. But I dunno. Vreeland's a sick fuck."

"That's quite a testimonial, coming from you."

"I could tell you some things . . . keep you awake nights. Federal shit, too."

"You wanna testify?" Raszer asked.

"From a furnished FBI safe house in Tempi, maybe . . . Otherwise, no fuckin' way. Anyhow, after that, Bronk got all supernatural. Told the boys he was givin' up all things carnal, from pussy to pork chops, and studyin' how to be 'quiet inside.' Pretty soon then, he got his 'call.' We moved camp to Kingman, Arizona, and the new boys rolled in . . . in a fleet of Lincolns with satellite dishes mounted on the roofs." He set his small, pink hands on his hips. "They had these 'minesweepers' . . . kinda like divining rods they used to check the ground for tunnels."

"Who were the 'new boys,' Karl?"

"Behold" said Lodz, *"a pale horse, and his name that sitteth on him was Death."* He smirked. "Voorhees. The Fraternity. They don't pick daisies and they don't brake for animals. They're in ev'ry picture, man, just like fuckin' Waldo. But I didn't make their grade, and I got no more to say." With that, Lodz returned his attention to the aquatic lettuce, and Raszer was left with a few questions answered and a hundred hanging.

9

THE HERMIT.

And GOD said unto Moses "I AM THAT I AM":
and he said, "Thus shalt thou say unto the children
of Israel, I AM hath sent me unto you"—
—Yahweh to Moses from the burning bush, Exodus 3:14

PROFESSOR Mathonwy emerged early that morning from his snow-dusted tin can of a hut, feeling not at all in a scientific frame of mind. He'd had a bad dream, and hoped the mean slap of cold air would purge its effects. It hadn't been the apocalyptic sort of nightmare that his jittery solitude often induced, but the common schoolboy's dream of being caught in the act of cheating on a test. The transgression had occurred in his own classroom, and the student whose answers he'd been cribbing had turned out to be April Blessing.

Once he got outside, however, something other than the sting of frost drove the shame from his head. Against the dead quiet of dawn, he could actually hear the mountain straining. As a scientist, he was not supposed to operate by his gut, but as Shasta's caretaker, he had come to know her habits. He closed his eyes, cleared his mind, and listened. Then a more immediate sensory jolt took hold of him: he could smell the sulfur dioxide on the mountainside. If not a phantasm, that meant that somewhere inside the volcano, magma was in motion and had come into contact with the atmosphere.

Mathonwy's hut was festooned like a tinker's shack with all sorts of cups, cones, and gauges for measuring gaseous emissions, one of the primary indicators of impending eruption. All but one, a makeshift instrument he had constructed from spare parts and a gasoline funnel, registered normal levels. His senses might be playing tricks. He determined to take a correlation spectrometer reading later in the day.

This afternoon, he was to meet the private investigator, and he was preparing as if for a long-absent friend. He had already made up the spare bunk, purchased a case of decent supermarket brandy, and had even added to his bookshelf a half-dozen more volumes of local lore. Now, however, he needed to check the night's readings on all his instruments and report in. Mt. Shasta was not currently on the vulcanologists top fifteen list of "decade volcanos," but it was bubbling just under. If it did erupt without adequate warning—even without oozing lava—the pyro-clastic flow of hot gas and ash that would sweep, silent and invisible, down the mountain's flank could kill the residents of the village in their beds. As he stepped into the hut, he was visited again by an image from his dream. He saw the answer he'd been stealing from April Blessing when caught. It was a multiple-choice question, and her answer was "None of the Above."

About twenty-three miles north of Redding on I-5, upon entering the Trinity Forest, there is a fantastically steep grade by which the road ascends thousands of feet in a few minutes. It's imperceptible at first, because the terrain still appears flat and featureless. Only the telltale clucking of the valves told Raszer that it was time to downshift the rented ragtop Jeep Wrangler.

He had shaken off the contamination of Karl Lodz on the last leg of the flight, and was trying to enjoy the snap of the October crosswind against his collar. Ordinarily, driving put his mind in cruise mode, but at the moment, he was stuck like a Buick in a mud hole. The previous night, he'd considered the possibility that Fortis Cohn's passing of the cryptic message to Rose had been a cry for help, the Hail Mary pass of a man far too proud to petition his father. Even the most outwardly devout cultists sometimes sent out unconscious rescue pleas, then denied strenuously that they wanted to be rescued. The Jeep's engine ceased clattering, and Raszer was sud-denly left empty of thought and breath by the sight he beheld as he crested the grade.

Mt. Shasta does not reveal herself coyly, as do the Rockies when approached from the east. At the top of the Trinity Grade, and in only the time it takes to check the gas gauge, she is just *there*. Raszer was not prepared for the torrent of memo-ries set loose by the sight of the mountain. For a few moments, although his car continued forward, time went retrograde. Every road sign, each natural landform was instantly animated with experience, and he found himself reliving in every cell of recall the aches and pains he'd carried on his first trip to Shasta. His load had been so much heavier then. He found it curious that not even the awesome responsibility for someone else's life—in this case, both Fortis Cohn's and April's—was as burdensome as a broken heart.

Ten years ago, the first glimpse of Shasta's almost mythical beauty had made his chest heave with hope of redemption. Today, it offered a more sobering kind of epiphany: the one hinted at by Madame Rey's deciphered verse and Karl Lodz's doomsday prophecy. Lurking in Shasta's shadow was her dark twin, the "lava plug" known as Black Butte, where a careless downhill step on a hike had first caused the injury to his left ankle that was now chronic. Shasta had granted him the rewards of reinvention, but he supposed that the Black Butte was his reminder of fallibility. As he nudged the accelerator, anxious to cover the last twenty miles, he was surprised by another reflex, moving slowly up from his belly and into his throat. He was also anxious for the smell and the sound and the sight of April Blessing.

As the volcano's enormous base filled his windshield inch by inch, Raszer was reminded of an old news item Monica's research had unearthed from the *L.A. Times* morgue. On a moonless night in 1932, a *Times* reporter named Edward Lanser observed Mt. Shasta from the club car of a passing train. In the article he subsequently filed, Lanser claimed to have seen "transcendent fireworks" on the mountain. He hadn't been the first. Three decades earlier, a modestly accomplished astronomer by the name of Edgar Lucien Larkin had written of witnessing nocturnal ceremonies that "flooded Shasta with an eerie red-green glow." And with his own approach, Raszer saw that in some ineffable way, it was the singularity of the mountain itself that made such visions seem not entirely delusional. Like Fuji or Kilimanjaro, it was not a place for mortals.

If Raszer was reliving by sensory stimulation a part of his own past, he was also aware that a novel history was unfolding with each mile he closed. Certain elements of the natural composition had changed, certain proportions were not at all as he'd seen them the first time. It was as if the image on his retina were being refashioned, pixel by pixel, by the author of this new saga, and he had to wonder how much of experience was shaped, not by any "objective reality," but by the interplay of physics and fate.

There were no fireworks, transcendent or otherwise, on the mountain as Raszer swung the Jeep into the parking lot of the Shasta View Motor Inn. Considering its proximity to the highway, the motel and its environs were remarkably quiet. He had selected the location for its very ordinariness, and because there was an unob-structed panorama of Shasta's massive southwestern flank from its second floor balconies.

He checked in and hauled his bags up the outer stairs to Room 23. He expected to find it empty, for not even the prospect of his arrival would induce April to hang around a motel room on a golden autumn day. Still, she'd made her presence known.

Despite the coolness of the day, every window in the suite had been opened to purge the room of its antiseptic odor. The cross-ventilation, however, hadn't dis-pelled her perfume, a concoction that was equal parts Oregon moss and opium smoke. Raszer would have sniffed it out in the middle of a spice bazaar. Across the carpet she had laid a trail of Hershey's Kisses leading to the balcony. The curtain and sliding door had been opened as if to lure him toward his first full-on view of the volcano, and out he went, bringing a small but high-powered telescope he'd purchased for the job.

She had set the cheap little patio table with a vase holding a single sunflower, an ice bucket bearing a bottle of Tattinger's *Comte de Champagne* (at $100 a throw, a liberal use of her expense account, but one of which Raszer approved) and a purple envelope to which she'd taped a big, fat joint. The envelope was addressed simply to "Wart." He opened it and read: *"Welcome to Avalon, my Liege. Get high and meet me at Lil's. Love, MLF"* MLF. Morgan Le Fay. Raszer laughed out loud. On the night—now long ago—when they'd made love, they had discovered a common childhood passion for T. H. White's Arthurian fantasy, *The Once And Future King*. Thereafter, Raszer had been "Wart," the young king, and April, "Morgan," his faerie-fey half-sister, seductress, and destiny.

Raszer pulled into Diamond Lil's Roadhouse at 3:52 P.M., showered and buzzing. The light had already started to ebb, but the village of Mt. Shasta always enjoyed a second sunset as the alpenglow reflected off the mountain's glacial face. Lil's was a beer, barbecue, and billiards joint on the fringe of town. A local favorite, but that's not why April had chosen it. She had chosen it because it was the place where ten years ago, as accidental lovers whose lives then seemed without any con-ceivable future junction, they had said good-bye. He stepped from his car and his eyes lingered on the blistered wooden sign, same as it ever was, same as on that day.

"I'm going to miss you in ways you can't imagine," he'd said to her.

"Maybe . . . maybe not," she'd replied. "I may not let you miss me too much. I may not be all that easy to shake off."

"I'm damaged goods," he'd warned. "You're eighteen . . . as light as that feather in your hair. You should steer away from men whose expectations of women have been severely lowered."

"I'll raise them," she had whispered, on tiptoe, into his ear. "And you'd never guess how damaged an eighteen year old can be. Maybe we can lick each other's wounds."

But he hadn't been ready to love again. Not the way April wanted to be loved. And it was true enough when she told him, five years later, that he'd forgotten how to love anything but the journey, forsaking both the place he'd come from and the place he was going. Raszer was leery of nostalgia and wary of banking too much on the future. She could see this clearly in him because it also described her. It wasn't for lack of kinship or chemistry that they'd never reprised their passion; it was that neither one thought history repeatable. Moreover, Raszer felt some psychic incest taboo, for April often appeared in his dreams as a sibling he'd never had.

In any case, not long after their brief encounter, they each became very different people. Raszer changed his name and discarded thirty-odd years worth of self-defeating personality tics. April stopped shaving her armpits, took a string of mostly Native American lovers, and became a kind of sorceress. They never stopped corresponding, and April's words had never stopped pulling on Raszer like the moon on the tide.

He strolled into the nearly empty roadhouse and glanced about, inhaling the sawdust and spilled beer. There was a small sunken dance floor with a jukebox, surrounded by varnished pine tables, and off in the dimness, a pair of pool tables at which some local cowboys were playing for drinks. No sign of a leggy blond in a tie-dyed skirt. He spun onto a bar stool and ordered a Rolling Rock, more because it suited the place than his particular tastes. The bartender was a flannel-clad local of about Raszer's age who mumbled through his bushy mustache. Raszer took a swig of beer and lit a cigarette, his habitual prelude to kibbutzing with bartenders.

"Town's pretty quiet, huh?"

"Yup," the barman answered. "Winter's comin.' Shasta's not much of a winter town. You here on business?"

"Sort of. I'm doing some research up at the Geological Survey station on the mountain. Routine stuff."

"She's not gettin' ready to blow, is she? You tell me if she is, because I will not be one of those crazy motherfuckers who sits on his roof and has to be hauled out by the FEMA team. No sir, I will be outta here at the first puff of smoke!" He threw a towel over his shoulder for emphasis.

"No," Raszer replied, "I expect she will one day, but you and I will probably be long gone." He tapped the ash off his cigarette and continued. "So tell me . . . weird stuff still go on up there on the mountain?"

"Hell," the bartender chuckled, "that's all relative, I guess. This whole town's a little weird. Nothin' special . . . just the usual German tourists looking for energy vortexes and the I AM stuff on weekends."

"I AM stuff?" Raszer asked.

"Local cult," said the bartender. "One of many, I guess. You know . . . the whole white robes and chanting routine."

Raszer had feigned ignorance in the interest of information. One could not live in his world and be unaware of the group which called itself the I AM Activity, a branch off the many-limbed tree of Theosophy. Founded in 1932 by one Guy Warren Ballard, during the last great period of Shasta myth-making, it was—in spite of the white robes and chanting—as American as apple pie and snake-handlers. Ballard's claim was that he'd received the gospel of his new church over a "sound and light ray" channeled directly into his home by an avatar of the mysterious and perennially reincarnated eighteenth-century occultist known as the Count de Saint-Germain, a character who seemed to pop up all over the Aquarian counter-cosmos. The I AM devotees, who appeared to have a rolling permit to make ritual use of the mountain, typified the way a certain kind of American soul—filled with Gnostic yearning and Protestant earnestness—was galvanized by a place like Shasta. Over the years, they'd, too, attested to visionary contact with the Ascended Masters, those angelic denizens of the alternate reality that infused the area.

"And now," added the bartender, "we've got these militia guys blowing off rounds at three A.M."

"Yeah, said Raszer. "I was told to keep my head down. They ever come in here?"

"The paramilitaries? Not really. They wouldn't exactly fit in. 'Scuse me for a sec."

He took another drink order from the dark end of the bar, a woman in a headscarf, cowboy hat and sunglasses whom Raszer suspected—for an instant—of being April in her redwoods Mata Hari mode. Then, his finger in the air, he returned to Raszer.

"Oh, yeah," the bartender recalled, "There was one crazy story a couple o' weeks back. Some local kid claimed he got zapped by cosmic rays while he was ridin' his bike up the Everett Highway."

"Zapped, you say?" Raszer asked. "How so?"

"Don't know exactly. Lost his memory for a while, and told the reporters he'd been abducted by aliens. That wouldn't make him anything special around here. Well, anyhow, he got himself the local paper."

"I'll be damned," Raszer said, "You don't remember his name . . . "

"Gimme a sec. It'll come to me."

As the bartender dried a glass and searched his memory, Raszer heard a quarter drop into the jukebox. The space behind him filled with the sound of castanet and clave, then the flamenco-styled opening chords of Bruce Springsteen's "Brilliant Disguise." It was his summons to spin around and take notice, for out on the dance floor solo was all five-foot-ten lithe inches of April Blessing, dancing in the jukebox beam, dancing for him. She wore a gauzy, floor-length skirt, its waist cinched loosely beneath her bejeweled navel, and a sheer red blouse, unbuttoned over a black satin halter-top.

Raszer shot a glance to the other end of the bar. The woman in the scarf was no longer there, but someone else was: a man of uncertain age in a wool watch cap.

He blinked and turned back to April. Her flaxen hair fell straight to her ass and her feet were bare. April had always been an unreserved dancer, the kind of girl invariably found at the center of any tribal drum circle. Today, she showed him something new, an invitation to an as-yet unvisited room in her imagination. The way she locked her hips into gear with each clap of the backbeat and found the song's perfect circularity; the thrust of her shoulder blades impelling her entire body into spin. It was more Tantric temple dance than hippie freeform. She was demonstrating just how well she had mastered her role. Raszer parked the beer between his legs and leaned back.

"Who is she?" Raszer asked casually over his shoulder.

"Our local white witch," the barman told him. "Her name's April. Lives up in the hills near Wagon Creek somewhere. Coupla' the local boys have tried their hand, but she's as slippery as a speckled trout. The Indians have had better luck. She'll come in sometimes, talk a little . . . maybe dance a little . . . and always leaves alone. Story is she still carries a torch for some guy who died years ago."

"Is that so?" said Raszer. He turned back to April as Springsteen's song reached its sobering coda, and the lyric that had stirred him even when he was too young to know its truth from personal experience. It was an elegy for his failed marriage and for the man he'd killed off a decade before.

Tonight our bed is cold
I'm lost in the darkness of our love
God have mercy on the man
who doubts what he's sure of

April finished her dance with a pirouette, emptied the glass of wine she'd left on a ringside table, then snatched up her jacket and headed crisply outside. The pool playing cowboys applauded enthusiastically and offered a few beery hoots. Raszer swung around to the bartender, put a generous tip on top of the loose bills he'd left on the bar, and rose from the stool. "What the hell?" he said, gesturing toward the door, "I might as well introduce myself. Six weeks on that mountain could get awfully lonely."

"Good luck, then, brother," said the barman, snapping off a salute. "Many brave and horny men have tried and failed before you."

He caught up with April in the parking lot, and pulled her behind an idled horse trailer. Once sequestered, she leapt into his arms with a force that took his breath away.

"Yee-ha!" she cried. "My number one gun is here!"

"Hey," he whispered, hugging her soundly and then taking a small step back. "A little less conspicuous, huh, partner? You don't want to blow my cover before I've even set it up . . . "

"Uh-uh, Wart . . . " she protested, her eyes following the after-image of his cigarette ash. "You played it just right. Now if anybody does see us together, they'll just make you for the guy who hit on me at Lil's. Hey, now . . . " She pointed sternly at the cigarette. "You swore you'd quit those things."

"Don't throw stones, sister," he reproached her, "I've seen you light up before."

"Only when I'm 'in character.'"

"Yeah, well . . . " he said. "Maybe I'm in character all the time."

"Aw, Raszer," she said, brushing his cheek. "I missed you, man."

"I missed you, too. Great song choice, by the way."

"Did you think I'd forget?"

"Nope." He flipped away the cigarette. "Women don't forget anything. Great dancing, too." He rubbed his chin thoughtfully. "Listen . . . maybe before we get into this we ought to take a drive and talk. A lot of stuff has happened."

"Okay," she said, instantly accepting his gravity. "Where do you want to go?"

"Let's see . . . I'll need to see Mathonwy before eight . . . "

"And I'll need to get ready for work. 'The Gypsy' is on tonight."

"Right. You know the entrance to the Pluto Caves. That little parking turnout at the trailhead?"

"That's north of Weed. Why so far?"

"Because it's a good place to get grounded. A good place to feel how dangerous this thing may be." He scanned the parking lot for any observers, then wrapped his arm around her neck and pulled her close. "I loved your welcome at the motel. We'll do the champagne when we've turned the first corner . . . okay, partner?"

By the time they'd both arrived at the dirt parking area near the Caves, all that was left of daylight was the memory. They sat in April's blue VW Bug, because the night air was dropping hard and damp, and her car had a roof. A hundred yards beyond the windshield, the scrubby meadow drained into three dry channels of eroded land known as lava trenches, and thirty yards later one reached the mouth of the nearest cave. These weren't caves in the usual sense, but "lava tubes," formed millennia ago, when the topmost layer of Shasta's volcanic effluent had crusted over, leaving the innermost part—still hot and seething—to push on like icing through a cake decorating tool. At roughly two hundred fifty yards into any of the three tubes, there were impassable walls of collapsed earth and boulder, though it didn't make sense that the caverns were named after the god of the underworld if that was as deep as they went. The lava flows that had formed them went all the way to Shasta's core, more than fifteen miles away.

Raszer cranked his window down and lit a cigarette to ward off the enveloping dark, while April found the local country station and lowered the volume to a murmur of pedal steel and Duane Eddy twang.

"So what do you know about this bicyclist who got 'zapped' up on the Everett Highway?" he asked.

"Jack Falconer," she answered. "A local kid who says his iPod got fried by the volcano. He's not the first. It's like an urban legend here that the Lemurians can jam up circuits. The Professor has some ideas. Some folks in town have been hearing a hum, too. Even Flo, my fellow dancer. Funny, though . . . I'm not getting it."

"Just as well. If it's anything like what my friend Madame Rey is getting hit with, I doubt you'd be able to find your way home, let alone maintain your cover." He recapped for her his session with Karl Lodz, as well as the murderous events that had occurred back in L.A.—events that he'd kept from her until now, when he could be present to nuance their telling and gauge her response. She was tightrope walking, and he hadn't wanted to yell, "Don't look down!"

"Jesus," she exhaled. "Why didn't you tell me?"

"Sometimes, ignorance is the best armor you can wear."

She started to object.

"But now," he continued, "I *do* need you to know how dangerous this is. It's bigger than we thought, and we'll have to limit our scope to what must be done."

"Fortis Cohn?" she asked, somewhat rhetorically.

"Fortis Cohn," he affirmed. "If we lose him, we lose it all."

"I want these assholes off my mountain."

"Try not to personalize it," he said.

"Saying that to a woman is like telling a duck not to quack."

Raszer laughed, but there was a measure of concern in it.

"All right," she said, after a pause. "You're sure this murder is connected to him?"

He nodded. "I am now. Rose was clearly involved with Fortis. He got the ciphered verse from him. I'm not sure that Rose understood what it meant—I don't know what it means—but he understood enough to want to unload it fast. His murder has the militia's fingerprints all over it, especially given the way he was mutilated, and how that links to Vreeland's clinical interest in your own anatomy."

"It did seem . . . clinical. Cold. I can't get a fix on his sexual orientation."

"Well . . . Lodz hinted at something. But I wouldn't sign our boy Bronk up for a Gay Pride March. It's probably more convoluted than that."

"I'd say so, yeah."

"What's he like?" Raszer asked. "Up close."

She thought for a moment. Longer than he would have wished.

"Not as despicable as I hoped he'd be," she answered.

"The really bad guys never are," he said. "But physically. *Psychically.* How do you make him?"

"Whew," she said, and pushed the hair out of her face. "All over the place. He's all about being hard and straight and clean, but . . . I don't know. Jude Law playing Rutger Hauer playing Attila the Hun. A sociopath, for sure, but not a typical one."

"Tell me something. You think he really buys that someone like you would be a fan of someone like him?"

"I'm doing my best to channel one of those blond right-wing bitches you see on cable news. I think he sees me as good, Aryan stock. And, honestly, I don't think he can imagine any woman—or any man—who wouldn't want to lick the polish off his boots. That part makes my skin crawl. But there's another place where we connect. He quotes this quietist mystic, Madame Guyon, and says he reads runes." She hesitated and bit her lip, and her eyes crinkled with a knowing tenderness. "Don't take this wrong, Wart, but in certain upside-down, inside-out ways . . . he's like you."

Raszer studied her for a beat, then nodded. "That's exactly what I was afraid of."

"Face it, Raszer," she said. "You wouldn't have it any other way."

"Yeah . . . " he said quietly. "Well . . . down to business. As regards your gig tonight. If Fortis Cohn is there again, get as good a read as you can. Make a mental hologram of his ticks, his body language. Watch the way he reacts to Vreeland reacting to you. If my hunch is right, he may get jealous, and that is something we can use. And if you find yourself alone with Vreeland, play offense. Yield only when you need to to draw him in . . . or draw him out."

She waited, sensing there was something else.

Raszer cleared his throat. "He has a daughter named Ori. According to Lodz, she disappeared shortly after Vreeland had his vision and hooked up with this 'Fraternity.' She couldn't have been more than nine or ten. From what you've told me about your first encounter, he seems to think you've got some oracular talents. Make use of that. When the time is right, maybe you tell him that you sense another person in his life . . . someone he cares about. I'd also like to know if he really believes in his prophecy about the hollow earth and his adversaries down below, or if it's just recycled Nazi mythology designed to fuel his cult of personality." He opened the car door and set a foot on the rutted ground. "And April, no matter what, do not go back to the compound with him. Not until we debrief. Can you handle him if he gets aggressive?"

"I can handle it," she said. "And my girl Flo and I . . . she's the other dancer . . . we worked out a buddy system. Neither one of us leaves the roadhouse without the other unless we talk first. No talk equals an S.O.S. So I'll see you back at the motel?"

"Yep," he replied. "It may be late, but I'll be there. Oh, by the way, I'm going to continue to keep Mathonwy in the dark about you. It'll be safer for both of you." He stepped out of the VW, shut the door, and then leaned in close enough to feel the heat of her breath. "Be ye as wise as serpents, Morgana. Don't work your spells too well."

She blew him a kiss, then roared out of the lot, leaving a cloud of dust hanging in the damp, night air.

The U.S. Geological Survey's outpost was at the very end of the last mile of fire road on the South face of the mountain, past Panther Meadows and the Old Ski Bowl. A month from now, snowplows would have to clear the way. Mathonwy's hut sat just below Sargent's Ridge at ninety-six hundred feet, a vantage point from which one could overlook the front third of the Klamath/Vreeland property. This could not have pleased the militia leader, but it suited Raszer's plans perfectly.

He pulled his Jeep in next to the professor's beat up Yugo and saw that the door of the hut was ajar and amber light was spilling onto the patchy snow. Raszer rapped gently on the tin-sheathed door, which rattled in response, and then peered into the hut. The professor was at his desk, wearing a jeweler's loupe over his eye and an old school headset over his ears, hunched over a long piece of graph paper. Raszer could hear the tinny overspill of an Irish tenor coming from the headphones, so he knocked again forcefully, shaking the entire structure. Mathonwy turned and rose immediately from his seat, removing the headphones and extending his hand. The crown of his head nearly brushed the ceiling, and his lankiness made Raszer think of a Daddy Longlegs. His long, silver-gray hair lay matted against his temples, and each of his features seemed to come to a point. His face had the luminous sagacity of a Welsh wizard.

"Mr. Raszer!" he lit up. "You've arrived! Come in, come in."

"Thanks," Raszer said, stepping in, "I'm glad to be here, Professor. Looking forward to an education."

"Me, too. May I pour you a cup of tea?"

"I'd like that," Raszer replied He marveled at the collection of instruments his host had found space for within the dimensions of the tiny hut. Not one cubic foot was unspoken for.

"This is quite a rack," he observed. "Where do you get your power?"

"There's a generator shack about fifty yards up the ridge. Have to keep it removed some or the vibrations will affect my readings."

"What were you, uh . . . contemplating when I came in?" Raszer asked.

"Spectrometer readings," Mathonwy replied, pouring the tea with practiced grace. "Analyses of the gasses belched out by the mountain today. Very odd. I got unusually high sulfur dioxide readings this morning, which usually indicates change inside the magma chamber. Then they dropped down to zero for the afternoon, only to shoot up at sundown. It's almost . . . " He paused. "As if the surges were being provoked."

"Is that possible?" Raszer asked.

"Not outside of a very farfetched possibility. But I'm trying to find out if there is a correlation of any sort between the SO2 levels and the intermittent seismic bursts I've been seeing."

"Bursts? How do you mean?"

"For the last two weeks or so, there've been earthquake swarms tracked all through the Southern Cascades, and in the midst of them the volcano has been emitting extremely low frequency—ELF—pulses of one to about three minutes in duration. Sound waves. They look like *harmonic tremors*, and an HT is a serious eruption warning. You feel it in the soul of your bones, as if someone had just wired your brain directly into the earth's liquid core. But HTs don't generally stop and start like this . . . "

Raszer accepted a mug of tea and perched on the edge of what he assumed was his designated bunk. He took a clasped envelope from his satchel and removed some documents and a laminated card.

"When you have a moment," he said, handing the items to Mathonwy, "tell me if you think these'll pass muster. Monica had them made up based on your specs." Mathonwy examined the phony USGS ID card and duty order, while Raszer's eye drifted across the overstocked bookshelf, its volumes of technical data intermixed with books on Indian lore and the lost continent of Lemuria, and settled on an odd little paperback titled *ELF Technology and the Human Limbic System*.

"May I ask you an oddball question, Professor?"

"I'm used to them."

"Is it possible for these ELF waves to get inside a person's head and affect sensory data? Aural hallucinations, for instance?"

"Yes, it's possible, particularly if the ELF is serving as a carrier wave for other signals. This is precisely what got the lunatic fringe so exercised about the Soviet "Woodpecker" experiments back in '76. They were pulsing at 6 and 11 Hz in the 3.26 to 17.54 megahertz range, and messing with some key brainwave rhythms. I'm no expert on this, but if you start stimulating the hippocampus in a concerted way, you'll have people hearing and seeing things for miles around!"

"And these . . . 'pulses' . . . that the mountain is giving off?"

"Have a basic carrier of 7.83 Hz, which is the Schumann 'fundamental,' and a strong rider at about 39, which is the earth's 'pulse' at the boundary of the solid and liquid cores. That one seems to have shape . . . in other words, it's modulated."

"I'm not following you," said Raszer. "The earth's pulse?"

"Oh, the earth is very much alive, Mr. Raszer. If you accept the Gaia Hypothesis, it's a kind of self-regulating organism. The core rotation produces electromagnetic signatures, like radio waves. But it is most unusual for Her to broadcast at this volume."

"You said the higher pulse had a shape. You mean like a coherent signal?"

"A very primitive one, but yes." Mathonwy sipped his tea and smiled.

"I'll be damned," said Raszer. "Could Vreeland's outfit be involved in this?"

"I'm beginning to wonder," Mathonwy said. "Step outside with me."

Raszer threw on his duster and followed Mathonwy through the creaky door. In just under thirty minutes, the outside temperature had dropped another ten degrees. There was some windblown snow dust in the air, but otherwise the night was radiantly clear. They walked about thirty yards to the crest of a small ridge.

"Look down there," Mathonwy said, pointing. "Those are the lights of Mr. Vreeland's compound. The old Klamath Company mining property." Raszer saw two clusters of bright light in the foreground that flared out what he took to be guard towers. "The back eighty acres or so," Mathonwy continued, "are dotted with dish antennas and radio towers, like a scaled-down version of the Navy's HAARP project. Whatever I'm picking up, they are, too. What do you suppose they're listening for?"

"Aside from the Fox Network, I can't imagine. Maybe it's not just incoming. He broadcasts over a local AM band, right? Suppose he's gearing up to go satellite-global. Hate speech and heavy metal could reach a sizable audience."

"I've had a feeling, Mr. Raszer," Mathonwy said, turning away from the wind, "ever since we first spoke. I did some poking around through county records. There are dozens of mine shafts on the Klamath property, most of them in existence for over a hundred years. But as far as the recorded claims indicate, not one ounce of usable mineral product has ever been taken out of this mountain. Why are there so many shafts?"

"Digging for Lemuria?" Raszer asked.

"Perhaps . . . " Mathonwy replied, with only a trace of whimsy. "But there may also be a more immediately profitable purpose."

"Such as?"

"Diamonds, Mr. Raszer. A by-product of volcanic processes, only recently appreciated as such. Certainly not widely known at the time the Klamath Company took possession of this mountainside, but they may have been ahead of their competition. The trick would be getting at them, and getting them out without anyone the wiser."

Raszer absorbed the new information, then told the professor of his plan to make a morning reconnaissance of the militia property. He was hoping to find vantage points where his binoculars would afford a closer look at the daily routine.

"Well," Mathonwy said. "We might as well get you into your role right away. I'll send you out there with a spirit-level and you can make some tilt measurements of the Shastina cone. That's how we tell if the volcano's pregnant—her shape changes."

"Spirit level? Sounds like it belongs in my kit bag."

"It's a surveyor's tool, essentially. You'll get the hang of it." There was a faint burst of automatic weapon fire, way down below in the dark section of the compound, followed by a disturbed, hyena-like cackling which stopped abruptly ten seconds later. "'What rough beast . . . '" Mathonwy muttered, " 'his hour come 'round at last . . . '"

Raszer kept his eyes on the lights of the compound. "Who's responsible for evacuating those maniacs if the volcano starts to rumble?"

"FEMA," Mathonwy answered. "With the assistance of local first responders. For Bronk Vreeland, that would be tantamount to an act of war. His paranoia validated."

"FEMA still pushes their buttons, huh? Funny, I don't see much ranting about it on their blog. I'd have thought that bogeyman died with the last century."

"Not for Mr. Vreeland," Mathonwy replied. "Not when you've spent ten years giving your enemy a name. And you may've noticed that FEMA rose from its ashes once we realized how much it was needed. Commander Vreeland certainly has." Mathonwy paused. "I wouldn't put too much stock in the blog or the radio program. That's PR, and when Vreeland does present, he's as smooth and coded as any politician. Tune in at five A.M.—when farmers, truck drivers, and soldiers wake up. There's a noxious fellow by the name of Latimer Bloch who'll persuade you that FEMA is the shock troop of the anti-Global Warming movement, with links to everyone from the United Nations to the Shriners. When the predicted coastal flooding begins, that will be a sign."

"A sign of what?" Raszer asked.

"Let's step inside," said Mathonwy. "It's getting a bit chilly."

"So the black helicopters are back . . . " Raszer said.

"For some people," Mathonwy replied, "they never went away." He turned to Raszer after sealing the door against the wind. "Will you be staying the night?"

"Not tonight, Professor," Raszer answered. "Thanks. I've got some research to do, and I'll need a stronger signal than I can get up here."

Mathonwy gave him a gnomish look. "You might be surprised," he said. "On a good night, you can hop onto Mr. Vreeland's wireless network!"

When Raszer returned to the motel late that night, April—long since back from work and three good hits into a joint—told him her "good news." She had been cleared to attend the following evening's troop rally as Bronk Vreeland's guest.

"You know what the son of a bitch said?" she asked.

"Let me guess . . . he wants you to peel for the troops."

"He said I'd make a good breeder. Shit," she remembered. "I'll miss my class."

"The professor'll manage without you," said Raszer. "Somehow. What do you suppose he wants to breed?"

"Little Bronks and Bronkettes, I guess."

"Tell me about the radio station. I could only get the Webcast in L.A., and it was pretty spotty, but I hear his signal reaches five states."

"'Radio Free America?'" she said, with a stoned laugh. "He calls it the 'emergency broadcast network of the Patriot Movement.' Between the metal thrash and fascist rap, they issue 'bulletins' about federal intrusion on property owners' rights. The usual manure."

"The usual manure," said Raszer. "Unless you use it to spread a very big lie."

10

WHEEL of FORTUNE.

WHILE Raszer slept, a clumsy ballet was being performed behind the drawn shades at the office of the County Recorder of Deeds. Fortis Cohn's gambit—to break into the Recorder's office and "fortify" the Klamath Company's deed to the Shasta property—had played out smoothly until now. He, Blottmeier, and third young recruit named Byron White had gotten in without a hitch. Now, however, there was a problem: the box containing the crucial nineteenth-century documents was not where it was supposed to be, and Fortis had begun to panic in a most unsoldierlike way.

The first hearing on the tribal claim against the Order of Thule and the Klamath Mining Co. was not to occur for a week, and the circuit judge assigned to the case had yet to review key documents. Beyond the dubious deed and the truism that possession was nine-tenths of the law, Fortis had little to show for his side, and he expected that any ambiguity would favor the Indians. In their brief, the claimants argued that the deed had never been signed by a duly authorized federal officer, merely initialed by a marshal awakened at three in the morning by a mining company stooge with a loaded shotgun. The militia—identified as assignee under the name Heritage Trust—had challenged this assertion as folklore, but the claimants had countered that regardless of the signature's legitimacy, the grant provided for a return of the sacred lands after a period of mineral exploitation, not to exceed without cause four renewable terms of twenty-five years." That would have been 1982, so the tribes had good reason for impatience.

But Fortis had an ace-in-the-hole by dint of his mother's legacy. In the Klamath Company archives—vaulted in Zurich under the aegis of Credit Suisse—there had lain a 1919 document petitioning the U.S. Department of the Interior for a fifth term of mining rights, and he'd insisted that an exhaustive search of county records would "turn it up." He had played the court for time and been given it. Now, he had to deliver the goods.

There was just one problem: the extension had never been granted. The request had never, in fact, been submitted, but that was just as well, for this was precisely the sort of history that could be rewritten with the stroke of a pen. Fortis had the document in hand. It was old, it was genuine, and all it was missing was a signature. He would provide it—in the name of the appropriate undersecretary— and cleverly misplace it in a neighboring file, thus insuring that a search would, indeed, turn it up. If accepted by the court, it would give them dominion through 2007, and that was all the time they needed.

Better yet, it would prove to Bronk Vreeland just how valuable an asset he was. Before this glory could accrue to Fortis, however, he had to find the missing box, for it contained not only the mining leases for Siskyou County 1875–1925, but the name of the federal officer whose signature he intended to forge.

Blottmeier assisted Fortis while White kept vigil just outside the front door. After five agonizing minutes, Fortis located the banker's box—not in the file room but on a desk in the front office. He gingerly removed the Klamath file and set it aside, then sifted one by one through the documents of a dozen other mining companies until he found a 1919 signature that suited his purposes. A few feet from the desk there was a dusty bookstand, the sort that county clerks once used to survey decades of birth and death certificates. Fortis set the two yellowed documents side-by-side on its angled surface, then drew from his inside pocket a forger's tool and the vintage fountain pen he would use to execute the forgery. The pen was a replica of a 1910 pump model, one of a hundred his father had had made to commemorate eighty years of the law firm of Cohn, Gottlieb, & Schuyler. The tool was of an ingenious design: stretched over a small, adjustable frame was a piece of synthetic vellum sufficiently transparent to allow for tracing but having the singular property of being semi-porous and holding ink in suspension for just long enough to be transferred to another surface, without bleed or fading.

He directed Blottmeier to hold the flashlight close and steady while he traced the signature, and though his hand shook, managed to make it to the last filigree by holding his breath. Fortis did not enjoy having Blottmeier so near. The young sycophant was pockmarked and sour-smelling and seemed to Fortis unclean, if only because it was widely rumored in the compound that he was Bronk Vreeland's dish rag. Worse, he was even more nervous than Fortis, and Fortis hated nothing so much as the mirror of his own frailty. The flashlight beam bobbed as its barrel kept slipping in Blottmeier's sweaty palms, and it was worse that the soft-bellied recruit kept repeating, "Sorry . . . sorry . . . s-s-sorry." How Fortis hated that word. In spite of his agitation, he lifted the tool cleanly off the authentic document and had just laid it over the signature line on the Klamath petition when there was a stir at the front door and White called out, "Shit! A cop car! He's turning! I think he sees the light!" Startled, Blottmeier jerked and the flashlight slipped from his hands and dropped onto Fortis's right hand, causing the ink transfer to smear and his left elbow to push the fountain pen off the desktop and into a side-mounted well designed to hold maps in the days when the land was all for sale.

"Idiot!" Fortis hissed.

"Sorry," Blottmeier whimpered.

Fortis felt his heart pound. The job had not been done properly, the police would soon be at the door, and on top of this, the flashlight had gone out and he could not find his pen. He fished frantically for it in the map well, managing only to pinch the nib for long enough to get ink on his fingers. He felt suddenly and overwhelmingly incompetent and ashamed, and the shadow of his father passed over him like a great wing.

"The fucking bulb!" Blottmeier moaned, hammering the flashlight on his palm.

As best he could, Fortis replaced the files, though there was no time to be artful about it. White whistled and called, "C'mon! We're outta here! Out the back. Let's go!"

"Blotto, you fool!" Fortis spat, hastily fitting the cardboard lid back onto the box. "I'll have your ass for this." Fortis felt entitled to use the recruit's diminuitive— the other men did—and entitled to berate him. Vreeland did. But Blotto, although raised to bear up under the rod of humiliation and ridicule, took his abuse selectively. He came to a halt and glowered at the lawyer, an immovable mass of bristling flesh.

"Watch your mouth, Jewboy," he snarled.

The lookout gave them a firm push and hustled them out the rear door just seconds before the village cop slapped his flashlight against a pane of glass on the front door. He remained there, deer hunter still, for a half a minute, until certain there was no movement within. Then he got back into his squad car and continued on his rounds.

Raszer awoke just before seven, his clothes on and his fingers still curled lightly around the spine of the book he'd drifted off with six hours earlier. He had slept on the sofa, leaving the bed to April, and awakened by a blast of cool morning air from the balcony, had opened his eyes to see her with bare legs propped up on the balustrade, wearing a white terrycloth bathrobe. He poured himself a cup of the coffee she'd made with her French press and went out to join her. She looked pensive.

"How long have you been up?" he asked, finding a knotted muscle beneath the robe's collar and kneading her sun-warmed skin with his fingertips.

"You've still got great hands, Wart," she said. "You always go right to the spot. About an hour . . . I couldn't sleep."

"Thinking about Vreeland?"

"Yeah, and other things. Weird guy. Tormented, I think. We're sitting at the bar, you know—after my show—and I'm trying to draw him out. I'm telling him about how the earth chakras mirror the body's and correspond to the Schumann vibrations . . . "

"And he was buying this?" Raszer asked, after a gulp of coffee.

"Like I said . . . he's a New Age fascist. And he's obsessed with these 'signals' he thinks are jamming his satellite hardware. He blames it on 'the rodents,' whoever they are, and the 'Underground.'" Raszer stilled his fingers for a moment and she shrugged. "I don't know yet," she said, rolling her head into his hands. "Lemurians, maybe . . . or a rear guard of the Weathermen."

They shared a laugh.

"Anyhow," she continued. "He gets real quiet . . . then he locks onto me like a laser 'n says, 'I could tell you things, but I don't know if I can trust a woman that much.'"

"And you said?"

"I know I should have encouraged him, but it was just too . . . intense. I'm not even sure I *want to know* his darkest secrets. Anyhow, I'm trying to recalibrate, and all of a sudden, I pick up a whiff of something. Like really old bronze. And I tell him . . . 'God, I don't know where this came from . . . that he's channeling Alexander the Great!'"

"You were riffing, April. That's good. How did he respond?"

130

"You won't believe it. He wrinkles his brow and says, 'Wasn't he a fag?'" Raszer shook his head and lit a cigarette.

"How did you handle that one?"

"I said that Alexander was adored by his men, and sometimes made a gift of his body . . . a sacrament, sort of like communion. He *liked* that. A *lot*."

She reached up, took the cigarette from his hand, and dragged deeply on it. "Hey, Raszer," she said. "Put your arms around me, would ya?"

He leaned in, wrapped himself around her shoulders, and kissed the side of her head. Her hair smelled like the morning sun.

"You know why I studied to be a shrink?" she asked softly.

"No," he said, though he had more than a clue. "Why?"

"So I'd never have to be alone. I'd always have visitors, and their stories would always be more twisted than my own. Isn't it ironic that I wound up living all by myself in a cabin in the woods?"

"The brave ones always go straight for what scares them the most," he told her. "You've got more guts than an army of Bronk Vreelands."

"Thanks, Wart," she whispered. He stepped around to the front and leaned against the railing, resting his hand on her bare foot.

"I want you to try something," he said.

"Name it, boss."

"You still pretty good at reading tarot?"

"Yeah, I'd say so," she answered.

"Next time you're alone with him . . . maybe tonight after the pep rally . . . read his cards. Mostly though, read him. See what makes him twitch."

"You got it," she said, and dropped her foot, letting it brush for an instant against the front of his sleep-wrinkled trousers. At precisely the same moment, the faintest tremor caused the balcony to shudder. He felt suddenly off balance, uncertain, and an absurd query crossed his mind: had the earth conspired with her flirtation or had his desire caused the earth to move? It was—of course—a ridiculous question.

Raszer urged April to sleep for a few more hours in preparation for her big night. This she did after receiving another twenty minutes of massage, with special attention to her tailbone.

"Why the hell do you suppose they were checking out your lower spine?" he asked, as he pressed his palm into her and cracked a vertebra.

"Don't know . . ." she answered languorously. "He said it was standard procedure. Maybe it has something to do with the 'breeder' thing."

"No . . . something else. It has to do with that part of the anatomy. It has to do with—" He paused. "—*the shortest is the root*. The tree of man has branches five . . . "

"What's that?"

"I'll fill you in later," he said absently. "Get some sleep."

Once alone, Raszer poured himself more coffee and booted up his MacBook. His wireless access to the Internet was via the same private satellite network which provided his GPS phone service and allowed Monica to track him with a reasonable degree of precision—if he bothered to carry the hardware. Much to her consternation, he often did not. When Raszer was offline, he made few concessions to technology, fearing that he could be trapped by the very thing that connected him. When they were online together, however, they were as much one mind as two people could be, and the server software Monica had bootlegged from an Interpol prototype enabled them to perform an array of Web navigations in tandem, from multiwindowed hypersearches of university libraries to hacking jointly into certain restricted sites. They shared a virtual hard drive in cyberspace. After a few moments, her face appeared on his screen. She wore a lightweight headset and her left nostril was newly pierced with a diamond stud.

"Good morning," he said. "You're on the air with D.J. Spooky."

"Morning, Raszer," she answered cooly. "You didn't answer your phone."

"Oh," he said, fished it out of his bag, and saw her message. "My mistake." He took note of the piercing. "Nice hardware. Must've been a good date."

"*Au contraire*," she said. "It stunk. This is my consolation prize to myself."

"Love hurts. Sorry, hon. Everything's cool here for now. How about down there? Any unwanted visitors?"

"You hired me a bodyguard who looks like some Baltic Steven Seagal, right down to the ponytail. Who's gonna mess with me?"

"How's Raja doing? Borges keeping an eye on her?"

"Yeah," said Monica. "I've been to the hospital twice and his man's been out there both times. Her tests came out negative. No clots, no scarring. They could release her as early as tomorrow morning."

"That's good . . . I think," he said. He opened her binder at his side, along with the brief on the tribal lawsuit given him by Abel Cohn. "I read your stuff. Solid work, as always. Appreciate the material on Fortis's Hollywood connections."

She smiled and spun her diamond stud.

Raszer grabbed the thick sheaf of documents from Abel Cohn's file and flipped through to a Post-It–marked page. "There's a pretty intriguing nugget

THE LAST DAYS OF MADAME REY

in the attachments to the Indian brief. It relates to something you dug up in your research on the whole Thule thing. Can you get to the page marked 'Appendix B11?'"

"Give me a sec," she said. A beat. "Okay . . . I'm there."

"All right," said Raszer. "Abel said that the first recorded tribal action against the Klamath Company was in 1882 . . . based on the Modoc claim that the deed was bogus . . . that the ceremonial grounds were basically stolen from them under cover of night."

"Sounds like Manifest Destiny to me," said Monica.

He paused and lit a cigarette.

"Right, well . . . one of the enclosures in B11—a plaintiff's exhibit from that dusty old case—is a page from the diaries of a U.S. Cavalryman named Augustus Leek. It's a bitch to read 'cause it's an old photostat of a handwritten page."

"I see it," she said. "It looks like it was water-damaged, too. Whenever . . . "

Raszer blew a tiny smoke ring and put his finger through it. "I'm not even sure what it's doing there," he said. "It doesn't bear directly on the deed, or any prior treaty or eminent domain issue . . . but if you scan about halfway down, there's a line that jumps out. Tell me when you've got it." He listened to the comforting sound of her lips buzzing, her mind at work. Then she cleared her throat, and read:

"'The KC agents seem little more than proxies for the Saint Joachim Brother-hood.'"

"Bingo," said Raszer. "I think we can assume that 'KC' is Klamath Co. and not Kansas City. So go with me here. You've got a Halgadom thread in your summary of the Thule tradition, right?"

"Right," she said. "Halgadom is the whole concept. The ideal. Like Plato's Republic or Utopia. It's the Aryan Nation." She turned her stud again. "But what's the connection?"

"One of your Halgadom hyperlinks goes to a FAQ page that says that the Pentecost meeting in 1914 that set up the parent of the Thule Society . . . the German-enorden . . . was held in a little Bohemian town called St. Joachimsthal . . . which at that time would still have been part of the Austro-Hungarian Empire."

"The Hapsburgs," she said. "Okay. Go on."

"I'd love to get a list of the supposed sixteen attendees. Maybe they picked the town because it was already the base of the Saint Joachim Brotherhood."

"It's a stretch, Raszer, but I'll work on it," she said. "This one'll take time. It's probably beyond the 'Net."

"Maybe . . . maybe not. Let's give it a try."

"Where are we going with this?"

"It's a hunch. Karl Lodz talked about the Fraternity and April's heard Fortis mention it, too. Fraternity . . . Brotherhood . . . Klamath Company . . . Saint Joachim. I'd like to know if there's a solid link between the Klamath Co and some right-wing fraternal organization with a central European pedigree and a pre-WWI vintage. If that lineage is still intact, it may tell us who's bankrolling Vreeland and give us a clue about what sort of millennial madness Fortis Cohn has bought into."

"You know, boss—Vreeland could just have used Thule because it suited him. Not every nut grows on a family tree. Sure you want to go looking for conspiracies?"

"Conspiracy is just history from a bird's eye view. My job is to get Fortis back to his law firm. Safely and without criminal charges, if possible. I have to give him an exit, and to do that, I have to tie these creeps to something that not even a con-flicted, self-hating guy like Fortis can stomach."

Her head was down, the streaked hair fallen over her face. He heard her typing furiously. "I have to rob you of my face," she said, "to let you see what I'm doing."

The screen went ultra-blue and then began to stream with search threads. It was an engine they'd designed, with the programming help of a savant from San Jose. They could synchronize up to nine related searches, cross-fertilized, and sort results by infinitely variable criteria. He watched the mice run, and heard her voice behind the maze.

"Let's see," she said. "We've gone as far as our access will permit into the FBI and Interpol files. We've been through all the cult watchers . . . Southern Poverty Law Center, Trancenet, F.A.C.T., Millennial Prophecy Nexus . . . "

"Fold in something else," Raszer suggested. "Good, old-fashioned capitalism. Multinationals. And businessmans' associations—even lame-sounding Rotarian-type things. Mix in threads for mining and mineral exploitation, and then . . . factor in *diamonds.*"

The search engine was potent. The programmer had told them that it was theoretically capable of locating all the albino hermaphrodites ever born in the city of Poughkeepsie to a mother whose maiden name meant sardine in Hun-garian, but, of course, only if that data had been seeded into the Web. It did little good to look for albino hermaphrodites if there were none in cyberspace, which was why Monica often had to rely on old school library-to-library cross-checking and legwork.

The two of them worked through the sortings for two hours, following every promising thread, until after three more cups of coffee and a dozen half-smoked cigarettes, Raszer was ready to call it quits.

"Let's pick this up tomorrow, partner," he groaned. "I'm glazed and I've got to get up on the mountain."

"Wait a second . . . wait-a-second!" she said. "Check this out. Something coming up from an old UPI photo file. It's really slow, but it's got all nine of our hooks. Hang on . . . " Raszer sat back and rubbed his eyes free of their myopic fixation.

"Do you see this?" she whispered. The digitized black and white wire photo was lousy, but the caption was clear. *"Rupert Francis Voorhees (center), South African mineral and newspaper magnate, and owner of the largest network of radio broadcast facilities in Eastern Europe, accepts the scepter of St. Joachim from other members of the Halgadom Fraternity at the Saint's Day festivities in Munich."* The photo file was dated August 17, 1984, the date that sixty-six years earlier, the Germanenorden had officially become the Thule Society."

"Raszer?" said Monica, breathless.

"Uh huh?"

"I just felt something with more than six legs crawl up my back . . . "

"I know that feeling," he said. "Voorhees. That's the name that Lodz mentioned. The Fourth Horseman . . . "

"What?"

"Nothing. Enough goose pimples for now."

"I'll bet you my stud," she said, "that his granddaddy owned the Klamath Co."

"Good work, pal. We've got our lead. Stay with it."

"I know what you're thinking," she said. "You couldn't live without me."

"Not any more than Astaire without Rodgers," he affirmed.

"Or Tracy without Hepburn . . . "

"Or Homer without Marge . . . "

"Go to hell, Raszer."

Mathonwy had been awake for five hours by the time Raszer hopped out of his Jeep, outfitted in an old British commando sweater and a pair of climbing pants.

"How's our mountain?" he asked. "Still gassy?"

"The sulfur dioxide levels are down again," Mathonwy replied, "but we had a 3.6 temblor this morning around eight, and she's been humming since. Did you feel it?"

"No," Raszer replied, then recalled the moment of vertigo on the balcony. "Well . . . yeah, now that you mention it. Do the quakes trigger the volcanic activity or vice versa?"

"Works both ways, or they can work in concert. Ready to do some surveying?"

Mathonwy walked Raszer patiently through the mechanics of using a "spirit level" to gauge the degree of swelling or "tilt" in the volcano's cone, though it was mostly for show. Before heading up the ridge, Raszer double-checked the contents of his pack: binoculars, a hundred feet of nylon rope and some basic climbing hardware, a pair of worn Scarpa rock shoes, a liter of water, and an apple.

"I guess I'm off then," he said to Mathonwy. "Back in around four hours . . . before the sun starts to dip. What's your day looking like?"

"Today I'm looking at magnetic field strength. There's a hell of a lot of electromagnetic energy being radiated. Sometimes you can feel the static electricity. Your hair will stand straight up."

"Cool," said Raszer.

"Oh . . . " Mathonwy held a finger up. "Wait there. Just one second." He ducked into the hut and returned with an artifact from the 1950s.

"Is that what I think it is?"

"I assembled it from a kit when I was eleven years old. Two dollars and five Post Toasties box tops. *'Kids! Build your own crystal radio!'* I've tinkered with it ever since, altering the size and composition of the crystal element. With a fresh battery, it can pull in AM radio from Chicago. And occasionally, some interesting transients."

"Such as?"

"Let me know what happens when you get up there. In any case, you ought to receive Radio Free America loud and clear. AM 88. Just in time for the midday prayer."

At about a thousand yards up Sargent's Ridge, Raszer got his first clear view of the summit and decided to try his hand with the spirit level. He felt obliged to bring back some data, even if it was data the Professor already had. Sighting through the instrument's scope and pivoting its barrel to center on Shastina—the oldest and most recently active of Shasta's cones—he noticed an outcropping of clean rock rising up out of Avalanche Gulch. With a little effort at triangulation, he calculated roughly that, from there, he'd be able to survey the otherwise hidden back half of the Vreeland property. It looked like a good hour's hike from where he stood, but it would be worth the sweat it if it yielded a better sense of how the militia was utilizing all that land, and how many men they had. He collapsed the tripod, threw it over his shoulder, and began walking.

The ledge he had sighted was higher off the floor of the gulch than it had appeared through the scope and could be reached without serious equipment only by free-climbing a granite wall steeper than anything he'd anticipated. Raszer was more hobbyist than serious climber, and for a moment, he questioned his prowess. What overcame his inertia was the same thing that nearly always did: a stubborn inability to turn back. He removed his boots, slipped on the Scarpas, and approached the wall.

The first twenty feet were easy enough—a good, wide crack to lever against and plenty of little ledges for his toes. After that, the crack narrowed and the rock went vertical and smooth, polished by the constant blast of wind and driven ice crystals. He realized that he would have a difficult time getting down without rope and should have taken the necessary few minutes to put on his harness and plant a couple of anchors along the way. *Damned impatience*, he thought. This was the point in a climb where it became less about impulse and will than about gear and skill. Resting in the crevasse, he looped one end of the nylon rope under his arms, knotted it, and hung the rest on his shoulder. If he anchored here, a fall would at least be stopped short of the hard ground.

From his pack, he took a half a dozen copper/steel "stoppers" and dropped them into the oversized front pocket of his trousers. One end of the stopper was a little steel wedge that was designed to be fitted into a crack and held fast by friction. Attached to it was a short length of galvanized steel cable that terminated in a loop, and through this loop passed the rope. It would have been an easier and far less hazardous climb with a partner on belay, but inch by inch and toehold by toehold, with the updraft from the gulch whistling in his ears, Raszer ascended to just below the overhang.

He hadn't brought gloves and was surprised by how cold and slick the face was, even in the full sunlight of midday. This was still glacial terrain. Before the final push over the ledge, he stopped for a moment to allow his heart to adjust to the altitude. The air was lean and bitingly dry. He flattened himself against the dimpled granite and contemplated his next move. Far below, he heard the report of gunfire.

For a full three minutes, he did not move a muscle, and anyone watching would have thought him stuck. In fact, he was plotting. Suddenly, he locked his left toe into the rock, let out a mighty groan, and simultaneously threw his right leg over the ledge, using it to scissor himself around the overhang. He collapsed, belly down on the sun-warmed shelf, and drank his first deep breath in thirty minutes.

When he lifted his head, he saw that it had been worth the effort. He also saw just how exposed he was. Three hundred feet below, laid out on the sweeping alpine plain, was the Klamath Ranch property. He rose to his knees, slipped off the backpack, and removed his binoculars. The main ranch house—presumably now the HQ—was a long, low frame structure located at the end of a dirt road that wound up through steep meadow from the south gate. There was a second gate on the east side, though it looked to be accessible only by foot or ATV. Dual sentry turrets flanked the gates, and the compound was bordered on three sides by a high fence crowned with razor wire. The north side was the sheer face of the mountain, and needed no other barrier.

Beyond the main building were four rows of bunkhouses which must once have housed the dusty Klamath Co. miners, and appeared able to accommodate a thousand men. Behind these were toolshed-like structures that might store munitions. The backfield of the compound, acre upon acre of rugged glacial moraine, was elaborately outfitted for war games. There were trenches walled with sand bags, sprawling obstacle courses with rope bridges and mudholes, and a target range arrayed with mannequins ripe for the slaughter. There were false buildings with dummy snipers in the windows, their door lintels bearing government acronyms like ATF, FEMA, and even DWP. This passed, he supposed, for humor in these parts. From up high, the whole thing looked like the sort of miniature action tableau a ten-year-old might set up on a few square feet of Midwestern backyard. But it wasn't a model. It was Afghanistan in California.

As Raszer surveyed the mannequins marked for death, he recognized a few perennial icons of the culture wars by the dime store plastic masks they wore. The militia seemed to have identified its enemies. Who, he wondered, were its friends?

Over this playground roamed tightly organized "platoons" of mercenaries, each conducting highly regimented exercises. Raszer stayed low and raised the binoculars to the far end of the property, right up against the skirt of the mountain. Spread along the baseline, just as Mathonwy had said, was an impressive array of satellite dishes, each with its own companion steel shack sprouting what appeared to be a transmitting antenna. Raszer couldn't be certain of the difference between a radio telescope and an oversized TV dish, nor between transmitter and receiver, but he guessed that all species were present. What was plain was that all but one of the dishes were aimed straight up at the ionosphere, and the sole exception was pointed at the Shastina cone.

He scooted back from the edge into partial shadow and reached into his pack for the apple. Time to think. Time to consider the question he'd ask Mathonwy: why aim a dish at the mouth of a volcano? His hand brushed the little transistor radio, and for a moment he forgot his hunger and his puzzlement. He took it out, extended the antenna, and spun the combination power/volume wheel on to a low level of static.

AM 88. It figured. And it hardly mattered if the assignment of that particular bandwidth was accidental or deliberate. Across the great Aryan skinhead nation, eighty-eight was a coded salute: the eighth letter of the alphabet. HH. *Heil Hitler.*

The screech of guitar feedback careened off the granite. Raszer quickly lowered the volume. Mathonwy had been right: the signal was loud and clear. A voice, sneering and adenoidal, over a hip-hop beat stripped of all its sultry blackness:

Two-by-two like a blue-eyed No-ah
I'm gonna load 'em in and get ready for Ra-ho-wa!
So don't come dirty bitch give it to me clean
Or you will feel the power of a full magazine!

He rolled the tuning knob back to static and scanned rapidly across the AM band. A country & western station out of Redding, some talk radio, and a little old time religion. The usual. No "interesting transients." Raszer dropped it back into his pack.

It was then that he noticed the six sets of parallel steel tracks extending from just behind each of the satellite shacks and vanishing over a rise in the land that seemed to drop right into the mountain. These had to be the mine shafts, and no sooner had he thought it than a small rail car trolleyed up over the hillock and disgorged three men in combat fatigues and one in a business suit. One of the soldiers stood a head above the others and had a scalp that glistened in the sun. Vreeland. The guy in the suit was easy. Even from this distance, he was recognizable as Fortis Cohn.

Raszer scrambled thoughtlessly to his feet to get a better look at the mineshaft entrances. Within a nanosecond a bullet ricocheted wildly off the granite wall behind his left shoulder, splintering the rock and sending a needle shower of tiny crystals into the soft flesh on the back of his neck. He dove and hit the ledge hard, shattering the left lens of the binoculars and sending an ugly jolt of pain from his right kneecap to his brain. Another bullet slammed into the overhang just beneath his pelvis. "Jesus Fucking Christ!" he shouted, rolled over the ledge, and hung there by his fingertips. If he could drop three feet in altitude, he'd be below the ridge-line and out of range, but at the moment his feet were dangling two feet out from the nearest purchase on the rock and he had no time for a graceful descent. He'd placed the last of his anchors two yards down the slack rope that bound his torso, and if he dropped from here he could not be sure that it would hold. Caution or guts, he asked himself. Another bullet answered the question. He dropped six feet with his heart in his mouth and jerked to a blessed stop, slamming into the rock face and earning a nosebleed for his trouble. The stopper had held. Now it was about getting down and the hell out of here before anyone reached his position, and doing so before nightfall. Suddenly, from six feet above, there came static.

He laid his forehead against the rock and cursed quietly. He'd left the pack up on the ledge, and in the scramble to exit, must have somehow jostled the radio back on. A lousy start, he thought to himself. Careless and hasty. And then it came, embedded in the white noise, not apart from it, but of it. A pulse. A pattern. He slipped his free hand gingerly into his pocket and withdrew the last of his steel stoppers. With its acute edge, he began to scratch out repetitions on the rock face. Now, perversely, he was relaxed.

From the moment April entered Vreeland's compound, she moved into a realm of hyper-reality. Dozens of spotlights threw the entire area into the high relief of a movie set, heightening every sullen feature on every hardened young face. Sounds and smells registered with jarring clarity: the crunch of a boot heel on frost-caked mud, the whine of a screen door being thrown open, then slapping to a close. She smelled the parade day scent of Kiwi boot polish and the summer camp bouquet of damp canvas and mosquito repellent, and she wondered: do these shades just come on stronger against the stark grayness of the setting, or had her paranoia pushed her senses up to a state of high alert? The whole camp resonated with a sort of hair-trigger stridency, like a ping off cold steel. April was being escorted through a milieu as different from her own as was conceivable on the same planet, and she realized that one cause for her unease was the total absence of any color, scent, or sound which was even remotely feminine. She felt sure she was the only woman in the compound.

She had driven herself to the South Gate, and from there had been taken by jeep to the main house. Now she was being walked by a six-man escort toward the rear of the compound, and at the point where they cleared the last of the bunkhouses, she was blindfolded. The effect was to augment her remaining senses still further, and she found herself very aware of the hand that gripped her upper right arm and guided her forward. They put her into an open car, as if onto a roller coaster, and she felt it jerk forward and clatter as wheels meshed with steel tracks.

"Don't worry, ma'am," said the boy whose hand held her arm. "We'll be there soon and you can have your eyes back." There it was again. A gentility at odds with intent. A sweetness that wouldn't brook dissent.

The cart rumbled down a steep slope and her stomach dropped. Her nostrils filled with the mineral scent of the inner earth and her ears clogged and then popped as the track leveled out and the car began to brake. She was aware now that darkness had given way to light, and as she stepped from the car and had her blindfold removed, she saw why. They were in an underground mess hall, a rectangular space of at least two hundred yards from end to end, carved from the rock but reinforced by huge struts and joists of timber. The ceiling rose to a height of about twenty feet. The gathered forces of the Military Order of Thule—about six hundred men, she guessed—were seated at long tables arrayed on the cavern floor. The hall was illuminated by gas fed torches that lined the walls and blossomed orange flame. On the opposing wall, flanked by two blazing Roman fagots and backdropped by an oversized replica of a battle sword— hanging blade down—was the dais from which she expected Vreeland would address the troops. It was bare but for an unusual piece of set dressing April could only construe as resembling the posts between which a man might be bound and scourged.

No sooner had she been led to the seat of honor in the front row than every torch in the room was instantly extinguished. The tables began to tremble with the dull throb of a loping trip-hop bass, followed by a jackhammer drum loop. Overlaid on this propulsive bed was an electronica pattern of machine gun precision. But only when the heavy metal guitar entered, accompanied by the arctic shriek of a heavily processed voice, did she recognize the tune as a techno-thrash version of Led Zeppelin's Hyperborean epic: *Immigrant Song.* The entire room began to pixillate with the white lightning of industrial strobe lights. *Oh, my God,* she thought, *it's a right-wing rave!* She knew the patriot movement was big on tent shows, but this . . . this was Nuremberg.

She turned back to see six hundred shaven heads bobbing rhythmically, insistently, reverently, like an army of Tibetan Buddhists on go-pills. If there was a utopian city within the core of this mountain, its High Priestess could not be pleased. On the stage, there was no sign of Vreeland, but she could feel his advent in the eager faces of his acolytes, as if they believed he could be evoked by their metrical rocking. Minutes passed, tension passing over the crowd in waves of muscular current, and even April began to hunger for the main event. He was toying with them—and with her. Then, the strobe lights began to slow to a mesmeric throb, theatrical fog enveloped the twin uprights on the dais, and the room went black and stone still. An arc of man-made lightning surged between the two posts, and suddenly, he was there.

He was dressed austerely in black—creased trousers and a silk shirt with hidden buttons—and lit by a single overhead spot. He wore a wireless headset microphone, but was otherwise without props. His demeanor was more that of a man at prayer than a showman. In the midst of the Sturm und Drang, he was *quiet*.

And all remained silent until Vreeland dropped the arm he'd held lightly aloft from the moment of his appearance, and began to speak . . . not in exhortation, but softly enough so that that every man in the room unconsciously leaned forward to hear. April felt a collective exhalation of breath around her, and shivered.

"There is a river," he began. "And its source is in ice. It flows beneath the ice like a virgin spring—clear, cold, immaculate, and carrying the memory of our past. No contagion can survive it; no obstacle can divert it. Gathering force, it enters the world and fills first the veins of the warrior, pure in heart. *Yes* . . . " he said, and paused.

It was as if the echo of his voice issued from every sector of the cavern. As if the rock walls themselves had become transducers of his speech, membranes vibrating in sympathy with every modulation of pitch and tone. And then, as she looked cautiously to her left and right, regarding the entranced Myrmidons of Thule from the corners of her eyes, it hit her. They were reciting. All six hundred knew every single word by heart.

" . . . *there is a river*," they all said. He came to the lip of the stage, not ten feet from where April sat, and slowly, the footlights faded up. "But nothing . . . nothing in this world remains pure unless chastened by fire and reborn in ice. Even this river must pass through the swamp . . . just as every man must pass through the womb."

He lowered his eyes, then closed them briefly. When he opened them, they were on her—whether to exempt or accuse her, she could not be certain. All she could be certain of was that the muscle at the root of her belly had begun to twitch again.

"I woke from a dream last night . . . soaked in sweat. I could not rise from my bed, so great was the strength of the Father's hand on my forehead." Vreeland's voice dropped. "In the dream, I followed a tall man in a long, white robe through the streets of an American city, knowing not where he led. At the edge of the city, he mounted a bridge that looked down on a great river . . . a river that flowed into the very heart of the city. And the robed man pointed down to the river . . . and I saw that it was six miles wide and sixty-six miles deep, and it was choked with vile human waste and the products of our rapacious consumption." His voice began to rise ever so gradually and mark out the cadences she had known as a child, seated in the front pew of her father's church.

"And the river carried a plague that slips like a tapeworm into the bellies of the sleepers, poisoning the souls of our bright children, pulling them down to the common denominator of the mud-person mind . . . until soon all they can hear is the babble of a thousand foreign tongues, melting into one incomprehensible universal language! And I wept for the children, and I wept for the lost treasures of this world, and for Halgadom.

"And the man in the robe turned to me and revealed himself as a mighty warrior, fair of face. And he raised his palm to me and said, 'Weep no more, but steel thyself for battle, for I bring not peace . . . but a sword. Believe not what the Cainites say of me, for Christ was neither Nazarene nor born of Miriam. On this day . . . I make my covenant with the Nation of Halgadom, for only those born in ice can withstand the fire of my wrath! And verily, Halgadom shall right the earth.' And I looked into the face of the true Christ, and saw not the pitiful beggar crucified as Jesus, but the face of a hero . . . and men—that hero is here with us tonight . . . *in-this-very-chamber.*"

Vreeland sprung from the stage and plunged into the crowd, seizing the chin of a wide-eyed recruit and hauling him up into the light. "Here! Look at him!" he shouted, turning the boy's proud, shining face to his cheering fellows. "And here!" he boomed, moving on to pull another gawky farm boy out of his chair. "And over there! You, soldier! Stand up and let them see you!" Vreeland raised his arms, the tendons in his neck taut as steel cables, and let the love of the crowd roll over him like the sea.

April's heart pumped a hot flush into her face. She began to feel the separation of her psyche into two entities: personal self and species self, and the personal was rapidly losing primacy. It wasn't Vreeland's oratorical skill. It was something else.

Then came the benediction, and Vreeland, now among his troops, returned to a silky purr, his lips hard against the microphone's diaphragm. "And this you know in your hearts: that to defend this false, fallen world . . . this Babylon . . . they have built a perfect Beast. A beast whose names are legion, but often as not, coded in the acronyms of government agency. You know what they are. They can creep into your hometown at night on the pretext of any little problem: flood, fire, drought . . . even tax resistance. But do the people see? No! And so we will prod and provoke this beast until the day it shows its true face." His voice began to rise again, but gently, bootstrapping its way back up by way of intensity rather than volume. "We will not relent until the prophecy of Isaiah 2:19 is realized: *'And Judah shall go into the holes of the rocks and the caves of the earth for fear of the LORD, when he ariseth to shake terribly the Earth!'*"

He strode back to the stage, his hand in the air, his shoulders back, and positioned himself between the upright posts. "Then," he said, "and only then will the eyes of the blind be opened. Then—and only then—will the sleepers awaken. Fear is the antidote to apathy. Fear is the spark of true awareness. When fear walks down every Main Street, the battle for this earth will be joined. Until then, we cannot cease our vigilance, because coiled beneath us—deep in the infernal bowels of the planet—our enemy waits. Where does she lay, boys?"

A mass of thumbs turned downward.

"That's right," he affirmed. "But hear now the secret of *our* strength . . . for we come not from the seed of Cain. *No!* We come, hardened by the clear light of Arcturus in the realm of the eternal, true North." He turned his eye squarely on April. "Show me, boys," he urged with a nod. "Where *do* we come from?"

Six hundred arms shot simultaneously up, index fingers pointed toward the Pole, and the sudden compression of air around April's ears brought her to her hands and knees. When she was able to raise her head, she saw that Vreeland had pressed his palms outward against the opposing uprights and that a current passed through his body, forming a corona of hot blue flame around his head and shoulders, and she felt something she would have preferred not to feel. It was the sort of thing that bypasses the organs of the intellect and imprints itself on the most ancient part of the brain. Vreeland stepped from the dais and approached her slowly, the aura still with him, the glow still present in his outstretched hand. The blood drained from her head as he helped her onto the platform and raised her hand with his.

"There was at Delphi," he intoned, "an oracle who prophesied with tongues of fire . . . " And as he continued, April's wits slowly returned, and she understood with the cold clarity of the newly anointed what her purpose was to be. Her sibylline reputation, embellished by his gift for hype, was to lend spiritual authority to his vision. She was to play Wendy to Thule's Lost Boys. He had called her bluff more adroitly than she'd imagined he could, and she was in a serious jam.

Afterward, he took her to an anteroom starkly furnished with an army cot, an old bath mat, two chairs, and a table lit by a tin swag lamp. Vreeland sat down and motioned for her to do the same. It was cold in the room and she realized her jaw was tight. Keeping her chin up and her eyes fixed on him, she lowered herself to the table.

"So . . . " he said. "Did you get your money's worth?"

She hesitated for a moment, the frisson of his commanding performance still too much present. He had made her his prophetess—whether by guile or mystical conviction—and she needed to play the part convincingly. She could not purge from her mind the image of the lightning bolt. She could not wipe its reflection from her eyes.

"And then some," she replied. "I didn't expect all the holy rolling."

"The first rule of hunting is to wear the colors of your quarry, and the first rule of conquest is to let the conquered keep their household gods. The Romans got a thousand years from that strategy. Most of these boys were raised Pente-costals. It's easier to put a new face on Jesus than to change twenty years of condi-tioning in one night."

"A new face," she said. "Your face?"

"No," he replied. "Their face. Their epiphany. I show them the way."

"Onward, Christian soldiers," she said, then broke eye contact to look about the room, noting the fastidiously made cot. "Is this where you sleep?"

"I don't sleep . . . " he answered, matter-of-factly. "This is where I reflect." He propped his hand on his thigh and leaned in. "Tell me," he said, "what'd your Daddy do for a living?"

She studied him for a beat. "He was a preacher . . . just like you."

"Did you love him?"

"It was my duty to love him." She stared coolly into his gold-flecked eyes. "Why?"

"Nothing reveals as much about a woman as how she and her father got along."

"You have this on the highest authority?"

"None higher," he replied. He stood up and walked around to her side of the table, then took her chin in his hands. "I want you to leave that shack and come to the mountain. Our mountain . . . yours and mine. There are dangerous times coming, but when it's all over, the world will be burned clean and you and I will still be standing. All I ask is your gift of sight. Do you understand what I'm offering in return, April?"

She swallowed, then said flatly. "I think so."

"We'll live forever."

She nodded slowly, and said, "Do you know what I need from you?"

"Ask."

"I need to be sure that your enemy is my enemy. You're a man with a mission. Who and what are we up against?"

"There are some things I can't say yet," he replied. "I'll tell you this. The world has strayed from true north. Our mission is restoration. But there's a clean-up to do first. *The enemy?* You already know, deep down, because you can feel them undermining your will like termites in the wood . . . moles beneath the foundation. Planting doubt . . . ambivalence . . . ambiguity. Malignancies of the mind. All products of a cockeyed world."

Suddenly, he stopped cold, and whispered, "Listen!" His eyes closed in concentration. When he opened them, he took her hands in his. "Can you feel that?"

She did, first through his hands, then through the ground beneath her feet and in the marrow of her bones. She knew what it was, not by dint of prior experience, but because the professor had described it so well. *As close to primal dread as any modern person is likely to feel.* A harmonic tremor: the volcano's quickening. The table rattled and the living rock around her groaned like a ship at sea. Vreeland's nostrils flared, as if sniffing the mineral air for a predator. As if, she thought, the man who'd held his troops in such total thrall was looking over his shoulder at the hellhound on his trail. Curiously, it was the first time she'd seen anything resembling vulnerability on his face. For the moment, he was mortal. She decided it was now or never.

"Sit down with me . . . while the channel is open between us. I want to try something. You're unsettled about something. You need to stay as true as an arrow. I can help, but I need you right here." She drew the tarot deck from the pocket of her skirt and spread the cards before him, pulling out the Ace of Swords and setting it midtable.

"No. No cards," he protested, waving away her display. "No Hebrew magic."

"The colors of your quarry, Commander," she retorted. "Trust me . . . it's not about the cards. You called me here, and I came. Now let me show you *why* you called me." He sat down grudgingly, drumming his fingertips on the tabletop. She knew she must assert her divinatory authority quickly or forfeit it.

"There was something you wanted to tell me the other night," she began in a low and even tone. "Something I think you need to clear from the past before you can embrace the future. Can you . . . for me . . . for Halgadom . . . try and put it in the form of a question?" She shuffled the deck, had him cut it in threes, and then laid the top card— The Wheel of Fortune—onto the Ace. "The Ace of Swords is the victory of righteousness. The Wheel of Fortune covers it. Which way the wheel turns may depend on the resolution of what's troubling you." He was watching her, still uncertain, but attentive. "See if this makes it clearer . . . because this next card *crosses* you. It's the thing that stands in the way of your destiny."

Even if April had been adept at sleight-of-hand, or such a powerful sorceress that she could will the deck into a prescribed order, she would not have chosen the card she laid next, nor could she have foreseen its effect. It was the Sun, the nineteenth card of the Major Arcana. Its rays fanned the horizon in all directions from an anthropomorphic face, but Vreeland's haunted stare was directed to a secondary figure in the foreground. A beautiful and naked young girl-child—her head wreathed in flowers and her graceful arms spread wide to welcome the nourishing rays—rode bareback on a white horse.

He leapt from the table as if stung, his features pinched, his bronzed face suddenly ashen. Here, she thought, was the opportunity Raszer had foreseen. The chink in the armor. Here was the thin line between visionary and psychopath. This was a gift.

"Get rid of it," he said, his authority now far less certain. "Get rid of it or get out."

"It's time, Bronk," she said, rising slowly from her chair, her fingers extended. "If you want me to be Delphi, then bring me an offering. Make yourself free. A man free of history can make it his own. I'll take your secret to the top of this mountain and give it to the wind. Do you know the story of Arjuna and Krishna? How the warrior Arjuna hesitated before battle, seeing the faces of his kin in the enemy lines? And Krishna said, *'Forget not your duty, warrior,'* and handed him the reins of the chariot." She moved a few inches closer, palms turned up and fingers curled as if holding invisible reins. "Here," she urged, her voice low and incantory. "Take them. Put whatever crosses you into my hands and take the reins."

He remained riveted in place, wanting not to see the card but unable to resist its draw. Spellbound, April thought: *this is what it really means.* And inside that crackling, fearsome, weirdly thrilling moment when he might either drop to his knees or snap her neck, she had her own little epiphany. She saw that spiritual power did not issue from any intrinsically moral source, and that the same might be said of the universe itself. They were at her command right now. She summoned them, scooped the card up from the table, and moved toward him, blocking any easy exit. "Now," she commanded him.

But she'd gone too far too fast.

He was on her before the breath had left her lips. He pinned her arms back and slammed her face into the table. She felt something splinter, and tasted blood. He wrapped her hair around his fist and gave a brutal yank.

"You gypsy bitch!" he said. "Don't fuck with my mind. You'll pay a very high price!"

She knew it was reckless—maybe suicidal—but she had to play her last card.

"Like Ori?" she said through the blood in her mouth. "Like Ori did?"

It was quiet. He backed up to the wall and froze there, arms limp at his sides. His jaw began to move, his lips to shape a vowel, but nothing came out. She drew herself upright and blotted the blood from her face with her skirts. At the sight of him, her courage returned. She went to his side, laid her hands on his breast, and put her ear to his mouth. The breath from his clotted throat curled around a sweet, two-syllable sound. A tear rolled down his unshaven cheek, dampening her face.

"Or-ee . . . " he said. And then she heard him speak as if entranced: "And the Lord said, 'Get thee into the land of Moriah, and offer him there as a sacrifice' . . . " Vreeland's chin sank to his chest and he spoke in what was little more than a mumble. "But the Lord never came," he said, wonderingly. "He never took the sword from my hand."

"Oh, my God," April whispered. She knew the verse, and what it meant.

April crept back into the motel room just after midnight. She thought Raszer might have drifted off to sleep, but he'd only returned himself a few minutes earlier and was on the sofa, hunched over the coffee table and studying a pattern of dots and dashes on a legal pad. He'd been up on the mountain, comparing notes with Mathonwy after his Tuesday class. She sat down on the opposite end and began to roll a joint, watching him from the corner of her eye as he scratched out another version of the pattern.

"What's that?" she asked.

"Something I picked up on Mathonwy's crystal radio," he replied. "It scans like Morse code but it doesn't read like it. Could be nothing. Or everything." He tossed his pencil onto the table and sat back, turning his attention to her as she drew hungrily on the reefer. Her hair hung down over her cheek. It struck him as odd that she hadn't yet looked at him fully. Like a child with something to hide.

"That scary, huh?" he said She conceded only a nod in his direction, but that was enough to reveal the bruised lip and the black and blue staining her cream-colored skin.

"Jesus!" he exclaimed. "You're hurt!"

"I'm okay," she said, shaking it away. "No serious damage. Things got a little intense when I read his cards." She exhaled the smoke and grinned through the curtain of hair. "But it was worth it. I nailed him."

"April . . . " Raszer said cautiously. "You're trembling. Why don't you let me run you a bath? We can debrief afterwards. Or you can talk while you're soaking."

She ignored his offer. "Did you get your reconnaissance done?"

His eyes stayed on her. "I got a good look at the property. Got shot at, too. I think Mathonwy and I have cooked up a way to get in, but that's for later. What did he—"

"Shot at? And you're coddling me?"

"Up on the rocks," he said. "These guys take private property *very* seriously. But you have to figure dozens of reporters and freelancers have tried to get a look at the layout. Anyway . . . they missed. Just got my face banged up."

"Then we both bled for the cause."

"Let me get this. You read his cards and he went off on you? Son of a bitch."

"Can I put my head on your lap, Raszer? You're right. I am a little shaky."

He pushed away the table with the toe of his boot and scooted back against the cushions. She laid her head on his thigh, her hair spilling to the floor, and drew her knees up to her chest. Raszer began to stroke her head, and she began, quietly, to cry.

"This thing we're doing, April," he said softly. "It does violence to the psyche. It's dangerous—and not only in the obvious ways. Cops who work deep cover, and spies . . . they know it. Some of them never come back from the other side. You go right to the edge of morphing into what you hate. But sometimes, that's the only way to win."

"He killed his little girl," she said, her eyes fixed on nothing.

"What?" Raszer stiffened, his fingers curling on her scalp.

"His daughter. Ori. He executed her. To prove to the Fraternity his fitness for command . . . that he was absolutely loyal."

Raszer drew a breath, held it, and counted silently through the exhalation.

"And beyond moral law," he said. "Go on." His tone was tender and even.

"He drew a card," she continued, "like all the other 'candidates,' back when he was in Utah, outside of Moab. Some kind of twisted game of Truth or Dare. Some of them only had to give up fingers or toes. They asked *him* to sacrifice his daughter."

"Motherfuckers," Raszer said icily. "They had big plans for him."

"Raszer . . . " She pressed her knuckles into her teeth to stifle a sob. "He cut off her head with a battle sword. She was eight years old. He buried her body out there . . . in Goblin Valley. And her head . . . here . . . on Shasta. Up near the place they call The Heart." She bit hard on her fist and dug her fingernails into his kneecap. "The Fraternity told him that his act set him above other men, and fit to judge them. But I think that deep down he just can't buy that. I think deep down . . . it's made him crazy."

"And even more lethal, because now . . . he has no soul to lose." He turned away, unaware that his teeth were clenched until his jaw began to cramp up. His thoughts were unavoidably with his own daughter, and because he was a man who looked at all the angles, he asked himself if there was any creed so compelling, any god so great, that it would finally accept such a sacrifice. His instinct told him that no such faith would be worth its name, and he understood that they were dealing with monsters.

"It sounds like the Yakuza," he said. "Or the Khmer Rouge. I've never heard of anything like this in the West. Murder, yeah. But a man's own child . . . *that* binds him totally, because the people who've asked him to do it are the only ones who can possibly ever accept him. And from what I discovered earlier today . . . "

He lifted her head and rose numbly to turn on the gas fireplace with its faux logs. The room had gotten suddenly chilly. There was a bottle of brandy beside the fire. He poured two shots and sat down on the carpet at April's side, handing her a glass and gently pushing the hair out of her face. "Anyhow, when you're ready, give me the rundown on tonight."

After a few moments and a sip of brandy, she cleared her throat and began, and he listened without interruption. When she had finished, he took the roach from her fingers, pinned it between two match heads, and fired it up. He blew it out and drew the stinging smoke into his nostrils until his eyes watered. Then he grabbed the legal pad.

"So, we've got reconstituted Christian Identity dogma, a new twist on the Hyperborean legend, and a mythos that connects some sort of subterranean demiurge with the forces of the New World Order. What a fucking goulash. It all makes a certain kind of paranoid sense . . . except for one thing . . . " He finished off his brandy. "Where the hell does Fortis Cohn fit in? What sort of marker do they have on him?"

"And Raszer," she added. "He asked me if I'd ever been to Morocco."

"Morocco?"

"Yeah. Said he might want to take me there. If I prove myself worthy."

"Morocco," he repeated, shaking his head. "Jesus. What is he after? And how have you gotten under his skin so fast? Is he falling for you, April?"

"Wasn't that the plan?" she said.

"Herod went for Salome, but he didn't ask her on a cruise."

"I'm not a cheap date."

"I don't know. The chemistry . . . sounds pretty volatile. Even the physicality, the violence. It's like he's laid a claim. I guess I should've expected—"

"Yes and no. It's not . . . carnal. He doesn't really seem *interested in me*—except as a kind of trophy and in this spooky, mystical way. He wants his own prophetess."

"Right," said Raszer, but he was more unnerved than he let on.

"The whole vibe up there," she said. "It's so . . . perverse. When I dance, they pretend to be into it, but I think they're really just into *him*."

He nodded. "Maybe it goes with the territory. They found photos in Afghanistan of the Taliban foot soldiers wearing mascara and dancing for their leaders. There's this heightened, hothouse atmosphere that comes with close ranks and the perception of an external threat. Men playing women are a lot less threatening than the real thing for guys who can't get out of their father's shadow. Make no mistake: it's a dangerous place for you to be, and I'm going to get you out of there as soon as I've made contact with Fortis." He ran his finger up her spine. "Listen. This is too big for us to process right now. Let's empty out. Sleep. We'll get up with the sun and check our game plan."

"Raszer?" she said, and bit her lip.

"Mm-hmm?"

"Sleep in the bed tonight, okay?"

April awoke with a start at three A.M., sat up, and lit a candle. She traced the faint arc of Raszer's bare shoulder, and had a ferocious desire to nuzzle it. She was aroused in some bristling, feral way that was new to her. She'd had a nightmare, and its colors were still very much present. On her knees on a grassy mound, her ten-year-old cheek pressed to the trunk of a cottonwood, she had been awaiting her father's punishment for some misdeed. A sacrilege. It was Sunday, and her mother had outfitted her in a puffy white dress, black patent leather shoes, and lacy white socks, turned down at the top. Expecting a beating, she had been surprised to feel instead a gentle pressure on her tailbone and a sensation of numbness from the waist down. She turned into the sun's glare, and shielding her eyes, was mystified to see that a part of her had been removed and lay still and fetus-like on a white handkerchief. There was blood and tissue, but the mass of it appeared bony, like a huge tooth freshly extracted. And indeed, there was blood in her mouth. A group of men in hoods and white shoes had gathered to examine the specimen for portents. One of them turned to her.

That was when she has awakened. She hadn't wanted to see the face.

She rose from bed and drew open the curtain, revealing a three-quarter moon whose light dusted the snowy crown of Shasta with diamonds. It was cold at this hour of the night, and she shivered as she peeled off the oversized t-shirt she'd borrowed from Raszer's duffel and dropped back down to the bed on all fours, gooseflesh breaking out on her arms and on the moonlit swell of her breasts. She eyed her slumbering prey like a lioness, considering which hunk of flesh to rip into first. Deciding upon his exposed shoulder, she prodded it with the cold tip of her nose until, obediently, he rolled onto his back. She traced her tongue down through silvery hair to the nipple of his right breast. She slipped her hand beneath the sheets and found his cock resting against his thigh, soft but thickening with blood. From the well of dreamless sleep she heard him moan, and her lips tightened around his nipple until she felt it harden against her tongue.

His eyes fluttered open and were stung by the hard moonlight; for a moment, still in another world, he thought he was back in Hollywood, and couldn't account for April's scent. By the time he registered that it was her, his libido had surged beyond the option of retreat. There was a moment when he might have drawn back, forced himself fully awake, and reminded her of what was at risk, but that moment passed as he instinctively reached for the warmth between her legs, finding her already moist.

She was so ready to be touched that her reaction was instantaneous and electric. As she bit down hard on his nipple and felt the jolt of his spine snapping like a whip, she realized that it all came down to who you were with. Raszer would take all of her: the whole, gloriously fucked-up package. The soiled Pentecostal girl from Southern Indiana, the self-administering psych major from U.C.L.A. who'd listed her father's occupation as "serial abuser," the ersatz sorceress with the patchouli bath oil, and now this: whatever she was becoming in the unsettling aftermath of her trip to Hades. She was a lamp inhabited by some new and vaguely sinister genie, and her skin fairly sizzled with her bedmate's touch. She was not herself—that's how people usually put it—or was she?

He threw the bedclothes back and pulled her on top of him. Running his sticky hands up the back of her thighs to her ass, he shimmied himself down to where his tongue could reach her sex. And then something went haywire. There was an electrostatic sizzle in the room, followed by a pop like eardrums snapping on a rapid descent, and suddenly he found himself nearly blinded by the glare from the light streaming from his own iris. "Come behind me, Raszer," he heard her say, in an unfamiliar voice, caustic and almost genderless. "C'mon . . . fuck me like a boy."

"April?" he said, slipping out from under her, drawing her up to her knees.

"Guess again," she answered, in the same acidic tone.

Intuitively, he understood her transformation, and admired her more than ever for her fearlessness, her shamanic madness. She might have played the enchantress before—and played it well—but this was an invocation of the profoundest sort: the kind that forfeits identity and risks immolation. She was inviting him to know his quarry from the inside-out. "Okay," he whispered, his hands supporting her belly. *"Here we go."*

Somewhere in the midst of their highwire act, Raszer became aware of a new scent, saline and metallic as a vein of ore. He tracked his eyes up the glistening arch of April's spine, the wild light in his eye pointing the way to the base of her skull, and saw the stigmata born of her catharsis. A fine red line encircled her neck like the most delicate of gold chains: a necklace of blood. He was deep inside her and still deeper inside the vision she had induced, but he felt a jolt of panic and reached up to caress the wound. His fingertip came away red. It was the shallowest of cuts, just enough to bring blood to the surface, but it was real and it was evidence enough of her immersion.

He returned his bloodied fingertip to the swollen spot amid her petals of flesh and called out to her, urging her back to him, and she started to come, hard and fierce and speaking in tongues only woman can master. As the sounds filled her throat, his climax came, and they collapsed together in the mingled perfumes of love and mortality.

But the light in his eye did not go out. It grew stronger and began to strobe until it was as if he could see the bit stream of photons that were the prophetic contents of his own mind. There was another *pop!* . . . then nothing.

In the deep space silence that followed, her heard her moan—a mourning sound—and wrapped her in his arms. The ring of blood had now disappeared but for a faint pinkness. He drew the sheet up to her neck and asked her if she was all right.

Her reply did not come right away, and when it did, it came in a glottal, gagging utterance that gave him new cause for alarm. There were stigmatics whose wounds vanished and those who bore them internally, like a cilice on the soul. He pulled her close and gently stroked her throat, saying, "Hush, now. Be still, baby."

"Aah . . . aahba . . . ahbra." She pounded the pillow with her fist, unable to get the sound past her larynx.

"You with me, April?" he asked.

"Aabra . . . Aaabrahh . . . Abra-ham," she sighed, her own, sweet voice having returned.

"Jesus," he said, feeling his heart speed, recalling his own seemingly nonsensical pronouncement on the massage table. "You really are a sibyl." He cradled her. "I'll have to give that sonofabitch credit. He knew it when he saw it."

Raszer lifted his head slowly and glanced out the window to see that the summit of Mt. Shasta was now bathed in a dusky, rose pink light, and he knew that Fortis Cohn's predicament was that of a man who waits longingly for his own killer.

11

Sexually awakened women, affirmed and recognized as such, would mean the complete collapse of the authoritarian ideology.
— Wilhelm Reich, *The Mass Psychology of Fascism*

I think maybe you should lie low tonight," Raszer said, reaching for a cigarette. "Put in a few hours at the bookstore. Talk to some normal people . . . if there are any around here. Get your bearings back." It was seven A.M.

"I can't," April replied, unconsciously stroking her neck, though it bore no sign of the night's sympathetic laceration. "I promised I'd meet him up there, and I'm so close to knowing what he's after . . . I don't dare leave him time to begin doubting me."

"I think we know pretty much what he's after," Raszer said. "We just don't know exactly how he intends to get it, or exactly who's footing the bill." He stuffed the Zippo into his jeans and exhaled a feather of smoke. "And he's going to doubt you to some degree no matter what. You're a woman. Even if you *have* turned his head, it's only *his* metanoia. He may be Caesar, but I'll bet you there's a Brutus or two up there, and you'd be right in the way of the knife."

"Maybe Fortis Cohn is Brutus," she suggested. "Isn't that what we want? Didn't you want me to stir him up . . . drive a wedge between them?"

"Trust me . . . you've already done that. Let it work its way in. Vreeland's decided he needs you, and a man like that doesn't question his decisions. A day won't make a difference, and it'll give me time to catch up. Remember, this is about getting Fortis back to Papa, not nailing Bronk to the cross. That'd be sweet—and it may happen collaterally—but it's not our main deal."

"C'mon, Raszer," she protested. "You wanna blow these guys off the planet as much as I do. They're toxic. Fortis Cohn just buys us in. You told me once, 'every job I take is the same job'—it's about making the world safe for the *sidhe* . . . the fairy folk . . . to come out of their hiding places again. You quoted Yeats . . . and William Blake."

"Which substance was I abusing that night?" he asked, unconvincingly droll.

"Probably a few," she answered. "Does that make it bullshit? *'You and I,'* you said. *'You and I will work together one day and the world won't be the same.'"*

"Don't do this, April," he said with quiet gravity. "Don't make this about you and me and what *we* dream. It's so much nastier, so much more dangerous." He watched her chin drop. "Okay, listen. Before we go hunting for more snark, let's look at what we've already bagged. You and I need to revisit our rules of engagement."

"Like the one you broke last night?" Her eyes danced, delighting in the bust.

"Among others." He smiled and flushed slightly. He couldn't help smiling when she looked at him that way.

"I love it when you blush," she said, her gaze remaining on him for a long beat.

"You bring it out, April. Once again, you've spoiled me for any other woman."

"Good," she said, batting her lashes. "After me they're all vanilla milkshakes."

"Hmm," was all he said. Her eyes had found his tender spot and drilled into it. He decided—because there was nothing he could say that wouldn't get him in deeper—to stay on point. He cleared his throat and began somewhat awkwardly.

"All right. What do we have that we can use to leverage Fortis? That Vreeland's Order is an operational arm—possibly one of many—of some larger organization with big-time mercantile interests. We know from all the hardware and from his obsession with these signals that they're well networked and—if his Morocco proposal means anything—probably global. We can infer from all we've learned . . . but especially from how anxious Christopher Rose was to lose that note . . . that they're planning something big, and that it involves the systematic provocation not only of their 'underground' enemies—whoever the hell they are—but of their supposed proxies in various federal agencies. And if Mathonwy's suspicions are correct, it may involve eco and geo-terrorism." He sighed, still not quite able to shake her voodoo. "And we know that Fortis Cohn is here to make sure that—by hook or by crook—they hold onto Mt. Shasta until it's a done deal."

"Right," said April, doing her level best to transition to work mode. "Right. And the whole Polar thing . . . I mean it's all so fantastic. So sci-fi. Can they really—"

"I don't know," he said. "It could just be a mythological prop."

He saw that there was something on her mind she couldn't yet conjure words for. Her eyes were those of last night's sorceress, not the morning after's all-too-human flirt. What unsettled him most was that those eyes offered him a well of salvation.

"I know," he said softly. "We're headed into a labyrinth, and the only thing we know for sure is that the Minotaur is a miscreant and that before we're through, reality will probably have a new look." He stubbed out his cigarette. "We have a few choices—none of them sure bets. If we involve the FBI we set off all the Homeland Security bells and risk another Waco—probably just what Vreeland wants. If we pressure Fortis legally on his possible complicity in the Rose murder, he may run and wind up dead, too. We can target Vreeland and flush out his Fraternity brothers, but then we become the targets. Or we can do what I do fairly well. We can try to give Fortis a reasonably graceful exit and hope that he tosses a grenade on his way out."

"Whichever way you go, Raszer," she said. "You need me. I'm inside."

"Yeah," he said, and paused for what seemed to her a long time. "You are. But we need to take some cooling off time, because now you know Vreeland's big, shameful secret. The next place he takes you may be one you can't come home from."

She took one of his cigarettes and paced, a hand parked on her right hip, in front of the balcony's open glass doors, the new morning sun gilding her hair. Then she collapsed into one of the room's ugly green armchairs and simmered.

"A penny for your thoughts," he said.

"Cost you more than that."

"All right," he said. "Dinner out tonight. We'll go as Groucho and Harpo."

She smiled, but the smile faded to wistfulness. "I'll say this once, Raszer." Her voice was deep in her chest. "If you'd only admit . . . to caring enough to be jealous . . . or worried about something besides losing Fortis Cohn . . . I'd quit running with the wolves and wash your socks. I *am* you. We'd be that 'alchemical marriage' you talk about."

He kept a steady eye on her until she returned his gaze. "Jealous," he repeated, mulling it over. "Well, I'll have to do some soul-searching there, because that really would breach the code of conduct. Worried? Oh, I'm worried. Worried that you don't understand that guys like Vreeland don't confess filicide to people they intend to keep around for very long. You're right about one thing. You *are* me. If we ever did try to fuse our lives together, we'd cancel each other out." He stood and walked over to her side. "And don't think I don't appreciate the offer, but I don't want anyone washing my socks who isn't being paid for it. I've tried that and it doesn't work." He sat down at her feet. "Besides, I couldn't give you the thing you want most." He paused. "Protection."

"I feel totally protected when I'm with you," she said.

He shook his head. "I'm talking long-term, April. Existential. There'd come a day when you'd look for me, and I wouldn't be there. And then the resentment would start."

Now it was her turn to shake her head, and there was a sadness in it. She cleared her throat and quickly recalibrated. "Listen, Wart," she said. "I think that knowing exactly what Bronk is up to is the key to turning Fortis Cohn. If I can get him to share his whole vision—and I think he has to now, because he has let me so far in—we can figure out why Fortis is willing to risk his soul to be a part of it. Give me another pass while I've got his confidence. He's promised to give me a tour of his listening posts. Maybe I can learn who he thinks is jamming his communications . . . or what that signal is that you picked up. Look, this may be way out there, but I think he connects me to Ori. I think he sees me as being able to offer some kind of redemption."

"After last night," Raszer said, touching her knee. "It doesn't seem so out there. Just don't mistake him for some fascinating case study you can do a clinical write-up on. Remember that Hiltler sent all the fortunetellers to Dachau when the tea leaves turned."

"I won't fuck up, Raszer."

"I know *you* won't, April. I'm concerned about that other person inside of you. I won't gamble either you or our mission, but I will take one calculated risk with you." He kneaded the skin on his unshaven face and took from his pack the cigarette she'd just returned. He lit it and inhaled deeply. "Was Fortis there last night . . . at the speech?"

"I assume he was around somewhere. I saw him before they blindfolded me. He made me sign a nondisclosure agreement and had this creep he called Blotto pat me down. More like grope me down. I don't get the feeling Fortis likes me."

"That's good," said Raszer. "He's not supposed to. Okay. You want high stakes?

Here's the deal. Mathonwy is setting me up with something called an E-40. It's a 'Notice of Geological Hazard,' a legal preliminary to an evacuation warning that the USGS issues and copies FEMA on. It gives me the right—so long as our boy Fortis doesn't go to court to block it—to inspect the mineshafts for signs of volcanic activity. I don't know whether it'll fly, but I'm gonna go up there with it around two P.M. What time did you agree to meet Vreeland?"

"One o'clock."

"All right. Go. Try to get some idea of what they're doing with those antennas. All that power . . . it's something we're not seeing yet. Then, take him aside . . . and tell him there's only room for one *consigliere* in his compound, and it's either Fortis . . . or you. Ask him if he thinks Alexander listened to his lawyers. Make a female fuss about it."

"Christ, Raszer," she said. "Talk about calling my bluff."

"It's one way or the other. The middle path doesn't work in our business."

"Now I'm hearing the man I'd walk through fire for," she said. "You're on."

"Speaking of, what's that *haute* sausage place out in the boonies you told me about? The one with the oak fire pit and the illegal menu . . . "

"Le Serpent Rouge."

"If we pull this off, we'll drink to our 'alchemy' tonight."

Raszer's cell phone bleeped and broke the brief resurgence of sexual tension. It was Monica with Abel Cohn on the line, calling after a string of sleepless nights. He sounded spent, and nothing could have prepared Raszer for the story he had to tell.

"Mr. Raszer," he began, hardly bothering with pleasantries, "I've remembered something from thirty-five years ago that I think I'd have rather not have."

"Tell me," said Raszer.

"I think it's possible that Fortis is not my son." He paused. "I'm a sober man, and I've based my career on what can be argued as common sense and common decency. I don't put much stock in the notion of recovered memory. But lately, I've been having some very unusual nightmares, and I think the real nightmare is that I'm not dreaming. I'm outside the maternity ward on the night of Fortis's birth . . . "

Raszer listened intently to Abel's remembrance, both for its details about the lunatic with the medallion and his ravings about the Fraternity and for the more typically dreamlike elements—the swinging doors of the ward, the tall, svelte man with the lizard's eyes, the oppressive heat—which might be just as telling. It was one hell of a story.

"I hope I did it justice," said Abel. "I'm a little the worse for wear at the moment."

"I can understand," said Raszer. "I can't imagine anything more—" He stopped himself. He'd made the mistake of empathizing too much and had been about to say that there was no hell like the hell of a man with reason to doubt his child's paternity.

"Anyhow," he picked up, "I'll have Monica check the records from the psych ward at Glendale Adventist and—if it still exists—the visitors registry from admitting. But I need to say this, Mr. Cohn . . . if I'm any judge of fatherhood, you're the only real father Fortis has. Hang in. He may need your help soon. I know I will."

At 9:12 A.M., Raszer arrived at the front door of the small frame structure which housed the Siskyou County Recorder of Deeds, only to find a Post-It note saying, "Went for donuts. Back in five." He turned and scanned the street for the absent public servant, observing the low-key bustle of a small town starting the day at a deliberately lazy pace. Lighting a cigarette, he stepped onto the square of undernourished lawn and squatted down to wait and smoke. The grass had been worn down to the black, volcanic dirt.

The village of Mt. Shasta was little more than a Main Street, now augmented by the usual assortment of supermarkets, fast food joints, and gas stations lining the access roads from the freeway. The original buildings were mostly utilitarian wood frame shells of the type thrown up haphazardly all over the west in the late nineteenth and early twentieth centuries. Whatever sort of Victorian, gingerbread charm they evidenced now, he guessed, had probably been added later in tourist-aimed renovations. Old World charm of the genuine sort seemed to come both from an integrity of design and an expectation of permanence. The towns of the Gold Rush West had been built like army outposts, designed to be functional for the period of occupation, and after that, home to wind drift and scavengers, their cheap single coats of paint blistering beneath the relentless frontier sun. West of the Rockies, nothing seemed permanent except the desert.

The town's distinctions—along with heavenly light and tonic air—derived from the determined nonconformism of its citizens and the visual sense that the whole town had been erected in homage to the mountain. The mountain was seen through every window and over every roof. It was inescapable. Raszer dropped his cigarette in the dirt, and as he stood up to crush it out, noticed a small collection of Newport butts clustered off to his right, and fresh footprints bearing the tread and insignia of U.S. Army work boots leading from there to the door.

He spotted the white donut bag from a half a block away. The clerk was a pale, gawky man in his early thirties with a ponytail, wearing beige trousers held up with a Navaho belt. The ponytail gave Raszer hope, and he hailed him on approach.

"Morning!" he called. "What have you got there . . . honey-dipped or chocolate?"

"Peanut caramel," the clerk replied, giving a chipped-tooth smile to the stranger at his office door. "My guilty pleasure. Can't start every day with prunes and granola. Howdy. I'm Doc Kane. What can I do ya for?" He peeled the note off his door and stepped inside. He hadn't bothered to lock it.

"Gary Powers," Raszer said, offering both his hand and the fake USGS ID that bore his latest nom de guerre. "U.S. Geological Survey. I need your expertise."

"You up there with the Professor?" Kane asked.

"Right. I'm mapping some rock slides and thermal vents up near the Heart, and I want to make sure I don't step on anyone's toes . . . or get shot at."

"Plenty o' toes to step on up there," Kane said, lifting his eyes to the mountain. "And plenty of ways to get shot, I imagine. Rock slides, hmm? She's not percolating, is she?" He set his donuts down amidst the clutter of his desk.

"Just a few little burps now and then. Nothing to worry about. But the Cascades HQ has asked us to prepare some pro forma evacuation plans. They're S.O.P. anytime you've got habitation near a natural hazard." Raszer took a seat in front of Kane's desk.

"Burps, eh?" said Kane, biting into his first donut. "Yep. I've been feeling 'em. Glad to know it wasn't acid reflux, otherwise I'd have to lay off these." He grinned and waited for a laugh that never quite came.

"Well, anyhow," Raszer continued, "the first order of business is to compile a list of people actually living on the mountain—squatters as well as property owners—beginning with that big parcel up near Avalanche Gulch. The one the militia boys are camped on. Do you happen to know who the owners of record are?"

"Well," Kane answered, leaning in conspiratorially, peanut chips decorating his moustache, "that depends on whose side you're on. There's a deed naming the Army of Thor or whatever they call themselves, but it's been challenged, as you may know."

"The tribal lawsuit," said Raszer. "Right. I'm looking for the folks who signed over the deed for a buck. The company that held mineral rights for a hundred years."

"The Klamath Company," Kane said. "And I personally don't think they'd let a spread like that go for a dollar. Not even to a relative. Not that my opinion means jack. Donut?" He held the open bag out.

"No thanks. I've eaten. So help me out here, because nothing wastes time like barking up the wrong tree. Who's in charge up there? Who do I contact for access?"

"Not exactly sure. Fella named Vreeland is listed as agent for the owners, but there's a young lawyer named Cohn representing them in this lawsuit by the tribes. He might be the one to see. I personally hope the judge evacuates those jack-booters before you have to. I don't like hearing gunfire in an avalanche district."

"Right," Raszer said. "Between you and me, they're a pretty serious environmental hazard. They've got more than target pistols. It's a wonder nobody raises hell."

"Well," said Kane drolly, "everything's live and let live in the great State of California. Nobody screams because nobody figures they've got a right to." He compacted the rest of the donut down his gullet with his index finger. "Until it's too late."

Raszer nodded agreement. He had his man. "Do you—by any chance—still have the original deed on file?"

"Sure do," Kane replied. "Nothing leaves this place except by fire or slow decomposition. And your timing's good. I'm just about to ship these old files off to the court. They've all been subpoenaed, but I see no reason you can't peruse 'em."

Kane stood and retrieved the bankers box marked *S.C. 1870–1880* which sat behind a pile of clutter on the far side of his desk, its lid still askew from Fortis's hurried exit. He lifted it and beckoned Raszer to a long rectangular table against the far wall, making room for the box by pushing aside his long-neglected "to be filed" stacks.

"What the heck," he said, sorting through the contents, mildly irritated. "This is out of order." He shot Raszer a look. "You can see I'm not exactly Felix Unger when it comes to housekeeping, but *inside* the boxes, we're as finicky as the Library of Congress." Finally locating what he was after, he removed a heavy cloth binder marked "1875" and carried it gingerly over to the bookstand with its attached map well. It opened with an effusion of mothballs and mildew to the very document they sought, as if it had been place-marked. "Well, I'll be damned," Kane said, "That's convenient."

"Mind if I take a look?" Raszer asked.

"Not at all. Heck, you're doin' me a favor by pulling out the pertinent documents. Like I said, I gotta pack this stuff off to that judge in Weed. Haven't been through this one in a while."

The deed was the same as the photocopy Raszer had seen in the files of Cohn,

Gottlieb & Schuyler in Los Angeles, hand-written in perfect schoolbook cursive. What he was after were ancillary documents: names of company officers, executives—anything that would put a face and a history on the mysterious tenant, especially if it provided a link to the line of "Rupert Voorhees," the mineral and media baron Monica and he had tagged in connection with Halgadom and the St. Joachim Brotherhood.

"What about the actual mineral claims?" he asked. "Weren't they required to file when they hit a vein and wanted to take their booty out of the mine?"

Kane fingered forward, dust rising with each brittle rustle of paper. "Those would be here, in these appendices . . . but if memory serves, they never got much out of those mines." The tabs were labeled Klamath 1, Klamath 2, and Klamath 3: one for each of the three shafts Raszer had seen from the outlook. The bent corner of a single stray document hung over the Klamath 3 tab. Kane pulled it out of the file. "What've we got here?" he said under his breath. "I must be getting sloppy in my old age."

Raszer drew closer. "What is it?" he asked. His eye had already scanned the petitioner's data, which located the U.S. offices of the Klamath Co. in Delaware, but the true origin of the document was betrayed by a date stamp with accompanying text in German. The year in the stamp was 1919, and it was initialed "Submitted 4 August."

"It's a standard filing with the Department of Interior for an extension of mineral rights," said Kane. "Except that . . . "

"They're asking for twenty-five years," Raszer said, pouring over the fine print. He pointed to the signature. "And it looks like they got it."

"Looks that way," said Kane, puzzled. He felt the paper up and down between thumb and forefinger like a merchant inspecting fine fabric. "Feels authentic. Looks authentic. Don't know how I coulda missed it, though. This changes everything."

"Maybe you didn't miss it," said Raszer. "What about that signature? Does that look genuine?"

"Genuine enough," said Kane. *'Cept that Mr. Silas R. McCabe apparently didn't know how to use an ink blotter.* "The signature can be tested . . . so can the ink and the paper. But this'll throw a monkey wrench into the tribal claim . . . 'least for a good while."

Raszer took his eyes from the document and lowered them in thought. The whole thing smelled to high heaven: from Kane's suspicion that the file had been tampered with to the hint of a jitter in the smudged signature.

And then he saw it.

It was on the backside of the Klamath 3 file separator, and visible only because a shift in the angle of morning light suddenly caused the windowpane behind the table to become semireflective. It was a fingerprint in black ink, and it looked fresh.

"My, my," he said to himself. "What's this?"

Then something more damning caught his eye.

It was winking at him from the deep well alongside the bookstand. As the breeze tossed the cottonwood leaves outside the window, letting dappled sunlight flicker through, he saw it again. A gleam off polished metal. A gold clip. He leaned in closer.

"You wouldn't happen to have a ruler handy," he asked Kane. "Looks like someone dropped his fountain pen down here. Nice one, too, from the look of it." Using the ruler through trial and error, he managed at last to roll the pen up the side of the trough. The ink in its nib had already gone dry, but the name engraved on its gold-plated barrel was fresh enough. He mouthed the legal litany: Cohn, Gottlieb & Schuyler.

"Gotcha, Fortis," Raszer whispered under his breath.

"Say what?" Kane asked.

"You mentioned Mr. Cohn," Raszer answered, holding up the pen. "This would seem to belong to his firm. Has he or anyone from Cohn, Gottlieb been here recently?"

"Not on my watch," Kane replied. "And it's a one-man office."

"It so happens," said Raszer. "that I need to see Mr. Cohn today anyway. I'll return it to him. You never know . . . it may have sentimental value."

Kane eyed Raszer as he carefully wrapped the pen in a handkerchief. "No prints, huh?" he said. "Are you sure you're not with the FBI?"

"Yeah," said Raszer, with a smile. "I'm sure." He closed the binder and looked up at Kane. "You mentioned more papers you had to ship off to the court. Did you mean other documents?"

"Side agreements dealing with water rights and access roads, and ninety-five odd years of mineral inventory forms, all amounting to the same thing . . . "

"Are there still men working those mines?" Raszer asked, shifting gears. "Those shafts are one of the things we're nervous about. We've had earthquake swarms all through the Cascades."

"If there are," Kane replied, "I sure don't know why. Like I say, those mines never produced. No surprise, really. What the heck they were doin' digging for uranium around here I cannot tell you. Closest deposit is probably Idaho."

"Uranium, you say? Not gold? Not diamonds . . ."

"Believe it or not." Kane shook his head. "If they'd been lookin' for diamonds, uranium would've been a great dodge . . . helluva a lot easier in the 1870s to stake a claim to something nobody thought was worth much. They did, though. The parent firm of the Klamath Company was a big European trading house whose founders were the first to discover uranium ore, way back in the 1700s . . . some-place in Bohemia, named after a saint whose name I can't pronounce. Whether the company still exists, I couldn't tell ya."

Raszer swallowed hard. "*Uranium?* You got all this from the mineral documents?"

"No, no." Kane replied. "It's all in the Journal."

And Raszer silently praised pack rats like Doc Kane who never threw anything away. They were the scribes of the postmodern age.

Kane strode with barely concealed glee to his desk and opened a locked file drawer. He delicately removed a worn, leather-bound journal. It bore the inscription: AUGUSTUS LEEK, U.S. CAVALRY.

"Thought I'd pack this off to the judge, as well," Kane said with a wink, and Raszer read in that wink a fundamental goodness, an expansiveness of spirit that was the sign that he had encountered a guide. "It's not strictly germane," Kane continued, "but I'd be concealing evidence if I held on to it, now, wouldn't I?" He placed the diary in Raszer's hands, laying his own hand on top as if to make a covenant. "You seem like a man looking for truth, Mr. Powers. If you've an hour to spare, you'll learn things you never learn in the history books." Raszer accepted the journal with a nod and carried it to the long table, accepting the chair that Kane thoughtfully brought over for him.

September 12, 1875

The members of the Saint Joachim Fraternity are a strange breed. They dress and comport themselves in public like European aristocracy, and yet a certain baseness of nature reveals itself when they are among their own. This is particularly true with regard to the female sex. One might almost say that they are absent of any-thing like what we call gentility. There is a certain fierceness around the eyes which I have seen before among certain of Morgan's deputies in Denver, and in some of the railroad barons in Wyoming. In spite of their finery and power, they have the look of brutes. They treat the Modoc and Wintu chiefs with contempt, and have even erected a brothel on a Wintu burial ground. They also evince a keen and

*—to my mind—unnatural interest in the human anatomy, subjecting all who
enlist in their service to an examination of the spinal column and posterior section. I fear some skulduggery is afoot. The Modoc chiefs have only recently cooled
the fever of the Ghost Dance mania, and the arrival of these men on their sacred
ground must confirm the darkest forebodings of that shared delirium. We shall all
learn soon enough.*

Leek, Raszer learned, had enlisted in the U.S. Cavalry in Topeka, after
having traveled there from Connecticut. He had risen only to the rank of corporal before his ardor for military service cooled. After two years of ambivalent
participation in a campaign to quell Indian uprisings on the Great Plains, he
found himself garrisoned in Southern Oregon, just outside a Modoc reservation.
It was there that he met Lalek, the aging chief who related to him the tale of
Llao, Skell, and Loha.

From Oregon, Leek and his regiment were ordered south, across the
border into California, where they were to oversee the relocation of the Wintu
tribes from their sacred grounds around Mt. Shasta to a reservation. The only
explanation given was that the Wintu land had been deeded to the American
subsidiary of a powerful European trading house for mineral exploration, and
that the resulting settlement of the area would establish a strong white presence in the midst of tribal territory, a breach in the fabric of the indigenous
culture which would eventually widen and push them out altogether. His
journal continued:

*The Saint Joachim elders have brought in a Dutch scientist who wears a mon-
ocle and keeps a Wintu girl as his concubine. His presence chills my blood. They
are looking for something within the bowels of Mt. Shasta, but I now surmise that
it is not solely precious minerals. Some peculiar vapor has settled upon this
region which gives a man over to unholy apparitions. The place seems truly 'twixt
heaven and earth. I have begun to feel that a phantom history, entirely unknown
to me, lies like a widow's veil across this entire enterprise.*

"Very illuminating," said Raszer, walking the journal back to Kane's care. "I
can't thank you enough."

"Il-lum-in-at-ing," said Kane, eyes widening. "That's the word, all right." He
opened his drawer, then froze, his right ear twitching. "Did you feel that?" he asked.

Raszer took note of a faint but persistent vibration rising into his bones through the soles of his boots. The ramshackle building gave out a groan. As the vibration swelled and hit his pelvic area, he felt a touch of nausea.

"That's an HT, isn't it, Mr. Powers?" Kane asked rhetorically. "Like some humongous snake slithering right beneath your feet."

"Let's hope not," said Raszer, shaking off a shudder. He had no reference by which to gauge a harmonic tremor, but as Mathonwy had said, one wasn't really required. You knew it as you knew the sensation of fear itself. Slowly, the contraction ebbed and the earth was released from its grip. He pictured Kane's python slipping off between the boulders, its tail giving one last twitch.

"You be careful up there, Mr. Powers," said Kane.

Raszer nodded tightly, then left and drove the six miles to Professor Mathonwy's outpost.

12

THE HANGED MAN.

Alienizing means being at ease with the aliens because one is an alien oneself

—Patrick Harpur,
Daemonic Reality: A Field Guide To The Otherworld

I'VE learned some amazing things this morning," Raszer said. "You and me both," replied Mathonwy. "Something triggered a harmonic tremor at about ten o' clock. She's still humming—tapering off, though. There was a landslide up on the Casaval Ridge a few minutes later. If this keeps up, your E-40 may turn out to be more than a bluff. We may be looking at evacuation of a limited area."

"And that would be FEMA's job."

"Ultimately, yes," said Mathonwy, getting up to brew him and Raszer a pot of tea, "I make the initial report, a deputation from Vancouver comes down and certifies my conclusions, and then FEMA takes over. They work through local authorities to make sure privacy rights are respected and no one gets too stirred up about 'men in black' pounding on their bedroom door in the dark of night."

"But I have a day or two before that happens, yes?"

"I'd say so. Volcanos pump themselves up over hundreds, often thousands of years. This one last blew from the Hotlum cone in the 1700s, but before that, you'd have to go back ninety-two hundred years. So, yes—you've got a day or two."

"Professor," Raszer asked, indicating the Department of Homeland Security form lodged in Mathonwy's typewriter. "In view of all this, and your reputation, you sure you're still okay to put your signature on this? I mean . . . I could really foul up the works."

Mathonwy paused to rub his chin. "I'm about due to leave this mountain, Mr. Raszer," he said. "I've done my time and now I feel called to other duties which—if fate sees fit—you and I may talk about one day. If issuing a somewhat pre-emptive E-40 shakes up that scorpion's nest down there, it'll be well worth the flack I'll take for not clearing it with Vancouver. Whatever that militia is up to is utterly at odds with the nature of this place. I don't say this to many for fear they'll write me off, but I'm convinced that this area represents a kind of *singularity*. A terrestrial 'Bermuda Triangle,' if you like. Sit with me for a few moments, and then I'll send you big game hunting with your E-40."

He handed Raszer an aromatic mug of black tea and motioned him onto a stool at his computer workstation. He loaded a file, and with a few swift keystrokes called up a graphical display of the continents in relief, arranged on the globe in their familiar configuration.

"We're going to look at a series of models. Models of the evolution of the planet's surface. All science is about models—always has been. The chaos theorists can even make the I-Ching work as a model." He maneuvered the map rapidly back through time, closing the Gulf of California, joining the Alaskan land bridge to Siberia, wedding Africa to South America, the landforms merging, fragmenting and reforming with the grace and fluidity of colored glass in a kaleidoscope, finally becoming the monolithic landmass known as Pangea. "You'll note," he said, "that as the land splits and the sea rushes in you see recurrent shapes and borders, some of them familiar from everyday objects and sacred designs. Fractals. Now, this is one accepted model of the very distant past. Let's make a subtle change in the fractal geometry and take it forward a few epochs."

Raszer watched with fascination as the waters of the southern Pacific parted as if by Moses' command and an enormous continent heaved up to fill the gap, spanning the distance from Indonesia all the way to the present-day location of the Baja Peninsula.

"This," the professor said with a grin, "is the Lemurian model. Decidedly *not* orthodox science—not yet. It was cooked up by a couple of dynamic systems theorists at UC Santa Cruz and allows for the existence in antiquity of a huge, temperate continent, separated from North America by a narrow sea and an expansive, marshy plain." Raszer glanced at the outline of the North American West Coast and realized that something was missing. "The mountain range which defines the east coast of Lemuria," Mathonwy explained, running his finger along it, "is what is now the Sierra Nevada-Cascade chain. If this model were to be accepted, it'd mean that all of California, Oregon—and a piece of Washington—from Baja to Mount Ranier, were once part of another continent altogether." He double-clicked his mouse and drowned Lemuria, summoning the mighty Pacific plate to shove up what remained of it and weld it to the West Coast, the tangent point more or less precisely at Mt. Shasta.

Raszer studied the map. "You said, *'if'* this model were accepted, right?"

"I did. In hard science terms, this is what is called a counter-factual. Something that—at least in the wonderlands of quantum uncertainty and chaos theory—might have happened with just a few jots and tittles and butterfly wings' difference from what we think *did* happen. For those who like the notion of parallel universes, it actually *may* have happened. We just wouldn't know it, because we're part of the accepted model!"

Raszer felt a dislocation deep inside himself: the silent crash of worlds colliding. The terrifying thought came to him that his daughter might be dead in the world he had once occupied; that only in his reconstructed universe had she survived. Madness.

"Professor Mathonwy," he asked. "Why are you showing me this now?"

"Because, my friend, if you are going to navigate this mountain—and terrains like it—you are going to need to make some allowances. Time, you see, can only be measured by change. If the change is other than what we've been led to believe, then our reckoning of time is altered, too. If there was a Lemuria, then there were probably Lemurians. Our dreams of altered realities . . . our myths—some of them, at least—may be things that have occurred on the other side of a very thin membrane of probability. Under rare circumstances, we find ourselves with one foot over the line."

"Like the shamans," said Raszer.

"That is certainly what they aimed for."

"But are you actually saying that it's possible to . . . 'step into a myth?'"

"I am," Mathonwy said, and paused, "only a middling scientist who dabbles in mythology. I'd give my right arm for the gift of poesy, but I can only speak of probability, and I believe it is probable that something extraordinary occurred on this land, and in some sense is *still* occurring. I can't otherwise explain the fact that the laws of physics seem to break down up here with some regularity. Clocks hold their time . . . stars don't seem to shift positions. I can tell you this, though. Forget about organizing expeditions in search of Lemurian tunnels or lost cities in the Maghreb. If such places exist, they are locatable only by coordinates which lie outside our familiar four dimensions."

"Uh huh," said Raszer, with a sigh. "I'll have to process this . . . " He pointed to the computer screen. "But I will cite this evidence the next time some smartass from the old world claims that California has no history."

"I personally know of only two people up here who seem to have 'processed' it," Mathonwy said. "One—ironically—may be Vreeland himself. The other is a young woman in my class. April Blessing. Amazing girl. She seems genuinely to understand that Shasta is suspended, like some mediating zone, between Heaven and Earth."

A faint smile drifted across Mathonwy's elastic face with the mention of April's name, a smile that gave Raszer just a moment's pause.

"Do you happen to have a 'model,'" he asked, "where the axis of the Earth aligns with the Pole Star and the Arctic is temperate?"

"Ah," said Mathonwy. "You're up on your Aryan folklore. That would, I suppose, be the Hyperborean model. Not handy, but we could always create one. I'd have to adjust the 23.5 degree tilt of the axis to zero and compute the climate change . . . "

"Twenty-three point five degrees?" Raszer wondered aloud.

"The incline of the axis from the ecliptic. That's why the poles are ice-capped."

"Right," Raszer said, wincing. *23.5>0: Fortis Cohn's scribbling in the margins of the Rose note.* "I suppose I should know that. And if it could be restored to true north— to zero. The North Pole would be green?"

"Well, now you're in Jules Verne territory. *The Purchase of the Pole.* It couldn't happen except as the result of some catastrophe of unimaginable proportions. We'd be eliminating earthly life in order to reclaim one questionable piece of real estate."

"Couldn't do it with geo-weapons—or some huge electromagnet?"

"Too imprecise," Mathonwy said. "But if you log on to some of the millenarist Web sites, you'll find people who believe that a slippage of the Earth's crust—a 'Polar Shift'—might cause the planet to flip back to Hyperborean state, and that . . . *that* might be accomplished—*theoretically*—by causing seismic chaos on a global scale."

Raszer shot his host a sidelong glance. "At the risk of presumption, Professor . . . you're not being coy with me, are you? It can't have escaped you that the Military Order of Thule has a polar fixation. Is 'seismic chaos' what you think they're up to?"

"It's hard to imagine they'd have the know-how, much less the financing—which would be unfathomable. They'd be operating on nineteenth century ideas which, though sound in principle, have never crossed the threshold into practice. So, the *ability* . . . doubtful. But the *ambition* . . . that's another thing. They seem possessed of a sort of limited bandwidth mindset that goes back to fellows like Cyrus Teed and John Cleves Symmes. They live *inside* their delusions. And then they proceed to *concretize* them."

"Which is exactly what happens within a cult."

Mathonwy tore the E-40 form from his old Smith-Corona typewriter and re-examined the language. "There are even people," he said, his back still turned, "who believe that the Earth is nearing something called 'Zero Point,' when her rotation will cease . . . and then reverse itself. If that occurred, anything could happen. But—"

"The first day of a new history," said Raszer quietly. "01-01-01."

Mathonwy signed the form with a flourish and cocked a bushy eyebrow.

Raszer took it from him. "Ever hear of a soldier named Augustus Leek?"

"I've used his transcriptions of local Indian legends in my class. Why?"

"I'd like you to tell me," Raszer replied, "what you know about tailbones. I've seen Leek's journal. He suggests that the Klamath Company progenitors had an interest in the human coccyx over a century ago. I've got evidence that they still do."

"May I think out loud?"

"I do my best thinking that way," said Raszer. "Let it rip."

"Lemuria got its name from the lemur, a little bushy-tailed proto-simian which some see as a common link to hominids. Nineteenth-century zoologists postulated a continent to explain why there were lemurs in both Southeast Asia and South America." He paused, tapping his pointed chin. "There is one variant myth that has the Lemurians, whose strengths were intuitive and telepathic, fighting a war over land and resources against a militaristic and physically stronger race . . . for thousands of years after the cataclysm that sunk their continent. The winners . . . well, they're still around. No consensus on what became of the losing Lemurians, other than the New Age notion that they built a network of tunnels under mountain chains." He winked. "Maybe the Klamath Company stewards were 'chasing the tails' of their old enemy."

"Right," said Raszer. "And maybe the war is still on."

Mathonwy gave Raszer a look that he'd seen before on the faces of great teachers and a Zen master or two. It was a sly yet benevolent look that said, "Bravo, son, you've just answered your own question," and it caused Raszer to wonder again just how much Niall Mathonwy really knew.

"By the way," he added. "Have you had any luck with that signal pattern I picked up on your radio?"

"Not yet," Mathonwy replied. "But I'm working on it. I agree with you that it's not Morse Code, but that doesn't mean it's not a cipher. Give me another day."

"I'm lucky to have found you, Professor," said Raszer.

"Luck had nothing to do with it, Mr. Raszer," Mathonwy replied.

At three fifty-seven that afternoon, a brittle ball of tumbleweed came to rest against Raszer's left foot and woke him from a light doze. He was sitting with his back against a twenty-foot-high security fence at the entrance to the M.O.O.T. compound, and had been so positioned since three o'clock, when he had handed the E-40 document to a sentry. Earlier, Mathonwy had faxed the completed form to the president of the Shasta city council for the required signature, and the president, an aging Deadhead, had signed it readily.

On Raszer's arrival at the compound's main gate, the lanky young guards had stiffened. He could not have been greeted with more suspicion if he'd been seeking access to Area 51. The stone-faced sentry had taken the document and told him to wait.

He was about to light a cigarette when he heard a half dozen electronic latches flip open in sequence. The big gate began to slide noisily across its track. He jumped to his feet and faced the humorless recruit, who carried an M-16 and said simply, "Follow me." The perimeter fence was shadowed by a second and shorter one about six feet distant, and the span between them was bridged by thousands of yards of tightly coiled razor wire. Once inside, he was led up a groomed dirt road that cut through a rugged meadow dotted with sunflowers and alive with hummingbirds. He could see the brown roofs of the compound buildings over the ridge, the satellite dishes looming beyond.

A short while earlier, if there'd been no mishap, April had entered the more restricted east gate for her "tour," and was now presumably in the company of Bronk Vreeland. Raszer couldn't shake the uneasiness he felt about it, and was pretty sure—notwithstanding April's implication—that it went deeper than jealousy. Something had gone off course. Ten years earlier, he'd detected his own wife's betrayal by seeing another man's attentions spelled out in the flush of her cheeks and the revival of her libido. Although April would deny it, Vreeland was working her. Somehow, he had sniffed out and embodied the deeply ambivalent feelings she had about her father.

They arrived at the weathered plank porch of the HQ, and Raszer was then escorted past a recreation room well stocked with videogame consoles and virtual warriors and into a makeshift "intake" office where he was instructed to sit.

A moment later, Fortis Cohn walked stiffly into the room with a uniformed older man and immediately staked out a position as far from Raszer as the confines of the office would allow. Raszer rose and offered his hand.

"Gary Powers," he announced. "U.S. Geological Survey." Only the older man accepted the handshake, albeit with some distaste.

"Latimer J. Bloch," he said. "Director of Security and sovereign citizen of the California Free State. This is Mr. Cohn, our legal counsel."

"Pleased to meet you both," Raszer said. "Quite a spread you've got. How's it feel to live next door to Vesuvius?"

Neither man replied.

"Let's not waste time," Fortis said brusquely. "I agreed to see you because I'd like to see what evidence you have to justify this 'alert.' I happen to know that this mountain has been stable for over two hundred years and it doesn't even make the bottom ranking of your agency's list. My clients would have every right to think that this constitutes just one more instance of federal overreach, and that your request to survey the property represents an unwarranted invasion of private property."

"Fair enough, Mr. Cohn," Raszer replied. "We've issued the warning because your client's property lies directly in the path of one of the most volatile slide zones on this mountain. They don't call it Avalanche Gulch for nothing. Just this morning, six tons of debris came crashing down the Casaval Ridge, and our meters are showing a fourfold increase in the usual seismic activity. If this keeps up, it won't take a full-scale eruption to cause you serious problems, but if Mt. Shasta does blow, bear something in mind . . . you do remember Mt. St. Helens, right?"

"Don't be coy, Mr. Powers," Cohn said.

Raszer could see that Fortis was coiled, his defense flipped to offense as a matter of both legal technique and personal temperament. "When the North side of St. Helens went, three quarters of a cubic mile of shattered rock shot down the mountain in a wall more than twelve hundred feet high. That's what'll be on top of you if the south side of Shasta goes, and that's where we've got activity. Now, the old Klamath mine shafts go straight into the mountainside. They're a window into the volcano's guts. By allowing me to make a routine examination for new fissures, we can probably eliminate the possibility of eruption and downgrade the warning.

An E-40 is standard anytime sulfur dioxide levels shoot above normal range, but it's probably nothing. If you send me away empty-handed, I'll have to file a non-cooperation report."

Raszer had delivered the warning in the dispassionately genial tone of an airline pilot, but with a difference. His eyes had not left Fortis Cohn since the men had entered the room. It wasn't a psych-out. It was his way of connecting with his quarry on another level altogether. He had no time to waste.

"This is private commercial property, Mr. Powers," Fortis said, nervously adjusting his glasses. "There are certain proprietary concerns. We are also, as you may know, facing a lawsuit. Is there some way we can persuade you to accept our good faith assurances that the mines are stable, so that you can, uh, feel secure in lifting this alert?" He shot Bloch a look, and the older man nodded. "Can we come to terms?"

"I'm sorry," said Raszer. "You're not hearing me. I'll need to take a look at those shafts, and file a report by tonight. We don't operate on our own anymore. Not since 9-11. I'm answerable to FEMA and the entire Homeland Security apparatus."

Fortis raised his palm. "Hold on, Mr. Powers," he said, and turned to Bloch meaningfully. "Let's get the Commander."

"Thanks, guys," said Raszer, with a smile. "Oh, by the way, Mr. Cohn . . . I'm just guessing on this . . . could be a coincidence . . . but I was in the Recorder's office this morning. Did you happen to lose a fountain pen?" Fortis blinked slowly as Raszer drew the handkerchief from his pocket and unwrapped it to display the souvenir he'd been forced to leave behind. "Cohn, Gottlieb," he said. "Senior partner, eh?"

"No," said Cohn, only momentarily stung. He gave the pen a perfunctory glance. "I'm not . . . and that's not one of mine. You're correct about the name, but there must be a thousand pens like that in California. My f-father—he's the senior partner—had them made up as gifts years ago and sent them to every government office in the state." He paused. "But I'll be happy to t—"

"That's okay," said Raszer, rewrapping the pen and pocketing it. "Finders keepers, then, I guess. You asked about 'evidence,' Mr. Cohn . . . of the volcanic activity, that is. Would you like to see it first-hand?" Fortis was unresponsive, and Raszer forged ahead. "Come up to the shack tonight if you like. I can show you some things it may be in your interest to know. Things you may want to inform your principals of. And the truth is, I wouldn't mind the company . . . the professor can get a little, well . . . Anyhow, we're here to help. And whatever we discuss is . . . what's the legal term . . . *sub rosa*."

He gave the subtlest of accents to the second of the two Latin words, and let it hang in the air like a scent. If he'd played it right, it was a scent Fortis Cohn would come sniffing after.

April came to with the whisper of tall grass in her ears, having temporarily forgotten what had triggered her loss of consciousness. She felt weightless and cradled, and even after she realized that Vreeland was carrying her, she did not immediately protest. He was murmuring something to her, low and urgent, and curiosity got the better of her alarm.

"Oh, yeah," he whispered. "You're the one, all right. I knew it in my blood."

Then she remembered. She'd been in the furthest removed of the satellite shacks with Vreeland and a pair of young radio operators when an intermittent, code-like signal had come in and they'd trained the big dish on a lenticular cloud that was sitting directly over Shasta's cone. Suddenly, Vreeland had gone Old Testament, pumping the air with his fist and exhorting his men to lock in on the faint waveform before it escaped them again. They had worked feverishly to clean up the signal, their backs to her, forgetting entirely that she was there, listening, framed in the door of the tiny trailer. She had gone to her knees when for ten seconds the signal stabilized, sending current cycling up and down her spine like charged neon. When she heard the voice—the song—everything had gone to limitless black, within which she had seen herself suspended. Now the experience was fading into that place in the subconscious where the memory of miracles is stored.

Vreeland set her down gently on the steps of the main porch. She dropped her head into the folds of her skirt and rested. After a few moments, she became aware of huddled voices nearby, and he left her side to add his distinctly gravelly timbre to the murmur. Cautiously, she looked up and saw—not fifteen feet away—her partner, Stephan Raszer. He was engaged in sober dialogue with Fortis Cohn, an older man whose uniform bore some emblems of seniority, and now Vreeland, who was reviewing a document Cohn had handed him. How Raszer had talked his way through the gates was an object of wonderment for April, though it ought not to have surprised her at this stage. He wore roles as easily as most men wore baseball caps, and he carried in his modest but persistent bearing a sense of having unrestricted entree to every private party. She'd seen him play a small town lawyer and a faith healer with equal facility. Now he was a volcanologist, and from all appearances, a worried one.

Raszer looked to be explaining to Vreeland the particulars of the document, while waving a sheaf of seismograms. An acute panic suddenly gripped April, the shame of a student who has forgotten her homework. Her mission was incomplete. She'd tranced out on the radio signal and had failed to deliver her 'it's Fortis or me' ultimatum, the dare she'd accepted from Raszer. She so badly wanted to please him, to erase his doubts. In her own way—there was no longer any question—she wanted to *be* him, and for April, this merging of identities was the deepest expression of love.

Lowering her head, she gazed at Raszer through the crook of her arm in a manner that not even a fool could misread. It was three seconds too late when she realized that Bronk Vreeland was watching her, and that Raszer was watching Bronk. He caught her eye fleetingly, but long enough to deliver a reproach with his eyebrows. She knew at that moment she'd made one of those mistakes you can't take back. Vreeland squinted and rubbed his chin, then turned back to the huddle and nodded his grudging approval of something that had been proposed. April took a deep breath.

"Okay, then," she heard Raszer say. "I'll wait for your decision. But I can't postpone this beyond noon tomorrow." Fortis nodded assent, but once again ignored Raszer's offered handshake. He's trying to prove his mettle to Bronk, she thought. The group broke up, and Raszer was returned to the gate by the sentries. Vreeland ambled over to the porch, kicking a small rock off to his left and raising a cloud of pink dust.

"Feeling better?" he asked her, but there was a chill in his voice.

"Back to earth, I think," she replied. "That was pretty intense. No wonder you've been up nights if *that* voice is in your head."

"You remember what you said?"

"Uh-oh. I hope nothing embarrassing."

"You said . . . at first I thought it was 'things in Attica.' Then you said it again, and I heard 'She sings in Africa.'" Vreeland paused. "So?"

"The sibyl speaks," she bluffed, "but the wise men interpret." She hadn't a clue.

"Right," he said. He gave a nod over his shoulder. "You know that guy? That Fed who was just here? You were staring at him like a general's wife."

"You're the only general here," she said. "I study people. That's how I get a fix on them. I studied you, didn't I?"

"I guess you did," Vreeland said guardedly. "Maybe I just didn't see it."

Le Serpent Rouge was located on an old stagecoach road, ten miles east of I-5 on County AA, halfway between Mount Shasta and Dunsmuir to the south, and probably as safe a rendezvous as could be found. It was run by a husband and wife, refugees from L.A., who spent their summers in Provence and had brought back a crusty little French chef from one of their wine tours. The restaurant's specialty was handmade sausage of every imaginable variety: sage-apple-pork, chicken with lavender and wild fennel, veal with oregano and pink peppercorns, all grilled to juicy, skin-popping perfection over an open fire of mesquite—or, when the moon was down, the forbidden fuel of seasoned California live oak.

Raszer had arranged to meet April here for an early supper, leaving the professor to await the militia's response but wanting to be back before too long—just in case Fortis Cohn decided to deliver it personally. April had taken a taxi, ordering it to wait, and he Mathonwy's Yugo—both for some measure of anonymity. Over dinner, he planned to inform her that her part in the mission had concluded, and he was expecting stiff resistance. April's momentum was a potent force. She always seemed to want to keep going until a brick wall stopped her. Recklessness and dedication were not separable in her. But Raszer feared that any further dalliance with Bronk Vreeland might backfire. He'd already fouled her idyllic life in Mt. Shasta by involving her this deeply, and by this time tomorrow, he expected to have ninety percent of what he needed to lever Fortis Cohn out. That was what he'd been paid to do. The loftier goal of breaking the militia and outing its mysterious patrons, the Halgadom Fraternity, might prove to be a lifetime's work. Nonetheless—and not least because she had gotten to him—he hoped to gather enough evidence to allow Lt. Borges to pin the murder of Christopher Rose on the Military Order of Thule, with Abel Cohn's son as the star witness for the prosecution. That would set them back for a while. To hope for anything more was vanity.

He waited for April on the secluded rear patio, at a picnic table that had been painted Cote d'Azur blue. Not far away, an electronic bug zapper, suspended from a locust tree, sizzled intermittently in odd concert with the crackling mesquite fire on the open brick hearth.

April arrived, carrying a Fed Ex letter that had been delivered to the motel. She took her seat opposite him, set the envelope on the table between them, and rested her chin on folded hands.

"Hmm. I wonder who 'R.' could be . . . " she mused. "From the handwriting, I'd guess it's not a business associate." Raszer glanced at the return address.

"Now who's jealous," he chided. "It's from my other sibyl . . . Madame Rey. A strictly professional relationship."

"And ours isn't?"

"Not after last night."

"Well," she said, pushing the letter to him. "It must be important. Open it."

"All right," said Raszer, and began tearing open the seal. He studied April's bearing and wondered if she knew what was coming. She had fixed herself up in a long black skirt and a loose-knit cotton sweater that lay revealingly against her bosom. Through the weave of the undyed fabric, he could make out the cream brown of her nipples, and found it difficult to resist reaching for her hand, particularly because he knew that she wanted him to. And also because it was trembling.

"You look especially beautiful tonight," he said.

"Thanks, Wart," she replied. "So do you."

"And I'll bet you know exactly what you want . . . to eat, that is. Let's get an order in. I should get back to the shack before nine."

"Right," she said, patting the closed menu. "I'll have the veal sausage with wild fennel. How about you?"

He set Madame Rey's letter aside and examined the menu.

"Let's see," he replied, running his finger down the list. "Duck sausage with juniper berry confit for me."

"Good choice," she said, collecting his menu and handing it off to the waiter along with their order. "Now open it. I'll bet she finished translating the verse."

He ordered a bottle of Freemark Abbey Zinfandel, then removed the folded correspondence. A look of consternation crossed his face.

"What?" said April. "Bad news?"

Raszer slipped it back into the envelope. "She still hasn't cracked the third verse, except for what she thinks is a reference to Alexander—"

"Alexander . . . the Great?"

"Not sure. And something about 'sleeping knowledge.'"

"Yeah," said April. "And?"

"Well . . . she has this notion that the Hebrew letters are a sort of acrostic for a tarot spread, and that it's *my* spread . . . "

"Wow." Unlike Monica, April did not find the utter imponderability and ludicrous coincidence of a cipher in Sanskrit—a language dead for more than two thousand years—relating to his present destiny to be cause for skepticism. She only smiled and said, "That would make you mythical. A man out of time."

"I'm out of time, all right. She's gotten to the seventh card—the future—and it's Death." The wine arrived and was poured, viscous and berry red. "Let's drink," he said.

They toasted their mission and drank before he spoke. "So, what went haywire this afternoon? You were on me like a laser beam. I'm pretty sure Vreeland caught it."

"I'm sorry," she said. "I fucked up. I wasn't thinking straight. He took me into one of their listening posts and I passed out after I heard . . . I think I heard the radio signal that's been jamming their airwaves. You wouldn't believe it."

"What is it?" he asked. "Who's transmitting it?"

"I don't know. But it spooked him. He really believes he's facing an enemy, and it's more than just the usual right-wing boogeymen. All this stuff about 'rodents' and 'the Underground.' It's not metaphorical for him." She sipped her wine and gave Raszer an apprehensive look, as if fearing he might judge her crazy after she said what she was about to say. "What I heard, before I tranced out, was a woman singing. Beautiful but sad, almost like those Portugese ballads women sang for their men at sea . . . "

"Fado," Raszer said.

"That's it. It means fate, right?"

"Yeah."

"Except this was in some more ancient language. Really primal. It went straight into my brain cells, and I just lost it."

"I'd give anything to know if it's the same voice Madame Rey heard, nuts as that sounds. Mathonwy says that these 'earth frequencies' . . . these Schumann Resonances can be used as carrier waves for radio. That they can get into the brain through the limbic system."

He studied her for a beat and became aware that his pulse had quickened with something that felt almost like fear. It might, he thought, be the same kind of wary reverence people must once have felt for those touched by the divine: the wariness that had given the word *taboo* its original meaning.

"Do you remember what happened last night . . . when we made love?" He'd noticed the delicate gold chain she wore around her neck, and presumed it held a cross.

"No," she answered. "I don't."

"You went away," he said. "A long way. It was a scary place. You really don't remember?"

"It happens, you know," she said. "After sex . . . "

He shook his head. "No. It was more than that. You were *with* someone . . . "

"Yeah," she said, in barely more than a whisper. Her mouth had gone dry. "I'm sorry, Raszer. I started with you. I wanted *you*. But then all of a sudden *he* was behind me . . . inside me. Inside my . . . And then it all got shifted around. I wasn't me and you weren't Bronk, but I was—" A look of terror passed over her face. "I was *her*. I was Ori."

He regarded her tenderly. "You were doing the work you were born to do." He leaned forward and touched her fingers, then sat back with a sigh. "Don't be sorry."

They watched silently for a few minutes as the chef expertly turned their sausages over coals that radiated warmth even to where they sat, ten feet away. Raszer steeled himself with a gulp of wine and edited his speech again. Then he threw it away.

"April," he began. "I've got to pull you . . . " There was a small combustion over by the locust tree as a large moth dove into blue fire, sending off sparks and a soft hiss. The sausage arrived a moment later, steaming and perfectly blistered, and the waiter set the hot platters down with a practiced little spin. Raszer observed, and nodded his approval, but April's eye had not left him, and her expression went from stricken to cold.

"Go ahead," she said, tonelessly. "You're pulling me out . . . "

He raised his eyes to the sparks still falling from the bug zapper, then looked at her gravely. "You don't get it, do you? We're *not* mythical. And the rightness of what we're doing is only assured so long as we keep our trust with the man who hired us. He's not financing some vision quest, and he's not staking a gambling junket."

She looked daggers at him. "You're the one who proposed I go for broke with Vreeland."

"Maybe I was wrong," he said. "He's knocked you off balance. You're not centered enough for—"

"Fuck you," she said, and pushed away her plate.

"April," Raszer said softly. "You miss one mark . . . make one more telltale move, and you will find yourself a hostage, or worse." He set down his fork and felt the damp drop heavily from the night sky. "I can't let that happen." She studied him from the shadows just outside the penumbra of the candlelight, gauging her next move.

"We were through this, Raszer," she said. "We had a new game plan."

"I know, April, but you didn't follow it. I would bet my life—and I may have to—that Vreeland suspects me. All it will take is for evidence to filter up from L.A. that connects me with that skinhead, and I will be cooked, and so, probably, will Fortis Cohn." He paused. "I have—at best—one day to make a play for him."

"And I'm the only one who can run interference for you," she insisted.

"Not against Vreeland, you can't. I didn't bank on his weak spot. A wounded predator is always more dangerous. Sure, I expected him to be dazzled by you, but I did not expect him to want you to be the mother of his child. I also didn't expect him to . . . that you would be . . . " He stopped himself. "Shit."

"That I would get so much into my role?" She leaned forward, and as she did, something shiny—whatever was at the end of her chain—slipped from the V-neck of her sweater and caught the light for just an instant. She closed her fingers around it and discreetly dropped it back inside, but her sleight-of-hand was not quite practiced enough. "Raszer," she pleaded. "C'mon, man. I wanna nail this motherfucker. We can't settle for taking Fortis as a prisoner of war. One more trip, Raszer . . . let me go back in."

Raszer watched her eyes grow moist and felt himself soften. It was wrong to have drawn her so far in only to deny her the kill she wanted so badly, but that was just the problem: she wanted it too much. His eyes went to the neckline of her sweater, where her fingers remained curled. "Is that new?" he asked. "The necklace? I didn't think you went in for jewelry."

"Oh," she said, suddenly short of breath. "This?" She shrugged gamely and then displayed a gold medallion roughly the size of a quarter. "Vreeland gave this to me just before I left today. It's his emblem. His top guys wear them, too. I thought I should accept . . . play along. I mean—" Raszer reached across the table and gently took the little disc in hand, running his thumb over its embossed surface. It was a depiction of a warrior on horseback, spearing a serpent to the ground.

"He gave you his fraternity pin, April." He gave her a little smile and let go of the medallion, but his levity was less than genuine and she knew it. "You're an amazing woman . . . that you got to him so fast, but I—" He left it to her to finish, and prayed that she would. When she did, he felt a volatile admixture of admiration and doubt.

"Yeah," she said, under her breath. "You're right. I can't go up there again. I didn't expect him to be . . . who he is. I can usually handle fanatics just fine, but this guy . . . he's like my shadow. And I can't handle that the way *you* can." Raszer drew a breath and held it in, hoping her self-assessment would take. His relief did not last long. "But," she added, "I'm supposed to dance tonight. If I don't show, he'll know something's up."

"No way," he said. "You'll be too self-conscious to be convincing. Call in sick. Get your friend Flo to sub for you. You'd have every right to be shook up after this afternoon. I'll put you on a plane tomorrow and you'll stay at my place with Monica until this blows over. Is there someplace other than the motel or your cabin you can crash tonight?"

"I'll stay at Flo's place. In town. Her boyfriend's a Hell's Angel."

"You've made the difference, April," Raszer said. "No bullshit." He gave her a real smile this time. "If things go well tomorrow, we'll have Fortis turned, and that's no small setback for Vreeland. We can both watch it unravel over the next few years. Give me Flo's address and phone number . . . I'll call you from the shack."

Raszer stepped back from the taxi after paying the driver, and stood at the edge of the gravel parking lot as it pulled off. He waited—as he always did when women left in taxis—for her to turn around. He wanted to see her face shine through the rear window, a little smile, a promise of some tomorrow. But she didn't turn, and it stung him. It stung him and it worried him deeply, because her resignation had come too fast, too easily.

The taillights were soon consumed by the rural dark, the engine's noise muffled by the thick pine forest, and there was nothing but him and the crickets. That, and a dizzying melancholy. If he'd listened to his heart, he'd have taken her in his arms and hung on for dear life, because she was him. She was his tarot. By not claiming her there and then, he feared he'd given both of them over her to an altogether different fate.

13

DEATH.

BREE Donahue lowered her dark glasses and peered into the hospital room, finding Raja fully dressed and sitting on the edge of the bed with her discharge papers. She gave three little knocks on the doorframe, though it was quite clear that Raja had recognized her in spite of the auburn wig.

"Oh," Bree said. "You're dressed." She hovered like a hummingbrd at the door.

"They're releasing me for good behavior," said Raja with a droll expression, and motioned her visitor in. She gave the actress a once-over. "The disguise isn't very convincing. How did you know I was here?"

"I came back to your shop and saw the 'Closed' sign and the police tape. Then I asked around on the strip. I finally found a cop who gave me the scoop in exchange for an autograph. I *really* wanted to see you." Hearing no objection, she invited herself in and sat beside Raja, setting her oversized handbag on the bedside chair. "He also told me," she continued, "that the guy who attacked you made bail."

Raja's expression darkened. "But he killed a man. How could they—"

"This is L.A., sweetie. They'll keep you in the tank for a DUI but bail you for a murder. Anyhow, I had my lawyer check. They said there was insufficient evidence."

Raja shook her head. "Then it's happening," she said.

Bree blinked. "What's happening?"

"I don't have much time," the gypsy answered. "That man has a mission."

"Back when I was doing soaps," said Bree, "I had a boyfriend on the vice squad. He told me there was one rule for survival in L.A.: no matter who you are, always carry the phone number of one really powerful person in your pocket. I'll bet you anything this guy has connections. This movie I was attached to—"

"I need to warn him," said Raja, highly distracted. She closed her eyes and put a hand to her temple. Her head was pounding.

"Are you okay? Are you still having those brain storms, because I am. I don't think I've slept three hours a night since I saw you. Humming, humming . . . all the time."

"They had me so full of drugs here, all I did was sleep. I've lost precious time." Raja turned to the actress and touched her hand. "Do you have a car?"

"I have my boyfriend's Hummer," Bree said. "If you can call that a car."

"That isn't a motorcycle, is it?" Raja asked warily.

Bree smiled. "Let me help you with your things."

As they passed the nurse's station, Raja noticed that the folding chair, which had been occupied for three days by her LAPD chaperone, was empty. Evidently, her V.I.P. status was no longer active. Nor had Stephan Raszer's pretty assistant come to see her off as had been planned. *Or had it been planned?* Raja was suddenly disoriented, and as they reached the elevators, she turned to the actress.

"What day is this?" she asked.

"Thursday," Bree answered.

"Then I'm off a day," said Raja. "Ah, well." She had last seen Monica two days before, when giving her the letter for Stephan Raszer. She'd told her she would call on Friday morning, but they were letting her go a day early. "Maybe there *is* time," she said.

Once they had left the confines of Hollywood Presbyterian Hospital and stepped into the parking structure, Bree became even more animated. "So, about the movie . . . the part . . . " she began. "I turned it down. Too creepy. And like you said, I—"

"I'm not sure I should be giving career advice—" But Bree was off and running.

"—have a better role coming. I'm sure you were right. But it gets weird. The producers filed an injunction, saying I breached a verbal contract—which I did not—and this jerk of a lawyer is putting the squeeze on. So I call my agent and I'm like—'get this fucking guy off me'—and she says, 'you're not gonna believe this, Bree, but an intern who read scripts for Christopher Rose'—the guy who got killed, you know?" Raja nodded. "Anyhow, this little bootlicker tells my agent 'you better warn your client . . . these people have resources.'" Bree paused to gauge Raja's atten-tiveness, then continued. "Resources. I'm like—what the fuck is that supposed to mean? Well, I'll tell you what it means. These lowlife Buzz Brothers who brought the script to Rose are into this Scientology meets the Sopranos crap and he knows this because he monitored Rose's calls and they had their hooks into him, too."

She broke stride for a moment to fish out her car keys. They had arrived at the car. "So I freaked," she concluded, disarming the security system with a series of robust chirps and opening the door for Raja. "And now, I don't know what to do." Raja stood stock still and considered how to board the vehicle with any degree of dignity.

"If you're going to drive something like this," she observed, "why bother with the disguise?"

As they were leaving the garage bound west, Monica rolled up to the gate of the visitor's lot in her Toyota and took a ticket. She was there to check on Madame Rey as she'd promised Raszer she would, and to dispatch any new progress on the decryption.

A few minutes later, Bree made a tentative left turn onto Western Avenue, heading north into Koreatown. Although not far off course, she was lost, and Madame Rey, who didn't drive and seldom left her Hollywood enclave, was no help. Bree, straddling two lanes, came to a stop at Third Street and innocently lowered the darkly tinted window to ask directions of an Asian couple in a Daewoo.

She called down from her commanding height at the steering wheel. "Excuse me! Do you—" The tiny Asian woman and her equally tiny husband reacted in alarm and rolled the windows up snug. "Oh, fuck," Bree said. "They think we're gangbangers."

"Ohh," Raja said with dull surprise. A third car—a big van, blacked out like an unmarked S.W.A.T. bus—had appeared from nowhere on their right, hugging the curb and nearly taking the mirror off. Bree turned to react with a movement that Raja perceived as like time moving through glycerine. She lifted her hand to shield her eyes from the glare off the van, and Raja heard the turquoise beads rattle on her bracelet like a snake in the brush. It all seemed familiar to Raja, even the rat-tling of the beads.

The man at the wheel was bulky and of non-descript white, ethnic stock. But from behind his blunt profile emerged a face Raja knew all too well.

The first bullet shattered Bree's wrist and sheared the bracelet in two. The second bullet entered Raja's temple just above the fine arc of her cheekbone. The third and final bullet shattered the safety glass and passed through Bree Donahue's left eye socket, emerging from the back of her skull in a pink mist of blood, bone, and tissue.

The van tore around the corner, hopping the curb and leaving a cloud of carbon monoxide, while the Hummer rolled silently and unstoppably through the intersection and into the plate glass window of a convenience store. In the cessation of time that followed the last beat of her heart, Raja saw mountainous terrain open to receive her.

Raszer had pulled off the road halfway up the Everett Highway and turned on the dome light. The FedEx envelope on the empty passenger seat had been too compelling, and the prodding of his curiosity too insistent. And then there had been the voice, which he now heard through the words of Madame Rey's letter.

Dear Stephan,

Before I tell you what I must, I ask you to promise me that you will keep this letter among your things and come back to it from time to time. If I have learned anything in my life, it is that prophecies—even the cheap sort that I offer —rarely mean what they first appear to mean. As this will probably have to serve as my last testament, it pleases me to think that it may provide in the future some wisdom that is lost on the present. I don't mean to sound like a melodramatic old gypsy, but I have been feeling for some time that my way of seeing has passed away along with dance halls and discreet love affairs. Intuition is not good enough when information is so easy to come by. I have laid your tarot in the old European spread of nine. I cannot prove that it is yours, but I am as sure of it as I am of my own father's name. You are known to me in some way that only memory can explain. The seventh card is the immediate future, and it is Death. In this case, I believe it is correct to read it as it lays, but don't be afraid. It is not your death. You will live for many more years and will one day find what you seek, though it may pass from your hands as quickly as it came into them. The eighth card is the High Priestess, and it is she who will light your path, though sometimes only with the pale moon. She is the meeting of opposites within you, but do not mistake her shadows for your soul. The final card is The Hermit. I wish, dear Stephan, that I could give you The

*Sun, The Star, The World, but these endings are for people who can be satisfied,
and you will never be. Take heart. You will be alone but never lonely. Many will pass
through your gate and be wiser for it. I am glad to have known you. In friendship,*

Raja

Along with her letter, she had enclosed the original note given to her by
Christopher Rose. In red pencil, Raja had written out her last and best translation
of the poem's second stanza. On the face of it, little new was revealed. Raszer
folded the pages together and slipped them into the inside pocket of his ski jacket.
Switching off the dome light, he put Mathonwy's Yugo into gear and pulled off the
rocky shoulder onto the narrow highway, ascending toward the USGS outpost at
the rate of a thousand feet per mile.

He cranked down his window to speed the defrosting of the windshield. From
the thick fog beyond the shoulder, he heard the howl of something more deep-
chested than a coyote, and shivered. He dropped the clattering Yugo into second
gear and negotiated another of a seemingly endless series of ice-glazed switchbacks. It was getting damned cold. A spray of ice crystals gusted in the open
window and stung his sunburned cheek. He hit the snow line at eight thousand
feet, and ten minutes later rolled into Mathonwy's long gravel driveway. A light
was burning in the window of his hut. It promised a moment's warmth before the
real cold came down.

"I've succeeded in stirring up my superiors with our E-40," Mathonwy said,
once they'd settled in with mugs of brandy-spiked tea. "There's talk of sending a
team down from Vancouver to look at the lava dome. Sooner than I thought."

"How soon?" Raszer asked.

"I'd say you have thirty-six hours at best," the professor replied. "Per regula-
tions, I've faxed copies of the E-40 to the county clerk and the chief of police.
They're not likely to get alarmed unless it's upgraded to an alert. People up here
are very slow to rouse. But we haven't a great deal of time. I doubted it at first, but
now I'm not at all certain that this volcano isn't waking up from her long snooze."

"How does she look today?"

"So far, I see little evidence that the cone is bulging. That's good. What's disturbing is that we are experiencing a lot of seismic activity, some of it quite
shallow. And we have incredible magnetic field strength. If you start seeing the
cone spitting lightning bolts like Mr. Tesla's coil, it's time to beat a retreat."

A thought fired into his brain. "Speaking of Tesla, you said this morning that it was conceivable that earthquakes could be artificially triggered. Don't the books say that Tesla experimented with some kind of seismic howitzer out on the tip of Long Island?"

"Yes and no. It was a potential application of his 'magnifying transmitter.' He called it telegeodynamics. He once nearly leveled a few blocks of New York City with it. Tesla said that, if he wished, he could 'split the planet in two,' but he loved to bait the press. Ever since, there've been rumors of Tesla Cannons which deliver huge 'slugs' of electromagnetism and could make geo-terrorism the next horror, but I—"

There was a sharp rap on the corrugated tin door. Mathonwy rose to open it, motioning Raszer to stay seated. Out in the cold stood Fortis Cohn, wearing a wool overcoat, accompanied by a pudgy young militiaman with an acne-scarred face. The two men—as different as could be in physical make-up, yet somehow joined in cause—made Raszer think of medieval grotesques by Hieronymous Bosch.

"Come in, come in," Mathonwy said. "It's bitter out there! Mr. Cohn, I presume?"

"You want me to wait outside, Mr. Cohn?" Blottmeier asked, the respect of rank restored to his tone. The professor waited on the attorney's response.

"No," Fortis replied, waving him off. "Go back to the compound. I'll call for you when we're done here." He stepped into the cabin and shut the door without turning.

"Mr. Cohn," Raszer began, "Niall Mathonwy, Senior Analyst, US Geological Survey. Professor, Fortis Cohn, legal counsel to the, uh . . . our neighbors down the hill."

"Please make yourself comfortable, Mr. Cohn," said the Professor, "if that's possible in this ice box. Tea? A bit of brandy?"

"Yes, tea," Cohn replied, surveying the hut. "Maybe a splash of brandy."

Fortis kept his coat buttoned. Raszer had asked Mathonwy to allow the coals in his wood stove to burn down to ash, the better to tempt Fortis with the false warmth of alcohol.

"Ahh," said Mathonwy. "I'll have one with you. Gary, will you be our bartender while I show Mr. Cohn the instruments?"

While Mathonwy introduced Fortis to the array of devices, describing the function of each with as much technical jargon as he could muster, Raszer stepped to the Professor's makeshift bar, his back to the room. He brewed their guest a cup of herb tea, poured in a shot of brandy, and then from the tea tin withdrew a pencil-thin plastic vial containing thirty milligrams of the muscle relaxant Temestal. It was tasteless, odorless, and 100 percent soluble. He sprinkled about an eighth of a teaspoon into Cohn's drink. It was not Raszer's intention to knock his guest out, only to put him at ease and loosen his tongue.

"To your health," he said, setting the steaming mug before his guest. "And to good neighbors."

Fortis wrapped his cold hands around it and took a sip. "So," he began, drawing the folded E-40 form from his inside pocket. "You'll be happy to know that we've agreed to let you take a look at one of the mine shafts tomorrow, on the condition that you advise us in advance of any consequent action. I think we have that right. After you've satisfied yourself, we expect you to rescind the alert promptly, or we are prepared to go to court and ask for an injunction prohibiting further harrassment pending a show of compelling scientific evidence."

"We can, of course," Mathonwy said, "give you no guarantee. But, believe me, my superiors have no desire for a confrontation with your people. Allow them the minor victory of examining your mine shafts, and I'm quite certain that you'll win the war."

Fortis gulped down the rest of his tea. "How do you people stay warm up here?" he said, shivering.

"A straight brandy this time, perhaps?" Mathonwy asked. "Believe me, you see why those St. Bernards carried cognac after you've been up here for a while."

The lawyer accepted. It seemed to Raszer that Fortis might, in spite of his loyalties, be the tiniest bit relieved to be out of Bronk Vreeland's shadow and in the company of less resolute souls. He was fidgety, but that was good. The more nervous he was, the more he'd drink, and the stronger the Temestal would come on. While filling his glass, the professor offered his own assessment of Mt. Shasta's condition, and Fortis sat surprisingly rapt, particularly when Mathonwy spoke of electromagnetic activity within the mountain. Mathonwy's professorial authority and scientific wizardry were proving very useful. As obliquely as he could, Raszer sized up his quarry.

Fortis Cohn was barely five foot-six, and had a face like a doll's. Despite his thirty-six years of life, he had not one wrinkle of character, and yet this very blankness suggested—if not the potential for good—at least a certain malleability. It was essential that Raszer find something in Fortis he could reach, and he found it in the downturned corners of his mouth. There was a boy there who'd wanted to be in the club but hadn't quite passed the initiation. As Mathonwy talked on, drowning his pupil in the arcana of volcanology, Fortis began to wobble and list slightly to the left. Raszer moved in smoothly to replenish his brandy, then returned to his place on the bunk beside the stove and waited for the lecture to conclude and the two men to take their seats.

For a few moments, he avoided Fortis's eye and stared at the floorboards, rubbing his chin and absently swishing the watered brandy in his mug. Then, as if seized by undeniable impulse, he looked his man straight in the eye and went for it.

"There's something I can't figure out, Mr. Cohn," Raszer blurted. "You're Jewish, right? Cohn is a Jewish surname." Cohn blinked but said nothing. "So am I, by the way—on my mother's side, which is the stamp of authenticity, I'm told. You seem like a bright guy, too. How can you bunk with those fascist thugs down there? How can you ally yourself with an anti-Semite like Vreeland?"

"You're being a little presumptuous, Mr. Powers," Fortis replied icily, with the barest hint of a mean drunk's slur. "I don't think we've discussed my religious affiliation, and as for my name, well . . . In any case, Commander Vreeland is an agent of the sort of change that will preserve America for the most enterprising, the most able—"

"You're right," said Raszer. "About my presumption, that is. I was out of line. To each his own, I guess . . . even thugs are entitled to lawyers, right? I shouldn't even assume that you buy his spiel, although it sounds as if you do. Your dad—he's the Cohn who runs the firm, right? The one on the pen . . . Gottlieb, Schuyler, whatever?"

"My s-stepfather," Fortis told Raszer, throwing him an unexpected curve. "My real father was D-Dutch. The great-grandson of the scientist who first staked a claim on this mountain."

"Your father is Rupert Voorhees?" Mathonwy interjected, confounding Raszer further. The name Voorhees had never come up in their discussions, and was nowhere mentioned in the Klamath records. "That's most interesting!"

"But I thought you said this afternoon," Raszer broke in, "that it was your father's pen..."

"F-force of habit," Cohn said quickly, and with an evident attempt to appear unfazed. "Anyway, it's not your—It's not why we're here."

"Right again," said Raszer. "Never discuss religion, politics or family secrets. But as a scientist, I am damned curious. How did your great-grandpa make his fortune? Our analyses of the area don't show much mineral—"

"Tin. Some small veins of silver," Fortis replied. "Not t-terribly productive. He was far more successful in Eastern Europe and Africa. I think this place held more of a . . . a historical attachment. His stake in the New World."

"That answers a question," Raszer said. "We'd seen uranium claims in the old files, and that didn't add up. What about diamonds? You get pockets of them sometimes in volcanic areas."

"Not here," Fortis said, lazily. "Mt. Shasta is a big, white elephant. Take my word for it. It's not worth its weight in dust."

Raszer poured himself a short brandy and sat down opposite his stray, who was beginning to fold over like an empty suit. He leaned in close "Then why," he said softly, "may I be so bold as to ask, are you fighting the Indian wars all over again for it?"

"Land is legacy," he recited like a schoolboy. "Property is identity."

"Ariel Sharon himself couldn't have put it better," Raszer said, and sipped his brandy. "And apparently, the Indian tribes agree with you." He let a moment pass. "I don't have a dog in this fight, Mr. Cohn, and it's no business of mine whose case you take or what you believe. I was just curious because . . . otherwise . . . you seem like a person I might like to know. I read people reasonably well. You don't strike me as . . . one of *them*." Raszer dropped his gaze to the trembling corner of Cohn's little mouth.

"Don't be mish—misled by first impressions," Fortis replied tartly. But something had been shaken loose. "People have been reading me wrong all my life."

Suddenly, the entire hemispherical frame of the hut heaved ten degrees to the north with a horrible gnashing sound, followed by fifteen seconds of shuddering and clanking. Fortis Cohn righted his leftward tilt and sat erect, blood draining from his face.

"Ah-hah!" said Mathonwy, as his seismograph began etching away. "There, you see? I'll wager that's at least a five-point-o." Fortis, temporarily sobered, stood quickly and began to button his coat.

"I think I'd better get back," he said, drawing a walkie-talkie from his coat pocket. He gave a curt nod to Raszer. "We'll see you in the morning, Mr. Powers."

"Wait a sec," said Raszer, setting his glass down. "No need to summon the sherpa. Let me walk you back. I know the path like a goat, and I don't especially want to be in this tin can for the aftershocks."

"Are you sure?" Fortis asked with a dubious tilt of the head. "It's not—"

"Positive," Raszer said, with a hand on Cohn's shoulder. "Let's go."

"All right, then," Fortis said warily, and pocketed the walkie-talkie.

As always after a quake, the California night seemed to Raszer virginal, somehow transfigured. The constellations shone brighter, and the windless silence at nine thousand feet was more starkly perceived. He had never figured out the post-quake afterglow, though he'd heard it had something to do with ions. He didn't particularly want a scientific explanation to dessicate its poetry. The earth had been violated, and was yet intact. Like the goddesses of old, she was eternally restored.

The two men walked along the descending path in silence at first, focused on their precarious footing and the beam of Raszer's flashlight. Above and behind them, an enormous hemisphere of rosy light materialized over the high ridge, jiggling like an alien mothership fashioned of luminous ectoplasm. Neither of them saw the min-min light emerge, as they were facing into the long throw of the compound's searchlights.

Raszer mused as he walked, watching as Fortis's determinedly stiff gait was challenged again and again by the rock-strewn path: the son had cast off his father and invented a genesis fantasy for himself, one which placed him in the lineage of a secretive Old World elite whose leaders probably stood waist deep in mineral wealth. Uranium, if Doc Kane was right. Raszer couldn't help but wonder why Abel Cohn wanted this ungrateful little bastard back at all. As they neared the fork that would drop them the steep last quarter mile, he paused to let Fortis catch his breath and broke the silence.

"You really believe in this guy Vreeland, huh?" he asked.

"As I told you," Fortis lectured, the thin air aggravating his impatience. "Vreeland is an agent of change. In that capacity, yes, I believe in him. The agenda itself is set, as always, by men who have a lot more at stake than the command of one garrison."

"You mean the politicians?" Raszer pressed.

"Only as proxies," said Fortis, his drug-dulled synapses firing faster in the frigid air. "Politics is a sideshow. The real players never show their hand."

"So you're talking about some kind of shadow government. A Trilateral Commission or International Zionist Conspiracy that's really pulling the strings? C'mon—"

"Enjoy your ignorance, Mr. Powers. This club is the only one that matters."

"Which club is that?" Raszer asked. "I might want to join."

"I doubt they'd have you," said Cohn. "You've counted yourself as one of the world's 'victims.' Those who think that their inadaptability to nature's cruelty entitles them to special treatment . . . to pity . . . to a handicap, so to speak."

"And you . . . you're beyond all that? Naturally selected . . . 'so to speak?'"

Fortis stopped and turned. "To be the object of pity is to be pitiful, Powers. To expect pathos is to be pathetic. These people are . . . yes, as you say . . . 'beyond that.'"

"Must be a swell club. What's the price of membership, Fortis? Your soul?"

"Like they say: if you have to ask, you can't afford it."

They began to inch down the icy, scree-covered rim of the bowl that enclosed the sprawling militia property. The trail here, though marked with cairns, was little more than a goat-path. Whether because of the Temestal, the rarefied air, or simply a determination to have the last word, Fortis strode purposefully ahead, promptly lost his footing, and began to stumble perilously close to the path's edge. Raszer scrambled down the path and broke his fall before it became a headlong tumble into oblivion, and there was an awkward moment when they were face to face, Cohn clutching at Raszer's waist for balance. Raszer gripped his shoulders to steady him and—from the look of surprise that passed over Cohn's face—got the strong impression that the lawyer had seldom, if ever, experienced simple, freely given masculine camaraderie. An instant later, an entirely different kind of surprise took possession of Fortis Cohn.

His eyes became blown glass baubles reflecting a giddy spectacle occurring just over Raszer's shoulder, and his mouth moved numbly to form the words, "What-the-hell-is-that?"

Raszer turned slowly and felt the air hiss from his own lungs. He had heard Mathonwy speak of "earthquake lights" triggered by temblors, but had imagined them looking more like the proverbial "swamp gas" of bogus UFO sightings. This was something else altogether: a semi-grounded aurora borealis, a genie freed from its lava lamp. It bobbed and wiggled like a technicolor amoeba. It was easily two hundred yards across, and so impossibly beautiful that it made him want to shout "Hallelujah!"

"I know about this," he said, though probably not with the confidence his shaken companion was hoping for. "It's caused by the earthquake. It's all right." He noticed that Fortis had not let go of his waist. "You got your footing?" he asked, then gently released himself so that he could turn around fully.

It had moved to the lip of the forty-five-degree incline, hopping a higher ridge and coming to a shimmering rest about fifty yards above them. Raszer wanted to get nearer, to touch it or at least to feel its warmth—if it had warmth. For the moment, Fortis Cohn did not matter. He tried to impel himself farther up the snow-slicked bowl but couldn't make his legs move.

Raszer felt his internal compass shift wildly and had a sudden urge to drop face-forward. All around his head, the air sizzled with static electricity and the ground beneath him hummed like a miswired appliance. Clumps of hardened snow rushed past his feet in a small-scale avalanche . . . only they were rushing up the slope. He thought of Mathonwy's *"the laws of physics break down here with some regularity . . . ."*

Suddenly, he found himself convulsed with vertigo and fell to his knees. He was aware that Cohn stood behind, but he could not be certain of whether the distance was five feet or fifty. As he hit the ground, he saw, within the bright heart of the aurora, what appeared for all the world to be a small, evanescent human form, alone and vulnerable.

Reflexively, he laughed from deep in his belly, because the last time he'd seen nature take such a bold turn he'd been eating peyote buttons in the Sonoran desert. If he'd tried to render it, he could only have done so—and badly—in the manner of those naïve, fantastical pastels of the vision at Guadalupe.

Amid the torrent of sound in his ears, he heard singing: like pirate radio picked up intermittently through a hail of static. Mathonwy had spoken of the min-min lights as electromagnetic broadcasts from the crystal core of the mountain, and Raszer knew from experience that he was all too receptive an antenna. As the perspiration trickled down the bridge of his nose, he tried to concentrate on the ethereal music, but then came an ear-splitting *pop!* like the one he'd heard in the bedroom with April. Instantly, all was as silent as midnight mass on a snow-blanketed Christmas Eve.

He realized after a few seconds that he'd automatically shut his eyes in reaction to the pop. When he opened them, his right eye was once again spinning out a pale blue thread of light. Only now—and for the first time in his singularly weird life—did he understand where the source of the energy lay. The break in his iris was a hole in the dike through which this maverick energy "leaked" when its voltage surged. Whatever was generating the voltage lay nested behind the lower center of his forehead.

He shivered uncontrollably. It appeared to him that he was umbilically connected to the rosy orb above, and the cord was the beam from his own eye. Stranger still, he was receiving information over that cord. He tried to stand, but was unable, and he suddenly knew how the prophets of old had learned prayer. Being on your knees was the only possible response to a miracle.

Even as it occurred, Raszer knew that he would never successfully describe the experience, which—for most people—would mean that it hadn't happened at all. Much later, the closest he would come was to say that it was as if his brain had received information enfolded in the big "spook light" like a digital bit stream, and that the information had registered before his eyes as a hologram, real as life. It was a meta-person, a virtual human: a ghost, and it was both inside and outside of him.

What he perceived was a small blond girl of not more than nine years of age. She was wearing a flannel nightgown with a Bugs Bunny print, just as Karl Lodz had described, and fuzzy pink slippers which seemed to leave no impression in the snow. She had one arm wrapped around a teddy bear and a scar that encircled her tiny neck like pearls. She was Bronk Vreeland's daughter, Ori, and he spoke to her, though he felt sure that Fortis Cohn saw only a man on his knees, babbling like Ezekiel to a flaming wheel. Outside this hallowed moment, his experience was madness.

"Hello, Ori," he heard himself say.

"Hel-lo," she replied, and smiled sweetly. "I got my head back."

"I can see that, Ori," he said. "It's a very nice head. Are you lost?"

"No," she replied, the corners of her tiny mouth curling up slightly, "but you are, aren't you?" She giggled and flickered. "Want to see a magic trick?"

Time elapsed, though in the uncertain increments of dream or highly altered states of consciousness. It could not have been long from Fortis's point of reference, because what broke Raszer from his trance was his companion's voice in his ear and a cold hand on the back of his neck.

"Powers! *Mr. Powers?* What's happening to you? Can you stand up?"

"I'm all—I'm okay," he mumbled. "Okay. Just need . . . get my bearings. Get my wind back." Fortis backed off warily, and Raszer got first onto all fours and then, with some difficulty, managed to sit. For a full three or four minutes, they said nothing to each other. Fortis just stared at him with his mouth hanging unlatched. It was impossible to know what he had or hadn't seen or heard, but his expression suggested some depth of affect. Finally, Raszer stood up, shook the snow from his boots, and said, "Let's go."

"What the hell happened to you?" Fortis asked, his lips blue with cold.

"I'm not sure, Fortis," said Raszer, his own words sounding foreign to him. "Some sort of electrical discharge, I guess. Maybe like getting shocked by a high tension wire and living to tell the tale." He turned. "I'm glad you were here, though."

"Who were you talking to?" Now, Raszer clearly heard suspicion, maybe alarm.

"I didn't know I *was* talking," Raszer replied.

For the remainder of the hike, he walked behind Fortis Cohn, lighting his path. At last, they reached the south gates of the compound.

Fortis turned uneasily to Raszer. "Well, you'll hear from us in the morning, then." Raszer eyed him intently, not yet ready to hand him back over to the forces inside. "Is there anything else, Mr. Powers?" Fortis snapped, but Raszer sensed that three or four defensive layers beneath his acid tone, he, too, was reluctant to step through the gate.

"You know, Mr. Cohn," he began. "I've been thinking about what you said earlier. They say the mark of true intelligence is the ability to hold two diametrically opposed ideas in the mind at the same time." He lowered his head and kicked a stone off into the gulch. A full five seconds later came its impact and echo. "You're an advocate . . . trained to see both sides. Think you'd ever consider being an advocate for a different side?"

"Only," Fortis replied, "if it became apparent that the future lay on that side, Mr. Powers. And that, I suspect, is not in the cards."

"You never know about those cards," Raszer said. "They change with every hand." He turned away, but not before seeing a troubled look cross Fortis's face. Raszer then began the trek back to the hut, the ground still far from firm beneath his feet.

Arriving at the shack, he wrenched open the ill-fitting door and stood in the half-light, uncertain of whether or not he belonged there. In his right hand, Raszer held a piece of drawing paper that he'd found in his his jacket pocket while digging for a cigarette on the last leg of the footpath. His first rational thought was that Fortis had, for reasons yet unfathomable, slipped it to him while he was out. The possibility that he'd gotten it from a spectral child was not one he could admit at the moment.

"Come in, man!" said Mathonwy, alarmed. He put an arm around Raszer's shoulder and pushed the door shut with his foot. "You look like you've seen a ghost!"

"Well," said Raszer, and laughed. "Hear me out while it's fresh."

"Of course, but . . . before I forget . . . your assistant, Monica, rang on your satellite phone while you were out. Said it was 'urgent.'"

"Okay," said Raszer, reaching for the brandy. "I'll get to her in a minute. I think, Professor, that maybe those 'laws of physics' broke down on me out there."

Mathonwy drew up a chair for him. He took the brandy from Raszer's unsteady hands and poured him a mugful. Raszer took one deep swallow, then another, and, setting the glass down, began to speak.

When the story was done, the professor said only, "Tell me again about the 'magic trick.'"

"She said I could move the 'eye' anyplace in my physical or subtle body . . . I don't think she used those . . . words. But that's what she *meant*. I'm sure of it. She asked me to move it . . . down here . . . the solar plexus, and tell her what I saw."

"And what did you see?"

"A sort of . . . latticework." He recalled the design on the Rose note. "All points interconnecting, and something woven through. Cellular. Like—neurons, dendrites . . ."

"A crystal lattice . . . but organic," Mathonwy mused. "Like a living geometry . . ."

"Right," said Raszer, fighting to retain the vision. "Sort of like . . . a mind."

Mathonwy pointed to Raszer's hand. "Let's take a look at what you've brought back from the other side of the looking glass."

It was a drawing. At first, it appeared a child's abstract, a labyrinth wrought in crayon, with anthropomorphic figures of the sun and moon in the upper left and right corners. Now, in the light, Raszer saw the autograph "Ori" distinctly visible at the lower right. It was Mathonwy who first perceived the order in its childlike chaos.

"It's a map," he said. "An underground approach to the core of the volcano. Look . . . at the upper left. That would be northwest." Raszer squinted. It was an arch, and inside it was written in tiny, lower case letters "pluto." "And this!" Mathonwy exclaimed, indicating a red X directly beneath the cone. "What do you—"

He suddenly leaned into Raszer's face as if to examine an injury. "You've got something," he said, "in your eye . . . and I do believe it's blinking at me."

"It's a kind of a . . . flaw. I've had it for a while."

Mathonwy smiled. "Did you know that the Greeks believed that the eye was an organ of both transmission and reception? 'We cast a pale light upon that we cannot comprehend, and retrieve the secret of its nature.' You are a most unusual man, Stephan Raszer. I think perhaps you have more than one foot over the line . . ."

Without the slightest forewarning, six or seven of Mathonwy's meters jumped into play and began recording activity. There was a deep fathomless groan like the creaking of an old clipper ship, and the shack was suddenly crackling with static electricity. The professor stepped to the sulfur dioxide gauge. "My friend," he said with practiced calm. "Hold on to your hat. This volcano is active."

14

XIV

TEMPERANCE.

HIS satellite phone rang at midnight, and he prayed it was April, calling to confirm that she was safely at Flo's.

"Raszer, where the hell have you been?" It was Monica. She sounded beside herself and that set his nerves jangling. "You've been drifting off and on the GPS screen and you *didn't call me back!*"

"I tried," he said. "I couldn't get a signal out. It's spotty up here right now. There's a shitload of interference from the volcano . . . yeah. Mathonwy says it's active . . . right."

Her voice dropped into static and returned to him as an echo.

"What?" he said, his face creasing. "Aw, Jesus, no!" Raszer closed his eyes and took a shallow breath. "Listen, I can't hear you well and I'm hoping I didn't hear you right. Say it again . . . and slowly." He listened, knowing he'd heard it the first time.

"I'm sorry, Raszer," Monica finished. "She's gone. Both of them were D.O.A."

"No witnesses? Not a single person saw a double-murder in broad daylight?"

"It was Koreatown. There was an old couple in the next lane. But Borges says they were too low to see the shooters over the roof of Bree Donahue's Hummer."

"What the hell was Raja doing in Bree Donahue's Humvee?"

"I wish I could tell you. Apparently they knew each other. She picked Raja up at Hollywood Pres. They discharged her a day early and she didn't call me."

"This doesn't sound right."

"I know. It stinks. But it doesn't sound like a set-up. At least not one Donahue had anything to do with. She's dead, too. It's all over the TV. What stinks is that the trades have been playing up a story about her getting sued for walking off a picture that Christopher Rose was developing. That's way too much coincidence for me."

"Goddamnit," Raszer groaned. "Goddamn LAPD. Borges was supposed to have a man on her. "

"He did. Someone pulled him off. And it gets worse. McGinty made bail."

"What? Fuck me. I should have hired someone. I should have protected her. I can't fucking protect anybody. I've gotta get April out of here, Monica, or this is going to go very, very badly. I told her tonight I'm pulling her out. I need you to get her to L.A."

"And then what?" she asked. "Chain her to the bedpost?"

"If you have to," said Raszer. "Put your Latvian Steven Seagal on her. Anything. She can't be here. I know where this is going. I'm going to give you the phone and address where she's staying. One of the dancers."

"You may need to put her on the plane yourself. You know how stubborn—"

"If I leave this mountain I will lose Fortis Cohn and these sons of bitches will walk. If there's an evacuation, there'll be total pandemonium and they will walk away."

"And if you stay . . . if you stay," she said, her voice rising to a rarely heard pitch of desperation. "You wanna know what I think? Borges says ten-to-one the killer is on his way back to his base. I think he's right. I think you get on that fucking plane with April—with or without Fortis Cohn—and cut your losses. *Do you hear me, Raszer?*"

"You know me better than that," he said.

There was a long pause and a crackling of static before he spoke again.

"Do something for me, will you?" he said.

"Anything," she replied. "But you know that, you bastard."

"Find out from Borges where they've taken Raja's body. There must be some sort of custom for a Roma burial. I'd like her to have that, and I'd like to pay for it." A thought crossed his mind. "Damn," he said softly, recalling Raja's letter. "She saw this coming."

The media began to arrive on Main Street just past six A.M., as if by spontaneous generation. There had been no public warning issued, no suspicious gathering of first responders or federal agents, and no telltale plumes of smoke. In fact, they had been clued in to Mt. Shasta's prenatal rumblings by an anonymous fax sent to radio station WSKU on Siskyou County letterhead.

At first, it was local cable teams and a handful of print journalists from Dunsmuir and Redding. By eight o' clock, however, the network affiliates with their minicams had already commandeered the cafes and cleared the bakery racks of the first batch of morning muffins. Someone had pulled an alarm: Shasta was about to do a St. Helens.

At 8:33 A.M., a redhead in a DKNY trenchcoat powdered her nose, scooped up her microphone, and announced dramatically that "Shasta Watch" had commenced. Down at the end of Main Street, Doc Kane enjoyed his second donut of the morning and watched it all unfold through his window, a smile on his lips and the E-40 in his hands.

The mountain, however, kept time in centuries rather than hours and was oblivious to the news cycle, granting not even a puff of steam as proof of bad intent. At nine thousand feet, she was as still as a Sierra Club calendar, and those on her flanks—both at the M.O.O.T. compound and at the USGS outpost—would remain unaware of the media siege for at least another hour.

Raszer set his feet on the cold plywood floor, cracked his neck, and watched bleary-eyed as Professor Mathonwy silently calibrated his seismograph. On the desk lay his Iridium satellite phone, still emanating last night's awful news like a wartime telegram left at the place of its first, terrible reading. Even this piece of sterile nanotechnology now seemed cursed. And the bad news had continued into a long, ragged night. Raszer had tried repeatedly to reach April at Flo's place, but without success. There had, in fact, been no answer at all, and this made him wonder if there was indeed a Flo.

Now, he tried again. Nothing. Prickly with worry, he realized nonetheless that he was stuck. He couldn't go searching up and down the mountain for her, he had to await his summons to inspect the militia's mine shafts, and hope against hope that the dumbest thing she'd done was to go back to her cabin to feed her macaw.

The mysterious little map was where he had left it. He might in some manner have hallucinated the giver, but the gift was "real," even if he was he was still in the dark about its purpose. Raszer thought about poor, numinous, dislocated Ori, about Rose's boyish, Armani-clad body, face down in the dust, and about dear Madame Rey, the most recent victim of this pestilence. His mood grew very grim when the dying started; it meant that the bad part of the trip had begun and that any grand epiphanies lay on the far side of Hell. The tin shack suddenly shook with the force of Thor's hammer, and Raszer heard a strident voice call from outside in the cruel blue cold of morning.

Mathonwy opened the door, and there stood Vreeland, clean-shaven, eyes honed to a pitiless cobalt sharpness by his morning regimen.

"Who're you?" he asked, with an accusatory glare.

The professor, not in the habit of responding to such discourtesy, stepped aside to reveal Raszer sitting on the bunk.

"Oh," said Vreeland. "There you are, Powers. Let's do this thing."

"Good morning, Commander," said Raszer, concealing his surprise at seeing the man himself on his doorstep. "I wasn't expecting you . . . so early."

Vreeland snorted. "The sun's been up for two hours, and if I'm not mistaken, you're on the taxpayers' clock." He glanced with disdain at Raszer's stocking feet. "Get your boots on. I don't have all day."

Raszer ignored the command and nodded toward the professor. "This is Niall Mathonwy, Mr. Vreeland. Now *he* gets up with the sun. Probably before you do."

Vreeland begrudged a curt nod. "Mathonwy . . . Mathonwy," he said, his hands on his hips. "What sort of name is that?"

"Welsh," replied the professor. "What sort of name is Vreeland?"

"Welsh," Vreeland repeated, ignoring the retort. "That's good."

"Would you like to come in?" the professor asked. "Have a cup of coffee?"

"I don't drink coffee," said the Commander. "It's a crutch. Arabian poison."

"Well, I do," said Raszer, getting up to pour himself a cup from the professor's thermos. "So you'll forgive me—"

Vreeland snapped a glance at his watch. "If you want to take a look at those mineshafts, we'd better get a move on. I can give you one hour, and that's it."

Raszer finished pouring with a flourish and took a slow sip, eyeing his adversary through the vapor that rose from his cup. Vreeland's face revealed nothing but the vanity of his practiced self-control, and his stance was a study in coiled tension, readiness to spring. Vigilance, Raszer guessed, would be the term of choice for a self-described "patriot," and yet there was something essentially defensive about his posture. Vreeland was out of his element—standing in a tin hut on government property—and it showed. For as long as Raszer could keep him waiting, he held the advantage of position. He set a cigarette between his teeth and sat down to pull on his boots.

"Jesus Christ," Vreeland muttered, shaking his head. "No wonder this country's a mess. Why don't you top it off with a Hostess Twinkie?"

Raszer curled his lips into a smile around the cigarette. "Would if I could," he said through clenched teeth, and and shot Vreeland a dead-on wink.

For a flicker of time, Vreeland was unbalanced. He shifted his bearing, then just as quickly straightened himself. Raszer finished lacing his boots, stood, and pulled on his coat briskly. "All right," he said. "Let's get this show on the road. Time's a wastin'."

"And you've already used up ten minutes of your hour,"Vreeland shot back.

Raszer zipped up his ski jacket and sighed pointedly. "Let's understand each other, Commander. I respect your position and your property rights, but right now those considerations come second to the public safety. Let me be the first to inform you that we've got confirmed volcanic activity here. The report's already gone in, and on my signature, a USGS team will be waking *you* up tomorrow. Now, it could be nothing, or it could be pre-eruptive. There's a range of conclusions I can come to, and unlike the way you may see things, it's not black and white. If you want to keep things status quo, I'd suggest you give me the time I need and not push my buttons. We clear?"

Behind Vreeland's shoulder, Professor Mathonwy suppressed a smile. Vreeland drew the cold air deep into his lungs and turned on his heel, calling out his marching song as he headed down the path, "Then forget the coffee and let's get on with it. The morning air'll get your motor running. Coffee! Cigarettes! Pussy and Death!"

Solipsist that he was, Vreeland couldn't have begun to sense the depth of enmity behind Raszer's slate gray eyes. He had harbored a hatred of bullies for so long that it almost qualified as a vocation. Raszer accepted from Mathonwy the compact aluminum flight case containing the field kit he'd assembled, along with a nod for good luck.

On his way out, his satellite phone jangled. He had set the ringer on loud so there would be no chance he'd sleep through April's call. The professor instinctively scooped up the phone and came after him. Raszer shot Mathonwy a look, shook his head, and nodded as if to say, "You take it." It wasn't until he'd turned back to the path that he realized Vreeland had stopped and turned on the path to witness the pantomime.

"Hold up, Commander!" he called out, feeling his advantage slip away with each step down the rocky path.

The sky above the ridge had begun to shift from sunrise pink to the cloudless azure of day, but below them lay a puffy quilt of low clouds that obscured the valley and village below. As they descended into Avalanche Gulch, passing the place of last night's epiphany, Raszer studied Vreeland for any sign that Fortis might have reported the incident, and saw none. He turned to look up at the passing mountainside and was unable to reconcile its stark realness with his otherworldly experience, yet he knew that otherworld was somehow enfolded in the atoms of granite and scrub. There was sudden movement to the left of a boulder lodged precariously in a gully, and he paused to watch a hulking form emerge from its right. It was a good two hundred yards distant, but there was no mistaking the animal. It was a mid-sized timber wolf of a type more likely to be seen in Europe, and it was watching him as intently as he was watching it.

"Take a look at that, Commander," he said. "Ever see one of those around here?" Vreeland stopped and followed Raszer's finger to the ledge.

The animal had vanished. "What was it?' Vreeland asked. "Black Bear?"

"No," Raszer said. "A wolf. I'm sure of it."

"No way," Vreeland insisted. "Had to be a big coyote. Or a wild dog. They come around the compound scrounging for scraps."

"Maybe," Raszer said. "But I don't think so. Anyhow . . . she's gone now."

They had walked another hundred yards before Raszer spoke up again.

"Can I ask you something?" he said.

"Speak."

"I've got no beef with the Fourth Amendment, or with the right of the people to organize militias if that's how they sleep at night. I'm a scientist, and I don't even care if people want to home school their kids and teach them that all this . . . " He swept his hand over the mountains. " . . . was created in seven days. What I do have a problem with is that guys like yourself . . . on your Web sites, your radio station—"

"You listen to my radio station?" Vreeland asked.

"It's about all we can get up here," Raszer replied. "Anyhow . . . that you seem to think I'm the enemy. That I'm a threat to your freedoms. What's that about?"

Vreeland shot him a dismissive glance. "You're no threat, Gary," he said, with needling intimacy. "What you *represent* is a threat. Clear and present."

"How so?"

"Dependence corrupts body and spirit. Anytime you hand over security and welfare to the state . . . to an agency outside your kinship group . . . it weakens the fiber of that group. Then you get this sick, unnatural situation where the weak can lord it over the strong because they've got armies—or tax collectors—working for them. That animal you saw up there . . . if it was a wolf . . . he's supremely selfish. Selfishness is survival."

"Wolves hunt in packs," Raszer said. "Interdependence is wired into nature. What do you mean by 'kinship group?'"

"The only bond that holds is blood," Vreeland answered. "The only tie that truly binds is tribe. That's why this country's losing the war."

"Now you do sound like your radio show," Raszer said. "I don't know . . . "

"I could show you how every place that's been declared a disaster area in the last eighteen years was left with a fully-staffed FEMA office more or less permanently installed. Why? If they came for the disaster, why don't they leave when it's over?"

"Maybe because disasters leave wounds that don't heal so fast—"

"Wrong, Gary," Vreeland declared. "Think about it. What does it remind you of? MacDonald's franchises? Starbucks? The way the Jews accumulated control over international banking? All that you hold dear is being undermined. Undermined, Gary . . . "

They crested the last ridge and the phalanx of satellite dishes came into view, arrayed along the far perimeter. "Why," asked Raszer, "do you people need so many dishes? It can't be just radio. Are any of them radio tel—?"

"I don't think that's within your agency's purview, Gary. Well, now," said Vreeland, as the huge electrified gates of the compound swung open for them. "Here we are."

"Right," Raszer said.

A minute later, an Army surplus transport pulled up and they were driven to the weathered porch of the HQ building where April had sat only a day before.

Vreeland lept out of the truck and called out. "Blottmeier! White! Front and center!" Blotto came promptly through the screen door with a strapping towhead who was introduced as White. Vreeland turned to Raszer. "There are three Klamath mine shafts. None currently in use except for supply storage and maneuvers. I'd suggest you work on Number Two. Same as the others, but the track runs deeper. When you're done, join me in the mess hall. You can brief me on what you found."

"It'll have to do . . . under the circumstances." Raszer nodded in the direction of Blottmeier and White. "Are they coming with me? They'll just get in the way. They can show me to the shaft and then get on with their duties . . . exercises or whatever."

Vreeland's eyes narrowed. "Why, Gary . . . protecting you is their duty. Those shafts are unpredictable. It gets slippery in there, and on the advice of our attorney, Mr. Cohn, I think you'd better have some assistance."

Raszer grimaced. "All right. Let's get on with it then."

Vreeland took him aside and spoke under his breath. "Do us both a favor. Don't mention this volcano nonsense to the boys. I don't want to start a panic."

"Neither do I," said Raszer, and returned to the young recruits. He handed White the instrument kit. Mathonwy had given him only the most basic primer in how to use it, but it didn't matter. They already had enough to back up the E-40. What Raszer was looking for were the keys to Fortis Cohn's extrication, for if he could present evidence that the militia was stockpiling exotic weapons and ordnance for some paranoid apocalypse, he believed he could get Fortis out before he dug himself deeper in. He was still banking on the presumption that an ambitious character like Cohn—a man who wanted to play on the winning team—would not risk his entire career for a lost cause.

When they arrived at the mouth of Number Two, a motorized cart was waiting on the tracks. It had a forward-reverse lever and an air brake on the right. White jumped in, took the controls, and motioned Raszer beside him. Blottmeier took the opposing bench.

"Why don't you boys stick with me to the first junction," Raszer suggested, "and then give me a little room to work. I'll give you the high sign if I need you."

"Sorry, sir," White said. "We've got orders not to leave you on your own."

"Well, all right then." He looked doubtfully at Blottmeier's girth. "But I may have to crawl through some pretty narrow spaces. Let's see what we find down there."

After rumbling slowly down the track for what felt to Raszer like half a mile, they reached a Y intersection above which the mine's granite roof vaulted to better than ten feet, unreinforced by timber. He asked to stop and got out to examine the arch with a high-powered flashlight. Raszer mumbled meaningfully to himself for a few minutes and jotted down some gibberish, then announced, "Looks intact here. Let's check what's down to the left." On that side, the track dropped steeply into inky blackness.

"Think we ought to go right, sir," White said. "If it's all the same. The track on the left ends after another quarter mile."

"Does the shaft continue?" Raszer asked. White hesitated.

"Yeah . . . for a while," he said. "But it drops real fast. And it's restricted."

"That's okay," Raszer told him. "I'm authorized, and the deeper in, the better."

"Aw-right, then," drawled White, shooting his partner a clandestine look. He got out to shift the century-old track switcher to the left, then returned and shoved the gear lever hard forward. "Hold onto your crotches," he said as the cart crossed the switcher with a jolt. The shaft went abruptly black and Raszer felt his stomach leap as the drop lifted him from the seat for a few dizzying seconds. The ride down was illuminated only by the cart's flickering, friction-powered lamp and its reflection off the crystal encrusted walls. After falling three hundred feet in less than five seconds, the track did indeed come to an end.

At the terminus was a cavern about the size of a two-car garage. Beyond it, the mineshaft appeared to continue for an uncertain distance, but on the left-hand side of the cavern, there was a narrow, rough-hewn portal, barred by a rusty iron gate. It looked to be as old as the mine itself, but it was padlocked with a fairly new Master. Raszer scooped up his kit and hopped out purposefully.

"What's over there to the left?" he asked. White looked to Blotto, who spoke up for the first time.

"It used to go through to Number Three, but there's a cave-in about a hundred yards down. Nobody's allowed in there any more."

Raszer shined his flashlight on the old gate. "A cave-in, you say . . . that's where I need to be looking. A little dicey under present circumstances, but the faster in, the faster out. You want to pop that gate open for me, Mr. Blottmeier?"

"Can't," said Blotto, jingling the keys on his belt.

"What 'circumstances?'" White asked, fidgeting.

Raszer looked from one man to the other. "You boys didn't know we've got a volcano acting up here? You wanna get out before she blows, better let me take a look."

"I'm sorry, sir," said Blottmeier. "We've got our orders."

"And I've got mine," Raszer retorted. "I can come back with a federal marshall, if you like, but I doubt your Commander would be too pleased . . . " He took a step in the direction of Blottmeier and aimed his index finger at his soft belly. "You," he said. "You seem to have your commander's trust. You seem like a man who can make a decision." He shined his light through the bars and into the narrow passage, then turned back to Blotto. "I'll make you a deal. I won't say a word to Vreeland . . . in fact, I'll make a point of saying how you reined me in. You let me do my job and everybody wins."

Blottmeier turned to White. "What's in there anyway?" he asked.

White shrugged. "Hell if I know. Prob'ly nothin'. Open 'er up."

Blotto fished through the keys. After a few misfits, the padlock sprung open.

"I'm going to take some sulfur dioxide readings," Raszer said. "Come for me if you hear any rumbles."

Raszer entered the tunnel slowly, feeling boyhood ghosts rush in behind him. The moist air smelled richly of minerals and of the earth's own roux, and the walls were bejeweled with tourmaline crystals as thick as barnacles. The passage narrowed to a width of no more than twenty inches, and he felt as much as saw his way down. Even the beam of his industrial flashlight was sponged up by the darkness. He had covered a hundred yards, and had as yet seen no evidence of a cave-in, but something was beginning to register on his eardrums. Water. Running water. An underground stream. He swept the beam across the floor until he picked up a reflection, then dropped to his knees in front of a narrow channel cut in the rock by an eon of erosion.

The spring's source was barely more than a large crack, but on his left was an oversized mousehole into which the stream flowed. He brought his chin to the floor and shone his light through the opening. It was then that he registered voices coming from the other side. The words were rendered incoherent by distance and reverberation, but they had the cadence of a command and response sequence. Raszer recalled that the Professor had dropped into his kit a kind of geomantic stethoscope for listening to the earth's own internal rumblings. Then he realized his world-class screw-up. He'd left the kit at the tunnel entrance.

He cursed and headed back up the passage. *Even these idiots are not gonna believe that a pro would leave his gear,* he chastised himself. As he neared the mouth of the tunnel, Raszer began to hear urgent whispering and what sounded like a minor scuffle. He switched off his flashlight, brought his cheek up against the damp rock, and peered cautiously around the corner. Ten feet away, Private White was up against the cavern wall, eyes closed, the dying light of the generator lamp on his face. Blotto was nowhere to be seen. Raszer crept out and noisily popped open the clasps on his fight case. With a small gasp, Blotto rose from his knees into the light, panic on his flushed face.

"Don't mind me, boys," Raszer said. "Like I said, I won't tell. Just give me another ten minutes here, all right?" He sped down the tunnel with his instrument in hand. He'd bought some time.

Back in position, Raszer brought his nose down to the small, water-cut passage, put on the headset, and snapped an eight-pin plug into its socket. The device resembled an old gramophone horn but contained a sensitive transducer for isolating selected frequencies and amplifying them by powers of ten. It was one of Mathonwy's junkyard originals. He passed the bell through the opening in the cavern wall, then set to work playing with the focus knob in an attempt to filter out the noise of trickling water. After skipping maddeningly over the sweet spot for five minutes, he finally managed to tune in the vocal frequency and monitor a brief series of commands. It was some sort of firing sequence.

"Charge the coil."

"Check. The coil is charged, sir."

"Clear the hole." A few moments elapsed.

"Check. The hole is cleared, sir."

"Mark your target."

"Target is marked, sir. Blue sky above."

"Fire!"

By what chain of instincts he could not say, because it all happened in the blink of an eye, but Raszer had the good sense to tear off the headset on the command of "Fire!" At first, there was nothing but what sounded like the hum of high voltage and the ping of a trigger mechanism, but within fifteen seconds there was a responding thud well below audible range, where hearing crosses over into feeling. Then the whole mountain began to tremble and Raszer found himself quickly covered with mineral dust. Mathonwy's mysterious "pulses" were at least partially explained, and Raszer had a card worth playing. It was time to have a serious chat with the Commander.

"We have a problem, Mr. Powers," Vreeland said, as Raszer drew out a chair to join him in the mess hall.

"Yes," Raszer said. "I think we do. You've got a volcano that's on the brink of climax and you're tickling its G-spot. I'll say that's a problem."

Vreeland raised an eyebrow, but hardly missed a beat. "The old Number Three mine is leased to an Idaho subsidiary of the original mining company. They still do occasional blasting. That's not what I'm talkin' about."

"I thought you said the mines weren't in use," Raszer reminded him.

Vreeland ignored the challlenge and aimed his index finger. "Main Street Shasta is crawling with goddamned TV reporters! We had an agreement. You promised me you bastards would keep this alert business quiet until we checked it out. What the hell happened?"

"I don't have the faintest idea, Mr. Vreeland," Raszer replied. He scrambled to make his own sense of the news. "This is no better for us than it is for you. Makes it look like we started a panic for no good reason." He thought for a moment. "Information has a way of jumping circuits, Commander. Before 9-11, everybody complained there wasn't enough information sharing between federal agencies, Now, with DHS, we're all just one big gossipy family. And half the time, the media know the gossip before we do. I can tell you this . . . if you're testing weapons in those mine shafts, they will be killing each other for the scoop. I didn't promise to keep that quiet."

"You're way off base, Powers,"Vreeland shot back. "Let me make it absolutely clear. The Klamath Company has a lease-back on Number Three that goes until 2005.They're clearing debris from cave-ins so they can reinforce the old shafts and get whatever tin is left out of this dirthill. Nothing but a few sticks of dynamite."

Raszer made a tactical decision not to challenge the assertion, though he was certain what he'd heard was no ordinary blasting sequence. It would not serve his larger purpose to corner Vreeland now. He was more interested in seeing whether or not the Commander had a move to make, a move that Raszer could counter with the proposal of a three-way meeting with Fortis Cohn. In that meeting, Raszer would lay out the exigencies in such a way that the lawyer in Fortis would see that it was time to head for the exit. Then, when the moment was right, Raszer would make private contact with Cohn and drop his Gary Powers cover. That was the way it ought to go down.

But Bronk Vreeland had ideas of his own.

"Now, listen, my friend . . . " he began unctuously. "You know what I want. I want this goddamned alert rescinded. I know exactly who you are and what you're doing."

Raszer breath stopped midway down his windpipe.

"You were right before about the feds. It's all interagency now. So maybe ATF, or the IRS or the fucking FBI think they can come at us using your two-bit agency as a Trojan Horse . . . get us off this land without firing a shot. Fuck that. I was in Angola, asshole . . . and Somalia, and worse. I've seen every trick this government can play.You're a pawn, Powers. A fucking pawn.Wouldn't you rather be a knight . . . or a bishop?" He pushed away from the table and stood up, hands on his hips. His voice dropped. "Now the feds will do what the feds will do, and we'll counter it with a lawsuit that'll make them wish they were back at Ruby Ridge, but before all that happens, how about you and me take some r&r. You got pretty grubby down there. Join me for a steam bath . . . pure, volcanic spring water.Who knows? Maybe we'll even part friends."

A sweat lodge experience with Vreeland hadn't been on Raszer's agenda. More than anything, he needed to confirm April's safety and try to determine the whereabouts of Buck McGinty, Raja's presumed killer. But this was a command performance.

The steam room, a vintage redwood cabinet the size of a toolshed, was set apart from the main house and connected to an artesian well via a byzantine snarl of old iron pipes. Raszer thanked Private White for the escort and stepped alone into a cramped locker room that smelled of sulfur, sweat, and seasoned wood. He undressed and hung his clothes on a hook next to Vreeland's, then grabbed a towel and wrapped it around his hips. The steamroom door was of solid wood and out-fitted with some kind of pressure lock, not—Raszer thought—unlike those on submarines. He gave it a pull.

Inside the chamber, Vreeland sat in Olympian clouds of vapor on the upper bench, naked but for a gold chain and medallion like the one he'd given April. A full sweat had already broken on his taut, nearly hairless body.

"C'mon in, Powers," he said. "And drop the goddamned towel. We're men here. Nothing binds men in trust more than nakedness. The Spartans knew it and trained that way. You like history?"

"Understand history," Raszer replied, tossing the towel away, "or be doomed to repeat it, right?" He joined Vreeland on the upper bench.

"You know the history of this mountain, Powers? This place?"

"You mean the whole lost civilization thing? What is it . . . Lemuria, right? I guess you can't be up here without hearing the stories."

"They're more than a stories, but the New Agers put so much fairy dust on them that nobody knows the truth anymore. Hardly anyone . . . "

"What do you know?" Raszer asked. "What's your truth?"

Vreeland, staring into the vapors like a seer, shook his head. "There was a time," he began, "before Babel, before the tilt . . . when you didn't need a foreign phrase book to buy a loaf of bread. One language. One creed. One race of war-riors, hair the color of the sun . . . "

"What went wrong?" Raszer asked.

"Things happened. Cosmic events." Then, his expression contemptuous, he added, "Chaos." He paused. "But the warriors, scattered by the Fall of Thule, weren't blameless either. They squandered their dominion over Earth. They lusted after the dark women. They sought to couple with their own shadows. The lower races were overbred, and gained ascendancy for a time. They will again . . . if we're not vigilant."

"That doesn't quite square with any history I've learned," said Raszer. "Unless your warriors are Lucifer and his outlaw angels."

"Forget what you learned . . . " said Vreeland. " . . . and consider this. You might've heard about that nine-thousand-year-old skeleton they dug up near Seattle . . . the Kennewick Man. Now the Indians claim he's one of theirs. They're hiding him because they don't want the truth out . . . but I know the truth. That skeleton has a femur nearly five feet long and the cranial structure of a white man.

It's all coming down. Right here in this place. This is the last stand. The lie will be exposed. We need to hate the lie—we need to hate like Phineas Priests—so that we can accomplish the task of restoration."

"Phineas priests?" Raszer interjected.

"There's a history they don't teach in public school," Vreeland said, intent on his lesson. "The Hebrew tribes of Benjamin and Judah—the slave tribes—got stuck with that worthless strip of land in Palestine, but the ten other Tribes of Israel left and never looked back. They founded places like Troy and Rome. The tribe of Manasseh came here. The left-behind Jews don't own scripture any more than a bunch of drunken Indians own Mt. Shasta. The Phineas priesthood? Numbers 25:8. God's covenant with Phineas. Sometimes blood is the only real baptism. Sometimes hate is the only love."

"Why's it come down to here?" Raszer asked. "Why this spot? Why Shasta?"

"Listen to me now, Powers. On the edge of the Shasta forest, not far from here, there's a group of standing stones. Stelae, they call them. Old as the hills. As old as the descendants of some of those Ten Tribes, who were themselves descended from the warrior giants of Thule. There's an inscription on one of them that translates 'Ceremony of Adoration to Gautama.' Know what Gautama is?"

"Can't say that I do," Raszer answered. "Are we talking Buddhism?"

"No, we're not," said Vreeland. "Gautama is what the Masters called America."

"I'm not sure I follow," said Raszer. "But you're a man of conviction. I can't deny that this country's seen better days . . . that sometimes I get angry."

Vreeland turned his head slowly and looked Raszer over. "Then you're on the edge of truth, soldier," he said, with an intimacy that set Raszer's teeth on edge. "Men of our race were meant to be kings. To have dominion over our homes, our lands, our women, our destinies. Haven't you ever felt it slipping away? Your birthright?" He paused while the steam rose, then looked straight into Raszer's right eye and found the chink. "I could bring out the warrior in you. I don't see that in every man. Don't ever make the mistake of thinking we're all cut from the same cloth."

In that moment, Raszer felt the most profoundly uncomfortable sensation he had ever experienced, an atavistic arousal that made his flesh creep. At once he understood why April was in such trouble.

"I don't know," he said. "I may just leave the soldiering to you."

Vreeland laid his hand on the back of Raszer's neck, and lifted a finger to touch the fringe of damp, ash-blond hair. It might almost have read as manly affection, except that everything Bronk Vreeland did seemed freighted with the threat of unimaginable violence. "You meditate on it while I go get us some water. You need to cook a little more. Purge yourself of all those toxins. Then maybe your mind will be ready for the truth." Vreeland slipped off the bench, patted Raszer's knee, and said, "Don't go away, now," and Raszer, reining in a growing panic, could only nod.

After waiting a scant five minutes for Vreeland's return, Raszer decided enough was enough. He had been ready to counter Vreeland's overture with a proposition of his own: that they sit down with the lawyer and draft a preliminary evacuation plan he could bring to his superiors as evidence that the militia had acknowledged the threat of eruption and was cooperating. The he would have offered to withdraw the E-40 if Fortis Cohn accompanied him into town to file the plan with local authorities. It was a decent gambit, but its moment had passed. He needed to get out, and he need to get to April. He had just risen to put on his towel when he heard the creaky pressure lock on the door being spun shut. "Vreeland?" he called out. There was no answer. "Shit," he said. When he pushed against the door and it didn't budge, he was not entirely surprised.

Still, the animal in him would not accept that he was trapped.

He threw his full weight against the door, but it was as tight as a cockpit. Only then did he process what he should have processed before entering: there was no reason to have a pressure lock mounted on the outside of a steam room, unless that room was meant to serve a purpose other than therapeutic. The small chamber was so thick with vapor that he couldn't see his own toes, and sweat was running from his forehead faster than he could wipe it from his eyes. It was getting hotter with each second. *Okay, Raszer,* he said to himself. *Breathe. Think.* He sat back down to make room in his mind for an answer. Panic could not be permitted to cloud his mental field.

"Hot enough for you, Powers?" he heard Vreeland yell.

"Perfect!" Raszer yelled back, trying to maintain his pluck in case Vreeland was playing with him. "What the hell are you tryin' to do? Purge my toxins or shrink me!?"

"I respect a man who's glib under fire," Vreeland replied. "Let's make it a little hotter and see how cool you are when it hits a hundred-thirty. And that's nothing compared to being roasted alive like those poor souls in Waco. At least you'll suffocate before the serious pain starts."

Any hope Raszer might have had that he was dealing with a frat boy in combat fatigues vanished into the vapor. "Hey, look," he shouted. "I wasn't at Waco. I'm a

215

scientist. And people know I'm up here. The office in Redding knows. You're too smart to kill me so you may as well tell me what you want." Raszer sat down to get his breath. He could not afford to waste it on unnecessary words. He was inhaling as much water as oxygen and his concentration was beginning to flag.

"A fucking scientist you may be," Vreeland said, "though I doubt it. But USGS you aren't. Think we're dumb enough to let you in the compound without checking your credentials. Yeah, there's a Gary Powers, but he was put on leave six months ago. How about you give me an ID before I serve you to my boys with drawn butter?"

Raszer saw that his forearms had flushed a disturbing shade of pink and that he could not stand without support. In a very short time, the steam would poach him. "Look, Vreeland. You want to know what I know, let me out of here. A man saved is an instant convert and a convert talks more than a corpse." He gasped in a scalding lungful of vapor and dropped to his knees. His only hope for staying alive was to stay low.

"Give it up!" shouted Vreeland. "Are you ATF? FBI? Fuck you. I'm putting this bitch up to one-forty and walking away. People drop dead in these old steamers all the time, Powers. It happens. The government really oughta put warnings on them!"

Raszer was now on all fours, mouth to the floor, sucking make-believe oxygen from the cracks in the plywood. Most likely, he would pass out within three to five minutes, and a minute or two later he would go into cardiac arrest. He'd been offered one small note of hope. If Vreeland thought it possible he was ATF or FBI, then he hadn't made him as Stephan Raszer. He considered silence, thinking that feigning unconsciousness might compel Vreeland to open the door, but then again, not if the man really intended to let him die. He tried a yogic breathing technique practiced by deep-sea divers in order to conserve oxygen, but the heat was so intense that his energy was sapped more quickly than he could store it. He wondered how Harry Houdini might have gotten himself out of this fix, and then realized that, alas, he was no Houdini. He was Stephan Raszer, and in the end, all that would save him was his muse. When his nose began to bleed, he decided to call on her. He rose to his knees with the last drop of stamina he had, and pressed his lips to the door.

"Hey, Bronk!" he called, in a harsh whisper that he prayed would penetrate the four-inch-thick door. "Karl Lodz 'n I were wondering. Was your little girl wearing those Bugs Bunny pajamas when you killed her?" With his mouth stuck to the door's damp surface like a suction cup, he slid down to the floor and passed out.

Raszer came to, naked and wet, on the parched grass outside the changing room. He didn't know how long he'd lain there, but a small crowd had gathered which included a distinctly ill-at-ease Fortis Cohn. He opened one eye and beheld Vreeland, eight feet away with his hands on his hips. The skin around his temples had darkened with rage. Raszer saw something else around the eyes, and wondered if it was fear.

Despite the fact that he had made it out of the frying pan, he was now truly in the fire, and so Raszer began to perform in his head his own kind of last rite, an assessment of his current station in the space-time continuum and a calculation of the odds of salvaging anything of value from the work that he and April had done. He had e-mailed summaries of everything he'd learned through last night to Monica, from which she edited daily progress reports for Abel Cohn. Therefore, they knew his approximate whereabouts, and they knew of Fortis's all-but-proven manipulation of the Klamath deed. They knew of his hunch that a plan for domestic terrorism was afoot, though what he'd discovered in the mine shaft today would die with him. There might be enough there for Abel to buy Fortis an immunity deal in return for testimony, but without direct account of Vreeland's complicity in the Raja-Rose-Donahue murders, or of some clear intent to commit mayhem, there was probably nothing that would cause the Order of Thule or its keepers more than expensive inconvenience in the courtroom.

Raszer's stock-taking was savagely interrupted by a blow to the ribs. Vreeland had opted for a new strategy. A second time, he drew back, ran full speed as if kicking a field goal, and slammed the steel toe of his boot into Raszer's side. The pain was so exquisite that his body reflexively contracted into a fetal lump and he blacked out again.

"Anything to say?" Vreeland said hoarsely. "Before you qualify for a handi-capped parking space." He dropped to one knee and leaned in close. "That's right. I'll break your knees and then I'll take a butter churn to your lower intestine. Who sent you here?"

Raszer winced and took the last arrow from his quiver. Pain had always brought him great clarity of mind. "Voorhees did," he answered weakly. "To assess your fitness for 01-01-01. Good report if you back the fuck off. Otherwise, the next man they send will have orders to terminate your command." Vreeland stood and raised his boot over Raszer's bad ankle, sending a jolt of anticipatory agony through the limb. He studied Raszer's poker face for a clue, wholly uncertain of whether he was looking into the eyes of a lunatic or his worst nightmare.

Raszer motioned Vreeland closer and, with measured precision, delivered the words. "They're not happy about the way you've let things go around here." Raszer saw from the corner of his eye that Fortis had gone pale and taken a step backward.

Vreeland turned stiffly, took Raszer's wadded clothes from Blottmeier, and threw them down. "Get dressed," he ordered. "Blottmeier. White. Take this trash to old Com Shack C and hold him until I get back. Shoot him if he runs." Then he delivered the *coup de grace* with evident satisfaction. "Gotta get to church. Don't want to keep my lady waiting at the altar."

Raszer made to speak, then thought better of it. He had no more arrows, and the last one—intended for his adversary—was now embedded in his gut.

"You're not smart enough for this line of work," Vreeland said. He mimed as if flipping open a cell phone and holding it to his ear. "Ding-a-ling-a-ling, asshole. You really have no idea what kind of machinery you've messed with."

Raszer slowly pulled on his t-shirt, feeling Vreeland's boot on every bruised rib, and replayed the sequence in his head. His satellite phone had rung as he was leaving the outpost—presumably April. The professor had fetched it, Raszer had refused the call, and Vreeland had observed. And now, that brief, abortive transaction had somehow cinched Raszer's collusion with April. With an awful certainty, he reasoned that the technology intended to protect him had once again delivered him to the lions.

He was herded to an abandoned supply shack, just beneath the ledge where he'd nearly taken a bullet a few days before. Blottmeier shoved him into the rear corner and began to shackle his wrists and ankles, while Fortis held Blotto's rifle— a spanking new Sig Sauer—unsteadily on him. Expensive artillery for a lowly private, Raszer thought, and worried that Fortis's uneasiness with the firearm made him all the more likely to squeeze its repeating trigger. He looked past his captor and into Cohn's eyes.

"Last chance to get out clean, Fortis," Raszer said. "You really think he'll let you stay in the club once he knows it was your cookie crumbs that led me here?"

"Shut up!" the lawyer snapped. "You don't have a clue."

"What's he talkin' about, Cohn?" Blottmeier asked. He took the weapon from Cohn's hands and held it steadily on Raszer.

"Bullshit," Fortis answered. "Just trying to keep his neck out of the noose. He knows enough to bluff and that's all he knows. Kill him if he keeps it up. "

The three of them sat for nearly two hours, exchanging few words. For a while, Blotto parked the assault rifle's muzzle on his fat calf while reading a *Spawn* comic, and Fortis conducted a fruitless interrogation, a series of questions to which Raszer would only respond, "You oughta know, Fortis." After a time, Fortis Cohn sat back and studied his captive as if he were from Mars, and Raszer gleaned that whatever the two of them had shared up on Sargent's Ridge had unsettled Fortis enough to give him doubts.

As any lover knows, a great deal can pass between two people in silence, and the lawyer's observation of his prisoner was not a one-way affair. Raszer met him stare-for-stare, and considered what he saw in light of what Abel Cohn had remembered about the night of his son's birth. He thought about the old AP photo of Rupert Voorhees, and about the strange history spun out by Augustus Leek's journal. He turned it all over in his head, assembling and reassembling the pieces.

It was hardly the *tete-a-tete* he'd hoped for, what with a third man present and an assault rifle aimed at his groin, but with every passing minute, Raszer feared he was losing April, and so he chose to reveal himself to his quarry.

"For my money, Fortis," he said softly, "you're nothing but an old marker your mom held on Voorhees. The king's bastard son and his share of the legacy. But once you've been cashed out, you're toast." He took a deep breath. "There's someone willing to buy that marker, though, Fortis. Someone who actually gives a damn about you."

Fortis sat stonily, his eyes revealing nothing, but the corners of his mouth— the feature Raszer had found the most telling—dropped slightly. Blottmeier scarcely took note of the exchange, which might as well have been in Russian. His only acknowledgement that something fishy might be going on was to bounce the rifle on his leg.

"Any chance we can get something to eat?" Raszer asked, his eyes still locked with Fortis's. "Contrary to the conventional thinking on torture, I'm more cooperative when I've been fed."

The mention of food got Blottmeier's attention, and he raised his head. "Yeah, Fortis, why don't you run over the the canteen and get us some chicken. I hate when I miss chicken day."

"I have a better idea, Blotto," Cohn replied. "Why don't *you* run over?"

"And leave you alone with *him*?" Blotto said.

Fortis glowered and put his hand out for the rifle. "He's in leg irons, idiot. Give me the fucking gun or we'll all sit here hungry for another two hours." Reluctantly, Blottmeier tossed down the comic and handed Fortis the Sig Sauer.

"The safety's off," he said. "Don't shoot yourself in the foot."

"Go," said Fortis icily. "And bring me a coffee."

Once he was on his way, Fortis stood, wiped the dust off his suit, and approached Raszer, the gun aimed at his heart. He dug the muzzle into Raszer's diaphragm, suddenly a man with both firepower and purpose. "Stand up," he ordered.

Raszer staggered up, his ribs on fire, and faced him squarely. "Nicely done, Fortis," he said, and nodded toward the open door. "Maybe you considered what it's like for a man like yourself to share a prison cell with a man like that."

Fortis's mouth twitched. "What do you really know about me?"

"More than you'd want me to know, I suppose," said Raszer. He moved a step closer to the barrel of the gun. "There's a guy serving time Lodi . . . three sixes carved into his forehead and an ulcerated rectum that has to be drained of pus three times a week. He was Bronk's man, too. Join a club where the dues aren't so high, Fortis."

Fortis dropped the rifle to his side. "Hit me," he said. "Hard. Right here." He indicated his right temple and handed Raszer the AR-15. "With the stock . . . Make it look good. Just don't kill me." Raszer nodded, very slowly. "The keys to the cuffs are over there on Blotto's pack."

"If you're going to let me go," Raszer asked, "don't you think you ought to tell me how to get out of here alive?"

"Maybe I don't want you to get out alive," Cohn answered. "Maybe I just don't want to be the one to kill you."

"I hadn't considered that."

Fortis nodded toward a small, recessed handle in the plank floor of the shack, and Raszer saw the faint outline of a trap door. "Where does it go?" he asked. "I don't stand a chance down in those mines."

"You'll figure it out. It was put there as an escape route in case the feds ever raided the compound. Now hit me before I reconsider. And make sure you knock me out cold. When I wake up . . . if I wake up . . . I want to be someone else."

PART THREE—CHAOS

15

THE DEVIL.

Here, in this wholly mineral landscape lighted by stars like flares . . . even memory disappears. A strange—and by no means pleasant process of reintegration begins inside you, and you have the choice of fighting against it and insisting on remaining the person you have always been, or letting it take its course

—Paul Bowles (The Baptism of Solitude)

RASZER'S Jeep careened around a steeply descending switchback on the Old Everett Highway, two wheels leaving the pavement as he swerved to avoid collision with a slow-moving fleet of oncoming media vehicles. "Jesus!" he cursed, wrestling the steering wheel to keep the roll-prone car on the scant shoulder that separated him from a two thousand foot chasm. The media, he guessed, were probably headed to the USGS outpost in search of a talking head, but at the moment, it was all a sideshow to Raszer.

Somehow, the militia had gotten his cell phone number and—possibly on a radioed signal from Vreeland—had rung it to make an ID. The GPS function would have further affirmed his coordinates. The one person they could have squeezed the number from was supposed to be safely out of their range. But what if she wasn't? What if Vreeland had not been bluffing with his taunt about getting to the church on time? *Don't want to keep my lady waiting.* Raszer banged the wheel twice and cursed again. He should have taken her straight to the local airfield. He should not have left it to her.

The trapdoor he'd dropped into after decking Fortis Cohn had led to a crude tunnel that brought him out in Avalanche Gulch, thirty yards clear of the security fence. He'd climbed out just in time to see Mt. Shasta belch her first sulfurous puff of smoke in over two hundred years. By any normal measure, that was the main event, but Raszer was not dealing with normal exigencies. He had to get to April before dark. There hadn't been a second to consider Fortis Cohn's motives for freeing him, let alone the possibility that the whole area might soon be covered in volcanic ash.

It took three stops for directions to locate the barely legible address that April had scribbled down for him. Looking at her scrawl now, in the aftermath, Raszer could see that she had been angrier than she'd let on. It was almost as if she had not wanted him to find her, but hadn't been able to bring herself to write down a phony address. With every block he drove, Raszer grew more anxious.

Flo's house was way up on the rural north side of town, an old Craftsman model wedged between a trailer park and Mt. Shasta's remaining heavy industry, a paper mill. The lawn had long since gone to seed, and there was a chopped Harley out front. April's little blue VW Beetle was parked at the curb under a eucalyptus tree. Cause for hope, maybe.

Raszer hopped the sagging porch and peered through the picture window. The living room was dark behind an army blanket which only half-draped it.

"April?" he called out, his face to the screen. He saw no movement

"Go away, man," answered a voice husky with hops and misery.

"Sorry to bother you, man," Raszer said. "It's urgent. I'm looking for a lady by the name of April. Or Flo . . . is Flo around, by any chance?"

"She left me, man. Have a little compassion, bro, and come another time. Can't you see I'm fucking bereft?" Raszer heard the man blow a noseful of sorrow into a rag and fall back with a groan. It was a voice he headn't heard in a long time: the hippie biker, tough and grizzled, tender and knowing—all in one package. His eyes adjusted to the murkiness and found its source: a big, bearded hulk of a man collapsed in a Laz-E-Boy behind a pyramid of Meister Brau cans.

"I'm sorry," Raszer said, cracking the badly hinged screen door and stepping through. "I've been there. Might be going there again soon. Listen . . . can you spare a beer? I need to talk to you. April may be in danger. Flo, too, for all I know."

"Sure, why not?" the man replied. "Only losers drink alone. Have a Brau. You'll wanna get as shit-faced as I am after you read this letter."

Raszer stepped in, his heart in his throat. He was now able to assay the human bear in the recliner, his generous belly hanging over a Harley buckle and his full beard frosted with beer foam. Raszer extended his hand.

"Stephan Raszer," he said. "Friend of April's. Did she stay here last night?"

"Not for long." The biker tossed him a warm can of beer from the iceless cooler at his side. "I'm Bo Gatz," he said, scooping up the scrap of notepaper that rested on his thigh. "Just read this." The paper had been torn from a drug store note pad and was bordered with fat little angels. "She and Flo went off to the club with those fuckin' Nazis around ten. I started drinkin' a couple hours before . . . it's the only way I can handle her workin' at that fuckin' place. When I got up this morning, I found this in the cat's dish."

Raszer took the letter into the light. *"I'm sorry, baby,"* it read. *"I've got to go away for a while. I know some things I didn't know before. I should never laffed at your wild ideas. They took April when she tried to give me her man's number. Lucky they let me go at all. Feed the cat, hon. I'll be back when it's safe. Dont come after me. Love, Flo."*

"Shit . . . " Raszer whispered.

"You said it," Bo agreed.

"Well, if it's any consolation, this doesn't sound to me like a Dear John letter. You say they left with the militia guys at ten. Did they go willingly? Was there a fuss?"

"Couldn't say," Bo moaned. "I was flat on my back. But if they've laid a finger on my Flo, I will rain more shit on them than that volcano. I'll call in my own personal fucking apocalypse."

Raszer took a seat on the threadbare sofa opposite Bo, sipped his beer, and mulled the possibilities, none of them good. Whether April had been abducted or gone by her own design to make some crazy, quixotic grandstand play against Vreeland, the likely outcome was the same. She was a hostage. In spite of all the precautions they'd taken, a series of small, very human errors had allowed Vreeland to sniff them out as a team. For all Raszer knew, he might have had a tail on April from the start. Catching April passing the cell phone number to Flo would only have sealed it for him.

And it was entirely possible that April had sensed none of this when she'd gone off with her military escort—that her zeal had trumped her fine intuition. It would be in character. She was a woman who figured she could always get the better of a man because she understood his appetites. But what exactly *were* Bronk Vreeland's appetites? Raszer suspected that he was beyond the reach of any stratagem based upon sex. He stood so utterly damned by his infanticide that his only hope for heroic stature lay in acting on the Fraternity's assertion that his crime had put him beyond moral law. Somehow, Raszer knew, Bronk had written April into that scenario.

Abel Cohn had described Vreeland as a man called to Mt. Shasta to await a "divine command," and Karl Lodz had said cryptically that Vreeland's overlords— the Fraternity—were "in every picture, like Waldo." Madame Rey's rough translation of the mysterious verse insinuated some schism in the human family . . . *to divide the wise man from the brute* . . . while Mathonwy's mythical conjectures seemed to support that. *"Don't ever assume,"* Bronk himself had said, *"that we're all cut from the same cloth."* The militia was desperately trying to squelch radio signals that seemed to issue—improbably—from the mountain itself, and April's hunch was that they weren't friendly to the militia. Was it possible that someone, somewhere was trying to send a warning?

If the source of the voice in Madame Rey's head—like the voice April had heard in the satellite shack and that he'd experience in his inexplicable communion with Ori—if that voice was in some manner an S.O.S. from Vreeland's adversary to anyone with the facility to receive it, then the Fraternity would do everything in its power to silence it before it exposed their grand plan. And whether Vreeland believed that April was truly a New Age Cassandra or simply a well-informed mole, he might well think that she could lead him to the enemy. Raszer could only pray she'd leave an Ariadne's thread behind.

"Bo," said Raszer. "I'm a private investigator. My name's Raszer. April was working undercover for me, trying to bust these creeps. It sounds like Flo got caught in the middle. If you're willing to get sober for a few hours, there's a chance we can both get back what we've lost."

"The spirit is willing," Bo replied, "but sober is an altered state for me, man."

"I understand. Just ride it out. Sober is a buzz in its own way. Listen . . . Vreeland said somethin' about 'going to church.' Mean anything to you? Church?"

"Sure, man. That's what the skins call the Temple. You know, that fuckin' dive where the girls dance."

"Then let's go see the preacher," said Raszer.

Bo gave a mournful sigh. A Hell's Angel with a broken heart.

With Bo's Harley in the lead, they found the Pink Temple Lounge tucked on the backside of the mountain, on the brow of the great Shasta forest. It was a monument to the lower urges, located on the perimeter of a region which local legend had populated with Ascended Masters. An old Buick was parked outside, next to a dilapidated neon sign in the shape of a voluptuous 1950s-style pin-up girl.

Raszer had never seen a strip joint so far off the beaten path, but then he recalled the entry in Augustus Leek's diary. *"They have even constructed a bordello on sacred Wintu burial ground."* So, this was the consolation the nineteenth-century Klamath Co. bosses had provided for their grimy laborers. A whore in those days had to have both a heart of gold and a stomach of iron. He stepped out of the Jeep while Bo dismounted from the chopper. Together, they climbed the bowed steps to a broad porch where two termite-infested porch swings hung from rusted chains.

Bo had insisted on bringing a sidearm, a shotgun sawed off practically to the nub, and Raszer had his knife and his kit of paralytic needles, arranged in a cracker-thin gunmetal case he carried in the inside pocket of his ski jacket. He intended to make no further pretense of being a USGS agent, though as the minutes passed, it was by no means certain that his cover had a thread left in it anyway.

The hot pink of the Temple's tired paint job seemed an affront to the surrounding forest's verdant serenity. They stepped through the front door into a small foyer, which must have served in days past for the hostesses to greet their customers and peel off their sooty overcoats. It was still furnished with a moth-eaten loveseat upholstered in faded Victorian red velvet. The walls were covered in bad Frederick Remington imitations, and there was one framed black and white photograph of a group of laborers surrounding a tall, well-dressed figure with a monocle. This, Raszer surmised, must be Augustus Leek's Dutch scientist, and Fortis Cohn's putative great-grandfather, the original Rupert Voorhees. His eyes were as black as a lizard's, a family trait he'd obviously passed on to the scion whose photo Raszer and Monica had seen on the Web—the man whom Fortis would make his grandfather. The succeeding generation had not yet made an appearance, unless perhaps in Abel Cohn's waking nightmare as the man briefly glimpsed through the swinging doors of the maternity ward.

The first sound Raszer became aware of was the drone of a television set mounted over the bar. As he and Bo padded in through the oak-framed entryway, the newscaster's words became more distinct.

" . . . that despite the ominous rumblings and occasional bursts of steam, neither the Federal Emergency Management Agency nor Mt. Shasta city officials are willing to talk for the record about an evacuation order. Informed sources tell us that a U.S. Geological Survey team from Vancouver, Washington is on its way down to monitor the increasingly hazardous situation, but the agency's local official, Dr. Niall Mathonwy, has so far refused to confirm the report . . . " Raszer glanced at the tube and saw the professor waving away a gaggle of reporters and mouthing,

"No comment" from the door of his little hut. He did not look at all pleased with his sudden celebrity.

Seated on a barstool directly opposite the TV, still as a taxidermist's trophy, was an ancient little man in overalls and red long johns. He seemed to be transfixed by the tube's cyclic flicker and oblivious to their entry, but then he spoke without turning, in a voice like the wheeze of a steam calliope.

"Bar's closed, fellas," said Grandpa Labin. "Ain't been open for day business since they shut down the mines."

"That's all right," said Raszer, approaching the bar. "We're just here for a couple of ladies who stayed out too late last night. You know April and Flo, your dancers?"

"Sure" replied the old man. "The Gypsy 'n Little Orphan Fanny . . . who doesn't know 'em. But they ain't here. Ain't been here. Left after the show."

"I don't doubt your word, gramps," Raszer said, "but I'd like to take a look in the dressing room. April's been known to pass out in the weirdest places."

The old man blinked slowly, one bloodshot eye on Bo's shotgun. "You can look," he replied, "but you won't find nothin'. I sweep it out every morning. There'd been a girl in there, I'd've swept her out, too." He nodded warily at Bo. "Looks like your partner here is after more than a look around."

"Never mind Bo, sir," Raszer said. "He's just a little irritated. Thinks Flo might have run off with one of the boys from the compound. She didn't make it home either."

"You seen her?" asked Bo, slapping the short barrel against his big thigh.

"No, sir, I haven't," the old man answered. "Like I said . . . "

With Grandpa held at bay, Raszer moved off toward the dingy backstage area.

The "dressing room" was no more than an old cupboard at the rear of the building: a cracked mirror propped against the wall, a single chair and vanity table, and an open toilet stall barely masked by a cheap oriental dressing screen. The smell of the place was equal parts urine, hard whiskey, and April's own forest floor scent, a fragrance that left an olfactory presence behind, as if, like Peter Pan, she'd dropped her shadow on the way out. There was nothing on her vanity but a matchbook and a cheap tin compact, both of which Raszer hastily stuffed into his pockets.

Standing before the mirror in the tawdry surroundings, inhaling her scent, Raszer felt shame that his mission had led April to toil here. It had been her inspiration, but it was his assent that had fixed the deal. He imagined her applying her eyeliner as Vreeland watched from the doorway, and it burned him. His eyes, newly adjusted to the darkness, suddenly fixed on a thick hank of auburn hair, spilling from under the lid of an old steamer trunk that had recently been shoved against the far wall. A shudder traveled the length of his body as he moved cautiously toward it.

Raszer squatted, weak-limbed, before the trunk and lifted the lid. There, on a heap of frayed chiffon and discolored faux silk left from days gone by, was April's outfit, along with the Queen of Sheba wig she'd laughingly described buying with her first expense allowance. He picked up the wig and fingered the thick ringlets, picturing how they must have spilled seductively down her naked back. Spellbound, he turned the wig inside out and sniffed the lining. Scent was as important as sight in Raszer's investigatory arsenal, maybe more important. Then he saw what he'd nearly missed, and gave a small gasp.

Protruding no more than a quarter inch from under the elastic scalp band was the folded corner of a paper napkin, stuffed in where the stitches had broken. He removed it gingerly. It was only instinct, made palpable by the finger of cold air on his damp neck, which kept him from opening it there and then. He shoved it into his inside pocket and rose from his crouch. As he did, the presence he'd just felt as a phantom was reified as gunmetal against his head, and a leather clad forearm cinched up against his Adam's apple. His heels left the ground and he was dragged away, flailing.

"Looking for something to wear tonight, asshole?" said a voice familiar from another night, another dark room. "Bet you thought you'd put me away for a good stretch, but all you need to make bail is one good friend."

William "Buck" McGinty's stubbly chin loomed over his head. The reckoning always came. Raszer had never once gotten out of a job clean, partly because he hadn't yet learned how to walk past a door marked "Keep Out."

As he was hauled out to the bar, Raszer tried to send Bo facial signals urging restraint. The burly biker, beer-saturated and clearly unschooled in the protocol of police action, went into combat crouch the minute he saw Raszer held captive, aiming his sawed-off squarely at McGinty. Grandpa Labin, observing all this with equanimity, sat quietly for a moment and then pulled his own shotgun from behind the bar, tilting both barrels up to Bo's bushy head.

"Oh, this is fuckin' beautiful," sneered McGinty. "We all die except Grandpa, and he should be dead already." He dug the pistol deeper into the soft flesh in front of Raszer's ear and sneered at Bo. "Take the heat off, fatso, or you'll never ride that Hog again. You keep him covered, Grandpa. You know who writes your paycheck."

Bo feigned as if to comply and lowered the sawed-off to his waist, then spun on his heels, swinging the stock into the barrel of the old man's shotgun and knocking him off the barstool. On impact with the floor, Grandpa Labin discharged both barrels into the saloon's acoustical tile ceiling. A stinging rain of asbestos dust and fiber poured down from above, and McGinty found himself suddenly with Bo's weapon against his own brainstem.

"Jesus, Bo," Raszer croaked, the skinhead's forearm still locked against his throat. "I'd hate to see you sober. Where'd you learn to move so fast?"

"I didn't spend my whole life on my ass," said Bo.

One man was down, but there still a gun at his head, and so Raszer, not willing to risk either man's hair trigger, decided to employ the only judo move he'd ever mastered. Wrapping all ten fingers around McGinty's thick forearm and gritting his teeth against the pain in his ribs, he stepped into the flip with his whole body and threw one hundred-ninety pounds of leather-clad meat over his head. The move was only moderately well-executed, but McGinty was so disoriented when he hit the plank floor that he began to fire wildly, in the process blowing the TV set to smithereens.

Raszer leapt onto his chest, shook the pistol from his hands, and spun around in search of Grandpa Labin, who'd managed to disappear in the melee. There was an eerie instant when the TV speaker continued to squawk, but it fizzled out quickly, leaving only the fiddle drone of mountain horseflies and the rhythm of rapid breathing. The brief silence was rent by a rebel yell as Grandpa Labin sprung up from behind the bar with an old hunting rifle and laid its muzzle on Bo's bald spot. He called for McGinty to get up, and then drew a plain white envelope from the back pocket of his overalls.

"I b'lieve you came for this, friend," Labin said to the skinhead. "Now take it and get before you do any more damage to my place. I'll keep these cowboys covered until you're down the mountain. Ain't gonna kill 'em for you, though. Not unless they try somethin'. My business is gettin' men drunk, not dead." McGinty rose to his feet and dusted himself off, then took the envelope brusquely from the old man and shot out the door, turning to give Raszer a backward look that said *Don't even think about it*. After a minute's pause, they heard a big engine turn over and tires spitting chat as his car tore onto the fire road.

Raszer took respites as they came, and was prepared to wait for his moment to disarm the old man. Almost immediately, though, he sensed that Bo was again contemplating something rash. Before he could bark an order, the big man ducked under the lip of the bar, forcing Grandpa Labin to choose his target. The instant Labin turned to train his sights on Raszer, Bo reached up, seized the barrel, and yanked it from his grip. Raszer stood up, more than duly impressed.

"Sorry for the mess, Gramps," he said. He took the rifle from Bo's hands with a grin of gratitude. "Man, do I owe you," he said. "Like I told you, sober is its own kind of buzz. Let's get outta here." The old man sighed and sat back on the stool where they'd found him, the scene unchanged but for the fallen ceiling and the gutted TV.

Raszer bolted out the door and jumped into the Wrangler. Bo kicked his bike into life and shot out in front of him. At that moment, they each had the same thing in mind: whatever was in the envelope, be it money, instructions, or lottery tickets, might in some manner provide clues to the whereabouts of two missing women. Six thousand feet above them, a thin, gray plume of smoke began to rise from Shasta.

Within three minutes, Bo was riding McGinty's bumper with Raszer churning up dust a few hundred yards behind. It seemed to Raszer that the Angel was tempting fate. Despite Bo's prowess, the Harley was a highway machine, not built for these dirt bike shenanigans, and would do better once they'd left the fire road. The rear end of the McGinty's old Dodge Charger fishtailed wildly, and at every switchback he braked hard in an effort to shake the tenacious biker whose front tire was buffing the chrome on his bumper. Raszer knew that if McGinty made it to the gates of the militia compound, he would find sanctuary, and was amazed to see the Charger shoot past the A4 cutoff road and onto the rough pavement of the Everett Highway, not more than a quarter mile southeast of the Geo Survey outpost. He appeared to be headed for town.

Now on pavement, Bo was in his element, and he roared up alongside McGinty's right flank and began kicking the door furiously with the cleated heel of his left boot. Raszer saw the skinhead turn in profile, a look of disbelief on his face. Real life did not generally dish out Yosemite Sam on a Harley. In any case, he'd met his match.

Now it was Raszer's turn to cozy up to the Charger's bumper, from where— if he could hold both the wheel and the killer's pistol steady—he was reasonably sure he could shoot out one of the tires. Up ahead, though, was a twenty mph switchback, the sharpest on the old highway. Raszer backed off the accelerator, certain that the little Jeep would roll at seventy. Bo, too, allowed the Charger to surge ahead for a moment, and rode up on the steep right shoulder in order to cut the curve. At precisely the instant Bo's Harley hit the dirt Raszer saw sunlight glint off the chrome bumper of a KSYS newsvan as it cleared the mountainside on its way back up to Mathonwy's hut. It was the first in a line of sixteen, lumbering up the narrow band of a highway in caravan. Raszer stood on his brakes and spun a hundred eighty degrees, his front fenders coming to rest against a well-dented guardrail. Fifty yards ahead, Bo surfed the rocky shoulder with a howl from Hell, his left leg fully extended, his heel striking sparks off the pebbles. For McGinty, there was a condemned man's choice: inglorious death by head-on collision or straight on through the rail.

Even if Mt. Shasta refused to cooperate with the news cycle, there would be newsworthy footage tonight. McGinty's Dodge Charger took long enough to hit the canyon floor for a handful of ENG cameramen to catch its precipitous descent live. By the time it met the equal and opposing force of the rocky ground, it had flipped eight times and its rooftop had been squashed flush with the hood. *Nobody,* thought Raszer, *survives a crash like that.* He had barely a moment to reflect on the rough justice of McGinty's demise when an even greater rumbling pulled his eyes northeast. The rising magma in the higher of Shasta's dual fumaroles had finally caused the cone to bulge visibly, bringing an avalanche of truck-sized boulders down Misery Hill, through The Heart, and on along the west flank of Sargent's Ridge on a vector that would take it directly to the door of Mathonwy's shack. "Jesus . . . " Raszer whispered, for he had never seen such enormous forces at play. "Mathonwy . . . " He turned away and scanned the roadside melee for Bo, who stood on the overlook, gazing down into the canyon at his kill. "Bo!" he cried out. "C'mon. He's gone. I need your help up on the Ridge! Now!"

Raszer's heart sank as they headed over the last rise and he saw that a twenty-ton chunk of the mountain had crushed the Professor's hut. "Nooo!" he cried out. "No one else can die!" He leapt out while the Jeep was still rolling, Bo right on his heels. Together, they wrenched open the accordioned doorway of the hut and stood while the dust cleared. Inside there was evidence of grace. With only his gray head protruding from a quarter of a million dollar heap of diagnostic equipment, he looked more like Ahab than Merlin, but Professor Mathonwy had survived. Looming over what was left of his hermit's lair was a glacier of rock more than fifteen feet high. Even given the hour it took Raszer and Bo to extricate the professor, the paramedics from Weed had still not managed to make it up the mountain, so Raszer decided against all medical wisdom to take his badly injured mentor to the hospital himself. All through the painstaking process of digging him out, Mathonwy, though conscious, did not—or could not—speak. Raszer presumed he was in shock. Then, as they laid him as gently as possible across the tiny back seat of the Jeep, Mathonwy motioned Raszer to bring an ear to his lips.

"A phone call," he whispered hoarsely. "On your mobile. It was . . . a student of mine . . . the one I told you a——? Miss Blessing. She said: 'Tell Raszer he's *in-fes'* . . . Cut off. Sounded as if she were trying to say . . . infested. Don't understand . . . was she working for you?"

"I owe you an explanation, Professor, but we'd better get you in a cast first." With Bo and his Harley serving as escort, they took off for the hospital in Weed.

Down the halls of Shasta County Hospital, Raszer hobbled alongside the gurney carrying Professor Mathonwy to surgery. There were multiple breaks and fractures, along with a collapsed lung, but Mathonwy was the son of a Welsh miner, and it would take more than stones to break him. He was full of morphine, but he was conscious and remarkably lucid. Moreover, against the doctor's advice, he wanted to talk.

"Professor," Raszer blurted as he ran. "I saw something when I was down in those mines. Or heard something. A firing sequence . . . then some kind of concussion that shook the whole mountain. That was less than two hours before the first puff of smoke. They're testing something down there, and when I mentioned it to Vreeland, he stonewalled. Listen . . ." He paused to catch his breath. "I know it's far-fetched, but could it be——"

"A Tesla cannon?" Mathonwy said, his voice frail.

"What would it take to build one?"

Mathonwy tried gamely to rise up on his good elbow, then collapsed with a groan. "It would take a subterranean shaft a half-mile in depth and a coil from three to six stories high."

"A half a mile," Raszer thought out loud. "Would the cone of a volcano do?"

"The cost would be astronomical."

"Somehow," said Raszer, "I don't think money is a problem for the Fraternity."

The orderly motioned Raszer to the side when they reached surgery. As the gurney rolled through, the professor raised his one good arm and called out as best he could, "By the way . . . I think I've cracked your code. It's a binary number . . . !"

A binary number? Raszer mused. From the same source as a Sanskrit riddle and a pagan lament? And then, things fired across his cortex and he recalled how Ori had come to him. As *information*.

Information with a soul.

Something was happening.

Outside, Raszer found Bo waiting beside his Harley.

"Where to now, Captain?" Bo asked, ready to do further battle for his lady.

Something about the way the biker looked at him, the expression of total trust, brought Raszer back to ground zero. He sat down on the curb and offered Bo a cigarette before lighting his own. "I think I'm on my own for a while now, Bo. But we'll find them. I promise you that. Thanks, by the way. You saved my life back there."

"My pleasure," said Bo, throwing his leg over the Hog. He kicked the engine into a steady rumble. "You know where to find me, brother. Anytime."

"Yes, I do," said Raszer, lifting his hand in farewell. "Yes, I do."

The Harley roared off, and Raszer was suddenly very much alone. His head ached, his bruised ribs ached, and his heart ached. He needed a drink. He took a deep drag on the cigarette, and only then remembered the articles he'd stuffed in his pocket back at The Pink Temple. He took them out one by one. The compact revealed nothing but a spent powder puff, and the matchbook bore only the name *Barbary Club*, in a gold, Arabesque font against black. The little cocktail napkin, however, held something dearer. It was a hastily written note from April, scrawled with eyebrow pencil.

I'm so sorry, Wart. Had to try. I don't know where he's taking me. All he said was "it takes a rat to find a rat." Don't give up on me. MLF.

It all catches up with you, he thought, and in the end, no one is spared. Nonetheless, as he slipped the napkin into his pocket, Raszer took some comfort from the closeness of her hand to his heart, and realized again that life on earth is mostly an endless round.

The lady had dropped her handkerchief, and he knew what that meant.

16

THE TOWER.

RASZER limped past the damaged Waffle Haus on the Shasta Village Main Street, his sense of mission as splintered as the broken glass that littered the sidewalk. Everything had changed. April and her mountain had changed it. She had scripted the very drama he hadn't wanted a part in. It wasn't any longer about saving a feckless young lawyer from his own demons. That seemed almost incidental. It was now about finding her and in the process facing Vreeland and the apocalyptic scourge he planned to loose on the world. Crafty girl. Now he'd have to play Orpheus to her Eurydice, and that, in a sense, was what she'd wanted all along: for him to follow her to Hell and back. Given his own complicity, he couldn't be angry with her. She had, in Serena Mankiller's words, "married spirit to will" and, thereby, made a new world.

He thought about her note, her phone call to Mathonwy. What had she meant by "infested?" But there was the more immediate matter of her whereabouts, and on that score, he hadn't been offered much help by the Siskiyou County D.A., whom he'd briefed an hour earlier on the apparent abduction, McGinty's death, and its connection to events in L.A. Nor had he gotten much from his tense conversation with Lieutenant Borges, who was no happier than Raszer about the way things were playing out.

"What the hell happened down there, Lieutenant?" Raszer had demanded. "You guys had at least two counts against that animal McGinty and you let him walk?"

"It's the system," said Borges, without apology. "You should know. I was trumped. A mob lawyer acting on behalf of some criminal rights group got them to lower his bail."

"Jesus. Well, his rights are gone now. Fucking L.A. Nothing changes, does it, Lieutenant?"

"You swim in this river, too" said Borges. "And you know there's only so far upstream we can fish before we hit a dam. This city has always listened to money. L. Ron Hubbard isn't the only bunko artist getting plazas named after him these days."

"You know the big fish are behind that dam," Raszer said. "Don't you want—"

"All I know right now," replied Borges. "Is that the State of California is relieved of an expensive prosecution. My job is to try and protect my little pond."

"If you do decide to go farther, try using the name Rupert Voorhees as bait."

"I'll make a note of that. In the meantime, keep me informed. And try to keep the lava off your gumshoes."

Borges was a good cop, but Raszer had gotten the message. He was on his own. Momentarily overwhelmed, he decided to find that drink. He needed a new strategem for the extrication of Fortis Cohn, and all he could do for the moment with respect to April's situation had been done. Local authorities were now faced with the more pressing problem of how to evacuate a fifty-square-mile area in less than twenty-four hours. The disappearance of a reclusive hippie girl was a subordinate matter.

He had dutifully reported his suspicion that the militia was testing weapons in a geological hazard zone. Then, after conferring with Abel Cohn, he had brought the D.A. into a three-way conference and detailed his evidence that a potentially crucial document in the Native American land use lawsuit had been planted by the militia's attorney and Abel's son, Fortis Cohn. The prefatory conversation with Abel hadn't been easy.

"Monica?" Raszer had asked. "Is he on?"

"He's coming," she said. "I've briefed him. He's pretty freaked."

Abel came on the line, gruff with worry. "Tell me Fortis is all right, Mr. Raszer."

"I can't promise that he's unharmed, sir. But in less than three hours the Sheriff's deputies will raid the compound. I *can* tell you this: he saved my life."

Abel sighed. "So you got through to him . . ."

"I think so," Raszer replied. "He told me he wanted to be 'someone else.' I'm interpreting that as a positive. But by doing what he did . . . he put himself at risk . . ."

"I understand, Mr. Raszer. I'm as concerned with my son's soul as I am with his body. If he's regained it, the rest comes down to the odds we all face."

"Listen . . . I'm betting he's still in the compound . . . even if Vreeland has him under house arrest. If we can bring him in, we'll need to make one hell of a deal in exchange for his testimony. I'll need your help with the state."

"You've got it," said Abel.

"Can I bring the D.A. on?" Raszer then asked, and Abel had assented.

Raszer said little about the broader story, and nothing about the Fraternity. He'd learned the hard way that if you offered a dish like that before it was fully cooked, you came off looking like an amateur. He avoided, as best he could, any conjecture that crossed state lines. The FBI could search every inch of Mt. Shasta, but if Vreeland had taken April out of the country, the trail was for him alone to follow. Just before the session broke up, the DA queried him about the badly burned contents of an envelope found in the wreck of William McGinty's car: two-thousand dollars in cash and the charred remains of an airline E-ticket receipt, itinerary indecipherable.

Outside, from a pay phone, Raszer had placed a call to Monica, on her way to Madame Rey's wake. After that, he'd decided he could go no further without a drink.

The village of Mt. Shasta was in the early stage of what would doubtless be a long siege. It was perhaps the most perilous stage, because residents were still inclined to think that it might all blow over. Although most of the shops had pulled down their shades and hung their hand-printed "Closed" signs, a few were doing record business selling coffee, soda, and bottled water to the media folks, whose numbers now rivaled those of the populace. The complacency of the press probably served to reinforce the illusion that the volcano was only a dramatic backdrop for what was otherwise a perfectly normal day. Parents were still allowing their children to linger in front of plate glass windows and climb atop mailboxes to gaze in solemn wonderment at the puffing mountain. The clouds had cleared and the late afternoon sky, though swarming with helicopters, displayed the usual shift from blue zenith to ruddy horizon. There was no visible explanation for the charged quality of the thin air or the fact that it smelled like the prelude to a thunderstorm of Wagnerian proportions. It felt to Raszer as if Mt. Shasta was gradually sucking all of the breathable oxygen into her cone. He was no vulcanologist, but he knew what Mathonwy would say. If the mountain did blow in their direction, the "pyroclastic flow" of super-heated gas would kill these people faster than Raid kills roaches.

He hobbled to the center of the street, his torso battered and the old tear in his ankle aggravated by the day's ordeal. A platform and public address system were being erected for the city council president and a FEMA agent to deliver what the press expected would be an evacuation notice. The area high schools and the junior college were already being readied to receive thousands. He brushed rudely past a cameraman, jarring the camera from his shoulder, and realized that he was in a foul mood. He was perturbed by his failure to turn Fortis Cohn away from Vreeland without putting him at legal or physical risk. This was the unwritten warrantee in his service contract, but it was also a matter of pride.

He was aware, as well, that he was now navigating a metaphysical grid for which he had no map in his glove compartment. No matter how he construed it, Ori's appearance to him on the mountainside was either evidence of a delusional disorder or a genuine revelation, and revelations were as rare these days as the kind of men who had once experienced them. As the hours passed, he became less certain of what he'd seen, but there was no doubt that he now possessed a little drawing that, if taken at face value, seemed to indicate the existence of passages to the very heart of the volcano.

Ahead, a small cluster of townfolk parted to let a man through, and Raszer instinctively glanced up. He stopped dead in his tracks, and so—six feet away—did Fortis Cohn. He looked nauseous, dirty, and scared.

"Can we talk somewhere, Mr. Powers . . . or whoever you are?"

"How about the D.A.'s office?" Raszer replied.

"No. This is for your ears, and you'd better hear it now," Cohn said, "because I'll deny most of it once I'm in custody."

"Okay, Fortis," Raszer said. "I know a place."

There was suddenly a commotion about a half a block away. They watched as a moving body of men rounded the corner, heading toward the platform. As the marchers drew closer and the press corps fell back, Raszer saw Fortis Cohn's eyes widen. The members of the procession were in full ceremonial dress, with the elders in the fore and the younger ones—at least thirty of them—following behind in solemn trios, heads lowered and holding aloft a banner. "Set Shasta Free," it read. They were representatives of the Indian nations suing the Order of Thule for land rights, and judging by the timing of their appearance and solemnity of expression, they had ideas of their own about how to cool the volcano's temper. They understood that the warrior god Skell had once again seized the maiden Loha, and hell would follow if she remained his captive.

* * *

"Come in," said the olive-skinned young woman in white who opened the door. "Everyone is in the back."

"I'm so sorry I'm late," said Monica, removing her dark glasses. Every curtain in the small house seemed to be drawn, and the effect was of stepping from broad daylight into dusk. "I always get lost in this part of town. The streets——"

"Are crooked," said the woman, with a little smile. "I know. They say that's why the gypsies gravitate here." Barely twenty, the dark-eyed girl spoke with the same rueful weariness Monica had heard in Madame Rey's voice. "Would you like a drink? I can offer you some peach brandy."

"Thanks, no. Well, some water, maybe. I just came . . . on behalf of Stephan Raszer . . . to pay my respects."

"That is very kind of you, Miss." The new voice belonged to an aged man in a gray suit who emerged like blown smoke from a hallway, spearing the green shag carpet with his ornately whittled cane. "We are all very grateful for the generosity your employer has shown to the kumpania. Even a modest funeral these days is no small expense." He approached to within three feet and tipped his head courteously, but did not offer his trembling hand. Though stooped, he was easily six-foot-two, with a magnificently full head of chalk-white hair and the bearing of a tribal elder.

"Stephan . . . er, Mr. Raszer felt that it was . . . " Monica hesitated as she searched for the words Raszer might have used. "That Raja had given him something invaluable, and that he should give something back. I hope everything has——"

"Yes . . . " the old man interjected. "Thank you. She will be cremated tomorrow at dusk. Our customs are ancient and precise, but we are frugal. I can assure you that Mr. Raszer will receive a full accounting."

"Please don't give it a thought," said Monica. She tipped her own head to him in kind. "I'm Monica Lord. And you——"

The young woman spoke up. "This is Mr. Rudari . . . our *Rom Baro*."

"A hereditary title," he said, seeing Monica's puzzlement and putting her at ease. "Not one, however, which conveys any status beyond our people, so call me Anton."

"I'm honored to meet you, Anton."

"The honor is mine," he replied. "Will you come with me? I'll introduce you to the others."

As they passed through the murky house, the Rom Baros's cane tapping softly on the carpet, Monica became aware of the absence of all reflected light, and of blankets draped loosely on the walls. "The mirrors," she mused out loud. "The mirrors are covered."

"A custom," said Mr. Rudari. "This is the *time between* for Raja. Have you ever stood before a mirror and seen a shadow pass behind you?"

"I think I know what you mean," said Monica, and the thought raised gooseflesh. She heard hushed voices—and then a sudden wailing—as they turned a corner.

"We do not make a romance of death, as the Irish do," he explained. "To die—especially as Raja died—is a great indignity, and the mulo of a Roma woman can become, in passage, a vengeful thing: a wolf, a bird of prey, or worse. Those who may have wronged her in life may have reason to fear her in death . . . Ah, here we are."

"Oh—" Monica's eyes widened. They stood at the threshold of a large recreation room that presented a tableau as alien to her as a borrowed dream. In the center lay Madame Rey in an open casket, her charcoal gray hair spread about her face, her nostrils plugged, the fatal head wound masked by the mortician's art. Around the casket were folding chairs occupied by women of all ages, each dressed in white like the young hostess, and so engaged in lamentation that they hardly noticed Monica's arrival. In the far corner, speaking in low tones, sat the men: smoking, drinking brandy from paper cups, and playing idly at cards. Opposite them, a television set blared and flickered with a Jackie Chan action movie that only a slender young man in a red vest seemed to be watching. Nearby, a furious game of round-robin ping-pong diverted the teenagers from the more serious business at hand. A group of dark-eyed children, some of them eyeing her curiously, clustered about a rented banquet table which offered a modest spread of pastries and stewed meats, though not one of the adults was eating. Monica turned to the hostess and smiled faintly. "I think I will have that drink," she said.

After she had been quietly introduced as the patroness of the nine-day pomano, or mourning feast, Monica took her brandy and sat down beside the Rom Baro and the hostess, who was, he revealed, his daughter. Their company was not unpleasant, but as they said little and remained entirely focused on the casket, the minutes ticked by slowly. As a cuckoo clock struck three, Monica happened to glance through a gap in the curtained patio doors and notice a group of young men gathered about a large fire pit in the back yard. The pit enclosed the newly lit kindling of what promised to be an outsized and flagrantly illegal bonfire, and stacked beyond the circle was a small apartment's worth of furniture and clothing. Monica tapped the Rom's shoulder and pointed.

"What . . . what are they doing out there?

"Those are Raja's things," he replied evenly. "All of it will be burned." He acknowledged Monica's mystification and continued. "Don't worry—the bubonic plague has not struck Los Angeles. Death carries its own kind of contagion, though. We call it marime. It's best that the dead take their worldy possessions with them."

"It's done that way in India, isn't it?"

"Not so much anymore, but once . . . India is the ancestral home of the Roma, though we are now cast to the four corners of the earth. We were once all people of the Rromani language . . . *jekhipe* . . . unity. One father. Now, we are three orphaned tribes. Ours . . . *Raja's* . . . is the Lomaruren."

"You . . . didn't say Lemurian, did you?"

"No . . . Lo-ma -rur-en."

Monica pondered this as the larger sticks reached their burning point. "She had some beautiful things . . . the bureau, the dresses. Do they all have to go?"

"No gypsy would possess them. But a *gadji* may. Is there something . . . ?"

She took a gulp of her peach brandy. "Her tarot cards," she asked softly. "The deck she kept at the shop. Was it retrieved?"

"There is a Marseille deck . . . very fine . . . that was in the car with her when she was murdered. Are you sure . . . " Monica nodded. The Rom turned to his daughter, who rose quietly upon his signal, then said: "I will make a gift of them—to you and Mr. Raszer. It was her *baxtalo* deck—lucky—hand-illuminated, she was told, by an old Jew in Morocco. In Fez. God knows if he's still alive he would have to be one hundred."

Monica blinked. "You say he lives or lived in Fez?"

"That's right," replied the old Rom Baro. "The birthplace of tarot."

Athough any number of dark taverns would have done, Raszer had chosen Diamond Lil's, and seen upon entering that he was not the only man seeking solace in drink. The place was doing good business, with three TVs blaring the latest makeshift news from "Shasta Watch." Raszer and his reluctant drinking companion had taken a table on the far side of the dance floor.

"Drink, Fortis?" he asked when the waitress arrived. Fortis shook his head no. "Well, I will. Scotch with soda back, please. White Horse, if you've got it." Once the waitress had gone off, Raszer turned to his stray. "All right," he began. "First things first . . . my name is Stephan Raszer. I'm a private investigator, and I was hired by your father to help you if you want to be helped."

"That much . . . " said Fortis flatly, " . . . other than your name, I'd gathered."

"Secondly. Thank you. I owe you my life. That means a lot, but it doesn't alter the facts. I don't need to tell you that you're probably guilty of any number of mis-prisions of felony, not to mention land fraud. Your clients are testing large-scale weapons in an active volcano. And there's a cop in L.A. who is very anxious to question you in connection with the murders of Raja Zlatari, Bree Donahue, and Christopher Rose. I'd say you're in about as deep as it gets. What do you have to tell me?"

"I'm a lawyer, Mr. Raszer," came the tart reply. "I know exactly how deep I am. You may not know how deep you are. These people have a stake in virtually every commodity that oils the world's machinery. They sit on the boards of Fortune 500 companies and control forty-three percent of the commercial radio spectrum. And that doesn't touch their influence in geopolitics and law enforcement . . . "

"Trying to scare me?" Raszer asked, and took his scotch from the waitress.

"I'm trying to wake you up," Cohn answered. "They are smarter, and tougher, and they are going to win. The fact that they're going to do it without me hardly matters."

"Who exactly are we talking about here, Fortis? Voorhees and his 'Fraternity?'"

"Don't get hung up on the name. They are people who share . . . a heritage."

"What kind of heritage? Hereditary? Political? Financial?"

"I won't get into that with you," Cohn replied. "Believe me . . . the less you know, the better a man like you will sleep at night."

Fortis chuckled darkly, as much—Raszer intuited—to preserve what was left of his vanity as anything. He'd traded so much for his privileged knowledge that he wasn't yet ready to relinquish his "I know something you don't know" smugness.

"And what kind of man is that?" Raszer asked. "You seem to have me figured."

Fortis laughed again, but nervously. If it hadn't been such a sad little sound, Raszer might almost have called it a giggle. "The kind of man," he said, "who really believes that the meek will inherit the earth."

"That was the other guy," said Raszer, and sipped his scotch. "Powers. The good-hearted civil servant. I know just how stacked the deck is in favor of the sharks."

Fortis was momentarily unbalanced, and gave Raszer a skewed look.

"The thing is," Raszer continued, "that it's *your* people who are going to lose."

"Oh?" said Cohn. "And why is that?"

"You quoted me scripture. I'll quote you right back. Proverbs 11:29. 'He that troubleth his own house . . . ' Do you know that verse, Fortis?"

Fortis looked down, his chin trembling just a little. "'. . . *shall inherit the wind.*' Of course I know it. It was my f—Abel's favorite passage. But I suppose you knew that."

"No," said Raszer. "I didn't." He let a moment pass. The jukebox kicked on with a Steve Earle song. "What finally turned it for you, Fortis? Why did you bail on Vreeland?"

"He had Christopher killed. To 'show me the price' . . . I told him Chris and I'd had a falling out . . . that he'd walked off with some volatile information. I was afraid he'd go to the police. I wanted him followed, not murdered." He paused and licked his lips. "But I needed time to think and—" He looked at Raszer. "—formulate an exit strategy."

Raszer nodded. "I doubt the police would have known what to make of that information anyway. But that's irrelevant. He lost his life, and he's not the only one, and I'm sorry."

Fortis shut his eyes as if to wall off tears, and held up his palm for a moment's time-out. Raszer leaned slowly toward him and lightly touched his arm. "Okay, now," he encouraged him. "I need context. The Halgadom Fraternity emerged from something called the Saint Joachim Brotherhood. Help me out with this."

"The original consortium was named after St. Joachimsthal, where uranium ore was first mined. The men who bankroll Vreeland still control the lion's share of uranium rights, as well as the enrichment plants. Globally. Get the picture?"

"Except for how someone like you fits in. Your father told me—"

"I told you who my father was," Fortis snapped. "That ought to answer your question. Like father, like son. Only I'm no longer fit for the family tree."

Raszer took a swallow, and said: "I don't buy it, Fortis. I see Abel Cohn's face—"

"You see wrong," Fortis shot back. "But again, it doesn't matter. They say dogs come to resemble their owners, too. I want out because I'm a coward. I don't have either the stomach to betray him as my mother did or the will to violate everything he ever tried to teach me. You see . . . he corrupted me." Fortis gave another caustic little chuckle.

"With love," said Raszer. "We should all be so corrupted."

"With his sentimental value system. Men like Abel can't see the world as it is. They see it as it should be. It's a delusion, of course. The future belongs to Vreeland."

"If you're so sure of that," Raszer asked. "Why not maintain your stake in it?"

"I don't have a stake. I've made myself expendable."

"Not as a star witness, you're not."

"Oh, right," he replied. "They'll have me killed just like Christopher."

"I'll take you in. You have protection and an immunity deal if you want it."

"Blanket immunity?"

"If you're state's witness, I think we can make the case for it."

Fortis put his hands up in mock surrender. "Then make me a prisoner of war." His expression was still a shade too glib for Raszer's comfort, but that might have been his pride. A surrender was a surrender, no matter the attitude.

"Just one more thing," said Raszer. "To make saving your ass worth my while."

"Yes?"

"01-01-01? It is a date, right?"

"It's a concept. The first day of the first year of the Restoration."

"And the earth'll be spinning on a new axis . . . the North Pole will be green?"

"Maybe not right away," Fortis replied with a shrug. "Maybe never. It's their foundation myth . . . like the Christian resurrection or the Jewish Exodus. But technology eventually answers to will . . . and they control a great deal of technology. Would you have guessed—even fifty years ago—that scientists would clone a sheep or teleport a subatomic particle? For them, it's no more daunting than putting a man on the moon."

"So what happens on the big day, then? What kind of hell breaks loose?"

Fortis nodded in the direction of the nearest television. "That," he said, "is just a preview."

"Geoterrorism." Raszer slowly drained his drink. "How soon?"

"Before the opposition makes its move," Fortis replied. "Vreeland's orders call for readiness by 2012, but these people are in no hurry. A hundred years is a short time for them. I was taught when I was young by my—I was taught that one way to look at history is as a series of pivots . . . points when things might've gone more the way people like Abel—and presumably yourself—would like to see them go. Only they didn't. The old order prevailed." His gaze drifted off with his voice. "The rats stayed in the sewers."

"The Empire never ended," Raszer added, though he doubted that Fortis Cohn had ever read Philip K. Dick. "Who's 'the opposition'—other than me and everyone else who loses if your guys win? And where has Vreeland taken April Blessing?"

"If you can answer the first question," Fortis said. "Then you may get the second. I'll tell you this. Their plans require precise synchronization of their global satellite network. They've been monitoring jamming signals that are playing havoc with that synchronization. Vreeland's charge is readiness. He's one of four commanders whose orders are to deploy when the time is right. That can't happen if the circuits are jammed. I suspect his current mission is to locate and destroy the source of those signals."

"Is he crazy enough to think April Blessing can take him there?" Raszer asked. "Or is she there to keep me off his tail?" He paused. "And what's in Morocco?"

A ripple crossed Cohn's face. "When you can tell me what you saw that night on the ridge," he said, pushing back his chair, "maybe we'll talk. Take me in now, Mr. Raszer."

"Fortis is in custody," he told Monica from the pay phone on Main Street. "The sheriff asked me if I wanted to go up to the compound with his deputies to serve papers on the militia. I said no. No way I want to see that fucking place until it's a mountain meadow again."

"Just as well," she said. It could turn into Waco. You should come home and let the feds handle this." He heard shuffling paper. Her pause made him feel she was holding a card, calculating its possible effect on his game. "I learned something pretty interesting about the Voorhees family," she said. "The old man . . . the guy in the wire photo. The son of the guy who staked the claim to Shasta. He died in 1984—the same year the photo was taken—but back in the '20s and '30s, when the eugenics thing was so big on the West Coast . . . all those forced sterilizations of poor women and 'undesirables?'"

"Go on," said Raszer.

"Well," she said. "Voorhees poured millions into it. He was a true believer."

"I don't need to hear any more. How quickly can you get me to Morocco?"

"Morocco?"

"Vreeland told April that he wanted to take her to Morocco. And then there's this crazy thing she said when she fritzed out on the radio signal: She sings in Africa . . . "

"Morocco . . . " Monica repeated. "That's kind of a stretch, isn't it? Where in Morocco?" But she seemed to be mulling over something.

"I don't know yet. It's a hunch," he said. "I still need more . . . "

"Don't tempt fate, Raszer. Don't do this without a solid lead."

"I'm working on it. I need to grill Fortis again. And Mathonwy."

"This may mean nothing," Monica said. "But then again . . . I never completely rule out the chance of divine intervention in your cases."

"I'm listening."

"When April tried to get that phone call through to you, and got cut off . . . Mathonwy thought she was trying to say 'he's infested,' right?"

"Yeah . . . something like that."

"I know. It doesn't make any sense. Could she possibly have been saying, 'he's in Fez?'" She waited for his reaction. "The old gypsy chieftain at the wake . . . the Rom Baro . . . asked me if there was anything of hers I wanted. I asked if I could have her tarot deck. You know, the hand-painted one she used for your reading. Raszer?"

Raszer was listening, but he was also remembering something Raja had said. She'd mentioned that her father had taught her "about the Jews of Morocco." About the connections between tarot and Kabbalah. "Yes," he said. "Go ahead."

"The Rom Baro said that the cards had been made by an old Jew in Fez . . . said he'd have to be a hundred years old by now."

Raja's voice came curling from Raszer's own lips in a plume of cigarette smoke. *I once met a man from Fez with the same gift . . . in Marseille, a long time ago.* She had been talking about his eye. His flaw. But he also knew she'd bought her cards in Marseille.

"What was that?" Monica asked. "You sound weirded out."

Empty your mind . . . and picture the name of your true . . .

"Say something, Raszer. You're scaring me."

He smiled. "Divine intervention," Raszer said, "thy name is Monica."

17

*A prisoner devoid of books, had he only a Tarot
of which he knew how to make use,
could in a few years acquire a universal science
and converse with an unequalled doctrine and
inexhaustable eloquence.*

—Eliphas Levi, *Dogma and
Ritual of Transcendant Magic*

BREE Donahue's Hummer had been subjected to a wide range of ballistics
tests. This much due diligence Lieutenant Borges could mandate without
interference from higher-ups with debts to someone other than the people of Los
Angeles. They had the bullets, and had traced their origin to three possible AK-47s,
one of which had found its way from Mozambique through two U.S. gun shows to
William "Buck" McGinty.

McGinty—who had been freed on a bail set in the murk of night and then had
executed his own death sentence on a mountain highway. Nice and neat. Borges, however, had made both a tactical and moral decision to pursue the avenues that were still
open to him, avenues which had been widened as a result of the events up north
reported to him by Raszer. Fortis Cohn had secured a broad use immunity, and state
law now trumped the hazy rules of war practiced in L.A. Borges had just a little leeway.

Assassinating a celebrity actress in broad daylight, when it would have been
easy to wait fifteen minutes and hit Raja Zlatari once she was alone, did not add

up. Not unless Bree Donahue had been a target, as well. And that smacked of *inside*. Hollywood *inside*. Borges had plans to see a few people at Paramount, including the producers who had recently filed suit against Donahue for her alleged breach of contract. He did not like where this was going, but he was going there anyway. People in his town had to be able to sleep at night.

Monica had returned from the wake with Madame Rey's tarot deck in her possession, but twenty-four hours elapsed before her desire to see the cards overcame the superstition induced by the Rom Baro's talk of marime and contamination. The deck had been in Raja's hands when she was murdered, and had been briefly held as evidence before being turned over to the gypsy kumpania. Though Monica was not the sort who kept a shrine to the kitchen gods or fingered her rosary beads before a blind date, it seemed illogical to her that an article that was considered viral by one culture could be entirely innocuous to another. By that primitive reasoning, she held off opening the velvet-covered case for a full day. When she did, she saw why Raszer had known that the law enforcement establishment would be clueless in a case such as this one.

Raszer had his bags packed and sat cross-legged on the floor of Room 23 at the Shasta View Motor Inn, surrounded by books. At the bookstore where April worked part-time, he'd emptied the shelves of anything having to do with tarot, magical alphabets, or Morocco. He had also scored a used copy of a hard-to-find book called *Subterranean Worlds* by Walter Kafton-Minkel, which surveyed—among other things—the stubborn myth that there existed an underground kingdom known as Agharta. He was tired, and not precisely sure of what he was looking for, but had a notion to make his own run at the last of the stanzas on the Rose document, using Madame Rey's numerological method and some computer assistance with the Sanskrit and Hebrew phrases.

The telephone rang. He expected it would be Monica, but not with anything more illuminating than prospective travel arrangements, and not with a carillon bell of excitement pealing in her voice.

"She did it, Raszer!"

"Who did what?"

"Madame Rey. The last verse of that poem. It was folded into her tarot deck. I don't even think the cops looked at it."

"Tell me," said Raszer, snapping immediately out of his haze.

"Okay," she began breathlessly. "She told you about how she was using gematria to substitute a tarot value for the Hebrew letters, right?"

"Right. I've got you."

"Well, there are different kinds of gematria, but the basic system assigns each leter in the Hebrew alphabet a numeric value and a relationship to the Tetragrammaton: the holy name of God. *Yod - Heh - Vau - Heh*. Yahweh . . . *I AM THAT I AM.*"

Raszer smiled. She was ahead of him. "Go on," he said.

"Well each word has a number, too . . . the sum of its letters . . . and any other word with the same number can be substituted for it. Once you find the right words, each one can be boiled down to a single number and letter—one of twenty-two letters in the Hebrew alphabet or twenty-two cards in the Major Arcana. That's how she came up with your spread. It's all here in her notes . . . but there's more—"

"You may have a future in divination. Keep going . . . "

"So I found this downloadable software on the O.T.O. site that sorts all the gematria combinations. It was only three hundred bucks and I—"

"Hold on," said Raszer. "You're getting ahead of yourself. You must've been sampling my herb garden again. Read me the last verse."

"All right. All right. I just wanted . . . Here it is." She sucked in a breath. "*There is a place where wisdom sleeps . . . and there a man who knew . . . The heir of Alexander's keep . . . the father of the Jew.*"

"Okay . . . " Raszer closed his book and cast a glance through the patio doors at the mountain, its double plumes of gray smoke twisted by the vortices into a helix. "*Alexander's keep* should be Alexandria. It was the greatest storehouse of spiritual knowledge on the planet for three or four centuries. It was sacked in the Middle Ages, and both Crowley and Waite say that the displaced magi migrated to—" He let Monica finish.

"Fez," she said. "Where the tarot was supposedly created."

"And the father of the Jew . . . " He pulled away from the phone and thought.

Empty your mind, and picture the name of your true father . . .

"Raszer?"

"Yeah?"

"Be-before you say anything. Just let me do this. The last thing in Raja's notes. This must've been just before she left the hospital. I think she figured out that the nine Hebrew letters were more than just a tarot spread . . . or maybe not a tarot spread at all. Some kind of geometry. A secret message within a secret message, one that you need a computer to decipher. So . . . I was telling you about that software—"

"You were about to when I butted in, yeah."

"It gave me one hundred and three possible combinations. You wanna know what combination number twenty-three is?"

"You bet I do. That's my lucky number."

"I AM BRAHMA."

"Okay . . . *I Am Brahma*," Raszer recited. "This I know. It's from the Sanskrit *Aham Brahmasmi*. It means 'I am one with god . . . with *Brahman*. But what does—"

"There's a hyperlink in the software that goes to a Web site called maguffin.com. It's a kind of search engine. A cyberoracle. So I type "I AM BRAHMA" and hit return. It says . . . wait a sec, there's a call on the other line . . . "

Raszer rolled his eyes to the ceiling.

"That was the travel agent," she came back. "They'll hold the seat for twenty-four hours. It says . . . I have to drop the "I" and the extra "M" because they're numerologically superfluous. That leaves ABRAHMA . . . the world's easiest anagram for—"

"Abraham," said Raszer. "The father of the Jew. Whoa. So, I'm looking for a hundred-year-old Jew named Abraham who paints tarot cards somewhere in Fez."

"In your world you are," she said sweetly. "Whether it's the real world is another one for the oracle to answer."

Professor Mathonwy was propped up in his hospital bed, his arm in a sling and his leg in traction. The nurses had groomed him nicely, as his long silver hair was not in its usual manic disarray. From the moment Raszer entered the private room, the deep furrow in Mathonwy's brow forecast a reproach. That could only mean that he'd learned about April. Raszer walked to the bedside and placed his hand on the Professor's.

"She was on assignment, Professor, and she was in very, very deep. To have told you about her involvement would have put both of you—and the mission—at risk."

"She was just a girl," Mathonwy said. "Why involve her in such nasty business?"

"You said yourself she was extraordinary, Professor." Raszer sighed. "Truth is, she's a human antibody, and if the plague these bastards have uncorked has been contained in any way, someone ought to write an epic poem for her." Mathonwy nodded sadly, and Raszer saw that he, too, had fallen under April's spell. "Anyway," Raszer said. "I am going to find her." He paused. "I have reason to think she's in Morocco."

"Oh?" said the Professor. "How did you arrive at that supposition?"

"Through a series of conjectures too improbable to meet any standard test of logic. But among them is one solid fact: Vreeland told her he wanted to take her there. On one level, she's a hostage, and he may want me to follow her there so that he can kill me. On another . . . this falls under the conjecture part . . . I think she's convinced him that she's some kind of Delphic bloodhound. That she can sniff out what he's hunting."

"And what do you suppose he's hunting?"

"I'm not sure how much of this I really need to tell you, Professor. But here goes. We speculated that Vreeland's people might be into geo-terrorism . . . the best evidence being whatever sort of device they're testing inside the mountain. It's no longer speculative. I think what we're looking at is a private, multinational strike force . . . an Armageddon scenario bankrolled by the world's most lethal venture capitalists. But somebody who knows is trying to thwart their plan."

Mathonwy shifted his weight, clearly itching to throw off his harness and go back into battle. "Go on," he said.

"All right. They've got a slew of satellite dishes trained on the sky above the volcano. Aside from relaying hate radio to the world—laying the foundation—the satellites synchronize their global command and control network. But it's getting jammed by persistent interference . . . possibly riding on the ELF carrier wave you picked up . . . and what this interference seems to be is a radio signal. I'm wondering if it's an S.O.S."

"Hmm," Mathonwy mused. His voice dropped. "My former student at Berkeley may have been on to something . . . "

"What's that?" Raszer asked, leaning in closer.

Mathonwy rubbed his chin, seeming to size up Raszer for his spiritual fitness. "Are you aware," he asked, "of the HAARP experiments the Navy does in Alaska?"

"Vaguely," Raszer answered.

"HAARP is High Frequency Active Auroral Research Program. It was a stepchild of Reagan's 'Star Wars' project, though I doubt you can find many taxpayers who are aware of it. Although the Navy won't admit it, it's basically Teslian science. The stated objective is research into the use of ELF waves to detect incoming missiles, improve communication with nuclear subs, et cetera, but it's the by-products—such as messing with weather and tectonic shifts—which have generated alarm out on the fringe."

"And you think . . . our bad guys might be using the same technology for offensive purposes?"

"It's possible. HAARP works by firing massive *slugs* of electromagnetism at the ionosphere, then using an aerial or dish to ping the signal back and forth until it builds up enormous resonances. It's called 'boiling the ionosphere' and is basically the operating principle of a Tesla cannon. Tesla showed that if you let such oscillations reach sufficient strength, you could do massive damage. Directing them repeatedly at the mouth of Mt. Shasta could indeed have made for a very irritable volcano."

"But how do the jamming signals find their way in? Timing-wise, they almost seem to coincide with the very ELF waves that the militia creates when they fire off their cannon. That'd be like calling out for an echo and getting someone else's voice back."

"Precisely." Mathonwy chuckled. "It must be driving them crazy."

"It's as if the volcano was talking back to them, and apparently to a few other folks, as well. How many of these 'human radio receivers' there are out there is a little hard to figure, but assuming there are more than just a few odd cases in California . . . how would the signals be carried to their brains?"

Mathonwy paused for thought, unconsciously registering on his face that same Buddha smile that had made Raszer wonder before. "All right. I'll add my thread to your 'improbable conjecture.' Mt. Shasta might just be a relay station . . . or even the 'head end' on a sort of telluric radio network. The signals would be carried along the old magnetic 'arteries' that grid the planet's surface . . . it's said that centuries ago men killed for 'maps' of these arteries because of the notion that everything from mineral deposits to auspicious trade routes lay along them. Some of the oldest roads in Europe follow them. Even today, you'll find underground cables and power lines tracing them. Of course, no one publically admits to it. It's geomancy. A 'crank science.' You might as well be out there with a dowsing rod."

"Like the people who believe in ley lines and that sort of thing . . . "

"Exactly," said Mathonwy. "Or, again, old Tesla, who believed—rightly, I think—that the Earth's crust was a natural conductor of electricity . . . and radio waves."

"And the seismic havoc that Vreeland's people are making could be inducing—"

"The cone of a volcano is a 'natural' transducer. If the militia does have a scalar weapon, and they've been developing 'slugs' powerful enough to shake the State of California, one of the results might be an enormous amount of stress on the bedrock . . . on the order of one thousand tons per square inch. The bedrock is veined with crystal formations, some of them growing for eons. Put that much pressure on a big vein of crystal, it's going to sing like Maria Callas!"

"Like the crystal in your old kit radio?"

"Yes," Mathonwy replied. "A crystal oscillates when electromagnetic force is applied. That's how radio worked until they invented the transistor. Depending on its on its size, how its facets are cut . . . its lattice . . . it can generate one hell of a wave. Theoretically, you could have planes, boats, and ham radio operators picking it up . . . "

"How about the fillings in someone's teeth . . . ?"

"Well . . . "

"Great," said Raszer. "So now we have—farfetched as it is—a way to generate a signal and a way to 'broadcast' it. We can even speculate that the militia's geo-terrorism experiments are causing it to be generated. But Professor . . . "

"Yes?"

"It's not just random noise. It's not even just a steady hum like those poor bastards who wear earmuffs around all day hear. It's a voice. It's . . . a song."

"Ah, well," Mathonwy replied. "There, I cannot venture with you. There, you will have to be guided by that 'improbable series of conjectures.' And by your heart."

"Professor . . . yesterday, before they took you into surgery . . . you said you'd made some sense of that pattern I picked up on your radio. A binary number, you said."

"Yes. Long pulses for ones and short pulses for zeroes. It's the only possibility I can't eliminate. It converts to three thousand, three hundred and three in base ten."

"Thirty-three-oh-three," Raszer said under his breath. "Any ideas?"

"None that I'm ready to send you off with. It could be a primitive algorithm, or the combination of a safety deposit box in Zurich. It could be anything or nothing."

"The words 'primitive' and 'algorithm' don't seem to belong together. As a matter of fact, there's a lot about this whole puzzle that's anachronistic. Very old and very new."

Mathonwy fished the control panel for his hospital bed from under the sheets and brought himself a little more upright. "Tell me, Mr. Raszer," he said. "Do you delve much into what they like to call 'maverick science?'"

Raszer laughed. "I'd say my life is a living example of maverick science."

"Indeed. Maverick science derives from an attempt to explain the inexplicable: how a subatomic particle can be in two places at once or alter its history after the fact. Or why the Pyramids align so precisely with certain celestial events, when even today, it takes the best minds and the fastest computers to program a radio telescope. Now, you're probably familiar with the 'many worlds' model in theoretical physics—that's not such maverick science anymore. But you may not be aware that there are some very sober-minded scientsts—not fantasists like von Daniken—who do not dismiss the possibility that highly developed human cultures existed in what we call prehistory."

Raszer found himself unconsciously scraping at the stubble on his chin, and moved his hand to the bed rail. "One more question, Professor. Then I'll let you rest. One of the first things I was told about Vreeland was that he'd had a vision that his archenemy was holed up a network of subterranean tunnels. Now, you and I have been mixing our myth and science pretty liberally, but tell me something. Those 'geomantic arteries' you spoke of earlier . . . are they believed to have certain, say, nodal points—like Shasta—in *other* parts of the world, as well?"

"That, friend, is the map on which science crosses into magic, and we're back in the Renaissance with Giordano Bruno—not a bad place to be, by the way. We're in the geographical realm of the Agharta Network . . . and on that map, yes . . . there are other waystations. I do believe you may be headed in the direction of one of them."

Raszer grinned. "I'll have to find myself a copy of that map. Godspeed, Professor . . . and get well soon."

18

THE MOON.

ROYAL Air Maroc carried Raszer across the Atlantic on a diagonal
from New York to Casablanca. Nobody stayed in Casablanca, other than
drug dealers, arms merchants, and misguided tourists, looking vainly for Rick's
Cafe Americain or some other post-colonial elegance long since gone to rot along
the wharf. The genuine romance of Morocco lay in points east, for which one
boarded a smaller jet: the Imperial Cities of Rabat, Meknes, Marrakech, and Fez.

The journey from San Francisco took only about fourteen hours as Monica
had booked it, but the culture shift was profound, for once Raszer left New York
he was aboard a floating mosque, where the avian fluttering of Arab tongues and
the conspiratorial rustle of kaftans replaced the boozy conviviality he associated
with trans-Atlantic flight. For the first couple of hours, there seemed to be much
commerce in play in the first class cabin, all of it of a high and serious order.
Later, the hum of the engines played like a tuned drone beneath the softly
plucked oud of Arabic discourse. The talk never ceased, but it did finally lull him
as only the babble of a foreign language can. As complement, he took good
advantage of the free-flowing wine and readied a sleeping pill for the long nap he
intended to have once the Airbus reached cruising altitude.

He had an infinite number of questions to consider, not the least of which was
how long it would be before U.S. intelligence and international law enforcement
were muddying the trail he hoped to follow. Those questions could wait until the

scent of foreign soil in his nostrils had awakened the Pandora in him; now, he needed rest.

On arrival at Kennedy, Raszer had placed a call to his daughter at her mother's place in Connecticut. It was a ritual. He rarely boarded a plane, and never left the country without contacting her, and she'd been on his mind almost continually since learning of Ori.

"Know where I'm headed this time?" he asked her.

"Timbuktu?" she answered.

"Close, baby. Mor-oc-co. The royal blue city of Fez, where the pipes play and the dervishes whirl."

"Hold on, Daddy," she said. "Let me find it. I have to check the gazetteer."

Brigit loved saying the word 'gazetteer.' It sounded exotic and very grown-up to her. He had taught her how to use one and to locate cities by latitude and longitude. She had a big map of the world on the wall beside her bed, and it was her habit to trace her father's journeys with colored yarn stretched between thumbtacks. In the beginning, it was she who derived comfort from gazing at the map, imagining herself riding his vapor trail. Now, it was Raszer as much as she who insisted upon the protocol. He wanted her to know his route.

"Are there wizards there?" she asked. "And flying carpets?"

"As a matter of fact," said Raszer, "I'm going to try and see a sort of wizard. I'll have to let you know about the flying carpets."

"Let's see," she said studiously. "Fez. Latitude thirty-two degrees north. Longitude five degrees west. Got it. Now I'll—"

"Brigit?" Raszer said, feeling the pulse throb in his temple.

"Yeah, Daddy?"

"Say those again. The map coordinates. Latitude and longitude."

"Thirty-two north, and five west."

"That's right, baby," he said. "I love you more than the sun, moon, and stars."

First Class was about three-quarters full and occupied mostly by businessmen from the Maghreb, a number in traditional Arab dress, others distinguishable from their pin-striped American counterparts only by their coffee complexions and abstention from vodka. One fellow, seated across the aisle and one up from Raszer, looked especially well heeled in Bruno Magli oxfords and a suit of hand-tailored British wool. Beginning with the shoes, Raszer tracked up the man's body, expecting to end on a profile of equally fine issue, and was unsettled to find a pair of opaque brown eyes, returning his stare in kind. The man turned away and lit a small cigar, an indulgence allowed—albeit unofficially—to Air Maroc's first cabin passengers. Raszer returned his attention to his foreign service Arabic book and sipped the glass of port he'd ordered after picking away at a flavorless lamb cous-cous. He cast an absent glance at the man in the Magli shoes and watched his left hand fall sleepily to his tray table. His fingers uncurled, revealing the book of matches he'd used to light his cigarillo. The print was clear, bold, and familiar. Gold letters on a black background. Raszer dipped into the pocket of his jacket and brought out the matchbook he'd taken from April's dressing room. Gold letters on black: *The Barbary Club*. Then he put away his pills and any hope of sleep.

"I'm told it's quite a place," said Raszer, standing in the aisle. The businessman looked up, surprised, and Raszer indicated the matchbook. After fifteen minutes of internal debate, he'd left his seat, bringing April's matchbook as an ice-breaker. *"Hael libs aes-saehra daruri?"*

"No, no," replied the man, immediately hospitable in the manner of his culture. "It is not formal. Sportswear is permitted. Men who come to the Barbary do not need to prove their net worth. But you would need more than an expensive suit in any case. It is private. Members only." He pointed to Raszer's matchbook. "If you don't mind . . . where did you get that?"

"A golf partner of mine . . . a distribution exec at Fox . . . told me I should check it out if I was ever in Morocco. Raved about it. But you know Hollywood types . . . they think they can get in anywhere. It figures he'd leave out the 'members only' part. Sorry to bother you." He began to turn.

"A 'Hollywood type' who has troubled to learn Arabic might fare better than most," the man said. "Have a seat. What are you drinking?"

The businessman moved over to the empty window seat and Raszer eased in, quickly cobbling together a makeshift identity for himself as a film producer scouting locations in North Africa. After ten minutes of guarded conversation, his companion opened up a bit and revealed that he was a Tunisian trader in phosphates whose firm was based in Hamburg, and that his name was Benani.

"Will you be staying in Casablanca?" Benani asked.

"Only for the night . . . hard for movie people to come here without saying they've done Casablanca . . . but we're due in Marrakech day after tomorrow."

"You're not traveling alone, then. Where is the rest of your, uh . . . entourage?" Raszer cocked his thumb back in the direction of the economy cabin. Benani nodded and said, "Ah . . . "

Raszer dimmed down the conversation after another fifteen minutes of talk about the odds of making a profit in movie speculation, yawned and excused himself to return to his seat and get some sleep. He didn't want to slip up and he hadn't planned on making any new friends, but the Barbary Club connection was too fortuitous not to jump at. He supposed that it could be a franchise, that there might also be a Barbary Club in Fez—or Riyadh, for that matter. No, he thought. Probably not. Just as chaos theorists looked for "strange attractors" beneath the surface of random events, experience had taught Raszer that when the planets lined up this way, it was time to pay attention. Now too pensive to sleep, and too excited to take a pill, he chewed nicotine gum and practiced his Arabic, the better to smooth his entree to the Club.

There was a brief stretch on the rim of pink dawn when Raszer found a sort of lucid sleep and recalled a moment on Main Street, Mt. Shasta, that he'd nearly misplaced in the smear of events leading to his departure. When he'd made his last trip into town to visit April's bookstore, he'd again encountered the tribal leaders, now holding a prayer vigil on the courthouse steps. He'd paused to show his solidarity with their cause. Raising his eyes after a respectful few minutes, he'd beheld the wizened face of the Modoc chief who led the vigil, and it had been as if the old man knew him as kin. He walked over, introduced himself, and suggested that if the lawyers representing their claim were still preparing the case, they ought to see a man named Kane in the County Recorder's office, and ask to see "The Diary of Augustus Leek." The chief nodded and thanked him, and as Raszer turned to leave, the old man had extended his arms and flapped them like a bird of prey seeking an air current on which to soar. The Modoc's eyes, which had been downcast and lifeless, now flickered with something like hope. He smiled, and with that smile told Raszer that his life would be one of constant flight, but that like the hawk, he would occasionally swoop down and rid the meadow of a snake.

The flight arrived in Casablanca at 4:53 on an October afternoon buffed to a glow by cool, moist winds. The connection to Fez was not available until the next morning, so even if not for the lure of the Barbary Club, Raszer would have been grounded for the night. As he waited at the crowded baggage carousel, the Tunisian approached him.

"If you have no dinner plans," he said, "I would be honored to have you as my guest at the club—"

"And my companions?" Raszer bluffed, gesturing toward two anonymous young American women on the far side of the luggage chute.

"Ah," said Benani. "I am afraid I am limited to one. And the Barbary is . . . a gentlemen's club." He grinned a little too suggestively.

"Ah," said Raszer. "I see. Then I'll quarantine the ladies at the hotel. Are you sure I'll pass muster?"

"Oh, indeed. They love movie people at the Barbary. I believe we may even have a few of your colleagues from Fox as members."

"Is that so?" Raszer said, his throat tightening. "Well, they say you never leave Hollywood these days." *Never, ever*—he reminded himself—*give them enough rope to hang you with.* "I'm at the Sheraton," he added.

Benanai handed him a business card with his mobile phone number hand-written on the back. "Call once you are settled in," he said. "I will have a car sent for you."

Raszer said, "Thanks. I look forward to it," then swallowed hard. He wasn't looking the least bit forward to it, but if there was the slightest chance of picking up April's trail, he had to go. It was hard to believe that the matchbook he'd found in April's dressing room had not once belonged to Bronk Vreeland or someone in his circle.

The Sheraton on the Place des Nations Unies was not Raszer's kind of hotel, but it would do for an overnight. He slept off the flight for two hours, then woke, ordered coffee, and phoned Monica in L.A. to let her know of the change in his evening's schedule. Like his daughter, Raszer's assistant vigilantly tracked his travels from afar, though not with thumbtacks and colored yarn. Monica maintained precision timetables for contact, which, if broken, would prompt her to summon immediate help.

His original plans for the evening had entailed dining alone and, later, having a nightcap with the local Interpol attaché and a mid-level trade representative from the U.S. consulate. He'd contacted them from San Francisco, thinking that one of them might have knowledge of Rupert Voorhees, and whether any of his presumably myriad fronts were operating in Casablanca. He'd known he would need help navigating the city, but had been wary of asking for it in a way that might stir up chatter on the wrong channels. Now, he had a more direct source of information, albeit one less assuredly sympathetic. He asked Monica to call his contacts and beg off, pleading jet lag and promising an update in the morning.

"Okay," she said. "I hope you know what you're doing."

"I hope so, too," he said. "What's happening up north? Are they evacuating the town?"

"Slowly," she replied. "CNN keeps showing live 'Shasta Cam' shots of the mountain, but it's the same picture every time. Just this thin plume of smoke going straight up in the air. No wind, even. It's eerie."

"Are they saying anything about the militia?"

"Not much. One of the cable news channels mentioned 'the likely evacuation of the compound' and played up the Waco connection. Something about 'local authorities treading lightly.' As for Vreeland, I jotted down the only reference I heard: 'Whereabouts of the outspoken white supremacist leader unknown.' It sounds like they're just getting into it, but sooner or later they'll get it wired and turn it into *Apocalypse Now*."

"Let's hope for later. I need some breathing room, and once he's officially labeled a fugitive from justice, the feds and Interpol will be all over it. If they trace him here, well—let's just make sure we clean our footprints as we go. No more satellite calls, no GPS, no e-mail."

"You can't go off the map like that, Raszer. I'd have no way to get to you."

He replied firmly and gravely. "I didn't plan on this turn of events. This isn't the way I wanted to see Morocco. But now that it's happened, I have to drop out. I have to assume at every step that *he* assumes I'm here . . . however illogical that may seem. So for now, I'm invisible. What you can do is use our contacts to set up a sham office and voice mail for me on the Fox lot. As Daniel Reznick, a production exec. You record the greeting in your best Hollywood assistant's voice. If I get into trouble, I'll leave a message there. And right now—" He looked at his watch. "I need to call Mr. Benani."

"Good luck, Raszer," was all she said. He knew she wasn't happy.

The Barbary Club was located three kilometers from the hotel, off the Avenue des FAR in a graying structure dating from the French colonial period. It was not possible to tell whether the building served any purpose other than to house the private club, but it was bounded on all sides by ten-foot cinderblock walls adorned with another two feet of barbed wire. It appeared to be the only distinguished architecture on this sad stretch of the Blvd. Hassan Seghir, which ran through the heart of the city's red light district. It surprised Raszer to see women working the streets in a Muslim country, until he recalled that Morocco was an anomaly, and Casablanca another thing altogether. Still, the presence of prostitutes near the gates of a posh private club seemed unusual.

In the heavy dampness of the coastal night, the building itself seemed to sweat an odor of internal decay, notwithstanding the presence of mirror-surfaced black

260

limousines and red-suited doormen with epaulets. He walked up the wide, car-peted steps and through a set of ornately carved wooden doors, and handed Benani's business card to the attendant.

"Please come this way," the maître d' said, in what seemed a Mitteleuropan accent. There was no music and no chatter that rose above the level of conspirato-rial murmur. Raszer's first impression was that he'd entered a den of assassins. The decor could be described only as *fin de siecle* gaudy, as if modeled after a club car on the Orient Express, or possibly the foyer of a Victorian bawdy house. In this regard, he was reminded of the entryway of the Pink Temple, and realized that the common element might be the venerable Voorhees family.

He counted only about a dozen patrons, mostly pairs, with the exception of a small private party at a dim, elevated table in the rear. As Benani rose from his table to offer a chair, Raszer became peripherally aware of the striking motif sug-gested by the club's choice of artwork. The dining room was hung like a gallery with expensively mounted paintings of ersatz German Romantic hyperrealism, one for each semi-curtained table, and every one of them depicting the sexual rav-ishment of a victim who appeared as passively resigned to its fate as a gazelle in the jaws of a lion. Most of the works bore the same trademark brooding skies and Olympian vistas. A few of them, though overwrought, were disturbingly erotic, as if painted by Caspar David Friedrich in a drug-induced sexual frenzy.

"Well," Raszer remarked, taking his seat, "I'm glad you advised me against bringing the ladies. When do the nautch girls come out?"

"Ah . . . stay long enough," Benani replied, "and you will discover that your American 'strip clubs' are only the lowest order in the hierarchy of erotic enter-tainment. We must first, though, look to our stomachs." He indicated the menu. "May I recommend that you choose from the house specialties? I sense you are a man who does not shy away from the unusual."

Raszer opened the velvet-covered menu and had to fight off a giggle. The dishes were exclusively fowl, but of almost ludicrously exotic provenance. There was "roast nesting swan with apricot glaze," "Norfolk Crane in aspic," and "baked puffin with date sauce," to mention only the least outrageous offerings. It was an absurdist's fantasy, but these people, Raszer sensed, were not absurdists. There was no *dada* here, not an ounce of irony. He glanced at the hors d'oeuvres and this time could not contain himself. "Ha!" he exclaimed. "I've heard about this. *Ortolan.* That's the little bird the French aristocrats pop into their mouths feathers and all, right? An endangered species, isn't it?"

Benani smiled and spoke with the air of the cognoscenti. "You may choose to call 'endangered' what other men simply describe as rare . . . and therefore, desirable."

"Well," said Raszer, closing the menu summarily. "When in Rome . . . I'll have the braised Corsican eagle. With a good Sancerre it may be just the thing for jet lag." He took out his cigarettes and sat back. He had to concede that the menu went with the décor. What the hell had he walked into?

"You won't be disappointed!" said Benani, and summoned the waiter. "Now then," he said, after placing the order, "tell me about your movie. I may be interested to make a small investment . . . if you are looking for partners."

"Thanks," said Raszer, heading off the subject. "This one's a studio picture. All the money's inside. But I'd be happy to keep you apprised of others." He gestured to the party on the dais at the rear of the club, a group of six presided over by a tall, princely figure in hand-tailored linen, who sat with his back to the room. "Who's that guy?" he asked. "A visiting duke? Sure looks like somebody important."

Benani smiled his self-satisfied smile once again. The man was a natural-born sycophant, Raszer thought. He'd do well in the movie business.

But the twinkle in Benani's eyes had barely dimmed when Raszer felt the gooseflesh rise on his arms. The tall man turned just enough to reveal a profile, and though in silhouette, the strangely elongated head, with its narrow brow and a nose that was hardly more than a line drawn from bridge to lip, was familiar enough. The family resemblance to the figure in the AP photo was more than striking, but no photograph could have captured the elegant menace in his cobralike face.

"Ah," said Raszer's host, his admiring gaze on the object of their mutual attention. "Indeed. That is a man you should know. I'm surprised your friend from Fox—the one who told you of the Barbary—did not mention him, because I suspect he could purchase the studio ten times over if he chose to. That . . . is Rupert Voorhees."

Raszer lit a cigarette, shook the match out slowly, and made use of the time to study his dinner companion, whose eyes remained fixed on the master of ceremonies. Was Benani what he appeared to be: a rich, credulous wannabe who'd been shaken down for the price of membership? Or had his presence on Air Maroc Flight 11 been much more than coincidence? It was impossible to distinguish—Raszer knew—between a genuine character and a skilled character actor, and in that uncertainty, there was paranoia. Now, to Raszer's horror, he seemed to be trying to get Voohees' attention.

"Hmm," Raszer said, and cleared his throat. "I suppose he's a member, too?"

"He is not only a member, my friend. He owns it! I must introduce you . . . "

Alarm bells went off in every sector of Raszer's nervous system. Every instinct told him that nothing good would come of showing Voorhees his face. He explained to Benani that he was jet-lagged, and that was true enough. He told him he had an early flight, and that was also true. But the Tunisian would not be deterred, and continued to signal the men on the dais, raising his glass in a toast when Voorhees finally and languidly acknowledged him. And Raszer knew then that Benani was no plant, and no actor. He was just a show-off, eager to broker a meeting between his powerful host and his new Hollywood friend. We are undone not so much by the clever as by the guileless.

"I'm quite sure he'll pay us a visit," he said proudly. "Rupert always makes the rounds and I . . . well, my firm is one of his recent acquisitions."

"Wonderful," said Raszer, taking a mouthful of wine as the waiter arrived with dinner. Any appetite he'd had was now as dead as the overcooked fowl on his plate. He picked up his fork and turned over what appeared to be a turnip. A shadow fell over the white linen tablecloth, and an odd scent—equal parts rosewater and formaldehyde—entered his nostrils. Benani rose from the table, wiping his mouth hastily.

"Ah, Monsieur Voorhees!" he exclaimed. "What an honor! May I introduce my good friend from . . . " He turned to Raszer, flushing slightly. "It is Fox Studios, yes?"

"It is for this movie," Raszer answered.

"Well, then, we may have mutual acquaintances," said their visitor. "Rupert Voorhees." He gave a nod. His bearing was somehow both effete and commanding.

"Daniel Reznick," Raszer said, offering a chair. Voorhees regarded the proposition cooly. "No, no," he said. "I insist that you and Benani join us at my table."

Raszer could not very well demur. Not now. He was already in the belly of the beast. By generational count, the Rupert Voorhees with whom Raszer was about to break bread had to be the third in his line from the monocled robber baron so chillingly depicted in Augustus Leek's journals, and the son of the mineral czar in the AP photo, but the filial likeness was uncanny, almost as if he'd emerged from the ancestral line by parthenogenesis. The small, widely spaced eyes and the edgeless features that seemed to melt together suggested—at the least—inbreeding. Still, he was impressive, more as a factor of height and presence than classic "good looks." It occurred to Raszer that it was a face only an Ayn Rand heroine could love. His dark hair was slicked back from a low, straight line and his age appeared fixed at a perpetual sixty-two by some combination of Botox, black magic and chemical preservatives.

"Reznick, is it?" Voorhees inquired as they walked. "I can't quite place . . . "

"I'm not in the trades much," Raszer interjected. "I'm a production designer."

"No, no," Voorhees corrected. "I mean the nationality. The *ethnicity.*"

"Polish," Raszer answered. "Abbreviated for Ellis Island, of course."

"Of course," said Voorhees.

"Voorhees is Dutch, isn't it? Or is it Huguenot . . ."

"Boer, actually," Voorhees said as he mounted the dais and invited the new arrivals to join the party.

There were five men already at the table. Three were older men in business attire, more self-assured and less indigenous than Benani, but at the far end, shoulder to shoulder in matching leathers, sat a pair of identical twins, distinguishable only by hair dye: one black, one bleached to the roots. Everything about them said Hollywood.

"Gentlemen," Voorhees began. "May I introduce Mr. Daniel Reznick of, er . . . a current Fox production. Daniel . . . Mr. Silvio Busconi of Banco Italia; Ahmed Rahman of Pioneer Exporting; Klaus Froeder of the Berliner Media Group . . . and you've no doubt heard of the Buzz Brothers, Reinholdt and Roger. They are preparing their first feature—as it happens—for Fox. The project had been set up at Paramount but, sadly, their leading lady, er, withdrew. Isn't that right, fellows?" He paused, and the Buzz Brother identified as Reinholdt nodded grimly. In afterthought, Voorhees added, "And you all know Benani, of course." Voorhees resumed his seat, leaving Raszer the last man standing. He intended to keep standing until he was out the door. He did not recognize any of Voorhees's guests, though they all seemed possessed of a certain intrinsic celebrity. It was clear enough why the Buzz Brothers had made the pilgrimage, just as it was clear who'd been developing their movie at Paramount, and why their leading lady was indisposed. He wondered how much they'd had to do with Bree Donahue's murder. They had the morally vacant look of German commercial directors who pimp for BMW and delude themselves they're making art. One thing seemed reasonably secure: none of these people would remember his own brief, tarnished acting career.

"I'm afraid I can't take you up on the drink," he said to Voorhees. then turned to the group. "We've got a five A.M. scout. Have to cover Marrakech before sunset. I'm sure the Buzz Brothers—" He nodded to the twins. "—understand."

"Yuh," the bottle blond affirmed. "Hate those early calls."

"That's a pity, Mr. Reznick," said Voorhees. "You'll miss our floor show. Hasn't Benani told you about our special entertainments?" He chuckled. "I had assumed that's what lured you here this evening. Tonight's performer comes all the way from your part of the world." Voorhees smiled thinly. "It is indeed a global village, isn't it?" Raszer remained outwardly impassive, but felt just the slightest surge in his heartbeat. "I'm told she's really quite unique," Voorhees continued. "In addition to her beauty and . . . athletic skills . . . they tell me she possesses the gift of prophecy. As you can imagine, our anticipation is quite keen . . . isn't it, gentlemen?" He polled the faces of his guests for their nods of affirmation, then turned back with a false frown that filled Raszer suddenly with both great sadness and anger. "So won't you stay with us?" Voorhees finished.

Raszer had honed his skills at forbearance to cutting edge. He was a chameleon. There were times, though, when his passions trumped all restraint, just as April's had when she'd made her fateful mistake on the porch of the militia HQ. Something passed silently between him and Voorhees, and it was not pleasant for either of them. The older man leaned into the amber spill of the overhead lamp, inspecting Raszer's face as if comparing fingerprints and finding a positive match. Raszer had made his own match. Voorhees's face—from the sagging bridge of the nose to the shapeless upper lip—-could have been superimposed on Fortis Cohn's with almost no variance. Now, he sat down.

Voorhees turned to the Tunisian. "Benani. Tell us the story of how you came to know Mr. Reznick. I always enjoy hearing how new friendships are formed."

"Well," replied Benani, sensing from the darker tone in Voohees' voice that some discretion was now called for. "I don't know that we are quite yet friends, but we had a most enjoyable talk on the flight from New York."

"I see," said Voorhees, His head pivoted slowly, like a gun turret, until eyes of cold fire were leveled on the Tunisian, who seemed visibly to shrink. "And you . . . my friend . . . you told him about the Barbary Club? You thought it would be nice to—"

"No, Monsieur," pleaded Benani. "Well, yes, but . . . you see, he—"

The tendons in Raszer's neck felt suddenly like steel cables. He saw the beads of sweat forming on Benani's upper lip, and decided to take him off the hook.

"I happened to see Mr. Benani's matchbook on the plane, and mentioned that a friend in the movie business had raved about the place. I begged him to bring me. I didn't expect the jet lag to hit me so soon. So, if you'll all excuse me—" He pushed back evenly from the table and stood. "—I'm going to catch a taxi and put myself to bed."

"Hmm," commented Voorhees, shaking his head in mock astonishment. "Well, you see, gentlemen, there it is again! Such a small world. Is it accident, or is it fate?"

Voorhees rose unhurriedly, but even in his practiced dispassion, there was urgency. He bowed and smiled to the table at large. "Would you excuse me for a moment, my friends? I need to check on the evening's entertainment." He stepped off the dais, and in three relaxed strides had vanished through the drapes at the rear of the room.

"Oh, dear," Raszer said, backing away. "I'm afraid I'm really not up to snuff. The rich food. The long flight—"

The Buzz Brother designated "Roger" pulled a prescription vial from his leather jacket and said, "You want to feel better fast?"

Raszer waved off the offer. "No, but thanks. Mr. Benani . . . thanks for the hospitality . . . " He took another step back, his hand on his belly. " . . . and the ride. I'll get myself home . . . " As he stepped off the riser, he turned back to the Tunisian. "And Benani . . . I'll call you about those film properties."

There was some murmuring, shifting, and clearing of throats among Voorhees's guests as Raszer made his way toward the door, reining in his flight instinct as tightly as he could, but when he turned at the bar to look back, they seemed almost to be in a state of suspended animation, awaiting the return of their host and the onset of the night's "entertainment." Nonetheless, he felt eyes on his back. From the barman. The waiters. The fucking pictures on the wall.

It had been foolish to come here alone, but it had yielded one bonanza: he knew where April was. If only he could get out and summon help. At this point, he didn't care where it came from. He wanted her out. What sort of performance they'd demanded from her was something he couldn't allow himself to imagine. No. It was something he couldn't allow to happen. Ten paces from the exit, he saw the red-cloaked doorman speak into a walkie-talkie and glance furtively his way. Raszer veered immediately right, following a busboy bearing a tray piled with the avian remains of someone's meal.

An unmarked gray door on the right offered one choice, but Raszer's intuition steered him with the busboy through the swinging doors and into the steamy kitchen, crewed almost entirely by locals. One by one, they glanced up from their chopping and stewing, and Raszer knew he must quickly perform some sleight-of-hand. He pulled out his wallet and held it open in the manner of a cop or an inspector, flashing his detective license and calling out, *"Services de Sante . . . inspection des lieux."* That bought him only a breath before the swinging doors once again flew open and the strident footsteps of two pursuers hammered the wooden floor. One called out, *"L' homme Americain . . . ou est il?"* Raszer darted into a narrow service hallway that offered just two outlets.

One door appeared to be for deliveries and might lead to the street, but he reasoned quickly that Voorhees would have that covered. Instead, with the shouts of additional men ringing behind him, he sidestepped into what looked like a large pantry, closed its heavy wooden door, and rolled a half-filled grain barrel against it. He took one breath, scanned the dimly illuminated room, and wondered, *Where is Vreeland?*

In Raszer's predicament, there was really no place to go but forward. In similar circumstances, he'd learned that a profound mental recalibration was required when one is truly facing death, and that with it sometimes came a kind of reckless intelligence.

He saw that opposite him was an oversized aluminum door with a spring-loaded handle. Presumably, a refrigerator, but possibly . . . In two leaps he was there and pulled it open just as the barrel hit the floor, spilling its contents of dry couscous. He stepped inside and shouldered the door shut, then felt its surface for a deadbolt or latch. There was a small button, which he pressed. A half-second later came the *c-click* of a lock tumbler turning, a bit of luck that made sense only if there was something in the room which merited restricted access. Only minutes, maybe seconds, until someone with the combination arrived. As soon as he turned around, he was aware of the odor of carrion.

Raszer felt the wall for a light switch while his pursuers surfed on spilled semolina in the pantry. He let out a curse when the flourescents came on overhead. He was in a vast meat locker; more precisely, a fowl locker, the carcasses of a dozen species of large bird suspended by their clawed, reptilian feet from row upon row of ceiling hooks. There were, he reckoned, at least six dozen of them, their gamey flesh "aging" to a state of tender decay worthy of the clientele. Eagles, condors, cormorants, albatrosses, peacocks, and ostriches, ripe for plucking. He turned off the overhead lights, flipped open his Zippo, and stumbled down the feathered aisles. If the refrigerator door locked from the inside, then there must, by reason, be another way to enter and exit this space.

He had just begun to perceive the faint outline of a big, retractable door, wide enough to drive a poultry truck through, when he heard, from his left and below, what sounded like weeping. He approached the sidewall and knelt, running the flame of his lighter along the baseboard. Placed at floor level, six feet apart, were two large air-conditioning vents, numbingly cold air blasting through at high pressure. He put his ear to the first, then the second, and then he heard her. From the right, farther down. *Go through the ductwork? No. Suicide.* He felt his way along the wall, trying to register through his palms the subtle vibrations of her sobs. He reached the corner adjacent to the delivery door. *There.* She was close enough to touch, but a wall separated them.

He heard sequence of digital chirps as a combination was punched into the meat locker door.

Raszer sprung for the garage door and fumbled for the button. At last, with a groan loud enough to summon the city's faithful to prayers, the door rose, exposing five feet of lamplit night and a steeply raked driveway before Raszer backed off the button. The locker door behind him burst open.

Exit to a loading area seemed sure to lead to capture, so he retreated instead to the darkness, where the hanging cadavers offered the only cover available. He grabbed the midsection of a plump ostrich, hiked his legs around its thorax, and hung on, praying that whatever bound its feet to the hook above would hold his weight and keep his feet off the floor. Its joints cracked and the bird began to swing precariously as one, two, then six gunmen tore into the room and rushed through the half-open truckport, fanning out in pursuit of their presumed escapee. After dangling for a full sixty seconds, Raszer dropped to the floor in a crouch, listened, then shot into the night air, swerved left, and squatted down. Shouts of pursuit echoed off the surrounding buildings, followed by a brief blast of automatic weapon fire. As the sound died out, he heard her again.

A narrow storm trough ran alongside the building. On his hands and knees, Raszer followed it until he reached a tiny barred window. He peered through the bars, seeing nothing but the murkiest gray. Then he tapped, and there was movement. Movement and the faintest outline of the face he knew.

"April," he called through the bars. "Oh, God, April . . . "

She returned a frail, prayerful whisper. *"Raszer?"*

"Yeah, baby, it's me. Come closer."

They had dressed her in the sequined outfit of a Berber temptress. Tears had smeared the heavy mascara. Her eyes were dull, her skin pallid. They had doped her, but still, she registered his summons as if it had come from the angel Gabriel. The footfalls of at least three gunmen sounded on the pavement beyond the open gate, twenty yards away. She drew the chair to the wall and stepped up on it, wrapping her fingers around the bars and bringing her face as close as she could. Raszer pressed his forehead into the cold iron. "Listen to me," he said. "I'll be on your tail every step of the way. Where are they taking you? Is it Fez?"

"Yeah," she said. "I think so. But it's just a—like a take-off point for wherever it is we're going." She moaned, "Oh, Raszer . . . I fucked up sooo bad."

"No, you didn't." He reached his hand through and touched her cheek. "You led me right to these bastards. And we're going to nail them. You and me."

Keys jangled in the hallway behind her. "They're coming, Raszer. You gotta go."

"I know," he said. "You may not see me for a few days, but you will see me." Another cackle of gunfire erupted beyond the wall. "Leave crumbs for me, okay?"

A caustic voice came from the corridor. "Time to hit the road, Gypsy! Show's cancelled tonight."

Vreeland.

"I love you, Wart," she sighed, so softly he barely heard. With all the strength left in her, she tried to pull herself up to him, but could only get close enough to feel his breath on her face. That was enough to bring the faintest of smiles to her lips.

"I love you, too, Morgana," he said. "I think I've loved you all my life."

Then they broke from one another, she to face her captor and he to make a wild zig-zag for the open gates of the Barbary Club and the Boulevard beyond.

He hit the Blvd. Hassan Seghir running at full clip; at the least, he wanted to be a fast-moving target. He dodged a bus, two taxis, and a mobilette and did not look back until he had reached the relative cover of a bus kiosk on the other side.

The gunmen had regrouped at the front of the Club, giving him the moment's free dash. Raszer could see Benani's driver and the other chauffeurs being questioned, as they huddled in a cloud of cigarette smoke. He doubled back to the west side of the fortresslike building, using parked cars for what little cover they provided, angling for a position from which he could observe both front and rear of the club. If pursuit was going to continue, he needed to know how fast and in which direction to run. Moreover, he wanted to ID whatever vehicle would be used to transport April.

A loonlike cry came from his rear. A fleshy whore with a swollen belly, half-hidden in a nearby tobacco shop entrance, fluttered her tongue at him. A second, farther down, wrapped herself around a lamppost and trilled as if signaling the pack that prey was in sight. He showed them empty palms and they moved on.

The running boards of a curbed postal truck gave him two more feet of height, and his line of sight just broke the barbed wire. A few yards beyond the sloped driveway leading into the meat locker was a loading dock illuminated by a single floodlight. A windowless black van had been backed up to the dock, and its rear doors stood open. A small detail of armed men—all in military khaki and all of North African appearance—emerged from the building, moving rapidly and clustered like Secret Service agents around a politician. In the midst of the moving huddle, Bronk Vreeland's bronzed scalp caught the floodlight's glare for an instant. Raszer rose up on his toes and squinted hard. *Was she there?* She had to be. A millisecond later, he got his confirmation: a flash of wheat-colored hair. Then she was in the van, and the doors were slammed shut.

The gates now opened completely with a motorized whine, and the full complement of henchmen trotted out with assault rifles, flanking the van as it lurched through and nosed out onto the boulevard, braking in mid-stream, its turn signal flashing toward the busy traffic circle at Avenue des FAR. The vehicle was completely blacked out: no grillwork, no license plates, nothing identifiable beyond its very anonymity. Once it had cleared the curb without ambush, the guards backed through the gates with rifles raised, drawing them closed again and leaving two sentries on the street.

Raszer watched through the filthy windows of a parked Toyota that had been stripped to the axles, drawing breath by shallow breath, waiting for the van's driver to make his decision. The sentries stood twenty meters apart, surveying the street, presumably ready to catch in a crossfire anyone or anything that gave chase. Raszer had no illusions he could do so on foot. He was still sorting out his options when the driver gunned the engine and spun sharply onto rue Mohammed Smiha, moving so fast that Raszer's usual presence of mind was left in the past tense. The geometry of his position was hopeless. If he moved one meter left or right, he would be in the sentries' sights.

From his left came the sputter of an old diesel engine: a newspaper truck was lumbering toward him down the side street. With one eye on the guards, Raszer timed its approach, calculating the moment—and the momentum—with which he would have to vault from the Toyota's trunk in order to make a running leap at the newspaper truck's rear bumper. No time for thought. *Go.* He landed hard in the street, a yard short. The nearest sentry pivoted and aimed. Raszer raced after the truck—a fusillade of .308 caliber bullets spraying the parked cars on his right—and leapt for the handle on the rear door, his legs momentarily flying into the air with the truck's acceleration. For a half a block, his toes skidded over rough pavement, but finally he pulled himself up on the running board. A single well-aimed bullet smacked into the truck, a foot from from his head, but the driver only gunned the engine and careened around a corner toward the relative safety of the Place des Nations Unies.

Two minutes later, Raszer dropped off two blocks from the Sheraton. The black van, which had been in his sights for a while, had sped ahead toward the inland-bound highway and vanished.

Raszer remained at the hotel's front desk while the porter retrieved his belongings from the room. He'd made a snap decision. He'd lost Vreeland's trail for the moment, but he was quite sure that Rupert Voorhees and the Fraternity had not lost his. By this time, the hapless Benani had surely told them he was at the Sheraton, and it was only a matter of minutes before his pursuers caught up. As he had only the vaguest idea where Vreeland was ultimately headed, he would proceed as if he knew where *he* was going. In six hours, his plane would leave for Fez. For now, the heavily guarded airport was the safest place to be. He didn't believe that Voorhees would risk an international incident by seizing an American amid U.S.-friendly Morocco's national guard.

After having passed a fitful night on a hard plastic bench, two feet from the comforting muzzle of an airport guard's Ruger Mini-14, Raszer arrived in the royal city of Fez with sore muscles, bruised ribs, and an unsettled mind. The low, pink sun of morning and the cleansing aridity of the desert restored him after Casablanca's dankness, but Raszer knew he was not yet in shape to begin searching the serpentine streets of the medina for a magus named Abraham, and much had to be learned before he could organize an expedition to wherever his final destination might lie. He had checked on his locator the map coordinates of 33N 3W suggested by Mathonwy's binary code-breaking and Brigit's gazetteer, and they placed him in the heart of the Middle Atlas mountain range, in an area which appeared entirely unpopulated. In this, there was reason for both hope and terror, for if a physical location was indeed what the numbers identified, then it was one the Fraternity was almost surely aware of by now. They had intercepted the pirate radio broadcast long before his own fortuitous discovery, and that would explain the presence in Morocco of Bronk Vreeland, Rupert Voorhees, and a small army of goons. Like it or not, he and Vreeland were to be fellow travelers.

Having checked into the comfortable but thoroughly native Hotel Palais Jamai, he awoke from heavy sleep with the muezzin's call to midday prayer, and for a few moments allowed his joints to sink back into the featherbed and his senses to attune themselves to the new spirits drifting up over the balcony and through the periwinkle-blue french doors. There was grill smoke perfumed with cardamom and coriander, the sweet smell of street market dates, plumped in the sun's rising heat; warm pistachios; the sound of thick gut strings snapping lazily against taut hide in accompaniment to a moaning voice which might easily have belonged to a Delta bluesman. And there was the light—a light so hard and sapphire brilliant that it seemed its radiance could be measured in carats. Not the gauzy light of Europe, or the pervasive golden blaze of Southern California. This was a light strained of anything but its primary blue, a light that hid nothing and everything. As he stood half-naked on his little balcony and looked out over the old walled city with its purported ninety-four hundred labyrinthine lanes, he knew that a great deal here was hidden. Somewhere down there, if a gypsy's divinations and a sibyl's prophecy held true, was a man with a good story to tell.

The Palais Jamai was on the north side of the Fes el-Bali, the ninth-century medina that was the heart and soul of the city, and pre-dated all else. The cheapest suite ran 3200 dirham—about $300—but it had been a small price to pay for a restorative sleep and a good meal. He suspected they would be his last for a while.

He had slept in his trousers and without bathing, and he felt far too fuzzy and dislocated for a standard hot shower to revive him. After splashing some cold water on his face and taking a clean shirt from his bag, he went down to the tiled lobby, where he accepted a cup of strong mint tea from an old fellow who was dispensing the national beverage from a silver tray. He inquired of the concierge whether the hotel offered a *hammam*, the penitential Middle Eastern equivalent of a spa treatment (a burly attendant scrubbed you head to toe with rock salt, herbs, and boar bristles, accompanied by water hot enough to disinfect wounds). *"Oui, monsieur,"* came the reply. "It is down the stairs and to the left." For good measure, he added, *"Aeg-aeb-nae!"* Enjoy.

When he returned to the room, purged, bruisingly exfoliated, and carrrying a fresh pack of cigarettes he'd purchased in the souk, he set about methodically organizing his day's work. On the ornately carved thuja wood coffee table, he set a tajine dish of dates and the military-grade map of the old medina that Monica had secured for him from the consulate. On the bed, he laid out clothing chosen both for its subtlety and functionality: the outfit had to serve as camouflage should he need to dissolve quickly into a crowd, and as protection through brick-oven heat of day and chill of evening. As always when he anticipated trouble, he selected one of six hand-tailored cotton shirts with vented side panels and a concealed inner pocket: this one was ivory, and long-sleeved. For footwear, he chose the pair of lightweight Scarpa Deltas he'd broken in at Joshua Tree. Then, there was the matter of defense.

He set his slim, reinforced flight case on the bed, snapped open the stainless steel latches, and surveyed his limited arsenal. His Swedish combat knife—its seven-inch blade ground from Viking steel, its hilt of gold and ribbed handle inlaid with pearl—was a given. Over the past few cases, it had acquired for him an almost talismanic value. Abjuring the traditional ankle sheath, he opted instead for a discreet new model, which strapped around his waist and nested the knife in the small of his back. The tiny gunmetal case that contained his paralytic-tipped needles and their carbon steel blow tubes was slipped into the hidden shirt pocket. Finally, and with great deliberation, he considered the gun. Not a conventional gun—Raszer wouldn't carry them. If he *was* required to kill in order to save himself or his comrades, he would kill up close. It was an elegantly downsized, semi-automatic version of the tranquilizer guns that zookeepers use on beasts run amuck. It was his favorite recent purchase, but even at fourteen ounces, it was still a lot to carry under light clothing. *Better do it,* he thought, considering his adversary. He strapped on the nylon armpit holster and shoved the gun in snugly.

Then he lit a cigarette, took a date from the mustard yellow dish, and knelt down to examine the map of the medina. His search would begin in the *mellah*— the Jewish quarter—with an eye to anyone selling hand-painted tarot cards. It was not quite as bad as searching Tel Aviv for a man named Chaim. Morocco's once plentiful Jewry, descendants of those whose erudition had fused with that of the great Islamic scholars and illuminated the Maghreb and Andalusia in the glory days of the caliphate of Cordoba, had long since left for Israel or parts West. The few genuine rebbes who remained in Fez were inclined to keep to tradition and to the mellah, especially in light of the continuing blood feud in the Middle East. But now that he was here, wandering rutted streets and dodging camels in search of a man who might be long deceased—if not entirely chimerical—Raszer began to question his judgement. His time and energy might be better spent in assembling a posse of Berbers to go after Vreeland, or even—worst case—involving agencies of the U.S. government. Along with his own instinct, he needed April's intuition. There was a moment near the Bab Bou Jeloud—the great western gate of the medina—when after fending off a pack of boys who'd offered to guide him through the souk for 100 dirham, he dropped to a bench and felt utterly foolish.

A whiff of saffron and turmeric from the market stalls had conjured her spirit. He'd taken heart, and gone on, and in a section of the boundless covered marketplace set aside for seers and mediums, Raszer found a few Domari gypsies who spoke English as well as Raja's Romany. It was evident pretty quickly that no Jew named Abraham traveled in their company. He was about to move on when he noticed in the rear of the stall an old woman, whose eyes were covered with the caul of blindness. She shuffled a tarot deck idly and expertly from hand to withered hand. An illuminated border and a flash of vermillion caught his eye; he leaned into the counter and called to her.

"*Sastimos, madame,*" he said. "Are you a *drabardi?*"

She cocked her head to locate the source of his voice, and as she did so, her egg-white eyes caught the light and reflected pale blue.

"Those are beautiful cards," he said. "May I see them?"

"Do you want to buy them?" she creaked, rising like a marionette from her wooden footstool. "I promise you . . . you cannot afford them."

"Then at least give me the pleasure of looking," he replied. "My offer may equal my desire." She came to him, the deck spread like an Oriental fan in her skeletal hands.

The cards were beautifully made but fairly orthodox in their depiction of the Major Arcana . . . until he came to the Fool and his heart pushed into his throat. In place of the usual feckless dandy was a hirsute fellow with a long tail curled into a spiral and a book under his arm that had on its cover a representation of a geometrical lattice—the same design rendered crudely by Fortis Cohn on the note that had sealed Christopher Rose's fate. Moreover, the same design had been dancing across his mind's eye for the past three days, though he was no longer consciously aware that a little girl had put it there.

Raszer sorted through the cards until he found Number 15. The Devil was a skeleton, seen from the rear on a field of slaughter, with a bloody sword in one hand and the severed head of a victim in the other. His coccyx was a truncated stub. Raszer glanced up at the gypsy, who was grinning toothlessly in spite of her blindness. He offered her 300 dirham on the spot, and she spat contemptuously. "I'll take no less than one thousand," she said.

"Five hundred," Raszer countered, laying the colorful Moroccan currency down, bill by bill, so that she could count by ear.

"My grandchildren will go without milk," the woman grumbled. "Nine hundred or leave without your treasure."

"Say good-bye to 600 dirham," Raszer retorted, fanning the bills in her face before turning away, though in fact he had no intention of leaving without the cards.

"Acchh!" she cavilled. "My husband will have his couscous without meat again tonight!" She hailed him back. "Seven hundred," she sighed pitifully. "You bargain like a Berber!" Raszer took it as a compliment and paid her. A small gaggle of curious children had gathered behind and followed him, chattering, as he left the souk.

It was nearly sundown by the time he found his way to the heart of the Fes el-Jdid, the once vibrant Jewish quarter, and stepped over a bootworn threshold into a place that was more cavern than house. He had passed the address no less than sixteen times before realizing that the *"Yasar al-bosta"* people kept referring to was "behind the post office" and not the proper name of some neighborhood rug seller. Like anyone lost in a foreign city, he'd become acquainted with certain shifting patterns of light and chinks in the mortar as he threaded the same alleyways again and again in search of the rabbi's dwelling. After four hours without incident, he'd acquired the false security of feeling he hadn't been followed, but in the medina, one never really knew. Any turbaned merchant or street urchin could be his shadow, and doubtless, *someone* was watching. As the light faded and color drained from the streets, he'd begun to think any hope of finding Abraham in a single day was pure vanity. He'd been selective in displaying the tarot cards, asking guidance mainly of cowled women in darkened doorways, of whom he inquired in French, "Do you know the man who made these?"

Finally, someone had answered yes, and now he stood in the doorway, almost afraid to speak for fear he'd walked up another blind alley. He cleared his throat softly.

The figure that emerged from behind a heavy, hand-woven curtain on the far side of the frontroom did not look to be one hundred years old. In harsh light, he might have passed for seventy, but age did not quite seem to apply. He was a tiny fellow who wore a royal-blue djellaba and an embroidered yarmulke, and looked a bit like Truman Capote in a monk's habit. He gave Raszer a quick once-over, taking note of the tarot cards in his hand, then stepped to the doorway and shooed the pack of tenacious children away with a hail of hard candies and a torrent of epithets.

"Like little ants," he said. "They can smell the sugar a mile away."

He whistled through his teeth, and from somewhere near there materialized a striking, olive-complected woman of about twenty-four, who wore a green tank top and combat khakis and carried an automatic rifle. He gave her a nod and turned to Raszer. "This is Ofra. She served with the Israeli Army for three years. She will see that our meeting is undisturbed. And now," he said, "do you have the coordinates?"

Raszer nodded a greeting to the Israeli woman, who acknowledged it with lowered eyes and took her position without comment. "Thirty-three degrees north, three degrees west," he answered his host. "Give or take a tenth of a degree or so." With that, the little gnome shut the heavy cedar door and addressed Raszer with sober cordiality.

"Welcome," he said, his hands folded. "You have been expected."

He brought two small, embroidered stools to a low table and summoned his porter, a gaunt, towering Berber named Latif, to bring a serving of mint tea.

"Excuse me, sir," Raszer asked, "Expecting me . . . *personally* . . . or someone?"

"Tell me this," came the non-answer. "How did you find me . . . *personally?*" Raszer laughed. He couldn't help it. The explanation would strain an imbecile's credulity

He began nonetheless. "Would you like the long answer or the short?"

"A short answer is generally best," said his host, "if it reflects long thought."

"Certain 'signals' were received," Raszer said. "By tarot, by intercepted correspondence, and by . . . other means. My partner, April Blessing, who is being held here—somewhere—against her will, was instrumental, as well as a Roma woman named Raja Zlatari who I think its possible . . . you may once have met. I'm sorry to say that she has been murdered . . . but before I go further. You *are* Abraham the Jew, are you not?"

"The answer is yes," he said. "And yes. You . . . Stephan . . . have been expected. In time, you will understand the mechanisms involved."

Before inviting him to sit, Abraham approached Raszer, placed his hands firmly on his shoulders, and looked him deeply in the eyes. He brought his nose to Raszer's lips, sniffed twice, and gave a nod. Then, with a perfunctory "Pardon me," he reached around to press his forefinger into the space beneath Raszer's tailbone.

"Should I cough?" Raszer asked. The rabbi said nothing, but leaving his forefinger in place, extended his thumb until it rested against Raszer's lower spine, pushing aside the knife sheath in the process. "Sorry about the weapon," said Raszer. "I didn't know we'd have an Israeli commando at our disposal."

"Mm-hmm . . . " said Abraham, removing his finger. "I believe you know that my interest is not, *er* . . . clinical. I am looking for a span of at least seven inches between the uppermost of the five sacral vertebrae and the tip of the coccyx. Without this, you are *rootless* . . . and ruthless, too." The rabbi chuckled at his wordplay.

Raszer recited aloud. "The tree of man has branches five . . . "

"Two arms, two legs . . . and a tail. Vestigial, of course. I am happy to confirm," Abraham pronounced, removing his finger, "that you are a member of the human family."

"As opposed to what?"

"Take its measure to discern the wise man—Homo sapiens—*from what . . . ?*"

"Why seven inches?" Raszer recalled Monica's discovery that the Voorhees family had taken an interest in eugenics.

"I think," replied the rabbi, holding up his palm, "that in this case, a picture may truly be worth a thousand words . . . or such was the thinking of my forbears, when they gathered on this very spot—eight hundred years ago—with the magi of the five great traditions, and first conceived the pictorial and mathematical language of Tarot."

"Mathematical?"

"Higher dimensional mathematics, if you like," said Abraham. He took the cards from Raszer's hands and shuffled through until he found The Fool, his grimoire bearing the exotic glyph. "This," he said, indicating the lattice, "is a simplified representation of the tarot's hidden geometry. Have you seen this . . . somewhere else?"

"On paper?"

"No," the rabbi answered sternly. "Think harder." He reached up and tugged hard on Raszer's right ear. "With this side of your brain."

"I think I need—"

"Before we sit and have our tea, let me see how far you've come. Answer me this. When does a traveler stand concurrently at both the beginning and the end of his journey . . . ready to embark, yet puzzled by the dust of travel already on his shoes?"

Raszer dropped to the cushioned stool, sighed, and lit a cigarette. He had a feeling that solving the riddle was a sine qua non of sorts, but he was so mentally spent that multiplication tables might have challenged him. He took a deep drag and dropped his eyes to the intricate design on the carpet beneath his feet, an infinitely repeating tiled pattern whose perimeter was nowhere and whose center was everywhere at once. He glanced off-handedly at the creature on the tarot card, and then, without exclamation, lifted his eyes to Abraham and said, "When he's The Fool, and his path is a circle."

"In two dimensions, yes," the rabbi agreed. "In three, it might resemble a spiral. Good work. There is no final *knowing* . . . only continual gnosis."

"So, then," Raszer asked. "Is The Fool the first . . . or the last card in the Major Arcana? Nobody's ever been able to give me a straight answer . . . "

"First," Abraham replied, " . . . and last." He lifted his crystal tea glass to Raszer, drained it, and handed it to Latif. Then he rubbed his hands together in anticipation and slapped Raszer heartily on the shoulder blade. "We leave in three hours. The Land Cruiser will be packed with provisions for three days. Ofra will collect your things from the hotel. It would not be wise for you to go back there. In any case, I'm sure you've had enough colonial luxury for the day! We'll eat a good meal before we depart."

"Depart?" Raszer asked. "For where . . . exactly?"

"For the desert, of course," he replied, "To see the wizard and find you a heart . . . and perhaps, your partner. This is why you came so far . . . is it not?"

The destination, as Abraham later whimsically explained, was thirteen kilometers and a magic carpet ride north of the desert town of Missour, on the far side of the Middle Atlas Range. The physical coordinates, he affirmed, were as Mathonwy's digits had indicated, though he suggested cryptically this was "only a starting point." They would travel as far as the foothills southeast of Boulemane in a 1981 Land Cruiser, with the Berber porter named Latif at the wheel and Ofra, who had the fierce beauty of a young Irene Pappas and the sinewy physique of a Patagonian trekker, riding a capable shotgun. It was to be just the four of them. They left that night after filling their bellies with a saffron-gilded Moroccan stew, rich and fatty with wine-soaked mutton. Abraham rode in the back with Raszer and alternated readings of the Torah with a Saul Bellow novel, in which he seemed to find just as many quotable passages. Raszer felt it somehow impertinent to grill him about how he'd come to know the nature of his mission, but he was beginning to have an inkling that "mechanisms" in addition to the supernatural might have played a small hand. It could not be due to oversight that Abraham had not even asked him his name.

Latif said little and Ofra, for her part, kept a vigilant eye on the side view mirror, speaking only to the rabbi and then only to affirm directions. Raszer was well-positioned to admire the firm line of her chin and her desert-singed cheekbones, but his few attempts at small talk were met with stony silence. She seemed to lack a smile reflex. Nonetheless, Raszer felt blessed to have her along and alert.

A few miles east of Sefrou, the land began to rise in pale gray steppes, and the last of the moon-silvered clusters of whitewashed houses receded from the dusty rear window. The moon itself was nearly full, and bright enough to mask the starlight. A few hours in on a badly paved road, straight enough to be one of Mathonwy's ancient grid lines, Raszer roused the dozing rabbi to point out two feral dogs who seemed, almost evanescently, to be racing them through the desert scrub. One was short-haired and yellow, like a ridgeback; the other was thickly furred and lupine, like the animal he had seen on the ridges of Shasta. "Look," he said. "They're tracking us."

"Spirit dogs," said Ofra, speaking conversationally for the first time. "From *raiyo* . . . that's what my grandmother would say."

A smile crept across Raszer's face, followed by the tingling of his scalp. The Israeli girl had Roma blood, and apparently recognized an escort when she saw one.

During the entire stretch of highway, only one set of headlights appeared behind them. As the vehicle labored past them, it was revealed as a poultry truck, likely on the way to market in Missour, but who knew? Only after its taillights had disappeared did Raszer's pulse drop and permit him sleep, a sleep troubled by the sight of the dogs. The wolf-dog might be Madame Rey's familiar, but whose essence was embodied in the other? Allah, Yahweh, and all the desert djinn willing, April Blessing was not in raiyo.

In a deep box canyon more than thirty miles from the nearest paved road, Bronk Vreeland stripped off his t-shirt and signaled the Algerian sentry atop the cliff that he was turning in. Oblivious to the hail of meteorites in the sky overhead, he checked the magazine of his Sig P226 pistol one last time and then strode to the tent where his captive was being guarded by a second hireling, the cousin of the first. He pulled the flap open roughly.

"No sign of him," he said. "My guess is he won't travel open desert by night."

"What makes you so sure," she asked coldly, "that he's 'traveling' at all?"

He squatted down and glowered at her. "If he was fool enough to crash the Barbary Club without a small army, then he's fool enough to come out here. And I—for one—am looking forward to welcoming him. Come to think of it, I'm sure you are, too."

Inside the tent, April pulled the roughknit blanket about her naked shoulders and said nothing. He watched, smiling when she shivered. She had escaped the humiliation planned for her at the Barbary Club, only to face a more rarefied brand of defilement.

"You stay put, now," he said. "I'll be back for midnight mass. It's amazing, isn't it, what two spiritually-attuned minds can accomplish together?"

She didn't dare respond, or even look at him, because her response could only have revealed her fathomless contempt, and survival required that April somehow retain her last measure of guile. It had gotten her into his unholy temple, and now it would have to get her out. She held one remaining card: his pride—if not his faith—demanded that he continue to put stock in her psychic abilities. He had, after all, bet the farm on them. She'd discovered quickly that her feminine arsenal was of little use here. Her sexuality both excited and disturbed him, but he was incapable of knowing what that meant. He found her beauty curious—the way a boy might—but like some little boys, he could acknowledge the butterfly's glory only by tearing its wings off. He fucked like a thief, taking everything, leaving nothing. The sterile intimacies he'd forced on her had torn her body, but of far graver consequence was the toll his misogyny had taken on her spirit.

He dropped the tent flap. She heard him stand and adjust his gun strap. When she was certain he had left, she rolled herself up in the blanket and put her ear to the ground. April shivered again, not from the cold, but from from anticipation of his return. She tried to banish the ugliness with thoughts of her little cabin, with its window boxes and its postcard view of the Shasta *masif*. She thought of Diogenes, her scarlet macaw. And she thought of Stephan Raszer, who had warned her not to get too close to the fire. She could redeem herself only by making Bronk Vreeland burn in it.

19

THE SUN.

LATIF brought a basket of dates around to Raszer's side of the car, and rested his beaklike nose on the half opened window.

"*Sabah ael-kher,*" he said. "Gud moor-ning, *Sidi Stee-fan.*"

"*Sabah ael-kher,*" Raszer replied. "Ah . . . *baeleah* . . . right? Fresh dates. *Shokran.* Thank you." He took a piece of fruit and nibbled it idly, instantly restored by the sugar. From the rosiness of the light and the chill in the air, he guessed it to be just past sunrise. They were in a shallow ravine, and the surrounding foothills looked a little like the arid slopes of the Santa Susana Mountains back home. There was little vegetation and only the salmon sky to lend color to the jagged rocks that had tumbled ages ago into the natural quarry. At the narrow end of the ravine was a wooden shed, barely more than a lean-to, and a stable in which Raszer could see the tails of horses and donkeys in motion, flicking away flies. Abraham stood midway between the Land Cruiser and the stable, arguing energetically with the proprietor.

Raszer eased out of the back seat, and as he approached, was able to make out fragments of Arabic, mostly references to Allah. It seemed an odd time to discuss theology, but then he realized that they were citing divine authority to haggle over the hire of donkeys for the trip over the mountains. The proprietor, a fleshy man in a black turban, wanted an exorbitant security deposit, as a dozen of his animals had already been taken and he had only six left. A few of them, he said, might not come back. That was when Raszer took notice of the torn strip of sequined fabric tied in a ribbon around the tail of the smallest donkey.

Cookie crumbs from April.

Vreeland surely had the rest of the mounts, and was out there, waiting either for Raszer to show him the way or walk into his ambush, probably both.

Once the matter had been settled and Allah had been praised for his mediation skills, Latif set about loading the donkeys while Abraham and Raszer had the obligatory tea with the proprietor. Ofra stood guard. After tea, Raszer took stock of the vast emptiness around them and marveled at the fact that though they were about to make one hell of a gold rush, there were no other prospectors in sight. The rabbi had said enigmatically, "others would follow," that he, Raszer, was the first. But if, indeed, some ragtag element of resistance to the Halgadom Fraternity's "restoration" was using "earth radio" to signal for help from way out here in the North African desert, how could such a widely broadcast summons have brought only one knight errant?

"Rabbi," Raszer said, as their sway-backed mounts were led out for saddling. "The ribbon on that third donkey's tail? It's a sign from April. What'd the owner say?"

"He said 'a dozen men,' just after midday yesterday."

"No mention of a woman?"

"It is not always easy to know the difference . . . in the desert."

"I have to assume they have the coordinates. Is there a way to get where we're going except by way of you?"

"God knows I'm not the only holy man around," Abraham replied, "but be assured, even if your Mr. Vreeland has a treasure map, he will not be able to go where *we* are going. The worst he can do is kill us . . . but that will not get him what he's after."

Seven hours on the back of an aging donkey is like twenty-four on any other mount, and so by half past one, Abraham had called it a day. The sun and the ceaseless wind in the high passes had wicked the moisture from joints and skin, and made the rabbi's Oz analogy seem apt: Raszer felt as stiff as the Tin Man between oil changes. "No bedouin," Abraham said, "rides much past midday, unless he is after a woman or a wadi . . . in either case, a place to dip his vessel."

Latif made camp in a sheltered canyon with a stand of gnarled trees that resembled bristlecone pines, but which Abraham introduced as thuja, source of much of

Morocco's fine woodwork. Just before dismounting, they watched as a procession of mendicant dervishes came surefootedly down a mountain path to the accompaniment of the *ghaita,* a raucous Berber pipe, and passed them on their way back east, saying nothing but *"La ilaha illa 'Llah"*—there is no God but Allah. The youngest of them might have been thirty and the oldest past reckoning, but between them there was little difference. The desert had made them all of a single age.

"Are they Sufis?" Raszer asked, after they had passed. *"Aissawa?"*

"Tinkers and clowns," the rabbi answered with a straight face, but Raszer sensed he was employing the mystic's dodge of making the sublime seem prosaic, so that a novice might learn to see it with his own eyes. A clown was a fool, and the fool was a seeker. And Sufis had long described themselves as tinkers, miners, and sellers of wool. As they marched off, one of the ragged monks began whistling *La Marseillaise,* and soon enough, the ghaitas and the others joined in, the tune diminishing and briefly returning as they crested and descended the folds of land, until it was as if they'd never come at all.

Latif had packed with great efficiency, but hadn't entirely forsaken luxury. A Berber knows that, in a land of scant comfort, the plush of a fabric can make the difference between sleep and stark insomnia. Raszer watched, enchanted, as he suspended an enormous silk tent between the thuja trees and carpeted the ground with woven rugs, wool blankets, and embroidered cushions. He offered to help hang a line for the airing of their sweat-soaked garments, but the porter protested, saying, "No, *Sidi Stee-fan* . . . you must let Latif do his work. This is what Allah has given me."

Raszer sat on a fallen tree and took out his journal, while Latif moved on to his next task, the digging of a fire pit. Ofra, meanwhile, had taken up sentry position on an outcropping high above the canyon floor. She had also her assigned tasks, but they included neither bedmaking nor food preparation. Raszer traced the nearly vertical crack she had utilized to get up to her aerie, evidently in a matter of minutes. He cupped his hand around his mouth and called out, "Nice climbing!" and then to his horror heard the accolade echo off the parallel rock faces a dozen times before dying out.

Ofra dropped to a crouch, her rifle at the ready, and put her finger to her lips in admonishment. He was sure he saw her mouth a curse as she turned back to the rock. Raszer sat back down, chastened, and Abraham appeared at his side.

"Don't worry," he said, patting Raszer on the arm. "She is, as you say, a 'tough cookie.' She saw her father and brothers killed in the intifada. Come. Have some tea."

Latif had prepared afternoon tea with a bundle of fresh mint leaves and a modest ration of the water supply. Abraham summoned Raszer to join him on the worn cushions that had been set about beneath the tent on rugs woven of reeds. Out of the sun's hammer, the air was surprisingly cool. He took from his pouch a drawstring bag of purple velvet, and poured out what looked like a few dozen irregular Scrabble pieces, though their manufacture had clearly been the work of an artisan, not a machine.

"These belonged to my grandfather," Abraham said, "And before him, who knows?" Raszer recognized characters from at least four alphabets: Arabic, Hebrew, Greek, and English, and a few glyphs he had not seen before. They spent the long, powdery afternoon in a way that afternoons are no longer spent, but must once have been for such wisdom as Abraham's to gestate in the human mind. While old Latif, in the background, beheaded, plucked, gutted, and marinated two plump, fresh hens in lemon and cardamom, the little rabbi taught Raszer the mysteries of language with a humble set of wooden chips.

Through a series of "games" that escalated in mathematical complexity, he performed riffs on the gematria, which, through Madame Rey's mediumship, had brought them together. There was *notarikon*, a method of encoding meaning through the creation of new words from first and last letters. Then he glossed a primitive but effective mode of encryption called *temurah*, in which the two halves of the alphabet were counterposed in mirror image, each letter replaced by the one opposite it. He alluded throughout to the links between the twenty-two character Hebrew alphabet, the twenty-two connecting paths of Kabbalah, and the twenty-two cards of the Major Arcana which had governed Madame Rey's divinations, all with their umbilical tie to the ultimate codeword, JHVH, the holy name of God.

"People take it now for some sort of acronym," the rabbi said with a laugh. "Like IBM. Or at best, as an all-purpose ABRACADABRA. But the name of God is a *concentrate* of sacred power . . . much closer to an atomic number or chemical formula."

"ADNI and AGLA are also salvific names. If your eyes are open, you see them over the entryways of temples and churches, carved in a solar disc with sixteen rays."

"Did you say sixteen?" Raszer asked.

"Yes. I did say that," replied Abraham. "Why?"

"I was once told by Raja that the symbol of the Roma Congress is a sixteen-spoked mandala . . . sixteen paths to illumination."

"The rota wheel, yes," said the rabbi. "Rota. Taro. More letter games. The fingerprints of wisdom lost are to be found everywhere." He sipped his tea. "It's a pity . . . that I was not privileged to know your Madame Rey."

"Ah, but Rabbi," Raszer said. "She seemed to know you. Or someone very like you . . . though she made you sound as old as Methuselah! "

"Let me ask you," the rabbi interjected. "How old you think I am . . . "

Raszer accepted the invitation to make his first, unabashed once-over of the man called Abraham, and the rabbi seemed amused by the scrutiny. "I'd give you," said Raszer, rubbing his chin, "Seventy-five at most . . . assuming a low-carb diet, B supplements, and thirty minutes a day on the Stairmaster."

The rabbi simply smiled. "We think ourselves distinct from our forbears, and lent a certain age by the passage of a time that God does not keep. But we are all grafts from our Father's stalk, given rain and sun by our Mother. There has been a Jew named Abraham fashioning tarot cards in the little shop behind the post office for twelve hundred years . . . just as there has been a man named Rupert Voorhees sowing discord on the Earth for the better part of two centuries. And you, Stephan Raszer? Where do you come from?"

"I'm not sure, exactly," Raszer said, feeling suddenly adrift. "My father was a Jew who outran the shadow of the 1940s only to run smack into Joe McCarthy's witch hunters. He cracked up when I was still on baby formula . . . left and never came home."

"And so you repudiate him?"

"I repudiate his not taking responsibility for what he'd created."

"Yes," Abraham said. "I understand. But consider where that has led you. Perhaps your father was, in truth, not what you think he was. Perhaps you will find him here. Maybe that is what the gypsy saw in your cards." He glanced up at the cliff where Ofra stood guard, her colors nearly indistinguishable from the rock. "Ofra's mother was also a *drabardi*. I fear, though, that these are the final days for that kind of divination. What is about to happen to history will require a comprehension of the formulations that lie behind the cards—and the ages of heartache and blind wandering they describe. No one will make a living telling this fortune."

The sun fell, turning the burnt brown hills a luminous red-gold. Aromatic puffs of vapor rose from the spit which Latif turned patiently over the fire. Abraham brought his lesson to a close with a demonstration of magic number squares. He showed Raszer how virtually any text, structure, or system— including tarot—could be represented by numeric sequences and the overlaying of geometric patterns. At one point, Raszer felt the warp speed rush of knowing, beyond doubt, that his teacher was speaking the language of quantum mechanics in a tongue as old as the Vedas.

"And here," Abraham said, having drawn a polyhedron in the sand, "we are depicting just two dimensions! What if we should sweep it out to twenty-four!"

"A lattice?" Raszer asked.

"We shall see," Abraham teased. He whistled for Ofra. "Let's eat."

After the meal, intoxicated with heady spices and a few draughts each of a meadlike brew Latif carried in his goatskin, they laid back heavily on the cushions and listened to their bellies gurgle. The smoke from the fire seemed drawn by the moon into a column of ether from which genies could be invoked. A dog bayed nearby and another answered more distantly.

Ofra had joined them for dinner and sat a few feet from Raszer, her knees drawn up and the Israeli Galil rifle snug against her breast, her dark eyes flashing with every random sound and scent. She smelled of palm oil and betel nut, a scent—he thought— as emblematic of this woman as April's was of her. The scent, and the desire it stirred, stung him with guilt, for by rights, sensual pleasure ought to be denied him until he had "taken responsibility" for what he'd set in motion. The rabbi watched him like a telepathic hawk.

"It was equally *her* will and *her* desire which brought things about," he said.

For some reason, Raszer was unsurprised. "Do you think she's alive?" he asked.

"I fear only what may happen once he discovers that she cannot take him where he wants to go." It was not the answer Raszer wanted to hear.

"Where exactly *are* we going, Rabbi? It may be time to shelve the metaphors."

"Ah," said Abraham, chuckling. "Metaphors and similes are all I have to sell today . . . perhaps an analogy or two. Where we're going is like where Enoch, and Ezekiel, and Isaiah went. Would you deny the 'reality' of their journeys because poetry rather than prose describes them?" Then, with a twinkle in his eye, he sent a shiver down Raszer's spine. "When intellect is husband to imagination, new worlds are glimpsed." He pushed himself up on an elbow and took a stick from the fire. "I will tell you a bedtime story. It may help your dreams prepare you for the morning." He sighed deeply and began.

"There is another history of the world. As bloody and rife with intrigue as those you know, but on a stage whose dimensions surpass imagining. Enjoy this moment's blindness: you are about to be given sight, and I can tell you it is no more pleasant than a baby's first moments outside the womb. Enjoy the soft, perfumed wind on your face. From tomorrow on, the wind will speak in tongues, as it does for those dogs you hear howling from 'raiyo.'" The fire popped and Ofra nudged unconsciously closer to Raszer's side. Abraham pulled the hood of his djellaba over his head. "It is the story of the secret battle waged behind every action, great and small. The battle for the soul of man."

Raszer lit a cigarette, and suddenly recognized it as a fear reflex. He'd chosen a path on which old habits and illusions of safety would eventually have to be cast aside.

"'In the beginning' . . . 'was the Word.'" The rabbi drew a closed circle in the sand. "Nothing existed until formed on the lips of God. Perhaps the true gift given to Eve by the serpent was the gift of naming . . . for by naming things, they come to be real. But then, once we have language, we have the problem of interpretation. You are here because of an interpretation you placed upon certain words . . . as it happens, the correct one. But think what can happen if a meaning worlds apart from your own is read from the same words, from a myth, a story . . . an article of faith. God did not figure on that." Abraham filled his mouth from Latif's goatskin and passed it to Raszer, as if to say "you'll need this." Raszer drank, and drank again for good measure.

"Nine thousand years ago," Abraham continued, "give or take a few centuries, there was a disaster in Eden. What the chaos theorists call a bifurcation. A fork in the road. The body of Man, as it were, was torn asunder, never again to to be assembled in quite the same way. But before there can be a split there must be a crack. Some millennia before that—perhaps many—a fissure had begun to form within the mind of the human animal, which until then had been communicating as well with God as any of his creatures. We don't know how or why it happened, and because this is not the 'official history,' science has yet to offer a theory. I will venture—if you will forgive the metaphor, Stephan—that it was a kind of trauma, and that an 'opportunistic infection' slipped into the wound. You may call this pathogen *evil* if you wish. I do. As with all infections, it found certain of us more receptive than others . . . those in whom the separation from Nature—by which I mean God's presence on Earth . . . the lady whom the Greek Orphics called Gaia, the Kabbalists' Shekhinah, the Gnostics' Sophia—was most profound."

Abraham leaned into the fire and engaged Raszer through the curtain of smoke. "And many generations later, when the bifurcation finally occurred, the descendants of these afflicted ones became a branch unto themselves . . . the carriers of a spiritual schizophrenia that alienates them from mankind . . . and that threatens the tenancy of Gaia herself." Beneath the hood of his djellaba, the rabbi cocked an eyebrow.

Raszer's jaw felt loose, his lips as numb as if he'd just had novocaine. It was an effort to form his mouth around words, and in this dumbness, he recognized what power they had. "When you say . . . 'a branch unto themselves' . . . are you really talking about—" He swallowed, searching for his tongue. "—something other than human?"

"We are all of the lineage of God," Abraham replied. "But don't presume we have remained cousins. The same genus, perhaps, but not necessarily the same species."

Raszer cleared his throat and crushed his cigarette in the sand. Bronk Vreeland, from the other side of the glass, had said the same thing. There was a small rockfall on a ledge some fifty yards above the canyon. Raszer flinched and brought his hand round to the hilt of his knife, and Ofra lept to her feet and pivoted in search of the source. From the edge of camp, he heard the joints of Latif's folding chair creak as he also stood, snapping the bolt action of his old Colt rifle.

A moment later, they heard the growls of wild dogs, fighting over some carrion atop the cliff, but it was warning enough to call Ofra back to her post atop the canyon wall, and to draw Raszer's thoughts to his partner.

April studied Bronk Vreeland's route of descent from the high ledge as best she could by moonlight. She took note of his prowess on the rock. With the exception of Raszer, she had never encountered a being with such transcendent stamina, and even Raszer was beginning to show some wear. Vreeland, she'd decided, had two opposing chinks in his suit of macho armor. One was an agonizing doubt, worthy of Macbeth, that what he'd done to earn the Fraternity's trust could be defended in the court of any realm, on earth or elsewhere. The other was a compensating delusion. He genuinely seemed to believe that—if offered the "straight story" and proper motivation—April might still *choose* to be on his side. He did not trouble to think that such a choice might be discouraged by either kidnapping or rape.

He'd come to her last night, asking permission to enter in the tent, and then informed her, with astounding naiveté, that he wanted to "make her his woman." She had taken this to mean he wanted to impregnate her. A curious thing about Bronk: the misplaced courtesy and the frontier bravado, as if his sole referent for how to be a man was old John Wayne movies. He slept on the ground with the Algerians, leaving her the tent for "privacy." Yet when she'd resisted his blunt seduction, he'd held a gun to her head and taken her anyway, ejaculating before he had even fully entered her.

Afterward, he'd mistaken her stifled sob for a snicker and beaten her with his gun belt. For April, the horror of it came from neither the pain nor the humiliation. It came from the fact that—after all these years and all she'd done to remake herself—she was back where she'd begun, Surely, she thought, life ought to grant a little more mercy.

Now he was there again. "They're in the ravine about a quarter mile west," he said, "and guess what? He's got a woman with him. That didn't take long, now, did it?"

April drew a sharp breath of the scentless air and recalled something Raszer had once said. "Life is an ad lib . . . play off every line you're fed."

"You remember," she said, "when we first met . . . and I told you I was sick of doubt? That part wasn't an act. All I've ever really wanted is to be sure of *something*."

"Then you understand," Bronk told her, "why I took you last night. That's the pure way. The warrior's way. Without remorse, without apology."

"Right," she fired back. "You also said that rape was for 'miscreants and mud people.'" A beat. *"Your quote*, Commander."

"That wasn't rape," he said. "That was testimony."

"I'll show you something," she said, and brazenly peeled off the sweatshirt he'd leant to cover the strap marks on her back: another gesture of bullshit gallantry. She had one gambit left. The firelight brushed the swell of her breasts with gold, and this did not escape his attention. "I want to show you what I can do with my hands. It's a kind of massage, but totally spiritual. If you're ready to trust me—and I can feel that coming off you—I'll be your sibyl *and* your concubine. Hell, nobody else has ever given me so much credit. Now lie down and shut up before I change my mind."

"Why should I trust you?"

"Because you want to," she said.

There was a loaded silence when she feared she'd missed her aim. But then he stretched himself out on the sand like a sated lion, and said, "Show me." She straddled him and began working down his spine, her firelit hair curtaining her face as she rolled her eyes left and right to gauge the dispersal of the sentries, the nearest of which had just gone off duty for his allotted two hours of sleep. Most of the men had fanned out across the ridge, where visibility was greatest, and were a good hundred yards from the campsite—easily five or six minutes when you figured time for the steep descent. That left just two in the camp proper, and one had just dozed off. The other crouched twenty yards distant, watching over the mules and the provisions, his Kalashnikov rifle pointed aimlessly at the bejeweled sky. There was only one unguarded means of escape from the canyon, and that was by way of the sheer wall that Vreeland had just come down.

"This'll open up your chakras," she said, playing the nerve endings tucked between his vertebrae, "and then I'll do some real magic." She thought it was likely that Bronk Vreeland had never experienced such treatment and was feeling for the first time what those on the other side of life had come to know as a healing touch. As April's fingers reached the base of his spine, she was startled to find a sort of dimple and a mass of soft cartilage where there ought to have been a tailbone. *Jesus,* she thought, reaching instinctively back to feel for her own, praying she would not find a kinship. She heard him begin to purr, and two minutes later she delivered the knock-out punch, simultaneously pinching the nerve bundles at the brainstem and the thirteenth vertebra.

He was instantly unconscious, but would not be for long. April had no more than three minutes to make her escape.

She pulled the sweatshirt back on and dropped to the cool sand, alternately crawling and slithering to the dark base of the canyon wall, searching with fingers and blind instinct for the big crack that Vreeland had spidered down. She was barefoot, and climbing would be painful, but she had acquired over the past eight hours a sure sense of her expendability. Any pain less than death was tolerable. Beyond that, her identity was fast coming unglued. Vreeland had violated her sense of self in every way, and she knew instinctively that these were the last hours during which she would understand the Stockholm Syndrome as an idea and not a personal experience. Her only hope for reintegration lay in being joined again with Raszer, and her desire for it was so fierce that it overcame even her concern that she might bring danger his way.

She found the narrow crack cleaved in the rock over centuries of baking and freezing, grabbed hold with her palms turned outward, and began to lever her way up.

The last thirty feet had to be free-climbed, but the exertion would not ordinarily have taxed her. The strain was doing it without alerting the sentries: no falling rocks, grunts, or heavy breathing. Each meter consumed ten times the usual energy. By the time her broken fingernails dug into the crumbling sandstone of the final overhang, she had reached that awful place of knowing that all her rockets had fired and she'd still not broken free of gravity. She laid her cheek on the cool stone and listened to the sentry's shallow breathing, barely fifteen yards away. It mesmerized her, that one small sound in the vast silence. She relaxed the burning muscles in her calves for just an instant, but an instant cruel enough to send pebbles skittering down. The Algerian approached, muzzle sweeping the ground like a dowsing rod, finding her ready to die. She lifted her head and screamed out Raszer's name. The least she could do was to warn him.

At once, she knew she'd done a foolish thing. The one thing keeping him alive was his knowledge; the one thing keeping her alive was her value in trade for it. But in this cold, heartless place, where a God of wind and fire tested men for sport, no one would hear her plea of contrition. She pressed her forehead into the cliff and wept, her tears making tiny rivulets in the soft, porous rock.

In a world apart—yet near enough to see by day—the rabbi's voice held Raszer as if by a spell. "The ground we sit upon," he said, "is the skin of a living organism: the first thing awakened by God's breath, and still flowing with that divine *pneuma* which science calls electromagnetism. Like a queen sold into bondage, she has been raped and ravaged repeatedly by the lust that men have for land—notably men of Mr. Vreeland's lineage. He thinks he's looking for 'a whore' . . . a Medusa he must kill in order to claim the planet for his kind. He has no idea that the enemy he seeks is his own mother . . . "

"So we are talking, then," Raszer said, "about a kind of sub-species. Is that what the tailbone thing is about? Or is it another of those metaphors you're selling?"

"With apologies to Mr. Darwin," replied Abraham, "not all selection is 'natural.' A mutation can mirror a very unnatural change of circumstances, and then be encouraged through aggressive breeding. Tyrants may call it 'ethnic cleansing,' scientists may call it eugenics. Our adversaries have so far not exceeded three to five percent of the population, but their influence far outweighs their numbers. Look at any chart showing where the world's wealth is." He allowed Raszer a moment to absorb this. "*Ah*, but God has placed an obstacle in their path! Their traits are passed only through the y chromosome. They can propagate only by making 'breeders' of genetically related females, and this—over the course of time—dilutes their strain."

"Until cloning," said Raszer darkly. "What's their kryptonite? What do they fear?"

"Anything they cannot bring under their control. And that includes . . . so far . . . the forces you are to encounter tomorrow."

As if from another universe, Raszer heard the echo of his own name volley off the canyon walls. A gunshot followed. He staggered to his feet and saw Latif do the same. On the ridge, Ofra pivoted. Abraham merely cocked his ear to the wind.

"April!" Raszer breathed. "Oh, God." He turned to Abraham. "She's close! I can't just—Jesus." He lost his balance. He could not seem to shake his lightheadedness.

The rabbi stood and took his arm. "She is *not* close, my friend. She is not in *our* time." He stepped to within an inch of Raszer's face. "You are not the first to travel this way," he said. "If you want to learn how much higher the stakes are than any one life, however precious, you must heed the lesson of Orpheus. You must not look back. For the soul of your friend . . . I *will* pray . . . but I think that you should get some sleep now."

Raszer studied his companion's face incredulously. There had just been a scream for help, a shot fired not a quarter mile away, and he was talking about sleep.

"They'll kill her," he said. "If they haven't already . . . I've got to try and get to her."

"With what, my friend?" Abraham asked, taking his place again at the fire. "One Israeli girl and your little knife? Sit down, Mr. Raszer. You are on the edge of the Sahara . . . and it is night. The only thing you can accomplish by action is to force the confrontation before its moment . . . and that would be a very great tragedy. Sit."

But Raszer could not sit.

After pacing the narrow canyon for thirty minutes, he finally began to gear down. The rabbi was right. There wasn't a thing he could do to alter the hurtling course of fate. He crawled into the tent and tried to empty his mind of her face, knowing he would not succeed in emptying his heart. Before dropping off, he lifted the flap to look out. Abraham sat silhouetted by the fire, rocking to and fro in the deepest of prayers.

Raszer had never received much in the way of a life lesson from his own father, who was too stricken by psychic debt to have anything left over for his son, and in any case, wasn't around enough. As he zipped up his sleeping bag, Raszer thought about Abel Cohn, a father of soul, and Professor Mathonwy, a father of mind. He thought about Abraham, a father of spirit, who would keep vigil for April and for a world in dire need of grace. And for an instant in time, they were all the man that Raszer knew his father had wanted to be. *Perhaps you will find him here . . . Maybe that is what the gypsy saw in your cards.* Finally, to the rhythmic sound of the rabbi's kaddish, he slept.

20

JUDGEMENT.

APRIL laid her head on the stone, took a shallow breath, and braced her trembling knees as best she could in the powdery sand. She wanted to be sure that the blade connected with its first blow. The Algerian pushed her hair roughly aside with the muzzle of his Kalashnikov, exposing her neck, and she shivered as the arid breeze instantly dried the film of sweat that lay over her skin. Bronk stood in the shadows nearby, his back to her in renunciation until the appointed time. She heard the guard's guttural summons and saw the glint off steel as Vreeland approached barefoot with the sword in hand and stepped around to her blind side. She heard him grunt with the exertion of raising the weapon above his head, and she closed her eyes, imagining her head in Raszer's lap. Her life did not pass before her, thankfully. Only perverse fragments: like Flo, her fellow dancer, saying, *"Wish I had your body, girl."* Then death came with a winged beating of air and a hail of steel and starlight.

For the length of a song, Bronk Vreeland stood with shoulders rolled forward and legs spread, regarding the eyes that stared from April's head. The eyes did not pass judgement; they left that for him to render against himself. The blade was planted between his feet, offering her blood drop by drop to the sand. Overhead, a swarm of meteors raced across the vault of the sky, passing witnesses to his infamy.

A few of the gunmen gathered around, all but one—the man with the Kalashnikov—fearful enough of Allah to keep their silence. The Algerian's gaunt, sparsely bearded face creased into a lewd grin. He could not have been more than twenty, but his teeth were as black as a beggar's.

He spat and said, "*La putain ... elle est morte.* God is great." Vreeland turned, seized him by the wrist, and severed his arm cleanly from the shoulder with one blow.

Just past three A.M., Abraham coaxed a flame from the last ember of the fire. He cocked his ear as there came, from the west, a long yelp of agony, its reverberation endless. *Aaiiieeee!* It might have been a dog, but he suspected it was a man.

Raszer sat straight up and yanked the tent flap open, his pulse racing. He could not make out either Ofra or Latif, but he watched as Abraham rose wearily and extinguished the fire with a handful of sand, as in benediction. Then he let the flap drop.

The rabbi sat in darkness for another hour, offering a prayer for the souls of the undeserving dead, for each innocent lost was a holocaust. Then, quietly and stealthily as serpents, he and Latif broke camp, loaded the donkeys, and roused their comrades from sleep. God grant, they would be two hours gone before the jackals realized it.

It was no wonder the ill-tempered stable owner had been concerned about losing his animals, for the descent into the deep, narrow cut between the front range and the high peaks of the Middle Atlas was precipitous enough to give a mountain goat pause. It seemed to continue forever, until the rough trail they followed was barely a meter wide and the canyon walls on either side rose to heights of more than three thousand feet.

They had been riding since four, and by Raszer's watch it was now almost one. All the while, despite the rabbi's assurances, he had kept an eye on the rear, although both Ofra, who rode backsaddle with the rifle on her knee, and the sheer verticality of the canyon seemed to preclude ambush.

They rode single file, with Latif in the lead, followed by Abraham, then Raszer, and finally their sentinel. Her dark hair swung from side to side as she rocked steady, her boots on the cantle and her back braced against the horn. An hour or so down the path, the walls converged to form a natural ogive, as if they were entering the pink plexus of the earth, and before long, they were operating on four senses, for the light was gone.

"All right, Latif," said Abraham, after they had continued for another fifteen minutes in darkness, "Will you tend to the animals?" Since in the blackness the pack-trained donkeys had continued stubbornly in single file, Raszer hadn't noticed that the trail, now completely overhung with rock, had widened into a kind of grotto. They appeared to be at the end of the line and sat waiting, pulled four abreast on their tired beasts. The rabbi dismounted first, and the rest of them followed, with Latif quietly leading the donkeys off into darkness. "Take my arm," Abraham directed, "and come sit with me. Your eyes will adjust to the light shortly." Raszer did as he was told, and sure enough, became aware within minutes of a faint, rosy glow filtering into the chamber through the hairline crack in the vaulted ceiling above. He could just now make out the strong curve of Ofra's jaw-line and the outline of Abraham's head.

"Rabbi?" Raszer said, and though he spoke softly, his words were amplified four-fold.

"Yes?"

"I've come this far on faith——"

"Don't lose it now," he interjected, and Raszer saw the faint curl of a smile.

"Are we near an entrance? I can feel . . . a current of some sort."

"Yes and no," the rabbi said. "Depending on how one defines 'near'."

"Even if Vreeland doesn't have the pass key to get in here, we should expect—shouldn't we—that he and his men will be waiting for us when we come out?"

"I wouldn't think to lead you out by the same way we came in, Stephan. I must ask you to put all of your questions in abeyance for the moment; there will be time later. If your mind is noisy with questions, you will be deaf to the answers."

Abraham removed a small, glazed ceramic jar from his satchel and pulled out the cork, releasing a scent that was at once pleasant and as pungent as old cheese. Dipping his index finger into the jar, he spoke the syllable "Yod" and applied the balm to the bridge of Raszer's nose. Incanting "He," he annointed himself. On the syllable "Vau," he ran his oiled finger across Raszer's lips, then repeated the "He" and applied the remainder to his own. He replaced the cork and slipped the jar back into his bag.

"Just you and me?" Raszer asked.

"Side by side," he said whimsically. "Ofra and Latif will remain here with the animals, and will rejoin you for the journey home."

"And you?"

Abraham put his fingers to his lips. "Shhh . . . " He broke a small, fleshy purple leaf from a stem which held a few more, and snapped it crisply in two, clasping each half between thumb and forefinger like a broken communion wafer. The bruised leaf oozed a thick, milky effluent and the distinct scent of the coital roux.

"Open up and say *'aah'*." Raszer complied, and Abraham swabbed the roof of his mouth with the torn edge of the leaf. The flavor was strongly alkaline. He repeated the process on himself with the remaining half and said, "Watch and listen closely. I'm going to teach you a little trick."

He began to chant, and at first, the tones were so deep in his gut that they were barely distinguishable from groans. As he moved the breath up into his windpipe, however, the repetition of the mantra *"Urim-Y-Tumim"* became recognizable as discrete utterance and his timbre became more lustrous and dulcet. By the time it reached his nasal cavities, it was the high register of a bassoon, bittersweet and plaintive. It was then that the grotto itself began to "sing" in sympathetic resonance, and from the fugal cascade of melodies, Raszer picked out a single strain: the same one he'd heard in Ori's presence on the slopes of Mt. Shasta. From some place twice-removed from his body, Raszer heard himself say, *"Uh-oh"* in exactly the way he recalled saying it the first time someone had slipped him a tab of pharmaceutical LSD. Now, he and Abraham were connected by the spider-silk of light issuing from their own foreheads.

Then came the rumble: deeper than Professor Mathonwy's harmonic tremors and as deep as the footfalls of God heard by a terrified Adam and Eve in the Garden. Raszer knew intuitively that it must be what Mathonwy had called the earth's brainwave: the lowest of the Schumann Resonances. Suddenly, there was not one Rabbi Abraham but three, six . . . then thirty-six! And there were the same number of Raszer's own replicated image, a polyhedron of mirrors, all seventy-two facets tangential and visible to him at once from all directions.

"Am I in the fourth dimension?" Raszer asked, uncontrollably giddy.

"For starters," said the rabbi.

Then, with an agility it had surely taken a lifetime to acquire, Abraham directed the axis of light which tied them slowly down their respective spinal columns until it appeared to emerge from the solar plexus, and Raszer thought to himself, *"Hey . . . I* think I know this trick." The fabric of space and time was suddenly shot through with an impossible cat's cradle of luminous thread, sweeping out a multitude of dimensions, until Raszer was no longer in any sense observing it but of it.

Then, as quickly as it had appeared, the lattice of the many-worlds dissolved like spun candy in the sun, and they were left, like boozy patrons at an after-hours piano bar, seated around a crescent-shaped terminal formed of particle beams and living posts of oscillating quartz crystal, at which a slight, brown-skinned man made fluid vertical "keystrokes" on an instrument more like a quantum harp than a computer. His body was draped in a loose muslin gown and his large head wrapped in a red, polka-dot bandana.

"Stephan," said Abraham, though his voice sounded a galaxy away, "may I introduce Mr. Tony Smith, senior theoretician of the Gaia Network and gatekeeper of Agharta." The rabbi cleared his throat. "Metaphysically speaking."

"*Tony Smith?*" thought Raszer, as he examined a face that had the endearingly inquisitive quality and vibrating nose of a gerbil. *Oh, April . . . If only you could see this!*

"You are more welcome than you can imagine, brother," Tony Smith said. His lips moved and the sound they produced registered as a voice, but Raszer heard it as one who is learning a second language and must "translate" before comprehending. "For years, we've been trying to clean the corrosion from the old arteries to the surface world. It looks as if we got through. What you and your *soror mystica*, Miss Blessing . . . accomplished last week should help revitalize the network . . . and none too soon."

"Where am I?" Raszer asked numbly.

"Would you like that as words, numbers, graphic display or a direct feed?"

"Let's start with the words. Then we can move to the good stuff."

"Well, all right," said Tony. "I'll have to use a little poetic license. You're inside the planet. Deep inside. The center, actually."

"So it exists, then." Raszer reflexively checked his pulse, which seemed steady. "The 'Inner Earth.' *Telos . . . Agharta* . . . all of that? This is unbelievable."

"In a word, yes," Tony replied. "But you won't find it with a pick ax or a drill . . . though at an early stage of mythogenesis that's how people pictured us: as little miners, Chthonic dwarves like the *Cabiri* of Samothracian myth."

He sang, "*Hi Ho, Hi Ho!*" in a lilting alto that made Raszer smile. "Now, you might be ready for something closer to the truth. To be a bit more precise, you're inside the mind of the planet. You can appreciate that we don't get a lot of visitors."

"Maybe I'd better see those graphics," said Raszer.

Tony made a few quick arpeggios in mid-air and sat back. "Look around."

They were suspended as if at the nexus of an infinitely vast constellation of stars, the space between interpenetrated by the same criss-cross lattice of luminous, vibrating strings conjured by Abraham's sacrament. Raszer felt like a canary perched in God's birdcage. He reached out to touch the wires, but it was like trying to grab the moon.

"It is difficult to wrap your mind around, I know," said the rabbi. "Kabbalists like Luria and alchemists like Paracelsus and Dee have tried and come close, but all ultimately fall on the sword of interpretation. The purest distillation may still be Plato's. We're looking at a geometrical exegesis of the laws of tarot."

"And it makes music, too," Raszer said, in Alicelike wonderment, for he was suddenly aware that what he'd heard as silence was, in fact, a perfect, sustained chord.

"But as exquisite as it is," said Tony, "it is all an apparition. No more the true nature of reality than a city is the lights one sees from an airplane."

"So take away the window dressing," said Raszer. "I'm ready . . . "

"I don't think so, Stephan. Your first look would be your last."

"Oh," said Raszer. "In that case . . . I'll wait."

"That you can perceive even this glorious illusion is a gift. In order to mistake phantasm for reality, a man must first have some notion of what reality looks like."

"Can I touch you?"

"Of course," Tony replied, and held out his long, elegant fingers.

"Are you . . . *physical?*"

"When I need to be."

"Are you . . . *sexual?*"

The rabbi chortled.

"Actually," Tony replied, unperturbed, "I'm *supra*-sexual."

"Are there others like you?"

"Oh, yes. We have our own 'fraternity.' No hazing allowed."

"Do you, or your kind, ever come to the 'surface?'"

"There was a time when we lived among you in enchantment. We are no longer as welcome. I'll be happy, however, to make you an ambassador." He smiled and his eyes twinkled. "But now . . . the conditions by which you've come can only be sustained for a very short while, so we need to get going. I'm going to ask you to receive information in the way you did when you were very little. The way all humans once did. Consciousness, you see, is a quantum-coherent effect, whereas thinking is simply computation. This will utilize brain functions that have long been dormant, so you'll 'wake up' later with what feels like a very bad hangover. You'll recall very little of this experience, and you will remember me only as—what is it they call me, Rabbi?"

"The current term of art is 'archetype,'" Abraham replied.

"An archetype I am, then," said Tony. "All right. Are you ready?"

Raszer's five senses must have been "on hold" during the lesson, because when it was done, perception returned with a bang. The seats they occupied levitated in thin air over a gaping chasm that plunged all the way to the iron crystal core of the earth.

"Holy shit!" Raszer cried out, and the rabbi grabbed his shoulder.

"Don't worry," Abraham said calmly. "It's only a reflection of what is above. See?" He leaned precariously forward and waved to his own reflection immediately below. "There I am. And there you are."

Raszer extended his leg cautiously and pressed the toe of his boot against its duplicate. The 'surface' of the mirror, if one could call it that, was gently yielding, rubbery. "I'm not sure the distinction is all that comforting," he said warily. "But I'll go along with you. What's it made of? It feels soft . . . "

"Ah," Tony laughed. "You have to analyze it, don't you? Hmm . . . let's call it some sort of petroleum compound, stabilized by heat and adhesive agents. You see, what you are feeling is the sole of your own boot pressing against its own antisole."

"You mean," Raszer said, a chill creeping over him, "it's not a reflection? It's another me? Jesus. How am I supposed to process that?"

"My advice," said Abraham, "would be: don't look down! It's dizzying to regard one's meta-self for longer than a heartbeat. We have only a short time before our carriage turns to a pumpkin, and there are questions you need answered . . . are there not?"

"Yes. All right." Raszer shook off his vertigo. "What do we call your adversaries? The people of the Fraternity?"

"Well," Tony replied. "We like to call them 'Stumps.'" He scratched furiously at the center of his forehead and then straightened his headscarf.

"Because they have . . . a stump," Raszer surmised, "where a tailbone should be. Which is some sort of mutation . . . not a pretty one, right?"

"Their lineage was genetically bifurcated from that of the lemur and other primates," Tony answered. "Here is a 'parable.' It's not precise, but it will do. Our forbears became predatory when they left the trees. All human aggression stems from this event, and human aggression is very different from animal aggression. But not all left at the same time, though eventually, of course, we all lost our tails."

Tony Smith cleared his throat. "Well, most of us. Humans of your type retain the vestige known as the coccyx. This is your mark—the link to your fellows and to creation. Something happened, however, out on the savannah to those earliest and most eager of predators. The Stumps, you see, have no affinity for life in the trees. The truth is they do not have much affinity for life."

"Are we still on the 'parable?'" Raszer asked. "Or can I spot these . . . Stumps . . . on Sunset Boulevard?"

"Oh, yes. If you know what to look for. I'm afraid that nearly all of you carry a trace of Stump these days."

"And they . . . the purebreads, or whatever . . . they have a foothold everywhere?"

"Almost everywhere," Tony replied. "They are especially adept at brute commerce and warfare, and do quite well in highly regimented, hierarchical structures like the military, the priesthood and cultlike organizations. As I've said, the nature of the mutation makes males predominant. Because novelty and difference are anathema to male Stumps, they are inclined to prefer the company of their own gender. They fear women, and are terrified by things like menstruation and childbirth. Even the females—the progeny of the 'breeders,' that is—share this aversion. Some institutions resist the Stumps more effectively than others. The most formidable obstacle they ever encountered was the belief system which peaked in 6000 A.D. at Catal Huyuk and made a last-ditch effort in Minoan Crete . . . the culture developed around the, er, archetype . . . of the Mesopotamian Goddess . . . Ishtar, Inanna, Isis . . . whatever you choose to call her. They call her The Whore. We call her Gaia, as the Greeks did, for she is patroness of the earth. It is her mind which the three of us now occupy."

"Cool," said Raszer. "I've always wanted to know what it looked like inside a woman's head." He glanced up, and then quickly down again, reeling with vertigo. "So . . . will Gaia's time ever come again?"

"We hope so," Tony answered wistfully. "The Orphics postulated three recurrent cycles of time. Chaos: none too pleasant, but as necessary as childbirth. Gaia: when created existence springs into fullest bloom. And Eros: the spiritual marriage of the foregoing two cycles. Like it or not, the planet is now in its Chaotic phase."

"And you, Tony," said Raszer. "You must represent some kind of bifurcation, too. I mean, I feel a kinship, but you're way beyond me. Are you . . . a Lemurian?"

"Last of a dying breed, I'm afraid," Tony replied. "Those who escaped the last polar shift . . . the 'Golden Age' that your adversaries Vreeland and Voorhees are so eager to restore . . . fled to the underground network. You see, although the Stumps did not emerge as a distinct branch until the current interglacial, this battle has been going on for a very long time. About forty percent of our network has been destroyed or fallen into their hands. Mining, drilling, underground nuclear testing. We've lost the Atlantic chain, and most of the Siberian. Mt. Shasta is a major nodal point, and we've been trying to hold them there. Our allies on the surface have put up a powerful resistance. People like Abraham here, and the ones you call . . . Sufis." The rabbi chuckled softly. "They retain some of the original marks of my kind. They remember the trees."

"The original marks," Raszer mumbled. "Such as—"

"A vestigial 'third eye,' for example. Ever have the experience of synaesthesia . . . tasting a color, smelling a sound?"

Raszer nodded numbly. "But on the outside . . . we all look pretty much alike. How do we tell the good guys from the bad guys without measuring their tailbones."

"You must learn to observe behavior," Abraham offered. "It's not the design of the face so much as its range of expression. Next time you're in the street and someone is hurt—a traffic accident, for example—study the reaction of the onlookers. Some will reflexively show empathy; others will draw a blank. You see, their souls have atrophied along with their tailbones. The clinicians will call them 'sociopathic,' but it's more . . . "

"Can you tell me," Raszer asked, eyeing the array of pulsing crystals that seemed to serve as Tony's motherboard, "if you know anything of my friend, April?"

Tony's black eyes softened and he spoke with an even gravity. "I can tell you this," he said, "though you'll recall it only as a half-remembered dream. Whatever has been put asunder we will restore. We will bring her home to us. In body, you see, she has one foot in each camp. That is why she served you so well. But in spirit—"

Raszer, recalling that Bronk Vreeland had wanted April for a 'breeder,' found it suddenly difficult to breath. "Then she . . . April . . . is—"

"The legacy of her father," Tony said softly. "Take a walk with me . . . and be comforted."

He rose and half-floated around the terminal, the hem of his gown dragging against its spectral reflection beneath, and offered Raszer his arm. Raszer stood up unsteadily, because there was nothing to walk on but the soles of his own boots. "You, too, Abraham," said Tony. As the three of them strode arm in arm, a fantastically tiled surface spilled out before them: a mosaic of perfection, grander even than the Alhambra in Spain. Grander still because it was both outside Raszer's head and inside of it.

"What would you have me do?" asked Raszer. "How can I help?"

"Gaia's magnetic field is exceedingly weak right now. The time is ripe for a polar shift, and they know this. If they can induce a slippage of the ice caps—both through seismic terror and global warming—they fancy that they can restore their Ultima Thule. They will fail, but in the process, cities will fall and half the population of the earth will perish. This is of no concern to them, and in any case, they believe they can wait it out in the tunnels they are busy seizing from us. What they really want, what they have always delighted in, is to instill fear in the hearts of people. This is their modus operandi. Their numbers are insufficient for outright dominion, but they will cow you with talk of global terrorism, third world chaos, economic catastrophe, horrifying weapons . . . all things which they, perversely, have created and which they control."

"How did they ever gain such an advantage?" asked Raszer, with growing anger.

"Advantage," Tony replied, "is something taken by those who covet it. Most people simply want to live, and love, and often, to be left alone. This, I'm afraid, will not defeat the Stumps."

Tony paused in midair and turned to face Raszer. "In the surface world, certain harsh rules apply which do not apply universally. But one must always master the rules of one's own world, and the Stumps excel at this. They have commandeered two important commodities. Diamonds . . . and uranium. All but one of the major diamond mines on the planet are in the hands of the Halgadom Fraternity. Raw diamonds are a by-product of volcanos. That's where they dig, and these are also crucial access points for us. They kill two birds with one blast. Thence, it's a matter of manipulating supply, something they do very well. That gives them financial power."

"Voorhees, " whispered Raszer.

"Yes. And control of the supply of enriched uranium gives them another sort of power. As long as the planet is kept in a state of nuclear terror, the Gaian plan cannot prevail. All it takes is one well-aimed neutron to split the unstable nucleus of Uranium-235 and produce U-238, and that will keep them in the driver's seat for a long time."

"That genie is out of the bottle, I'm afraid," Raszer said.

"We're working on a way to get it back in. But time is not on our side."

"But you are frustrating them somehow . . . with your radio signals. Where do they come from? What's Vreeland looking for out here?"

"The crown jewels," Tony replied, "But he would not know where to look, let alone what to look for. My ancestors, you see, were blessed with foresight. They loaded their most essential wisdom in a series of . . . 'storage batteries.' Organic 'hard drives,' each of which is a cousin, in molecular structure, of the solid iron crystal that spins at the center of the earth and regulates the pulse of the planet. One such 'battery' sits encased in a column of basalt, a mile beneath the cone of Mt. Shasta, and barely five hundred meters from where the militia has been test firing its scalar weapon. When they fire, it chatters, and that makes it impossible for them to synchronize their weapons globally as required for their 010101. A bit of 'luck' for us. Would you like to see it?"

From the streaming web of information that vaulted above them like a multi-dimensional aviary, Tony drew down a holographic image of striking realism. It was a facsimile of a human skull, thirty inches in height, and cut from a solid piece of quartz crystal. The shape was slender, the features elongated, the impression of great beauty.

"There were originally sixteen of these," he explained. "Relay stations, placed at geomantic nodes, where telluric currents generated by Gaia would cause them to oscillate at key points in evolution and transmit information directly to the human mind. Ten have been destroyed, either by sabotage or cataclysm. Four are in the hands of our enemies. Two remain. One, here . . . and one, within Mt. Shasta. Now, a crystal oscillates in proportion to its facets. If you take a look at the lattice within this one, you may get a sense of how much information it holds. The Shasta Skull is one of the most sophisticated transceivers ever created, and it is currently firing off random bursts in response to the seismic disturbances created by the militia—among them, the 'song' which some of you topsiders have picked up through the old receptors. The Stumps think the signals are coming from *here,* because we have a stronger transmitter, but it is only a matter of time before they realize that the source is right under their noses."

Raszer held up his palm. "Before you go on . . . Tony," he said. "There's a basic disconnect here. You're describing technical processes and material things. 'Batteries,' 'oscillators,' 'transmitters' . . . and *tunnels.* But you and the rabbi here have told me that this . . . is all an apparition. That you can't find this place 'with a pick axe or a drill.'"

"Plato taught," said Tony, "that all things are form before substance. Anything well conceived can be physicalized. The batteries are real. As for the tunnels, no, one cannot simply 'dig' to them, though God knows they've tried. But that doesn't mean they don't exist. Even *I* must obey the physical laws of the multiverse. One has to know where and how to enter. One must have access. For millennia, this riddle 'stumped the Stumps,' but they're beginning to grasp, due to modern science, an aspect of reality that many children intuitively grasp: when your ball rolls

303

through the fence and doesn't come out the other side, it hasn't 'disappeared.' It has simply gone—by chance—*somewhere else.*"

Raszer shifted his weight and scanned the surroundings. "Oh-kay. I guess it's an empirical fact that I got here." Then it hit him. "The map. Ori's map . . ."

"Yes, Stephan, the one that Fortis Cohn gave you. Do you still—"

"Fortis?" Raszer broke in. "So he *did* . . ."

"She dropped it in the snow, friend," said Tony, "and he put it in your pocket."

"And you want me to retrieve the last of the skulls before the Fraternity does?"

"'X' marks the spot," Tony answered.

"You know that the volcano is in pre-eruption . . ." Raszer mentioned.

"Yes. You'll need to move fast."

"If they get their hands on it . . . what will they learn?"

"Assuming they can get it to oscillate properly and break the cipher—neither of which is beyond their means—a great deal. Quantum leaps in human knowledge— in the fields of mathematics, medicine, and psychology, for instance—have been abetted by transmissions from the skulls to those of you who were still able to receive them. Pythagoras, Hypatia, Plato, Newton, Da Vinci, Einstein . . . Tesla. The Shasta skull contains the full explication of an idea first intuited by Mr. Tesla: that harmful forms of radioactive decay could be prevented . . . and potentially reversed. We believe that the conversion of all fissionable U-235 back into *stable* uranium hexaflouride is possible. Neutralization of nuclear stockpiles . . . and the major source of the Fraternity's wealth. But human cognition must catch up a bit before even your greatest minds will recognize the formulae. We must preserve the skull before . . . eh . . . Stephan . . . *Stephan?*"

But the clock had run down on the rabbi's spell, and the image that Raszer retained as he merged painfully back into the surface world was of Tony Smith, striding toward his terminal as the magnificent fractal mosaic rolled up behind him, his thick, furry tail dragging behind him like the train on a bridal gown. Abraham acknowledged Ofra and Latif, who sat quietly smoking on top of the pile of provisions. Then he turned to Raszer, smiled puckishly, and spread his hands as if to say, *"Voila!"* He drew close, grasped Raszer's shoulders, and spoke then in deepest earnest.

"I must remain here for a while, my friend. One cannot go breaking into other worlds without making sure the doors are closed behind. Latif and Ofra will guide you back to Fez by a safe route that the Sufis use. Perhaps we shall meet again . . . in less perilous times." He paused for a moment, then pressed his palms together in blessing. "In fact, Mr. Raszer," he said, "I'm certain that we will. Go with God. And honor Gaia."

"Rabbi?" Raszer said, with a look of profound puzzlement. "Just one thing?"

"Yes?"

"The lattice . . . I understand that it's a mathematical construct . . . but . . . But—"

The rabbi raised his palm in caution. "Give it time, Stephan," he said. "I can tell you this: you were just now a *part of it*. Your body waited patiently here for the return of your consciousness, which had business elsewhere. Ofra and Latif will attest to the fact that your physical being never left this very spot. The lattice . . . the lattice is what is spelled out by the seventy-two syllables of the holy, unutterable name of God." And with that, Abraham vanished, leaving behind the trio of pilgrims.

"Ofra?" Raszer asked through a net of cedar smoke. "Look at me. I feel like I'm fading in and out. I'm not dead, am I?" After six hours of traversing rugged terrain under merciless sun, Raszer had still not fully ascended from the underworld. Moreover, though he had no proof of April's death, her phantom heart beat faintly in his solar plexus, and he felt the ache of knowing that a part of him was gone.

"No," the Israeli girl answered laconically, stirring the fire pit with the barrel of her rifle. "You're not dead." She regarded him warily from beneath dark lashes. "I know what death looks like."

Twenty yards away, at the mouth of the wadi, Latif had nodded off in a cheap, aluminum beach chair, the loaded carbine in his lap. They had ridden until nightfall, making it out of the mountains and two hours beyond. Now they were in an expansive high desert valley southwest of Missour, where they could spot potential trouble from a considerable distance.

Raszer nodded. "You lost your family. Abraham told me. I'm sorry. I didn't mean to be flip." She sat back on her haunches, the Galil rifle across her thighs, and acknowledged his sympathy stoically.

"Not all of them," she said. "My mother is still alive."

"Your mother . . . she's Romani, right?" He offered a cigarette and she accepted, breaking off the filter and lighting it with a piece of kindling.

"Yes." She drew the smoke into her lungs. "I am twice hunted . . . as a Jew and as a gypsy." A rueful smile passed over her lips, and Raszer was reminded of Raja.

"Did she practice tarot? Is that how you—"

305

"Yes," Ofra answered presciently. "She was, for a time, the rebbe's woman. We came here . . . to Maroc . . . after the intifada. I was eighteen. I would have stayed to fight, but my mother insisted she would not lose another child." She blew the smoke out harshly and gave a wry little laugh. "Now, I have lost her. She went off with a kumpania from Tunis, and left Abraham to see to my education."

"She could not have found you a better teacher."

"No."

"And he . . . has found himself a soldier."

"Yes. But our enemy is not so easy to identify as Hamas." She paused, pivoted slowly on her toes, and cocked her ear to the wind, her spine straightening. The reflexes were those of a gazelle sniffing danger. Her nostrils briefly flared.

Raszer rose slowly to a crouch. "What is it?" he asked her.

Her eye was on a black horizon that could be surveyed only with senses other than sight. "Probably nothing," she said. "They could not know this route unless they had followed us from the gorge, and I would have seen something."

"Oh, he's out there all right. It's just a question of how close."

She stood and plowed a pile of sand into the remains of the fire with her boot. Although they were banked on three sides, the fire was a risk. "You should get some sleep while you can," she said. "I'll take the next hour."

Raszer cupped his hand gently around the breech of her rifle. "No," he said. "You haven't slept in twenty-four hours. I'll take this watch." For a few moments, she held resolutely onto the weapon, but when he neither blinked nor averted his eyes from hers, she slowly released it into his hands. Raszer strode beyond the smoke and tilted back his head to drink in the Saharan sky, shiny and hard as polished opal. "All right, you sonofabitch," he whispered, praying his courage would match his words.

Bronk Vreeland had watched Raszer's party descend into the gorge from a distance of a half-mile as the crow flies, but he could get no closer than the lenses of his binoculars. Notwithstanding his military maps, his Algerian mercenaries, and two Libyan trackers who had done time in Afghanistan with the mujaheddin, he hadn't been able to figure out how the pathetic mule train had made it over the massive front range so quickly. And so, separated by a two-thousand-foot chasm and miles of switchbacks, he had been forced to wait them out, hoping they would emerge by the same route. When they did not, he'd made the risky but necessary decision to split his forces into three, so that all passable returns to Fez could be covered. He took four men, and just before sunset, he spotted them, headed into a wadi fifteen kilometers SW of Missour.

At night, in the desert, where humidity is nil and all warmth dissipates quickly from rock and reptile after sundown, even his infrared goggles were of little real use. Not until something warm-blooded was in range. Vreeland was forced to rely on the predatory instincts of his Algerians and the remaining Libyan's eye for even the slightest disturbance of the sparse fauna to follow Raszer's trail from two hours behind. There are no hoofprints in the Sahara and no scent remains for longer than five minutes. All is erased by the ceaseless wind that rises with the setting sun. Nevertheless, at 10:01 P.M., Vreeland's lead guard spotted the faint flicker of a cooking fire a kilometer away. A moment later, the fire was out, but the mercenary had fixed its rough locus by triangulation off the bright star called Sirius, and they advanced.

Raszer roused Latif after allowing the old porter a decent catnap. They shared a draught from his wineskin of the strong fermented honey drink that Abraham had passed around the night before, and made what quiet banter they could. Raszer's Arabic was rudimentary, his Berber nonexistent, and Latif's English was limited mostly to "okay" and "thank you." They had just realized that they could manage a serviceable conversation in French, when Raszer heard something *crrack* like a dry joint, followed instantly by the rapid *shh-clkk* of Latif's bolt action. The porter was quick, but Raszer had no illusions that his sun-scorched eyes or his antique rifle would be a match for a squad of Fraternity commandos. They froze and listened. It might have been the pop of a latent ember in the fire. Raszer knew you had only one chance to recognize noises in the open desert. There are no echoes.

Raszer entrusted Ofra's Israeli rifle to Latif and signalled him to wake her and cover the back end of the horseshoe shaped wadi, while he went to retrieve his weapons case from the saddlebag. They had tied up the donkeys at the open end of the windbreak, reasoning that anyone sneaking past the temperamental beasts would be likely stir up a chorus of braying. Raszer crept slowly round to the head end of the fair-haired donkey he had named Diogenes and reassured it with a stroke on the nose. He slipped the aluminum case from the loose-woven saddlebag and set it gently on the sand. It occurred to him that the clicking of the latches might flag his location, so he pressed his chest into the lid to muffle the sound as best he could. *Clk-clkk.* He waited, holding his breath. Nothing. He removed from the case the tranquilizer gun, snapped in its rotating four-dart magazine, and eased off the safety. Then he rose cautiously to a crouch and reached behind his back to make sure that his knife was in its sheath.

He realized now that he was inadequately armed. The dart gun was better suited to holding off thieves than trained assassins and a knife was no good against a sniper. Raszer had a habit of underarming himself in the fond but perhaps suicidal hope that he could avoid doing any personal killing.

From the enclosed end of the camp, there was a *crrrack* and a flash of muzzle fire from Latif's rifle. Fire was returned instantly from two locations atop the embankment, followed by a yelp. Raszer heard a body hit the ground. *Whose?* His pupils had momentarily contracted and he couldn't see the perimeter at all. Not ten feet from where he stood, the sand squeaked with the friction of a rubber sole, and the hair bristled on his damp neck. Nearby, Latif's donkey brayed and flicked its tail. Raszer leaned into Diogenes's flank, both hands on the gun, and locked his elbows against the slopes of the saddle. The squeak registered again, twelve degrees off axis to his left; Raszer pivoted, leveled the barrel at the height of a man's heart, and squeezed. *Kkpffftt!* The tranquilizer dart passed almost noiselessly into muscle. There was a groan, followed by the clink of gun metal against a rock. A shudder ran through his donkey's sloping spine.

Raszer stepped back, the gun extended at shoulder level, and turned degree by degree in a semicircle, every instinct phased to the moment. He listened, smelled, and felt for any movement of air that betrayed trespass of his space. Sensing nothing close, he backed slowly toward the fire pit, calculating that the best defense against greater numbers would be the three of them firing from the center out. As he drew near the place where fifteen minutes earlier they had rested, there was another exchange of fire from the embankment directly opposite, and now he was certain he heard air escape a woman's lungs. *Fuck! Fuck! Fuck!* His pulse hammered his windpipe as he aimed the gun at where he'd seen the muzzle flash that lingered on his retina, and fired twice. For two purgatorial seconds, it was utterly quiet, and then, from a few yards to his rear, came a macabre gurgling sound, followed by a thump and a whisper of sand as something came heavily rolling to his feet.

With the gun, and its one remaining dart, aimed into blackness, he turned slowly from the waist and rolled his eyes down.

The faint glow from the last live ember of the fire illuminated a drawstring sack the size and shape of a soccer ball, its leather cord cinched to contain whatever it held, and whatever it held could not be good. He felt the dope of fear flood his veins like a lethal injection. There was every reason to believe it was a bomb, and that he was about to be blown to pieces like some poor sonofabitch at a Jerusalem street market, another quickly forgotten casualty of jihad. But a second look, and the terror-honed sharpness of his senses revealed what his mind would have split itself in two to deny.

From the mouth of the sack there spilled a lock of wheat-colored hair. April's hair. April's head.

"Latif?" he called raspily, his eyes bound to the sack, his voice surely betraying some debilitating combination of dread and despair. "Ofra?"

He'd called out not because he wished them, if alive, to expose their positions by reply. Nor had he called for the cover to crouch down and examine the sack, to make sure it wasn't some grotesque decoy. He knew from the awful pull of its gravity on his heart that it must be what he thought it was. No, he had called out for the same reason a child will call out from its bed for a parent.

The answer he received was no lullaby.

"Sorry, hero," said Bronk Vreeland, "It's only me."

He was naked and slick with sweat, painted from scalp to calve with red ochre. Against his shoulder was a Ruger Mini-14 automatic and around his waist was a leather belt strung with human tailbones and a sheathed Navy Seal knife.

"Where's the Jew?" he demanded. "Come sunrise, you two are going to guide me back to that tunnel. Then, if I don't decide to kill you, maybe we'll strike a deal." He folded his hands in mock prayer. "Allah is merciful . . . "

"What whore from hell," said Raszer, his voice unsteady with fury, "carried you in her belly? When you need to bargain, Vreeland, you don't kill your hostage."

In the harsh silence that followed came the howl of a feral dog. Raszer prayed for the snap of the Latif's bolt action, then realized with cold certainty that the gurgling he'd heard had to have been the sound of his guide's throat being cut.

"The cavalry isn't coming, Raszer. Your pals are dead. It's just you and me." He aimed the Ruger at Raszer's heart. "Now drop the fucking paint gun."

"You are going to burn for aeons, motherfucker," Raszer said, and complied.

In his mind, there was but one uncomplicated desire. Nothing so altruistic as wanting to rescue the Shasta skull or prove himself Gaia's chosen centurion. Raszer wanted to kill the man who'd killed April. The knowledge that it was at this primal level—of blood and tribe and vengeance—that eighty percent of the world functioned came to him all at once, as did its terrible irony. There could be no peace, no "Gaian plan" as long as this was so, and it would be so as long as there were aggressors on the planet. He knew now the root of that aggression: it was born of an alienation from humankind itself, and it could not be tolerated for a moment longer.

With darkness and surprise his only allies, he hit the sand, rolled for the shadows, and drew his knife from its sheath. As Vreeland spun, Raszer scrambled behind him and plowed full force into his calves, robbing him of his center of gravity and knocking him headlong into the smoldering fire. Bronk's knuckles hit the hot coals and he howled, fumbling the Ruger as he staggered to his feet. Raszer rammed him again from behind, jarring the weapon entirely from his hands. Vreeland stumbled about the coals, pawing for the fallen rifle, but Raszer, unrelenting, prodded his ribcage with the tip of his knife, driving him toward the embankment, the gun left behind in the cold sand.

"C'mon!" Raszer growled. "C'mon, you sonofabitch! Turn around and show me that grit." He circled Vreeland, who had unsheathed his own knife and now faced Raszer with combative relish.

Vreeland feinted right, causing Raszer to lose his balance for an instant. Before he could recover it, he felt the honed edge of Vreeland's blade slice a bloody filet from his shoulder. Bronk widened the circle of combat, defining it, trying to keep Raszer in the center. He stuck at first to the shadows, where neither his eyes nor his blade would reflect the dim firelight. He must have seen that his first strike had only given his opponent the gift of an endorphin rush, for Raszer now took the offensive, rushing him wildly and forcing him back on his heels. Vreeland lept atop an angled slab of rock half-buried in the sand, where the silver moonlight spotlit him and made the beads of sweat on his hairless chest look like costume pearls. By commanding the high ground, he had forced his opponent to strike from below, enhancing his six-foot-plus advantage.

Raszer orbited the mound in a crouch, knife held palm up, his breathing finally even, winding Vreeland up like a music box. He had a measure of control, but he had no opening, and sooner or later, his bad ankle would weaken and he would falter. He slowed his pace and began to taunt the man on the hill. "How old were you when you stopped sleeping with the lights on, Bronk? When you stopped looking under the bed?" He slowed still further. "The rats are coming out, Bronk. They're all around your feet . . . " Vreeland lunged and wobbled the tiniest bit. "I've got a message from Ori, Bronk—"

But before he could drop the bait, there came from atop the embankment— just fifteen feet away—the pre-attack growl of a wild dog. For one critical second, Bronk rolled his head left to see what might be coming at his heels. When he turned back, it was into the muzzle of his own assault rifle. Ofra held the weapon as steady as a truck axle, in spite of what Raszer could see was a gunshot wound to her left shoulder. She flipped the hair from her eyes and nodded to Raszer. "Do you want to finish this pig?" she asked. "Or should I?"

Bronk Vreeland gave his own decision no more time than he gave any other thought, and sprung from the rock toward Ofra as if executing a belly flop. Raszer torpedoed in beneath him and drove the knife into his gut with such force that it kept him airborne until the hilt had locked against his ribcage. The instant he touched down, Raszer plowed him against the rocky embankment, forcing the knife still further in, until he could feel the tips of his fingers inside the wound. Bronk flailed wildly with his right arm, and when his own weapon did finally connect once more and graze his attacker's other shoulder, Raszer let go his last measure of civility and opened Vreeland's entrails to the night air. His knife finally hit bone against the saddle of Vreeland's sacrum, and then he withdrew and staggered back, his forearms covered with blood.

The Supreme Commander stood, spread-eagled, his bowels spilling onto the sand like fish from a damaged net. His face bore the grotesquely bemused expression of a man surprised by death, a creature going rapidly into irreversible shock.

"Tell your friends in Hell," Raszer said, with a voice that he hardly recognized as his own. *"Tell them:* the meek *will* inherit the Earth. I'm going to see to it personally."

He dropped to his knees, stuck the knife in the sand, and watched Bronk Vreeland die. Behind him, her rifle still at the ready, Ofra blinked in astonishment.

She caught movement from the corner of her left eye and wheeled around, raising the telescopic sight to her eye, only to lower it again in awe. "Look!" she cried. "Over by the fire."

Raszer turned almost casually, as if the appearance of the Devil himself could not have disturbed his deathwatch. There, beside the firepit, stood a mongrel wolf, its eyes phosphorescent. It lifted its long, slender snout and howled, and then at once seemed to dissolve into the plume of smoke rising from the fire, ascending to the pitchy ceiling of the desert, freed from raiyo to roam through another one of the many worlds.

"So long, Madame Rey," he whispered, a faint smile crossing his lips.

He rose from his knees and shuffled through the sand until he found the body of Latif. His throat had been cut from ear to ear, but Raszer checked his pulse nonetheless. Allah had been with him in his last moments, for he had gotten off a couple of good shots. Ten feet away lay the bodies of two of

Vreeland's men. He walked back to where Ofra stood and brushed her shoulder with his bloodied fingers.

"Are you all right?" he asked.

She nodded. "I'll make it." She eyed his wounds. "What about you?"

"Okay while the adrenalin lasts. Let's clean that gunshot wound of yours and tend to the bodies. We'll head out of here before the sun rises."

Grim and silent—for neither had words—they buried their foes and their fallen comrade and bound the still-tranquilized Libyan tracker. When it was done, they went to the fire, beside which lay the crude sack holding what was left of April Blessing. If ever something was marime, Raszer thought, it was this awful trophy. Yet he picked it up and tenderly tucked the loose strand of hair back inside. He had no need to see the rest. From his father's tradition, Raszer had learned a Jew's respect for the saving power of ritual, and from his Irish Catholic mother, a Celtic reverence for the head, though it wasn't within his powers to make April whole again like the martyred St. Winifred of legend, whose rapist had severed her head at the very threshold of her church.

While Ofra cleaned and bandaged his wound by the light of the restored fire, Raszer held the sack against his heart and rocked slowly back and forth. As in that earlier moment of terror when he had called out for his comrades, he was a child again. Sometimes he mumbled things, and sometimes he wept. After a while, Ofra left him and returned to her tent to sleep, knowing that when morning came, she would be the designated driver. Raszer himself did not sleep for what remained of the night, though the fire died and the canyon grew bitterly cold. Just before Venus rose over the jagged rock, Ofra heard him cry out, and it was the loneliest sound she had ever heard.

On the way out of camp, Raszer took a straw basket from Latif's mule, and buried it with April's remains in a hermit's cave, the better for her tongue to prophesy to other pilgrims seeking some tender truth in the harsh and boundless desert.

Raszer had learned starkly what all seekers come to know: that the thing sought, be it truth or treasure or eternal youth, is at best a glittering substitute for something once possessed, and lost. It wasn't the hunger for gnosis alone that drove men like him on, or a thirst for redemption, or forgiveness for some ancient sin. It was a kind of grief. As they tracked the ancient Sufi route back toward Fez, he did not torment himself with visions of what might have been had he embraced April as his mate and soul's complement. Instead, he resolved to restore Gaia's marvelous crystal skull to its rightful stewards before his enemies profaned yet another goddess, and he prayed that in doing so, April Blessing would in some way also be restored.

21

THE WORLD.

WHEN Raszer entered the Pluto Caves with Ori's map in hand, he took four hired marksmen, three Modoc trackers, an archeologist, two young scientists from the U.S. Geological Survey, and three enforcers from the Shasta-Trinity chapter of the Hell's Angels, including Bo Gatz, who had still heard nothing from his beloved Flo. Professor Mathonwy himself was recuperating, and so could be present only by way of his geological expertise. The entire team had been assembled over forty-eight hours with the guidance of Mathonwy, County Clerk Doc Kane, and the old Indian chief with whom Raszer had had a brief but telling encounter before his departure for Morocco.

Aside from the Geological Survey agents, whose first loyalty was to science, there was not a state or federal employee among them. Raszer intended in short order to brief the authorities fully on what he'd learned of the Fraternity's global agenda, but this particular mission was outside their purview and would never have been approved in light of the hazards of entering an active volcano. Moreover, he was seriously concerned that inviting the U.S. government in might result in the removal of the Gaian skull to some DIA or CIA laboratory. He doubted that such an exotic songbird would sing in captivity, and wondered also about how far the Voorhees cancer might have spread into the organs of the national security establishment.

Except to Mathonwy and the Chief, Raszer was vague about the expedition's rationale, saying only that the militia was suspected of having cached certain precious artifacts in the tunnels, and that he had been directed to make a reconnaissance. He justified the firepower by explaining that, although the National Guard had evacuated the miltia compound and the Sheriff had many of the grunts in a temporary detainee camp in Weed, they couldn't be certain that the tunnels did not still harbor a rear guard of Vreeland's elite. His self-defined mission was to confirm that the skull was in place and intact, and to secure its perimeter with a radio-controlled alarm system which would, at least temporarily, flag any attempt by the Fraternity to approach or tamper with the treasure. There was no telling what would happen if Mt. Shasta did erupt, but he had to assume that if the skull had survived eons of geological tumult, it could survive this.

At 9:16 A.M. on October 31, Raszer and his team entered the fifteen-foot mouth of the Pluto Caves, with a child's hand-drawn map leading them. It had revealed its true and ingenious design only when Mathonwy suggested that they illuminate it from below, to see if the paper had been impregnated with an invisible ink. Embedded in the fibers of the parchment was a fantastically precise diagram of Shasta's hidden labyrinth, which had later been traced over and embellished with Crayola. The map displayed not only the horizontal layout, but verticality in degrees of ascent or descent. Certain junctions were marked with icons that resembled an old Celtic spiral—the symbol of a passage that transcended the coordinates of ordinary travel.

Raszer took along a minicam to document the search for Mathonwy—and just in case a doubting world later required proof. It seemed more likely that such a clip would be aired at two A.M. on the Sci-Fi Channel than by CNN, but Mathonwy had persuaded him to do it. "Public awareness often begins at the lunatic fringe," is what he had said, a statement that Raszer was now less inclined to challenge.

The volcano had been active, groaning and spouting steam, for nearly two weeks, but hadn't yet blown a major gasket. The town had been evacuated to an eight-mile radius, and only the National Guard and the media remained closer in. The Geo Survey experts were cautiously hopeful that enough pressure had been released to stem the immediate threat of eruption, but Mathonwy was not convinced. Magma was like excrement, he said. It might get stuck for a while, but once it was on the go, momentum had a way of taking over. Nonetheless, most of the major news organizations had decamped, lured back to their hubs by more pressing and profitable stories. The National Guard and FEMA, however, remained on site and in force. Had the entrance to the caves been any nearer the base of the mountain, Raszer and his troops would not have gotten past the barricades.

Raszer's operational plan, such as it was, had evolved in part by intuitive conjecture and in part by way of a "letter of instruction" from Rabbi Abraham, given to him by Ofra en route to Fez. Under the subheading of "What You Have Learned," the communique summarized a lesson that Raszer did not quite recall having received but knew to be authoritative. It was a singularly weird sensation to read a third-person account of his own shamanistic descent when he himself could only cognitize it as a sort of déjà vu. He had shared the rabbi's missive with Mathonwy, whose grief and indignation over April's murder had trumped any scientific skepticism he might have been expected to show. Furthermore, Abraham's carefully worded exegesis accounted for everything Mathonwy had been seeing on his gauges for the past two months.

The men wormed one by one down the first of many narrow vertical shafts, with Raszer in the lead. He dropped lightly onto a soft carpet of volcanic ash, letting his heels down easy. His flashlight revealed a steeply raked ceiling and a passage littered with blocks and boulders of basalt, some more than six feet high. The usual reverberation was damped by the heavy steam that filled the tunnel like acoustical foam.

"This is not a good sign," observed one of the Geo Survey agents as he landed at Raszer's side. "We'd better make this fast." The team padded along a path cut beside a simmering subterranean river, the marksmen flanking them with weapons drawn. The second geologist took the stream's temperature with a digital thermometer and flashed a cautionary look at his partner. Shasta's fever was up seven degrees from the last reading. The heat of the rock allowed the team's archeologist to snap a handful of infrared photos of cave paintings found along the way, rendered in long-faded cinnabar and depicting godlike figures, some with long, spiral tails. The Modoc guides shot each other knowing looks, and Raszer felt a tickle deep within his limbic system, for a new "archetype" had been added to the dramatis personae of his own subconscious.

At 3.5 miles in, with the mercury having risen to 103, they descended the final long leg down to the skull's indicated locus. The group now traversed a broad avenue of stone that to Raszer's eye did not appear of entirely natural design. On either side, the moist rock face was extravagantly jeweled with growths of quartz and tourmaline, sprouting like pink heather on the shoulders of a Scottish Highland road. With each ten yards they advanced, the ceiling widened and vaulted higher and higher, as if mounting toward the great dome of some chthonic mosque. Raszer, his sense of place and distance still skewed by the aftereffects of his experience in Morocco, had to be alerted twice by the geologists to the fact that they now stood almost directly beneath the active Hotlum cone of the Mt. Shasta volcano. "We're within a degree or two," he was told.

"But that's impossible," he said. "The summit is at least eleven miles as the crow flies from the cave entrance . . . "

"Well," replied the geologist, displaying a wrist meter which gave a luminous readout of latitude, longitude, and depth, "then explain this. I sure as hell can't. Somewhere, we took a shortcut." The chamber groaned ominously as Bo Gatz and his Angels, with the marksmen, fanned out, rifles at the hip. Raszer shined his flashlight up into the billowing clouds of steam, and a fine rain of basalt dust crossed its beam.

"You realize," whispered the geologist, "if the lava dome cracks while we're down here, we won't even have time for a Hail Mary."

"Five minutes," Raszer said. "No more. I promise."

Five minutes, possibly ten, is what he believed it would take to place the two dozen radio alarm contacts around the perimeter of the skull column, once he'd located it. The scientific crew and Raszer donned infrared goggles and dispersed to survey the enormous chamber, but the target was as obvious as a sequoia in a living room. In their midst, the steeply vaulting ceiling appeared to be buttressed by a natural column of living rock, rooted in the cavern floor and shooting up into the unmeasurable darkness. Raszer looked at his map, and the coordinates that Mathonwy had jotted next to Ori's big X. He glanced at the geologist, who checked his readout and nodded. They were about to approach the column when he heard Bo call from some distance away.

"Hey!" he cried. "Take a look at this. It's like fuckin' Moonraker!" Fourteen high-powered flashlights turned at once on the source of Bo's wonderment, illuminating some two hundred yards away what was assuredly the highest security fence Raszer had ever seen. It was, however, what lay on the far side of the steel mesh that had drawn Bo's comparison. Three sheer stories below, its pylons sunken into the lava cap that had receded a mile beneath Shasta's largest fumarole, was an enormous structure which did, in fact, look like a NASA launch tower. The scaffolding enclosed a massive conical structure with a huge dish aerial, which in form and structure met nearly all of Professor Mathonwy's specifications for a Tesla Scalar Weapon, a magnifying transmitter capable of resonating the mountain to its roots. Here, not even a scant eighth of a mile from where the skull had been singing out its apocalyptic warning.

This was the house that the Voorhees diamond fortune had built, and the horrifying thought was that it might not be the only one on the block.

Raszer took it in quickly, his desire to linger and gawk overcome by the urgent vibrations he felt through the soles of his boots. He grabbed two of the scientists and hustled back to the column. They reached the base and lit it up from all sides. Then, suddenly, all the energy hissed out of Raszer's limbs. The column had been chipped and chiseled and blasted away, and there was only a gaping emptiness at its center, where the treasure he sought had once presumably rested. He was too late. Standing abject before the empty space, the fate of nations and the future of his own child suddenly in grave doubt, he failed to notice that the cavern was rapidly filling with steam. All around him, a torrent of dust and stone began to fall, and Mt. Shasta, grievously provoked, at last came out of its long slumber.

Like miners in a collapsing shaft, they all froze for a moment, each one acknowledging to himself that it might be too late for anything but acts of contrition. Then came the sound of gnashing, screaming steel as the lava cap was convulsed by the column of moving magma below. The Tesla tower was wrenched from its sixty-ton base like a child's erector set and the massive coil collapsed like one of Bo's beer cans. Raszer felt a beefy hand clap his shoulder and shove him narrowly out of the way of a sixteen-foot stalactite that had shaken loose from the ceiling and came crashing to the cavern floor, spitting shrapnel. It was Bo, but Raszer did not get leave to thank him for once again saving his life. Mt. Shasta was erupting, and if the rockfall didn't crush them, if the lava flow didn't fry them, the heat and the gas would kill them soon enough.

Time congealed the way it must have for thousands on a certain September morning in New York. With no lack of alarm, Raszer realized that they were all looking at him for direction.

"Let's move!" Raszer shouted, and they were off, minutes ahead—if they were lucky—seconds, if they were not, of a monumental meltdown. Not one of them looked back. The pervasive steam, blowing through all chambers as if through the arteries of an ancient boiler, reduced visibility to a few feet, and Raszer felt himself grow clumsy as the already minimal oxygen supply was rapidly swallowed by the volcano's vortex. They prodded and pushed and heaved and hauled one another up chimney after narrow chimney, becoming one long, linked chain of cooperative human muscle and will. If not for the "shortcuts," those odd spiral road signs on Ori's map which seemed to squeeze time and space unaccountably, it is doubtful they'd have made it.

At 1:15, the team emerged from the Pluto Caverns, muddy, singed, and bruised, and high-tailed it for the fleet of sport utility vehicles left at the roadside. At 1:23, just as Raszer's Jeep was mounting the I-5 south ramp, the entire north-eastern wall of the Hotlum cone that formed Shasta's summit blew out. The blast was followed by a tidal wave of incandescent gas and shredded magma which in fifteen minutes leveled three hundred-twenty square miles of the Trinity National Forest, and a mushroom cloud of ash and rock which hit the stratosphere in seconds and turned day into night all over the Pacific Northwest.

From a wheelchair parked atop the flat roof of a makeshift medical clinic in Dunsmuir, Niall Mathonwy watched the world he'd known for the past five years come to a violent end. Beside him stood the Modoc chief. "Chaos is the mother of Creation," Mathonwy whispered, to which the chief added, "Skell has taken back the maiden. Maybe now there will be peace."

0

THE FOOL.

THE rain pelted L.A. like pigeon droppings, from Barstow to the sea, glazing the black BMWs and the white columns of Bel Air with a thick, gray paste of liquid ash. Nothing and no place was spared, and only Hollywood's timeless trashiness adapted to the aesthetic assault, acquiring a sort of patina with the frosting of filth. No cleansing, millennial downpour was this, purging the city of vice, leaving it polished and fresh for the dawn of the Aquarian Age. It was a dirty rain, forced through a cloud of volcanic dust eighteen miles high. The cloud had drifted down the coast within a week of Shasta's eruption, and then nestled into the basin between the San Bernardino Mountains and the Coast Range, remaining there for the past three weeks. It would take a Pacific storm to move it, and then the cloud would circle the planet six or seven times before its load was brought to earth and reclaimed by her remarkable economy.

The vulcanian gods had allowed a measure of grace, though not for the thousands of old growth trees destroyed or the millions of dislocated animals. Mercy was present because not only had the explosion relieved more than two hundred years of pressure, it had blown toward the unpopulated east. Only six people had been accounted as fatalities. Still, it was a hell of a mess, and in the last, ragged weeks of the year, California once again became The Grateful Dead's *Estimated Prophet* of Apocalypse.

Raszer himself suffered little material inconvenience from the ever-present

Cloud of Doom. His work didn't require him to use the freeways much, and he had managed to fly his daughter in for Thanksgiving before they had cancelled all incoming flights and shut down LAX. Brigit thought the cloud made Los Angeles look like an old black and white horror movie, and for a while they made the best of it, lighting fires and drinking hot cider in his living room, playing out their own version of London during the Blitz. But the darkness at noon had begun to have an insidious effect on Raszer's mood. Overnight, an army of self-anointed Jeremiahs had materialized, proclaiming the End Times at Hollywood and Vine, ranting that Babylon had at last gotten its just deserts. They read their lines so well and with so little recourse to text that Raszer half-suspected a few of them were out of work actors, using the transfigured streets like passion players of old, but still, they got under his skin. The change of heart came over him slowly; one day he simply woke up feeling that the world might indeed be done for, that despite some successful containment, the bad guys might be destined to win.

On the way home three weeks earlier, he had taken what consolation he could from his half-remembered epiphany in Morocco and the fact that, thanks to Abraham, he now knew the name of the Beast. Lately, however, he had begun to think that it did him little good to know the dragon's nature if he was going to be eaten anyway. Worse, he was needled by the sense that April's unmoored soul had drifted into the feeding ground partly by the glimmering of his own lure. Her death weighed heavily on him.

In Fez, Raszer had casually suggested to Ofra that on Abraham's return, she and the rabbi pay a visit to Los Angeles. Although she felt certain that Abraham would demur, citing age and a longstanding aversion to air travel, Ofra announced that she had an uncle in San Diego and that it was, at long last, time for her to see California.

She flew back with Raszer and en route, the Air Maroc flight bound for New York was diverted to Charles de Gaulle in Paris due to a bomb threat. Unable to get an L.A. connection until the next morning, they checked into a small hotel in the Marais and gorged themselves on veal ragout and *Cotes de Rhone* at the bistro next door before staggering up three flights to their tiny suite, determinedly singing Piaf's famous chorus, *"non, je ne regrette rien"*—although Raszer had more than a few regrets.

After what they'd been through, lovemaking would have been a fitting coda. But when she arrived, chilled, at his bedside, her bare brown shoulders draped in his old coat, the best he could offer her was his arms. He couldn't shake the memory of his last meal with April, or the words she'd breathed to him through the bars of her prison. He couldn't forget the sound of the shots echoing off the canyon walls on what must have been her last night on earth. He wasn't sure he ever would. So he held the Israeli girl until morning, inhaling from her hair the hope of some future revival.

On this day, the Friday after Thanksgiving, he sat on his front deck overlooking the cul-de-sac and the mud-clotted canyon, the fir branches heavy with ash. Brigit was at the dining room table, eating leftover pumpkin pie and attempting to trace Ori's map, and Monica was at her terminal just inside the screen door. Raszer's Avanti was in the driveway, its restored finish hopelessly spattered with muck. He had lacked even the stamina to take it to the car wash. The screen door creaked open.

"Hey, Raszer," said Monica. "A little something to cheer you up."

"What's that?" he asked.

"Just got a fax from Doc Kane in Shasta. No surprise, really, but the judge in that Indian lawsuit ruled decisively against the Order of Thule. The land'll be handed over on Christmas Day to a multitribal council. He wouldn't even hear the militia's brief."

It wasn't a surprise, but it was good news, and it added another item to the plus column of small victories. Although the mainstream media, lacking any confirmation from Washington, had so far hedged on the geo-terrorism story, the *National Star* had run a front-page exposé, entitled GEO-WEAPONS CAUSED SHASTA BLAST, and subheaded *Shadowy Global Cult Controls Weapons of Mass Terror*. The cover picture was the mountain, but the inside pages were sprinkled with wire service photos of Bronk Vreeland (described as "missing and presumed a fugitive") and Rupert Francis Voorhees, international mineral magnate. The article's sources were given as anonymous, but Raszer knew that Doc Kane and Bo Gatz had each received five thousand dollars for their personal accounts. Raszer himself was not mentioned and had not contributed. He would have happily provided visual proof of the Tesla cannon, but in the heat of the moment, he'd never turned on the minicam.

Brigit slipped past Monica's skirts and hopped into Raszer's lap to ask about the little spirals on Ori's map. She might have received an eye-glazing dissertation on Afro-Celtic afterlife beliefs, but at that moment an unmarked squad car rolled up Whitley Terrace and pulled slowly into Raszer's drive. Borges got out.

"Hang on, honey," said Raszer. "I need to talk to the policeman."

He trotted down the steps and crossed the front lawn. Borges was looking askance at Raszer's filthy museum piece of a car, and had leaned over thoughtfully to remove a mud-spattered yellow handbill from beneath his windshield wiper.

"This is a beauty," Borges said, indicating the Avanti. "You ought to take better care of her." He passed Raszer the yellow flyer and they shook hands.

"I know," said Raszer. "I've been remiss. What's up, Lieutenant?"

"Couple of things I thought you'd like to know," he replied. "For one, Fortis Cohn has fingered Bronk Vreeland for ordering the murder of Christopher Rose. You wouldn't happen to have picked up any leads on Vreeland's whereabouts, would you?"

"I'm afraid not, Lieutenant," said Raszer. "I'm out of that loop."

"Uh huh." Borges wiped the mud from his boot. "And, based on Cohn's involvement in the drafting of Bree Donahue's movie contract, we may . . . I say *may* have the beginnings of a conspiracy to commit murder case against these punks who call themselves The Buzz Brothers and something called Arctic Entertainment, Inc. It's a hall of mirrors, but you know . . . we look in one mirror at a time. Any, uh, help there?"

"Only that I'll wager that if you can get to whatever offshore account underwrites Arctic Entertainment, you'll find yourself nearer to Rupert Voorhees."

"Right," said Borges. "And here's something else. We subpoenaed those old medical records from Glendale Adventist. There *was* a man present at Fortis Cohn's birth. He registered as R. Francis. I think we can lay odds that's our man, right? And the Psych Ward logs do show that a patient—a John Doe—left the ward without permission that night and was later found at the bottom of a sixth floor stairwell with his neck broken. So if you wanna tell Abel Cohn that his 'nightmare' is real . . . "

"Do you think I should, Lieutenant?"

"I wouldn't. In this world, a man's paternity can be his last article of faith."

"I'm with you," said Raszer. "It's hard enough to be a father."

Once Borges had pulled away, Raszer took a cursory glance at the dirty yellow flyer that had been under his wiper. No doubt some carpet cleaning franchise run by an immigrant father and son, hoping to catch hold of the last whiskers on the rump of the American Dream. Ordinarily, he tossed them out without a thought, but this one drew his eye. It was a hand-stenciled invitation to "Come Ride the Caravan" at a little strip joint on Wilcox called *Bob's Frolic*. It was the second glance that nailed him.

There was a hand-written inscription in the lower right corner. It said simply

"Fri. - 2:30." It was signed, in letters almost too tiny to make out, with the name "Gypsy."

"Monica!" he hollered from the driveway.

The screen door opened. "Yeah, Raszer?"

"I'm going for a ride," he said. "Back in an hour. Why don't we, uh, order in some Indian food?" Brigit, who had squeezed next to Monica in the doorway, rolled her eyes.

"Not again, Daddy!" she protested. "Pizza!"

"All right," Raszer said, climbing in his car. "Pizza. But make it interesting."

"Anything I should know about?" asked Monica, ever vigilant.

"Naw," he said. "You might get the wrong idea." He closed the door firmly and took off down the hill for Hollywood Boulevard.

Raszer detoured down Franklin Avenue on his way into Hollywood so that he could cruise past Madame Rey's old storefront. Ten days earlier, Ofra had taken one look at it and then persuaded her uncle, who owned a chain of falafel stands, to lease it for her. A "Closed" sign remained in the window, but she had already repainted the marquee, which now read: *Madame Rosa, Diviner of Dreams.*

He parked the Avanti at a meter two blocks north of Bob's Frolic and opened the umbrella that had become standard equipment for anyone heading out in the muck-storm. He didn't like umbrellas, but he liked cleaning Plaster of Paris off his coat even less. Hollywood was deserted save for a scattering of tourists who looked even more disappointed than usual, having found themselves in the midst of Tinseltown in a torrent of mud and ash. Good weather or bad, nearly everyone was disappointed by Hollywood, except for those who were privy to her occluded charms and could imagine Nicole Kidman behind the hooker's Kmart makeup. Raszer always had an itch to grab the long-faced tourists by the sleeve and say, "Excuse me . . . I think what you're really looking for is Las Vegas."

He leaned against the grimy brick wall of Bob's and lit what he had impulsively decided was his last cigarette. Eight hundred years from now, if the city hadn't turned itself to powder, the little fleshpot of sin and sacrament known to its early Anglo inhabitants as "Hollywoodland" might almost look to an alien visitor as the medina of Fez had looked to him: a place of impenetrable mystery where once something magical had occurred. He knew that's what the old intellectual priesthood of Hollywood—people like Annie Besant and Ramakrishna and Aldous Huxley and Christopher Isherwood—had longed for it to be. In those days, they'd thought of the cinema as rekindled alchemy, an alchemy that was to conjure the twentieth century's own Alexandria. They'd even begun to erect its temples—the Vedanta church up on high Vine; the Krotona Institute, perched in Moorish splendor on the bluffs overlooking Beachwood Canyon. None of this had lasted past 1930. What had snuffed the Orphic fire? Some blamed the Depression, others the movie industry's flavor-of-the-month infidelity. But maybe—just maybe—people like Fortis Cohn's mother and Rupert Voorhees had played a role in extinguishing it.

He'd learned from Monica's Voorhees research that between the years of 1907 and 1940, more than thirty-five thousand involuntary sterilizations had been performed in the United States on poor women, gypsies, and "undesirables," most of them in California, all of them in the name of a eugenics championed by the richest tier of Southern California society. Had they—at least in part—been breeding out tailbones and breeding in "stumps"? He stamped out his cigarette and had just considered making discretion the better part of valor and going home to his daughter, when he heard the music: tinny and distorted, but every bit as seductive as it had been at Diamond Lil's. Springsteen's "Brilliant Disguise."

It pulled him into the tiny lounge, four small tables and eight cracked and creaky stools lined up at the foot of a stage that also served as the bar. He took the stool farthest to the left, paying little notice to the dark and haggard men to his right. Like most daytimers with any kind of reputation to uphold, Raszer did not particularly want to be seen in a skin joint, much less one as tawdry as Bob's. Likewise, he avoided eye contact with the dancer, knowing that it would only draw her to him in pursuit of tips. As soon as he saw her, though, he needed a drink.

She had a round and common face, sweet like an overripe peach. Too sweet to age well. She wore a henna-colored wig, and had drawn the eyeliner from the corners of her eyes in the manner of an Egyptian queen. The eyes themselves were kind and sad, full of memories she'd probably rather be without. It was her body that grabbed him. It didn't go with the face. It was lithe and fluid, with the long, flat leg muscles of a climber or a gymnast. And the way she moved; the way her hips impelled her across the floor as if it were oiled glass . . .

He ordered a double scotch and put it down in a gulp, watching the girl move to the far side of the stage and dip low to receive an offering from a furtive man in a blue stocking cap. The man whispered something in her ear. She rolled her temple dancer eyes to Raszer, and shimmied down the bar as the song reached its climax with Springsteen's wounded concession that in the *"wee, wee hours . . . maybe, baby . . . the gypsy lied."* For a few seconds, she was his private dancer, and as she lowered herself gracefully to a squat, her stiletto heels never touching the floor, he breathed in